PUTTING OUT THE STARS

Roisin Meaney was born in Kerry and has also lived in Dublin, Tipperary, London, Zimbabwe and San Francisco. Her present home, and her main place of residence since the age of 8, is Limerick, which is a much nicer place than you might think.

Putting Out the Stars is the second of, hopefully, many books.

Also by Roisin Meaney

The Daisy Picker

Putting Out the Stars

Roisin Meaney

Tivoli
an imprint of Gill & Macmillan Ltd
Hume Avenue
Park West
Dublin 12
with associated companies throughout the world

www.gillmacmillan.ie

0 7171 3676 0

Print origination by O'K Graphic Design, Dublin
Printed and bound by Nørhaven Paperback A/S, Denmark

The paper used in this book is made from the wood pulp of managed forests. For every tree felled, at least one is planted, thereby renewing natural resources.

A catalogue record is available for this book from the British Library.

1 3 5 4 2

To the Meaney and O'Grady clans,
past, present and to come.

Thanks to all at Tivoli, and to Faith.
Thanks to Annaghmakerrig, for taking me in again.
Thanks to Liz and Desirée for the biology lessons.
Thanks to family and pals, for encouragement and kind words.
Thanks to all who bought *The Daisy Picker*. Here we go again.
Thanks to Limerick for the inspiration.
Thanks, and apologies, to anyone I've forgotten.

Roisin Meaney, October 2004

The stars are not wanted now: put out every one;
Pack up the moon and dismantle the sun;
Pour away the ocean and sweep up the wood,
For nothing now can ever come to any good.

W. H. Auden

before

Heaving herself into the car, pulling the door closed with an effort, she thought *toothpaste*; *I forgot toothpaste*. Everything else was on the list – bin liners, milk, washing-up liquid, coffee – just the few things that couldn't wait until they did the big shop at the weekend. Not that *she* needed coffee – just the smell made her gag these days, and she'd been so addicted to it before – but she couldn't expect John to give it up too. He had enough to deal with right now, all those extra hours at work he'd put in for, heading off at eight every morning and often not home again till after nine. Of course they were glad to have them, God knows they could do with the money, with her contract finishing up just before she'd have had to leave anyway, and nothing else in sight for when she'd be ready to go back to work, but still . . .

She switched on the engine and put the wipers to the fast setting – would the rain never stop? – before backing the car carefully out of the driveway, conscious of her stomach sliding along the steering wheel as she swivelled both ways to check the road. She shouldn't be driving at all, the size of her, but if she didn't get the things they needed, who would? And her legs, swollen to the width of tree trunks, wouldn't take her as far as the end of the road. One month to go, one more month of feeling like a hippopotamus every time she moved, of hardly being able to turn over in the bed, of heartburn and backache and at least three trips to the loo every night – and they talked about pregnant women blooming.

Toothpaste. Toothpaste. If she didn't keep repeating it, she'd forget it. Nothing stayed in her head these days – she couldn't remember from one episode to the next what had happened in *Coronation Street*, kept walking into a room and then wondering what had brought her in there, forgot to feed Bonkers – or fed him two breakfasts in a row; the poor dog didn't know if he was coming or going. Wait till the baby arrived.

She drove through a log of water, sending a wall of spray out to the side and feeling the car sliding on the wet ground for a terrifying second. She clutched the wheel tighter and dropped her speed, kept her eyes riveted on the road ahead as it went from blurry to clear with every rapid slash of the wipers. *Toothpaste. Toothpaste.* A car turned out from a side road and came towards her, blurry, clear, blurry, clear. It looked like it was wavering, tilting from side to side in the rain.

No – it wasn't the rain – with a lurch, she realised that the other car was swerving across the central line, now back into its own side, now coming straight towards her. And she was suddenly terrifyingly helpless, frozen with her fingers white on the wheel, foot pushing down so hard on the brake pedal that she must stop, she must, and the brakes screamed loudly but she kept on going, wipers still flicking madly from side to side, and the other car was still heading straight for her . . . God . . . now her hands were flying to her stomach, curling around it, her body bracing itself, her mouth open in horror, her eyes squeezing shut –

And then it was all over.

during

You could say it began with Laura and Ruth in a pub in the middle of Limerick, one mild and drizzly September afternoon. Ruth had recently got back from Crete; the table in front of them was scattered with photos. Laura picked one up.

'God – what I wouldn't give to be on that beach right now, instead of here in the rain.'

Ruth smiled. 'I know – imagine waking up to that view. Every morning, first thing, I'd go out onto the balcony to make sure I wasn't dreaming.'

Laura arched an eyebrow. 'First thing every morning? Really?' One side of her mouth slid upwards. 'Before you did anything else?'

Ruth immediately blushed scarlet and ducked her head, letting her pale blond hair swing forwards as she started fiddling with the photos. Laura gave herself a mental kick – she kept forgetting what a bashful creature her new sister-in-law was. Imagine blushing like that though, at her age – you'd think she was fourteen instead of thirty. Mind you, just because Laura and Donal had hardly got out of bed on *their* honeymoon didn't mean that everyone else did the same.

'Sorry, Ruth – me and my filthy mind; take no notice.' She swept up the two empty glasses. 'One for the road, as long as there's no sign of your chauffeur?'

Ruth, new wife of Laura's brother Andrew, checked her watch as the blush died. Then she shook her head. 'No more for me, thanks; I'd better be sober going home to your mother.'

'You mean your mother-in-law.' Laura grinned. 'Better get used to it; you're stuck with her now. Right, one more beer for me, and I'll get you a Ballygowan.' She turned with the glasses and headed for the bar.

Laura and Ruth had known each other for eight months. They'd met when Andrew had brought Ruth home to meet his mother, and arranged for his sister Laura to be there too, to help break the ice. Laura's husband Donal had been included in the invitation, but he'd managed not to be available that evening.

From their first meeting, Ruth Tobin and Cecily O'Neill had seemed to hit it off. Laura's watchful eye could detect no obvious tension between the two women, despite the fact that they could hardly have been more different; nobody could accuse Cecily of lacking in confidence. But she and Ruth chatted pleasantly, if a little formally, over Cecily's perfectly cooked salmon steaks and char-grilled vegetables. Ruth wasn't exactly the life and soul of the evening, but she coped quite well under the circumstances, Laura thought.

She used the right cutlery without hesitation. She didn't speak with her mouth full, or drop anything. She complimented Cecily shyly on the meal, and refused second helpings of the light-as-a-feather pineapple soufflé. She admired the Lladro collection in the cabinet in the hall, and pointed out a few books on Cecily's shelves that she'd read too.

And Cecily responded, offering to lend Ruth a recently-read William Trevor that she herself had enjoyed.

'It was my book club's choice for this month; I thought it was his best so far.'

Altogether Ruth was perfectly behaved – the ideal guest in Cecily's genteel home. Laura had watched and listened, and marvelled that this demure girlfriend of Andrew's – so unlike his usual choices – had somehow found favour with the woman who'd managed to get rid of all his previous ones. And then, towards the end of the evening, she'd suddenly thought: *of course – she'll never lose him if he marries Ruth.*

When she left that evening, Ruth had tucked William Trevor into her bag and thanked Cecily for the meal; and the second time they all met, she'd finished the book and agreed to marry Andrew.

Laura saw her often after that, whenever Ruth came down from Dublin for the weekend; she usually invited the two of them to dinner with her and Donal on Saturday night, so Ruth wouldn't have to endure a whole two days of Cecily.

'Bet Andrew is sorry now he never got his own place; there's Ruth in the spare room, and God help them if they try anything under Mother's roof.' Laura was melting dark chocolate over a pot of boiling water for a mousse.

Donal raised his head from the paper. 'Quite right too. Time enough for all that carry-on after they're married.'

Laura grinned, turning a spoon gently through the softening chocolate. 'You mean, like the way you stayed away from me until we were legal.'

He dropped the paper and came over to the cooker, putting his arms around her waist from behind, leaning into her. 'That was different. You were completely irresistible – it was beyond my control.'

'Good answer; here.' She dipped a little finger into the chocolate and turned around to slide it into his mouth.

Laura met Ruth's mother and three sisters for lunch in Dublin a month before the wedding. The women washed down fettuccini and roasted vegetables with several glasses of Chianti, while Andrew took his future father-in-law off to watch a match and eat pub grub.

And then Ruth and Andrew got married, and Ruth moved into Andrew's room in Cecily's house.

But just until their own was ready. Unlike Laura, who'd moved out to share a house as soon as she started her course at the Art College, Andrew had never felt the need to leave home; the subject had simply never come up. And of course there was no question of leaving Cecily on her own after their father died suddenly, two years into Andrew's first computer programming job, so he continued to sleep in the room he'd taken over when Laura had moved out, bringing home the occasional girlfriend to meet his mother.

And now everything had changed, and Andrew was twenty-eight and married, and he and Ruth would be moving out of Cecily's as soon as the house they'd bought was ready – a month or two more, according to the builders who were doing the renovations.

Or maybe a little longer, depending.

Ruth had lived all her life in Dublin. Born and bred in the same little Northside neighbourhood, she finally moved into a flat two streets away from her parents when she turned twenty-seven, tired of feeling slightly ridiculous whenever she admitted that yes, she was still living at home. Two years later, her flatmates persuaded her to go on her first ever sun holiday. She hadn't fancied the thought, not at all.

'Look how fair I am. I'll burn as soon as I step outside. Or get covered in freckles, which is worse.'

'Course you won't – you'll slather on the sun cream and wear a giant hat, and you'll be fine.' Claire was big and rosy-cheeked. 'And you've a lovely figure – you'll look brilliant in a bikini.'

'Ah come on, Ruth – Crete is fabulous; you'll love it.' Maura lifted a handful of ginger curls. 'If I can survive in the sun with this mop, so can you. And we might even find you a hunk to have a fling with.'

And Ruth, who'd never had a fling in twenty-nine years, whose few short-lived romances had been spectacularly disappointing, shrugged and said she'd think about it, wondering what excuse would sound the most plausible.

But of course Claire and Maura hadn't been fooled, and she'd finally run out of reasons why they should leave her at home and go themselves. And then they'd hardly arrived in Crete when she met Andrew, and now she was living in Limerick, never having been further west than Portlaoise up to this.

Laura came back with the drinks. 'I got the fizzy stuff – hope that's OK.'

'Thanks.' Ruth smiled and took the little bottle and the glass full of ice and a lemon slice. 'You know, I'm so glad Andrew had a sister. After growing up in a house full of girls, I don't know what I'd do without a bit of female company.' She blushed faintly again.

Laura pushed an auburn curl behind her ear. 'Mmm; I'd have liked to have a couple of sisters myself – especially since Mother and I were never what you'd call close.' She lifted her beer and drank, then seeing Ruth's look of concern, grinned and shook her head. 'Oh, it doesn't bother me really; I'm just glad I don't have to live with her any more.' Immediately she realised what she'd said, and added quickly, '– but hey, that's just me; you seem to get on fine with her, don't you?'

Ruth nodded. 'Yes; Cecily's been very nice to me since I moved in.'

And Laura looked at her sister-in-law and thought *most people would be nice to you . . . what's not to be nice about*?

Pity Ruth hadn't more of a spark about her though – nice was all very well, but when you had to watch what you said all the time, make sure you didn't offend . . . She wondered what Breffni would make of Ruth. Chalk and cheese, definitely. But maybe Breffni would be charmed by Ruth's shyness.

Yeah, right. Laura started to gather the photos together.

'We'd better put these back before they get drink spilt on them. When did you say the album proofs would be ready?'

And Ruth, having no idea of the nightmare that lay ahead – how could she? – began to talk about her future.

✡✡✡

Cecily O'Neill clipped the wafer-thin metal bookmark over the top of the page before closing her book. She turned her head and looked out the window. Not yet five o'clock, and already the day was starting to give up its brightness.

She always dreaded the winter. Biting wind drying up her skin, chilling her right through to her bones, no matter what she wore. Long, long, dark nights spent alone in her wide double bed, curling up to keep warm – electric blankets were so unhealthy – trying to shut out the sound of the interminable rain.

Having to pile on layer after layer of clothing – those horribly unfeminine thermal vests – hiding her neat shape. Cecily had always taken great care with her appearance, proud of the fact that she looked years younger than her age. She was fairly sure that everyone at the book club assumed she was in her mid-fifties – not, of course, that she would dream of discussing the subject with any of them.

It had never come up with Brian; he'd never asked, she'd never said. He almost certainly thought she was younger than thirty-three when they met; and she, having long since lost patience with men but longing for the respectability of marriage, had never told him otherwise.

She hadn't commented when she'd come across his passport one day and discovered him to be four years her junior. She'd simply made sure that her meticulous skincare routines, and her careful diet, never varied: cleanse, tone and moisturise every morning and night, with a weekly facial and a full body massage every fortnight. Lots of chicken and fish and fresh vegetables, very little red meat. A carefully controlled amount of milk and cheese for her bones, plenty of water.

No sweets or chocolate – dessert on special occasions only – and never more than one small gin and tonic before dinner. A daily walk, whatever the weather. And, of course, no direct sunlight – the ruination of so many complexions. She thoroughly disapproved of Andrew's tan when he and Ruth had come back from their honeymoon – not that she had mentioned it, of course. And Ruth had obviously exposed her pale skin too – face covered in freckles, nose peeling most unattractively. She'd be sorry eventually, particularly as she was no Venus to begin with. Presentable enough, certainly, but had probably never turned a head in her life – or looked a day younger than her age.

Cecily assumed that her own husband had probably discovered how old she was at some stage – a marriage of twenty-three years has few secrets – but if he had, he'd never spoken of it. He was naturally quiet, not given to much in the way of small talk; and she, never one for idle chatter herself, was thankful for it.

So it still surprised her, whenever she thought of it, how quiet the house seemed after he'd fallen from a ladder five years ago and broken his neck. It wasn't as if he'd ever made much noise when he was alive.

She set her book down on the little table beside her, then got up and drew the heavy curtains together before switching on the standard lamps. The room was softened with golden light. Still half an hour or so before Andrew and Ruth got in; then just enough time for a pre-dinner drink before her Basque-style chicken was ready. Cecily rearranged her cushion, sat back down and returned to her book – Ann Tyler's latest, and up to standard – with a satisfied smile.

Everything as it should be, as always.

✡✡✡

'Hello?'

'Bref, it's me. What's happening?'

'Hey Laur. Not much really. Poll's just over a cold. We had a couple of broken nights – she was really choked up.'

'Ah, the creature.'

'Yeah . . . she's fine again now though. What's up with you?'

'Just wondering about yourself and Cian coming to dinner here on Thursday, if you're happy about leaving Poll.'

'Happy and more than ready for a break – Granny Mary will hold the fort. What's the occasion?'

'You have to meet Ruth; they got back the other day.'

Pause. 'Oh . . . right.'

Had Laura imagined that hesitation? She decided to ignore it for the moment. 'I've told her all about you, so you need to come and show her you're not that bad really.'

'Har de har – you should be on stage. How's she getting on with the dragon lady?'

Laura smiled. 'Hey, watch it – that's my mother you're talking about; she's no lady.'

'I'll tell her you said that next time I see her. Anyway, she's not that bad – "dragon lady" is actually a term of endearment. I just wouldn't fancy living with her.'

'Hmm – and so say all of us. Ruth seems to be getting on fine with her so far. But then, she's the kind who'd get on well with anyone – you know, nice. Friendly. Easygoing.'

'You make her sound like a sheepdog – or someone who crochets. Does she crochet?'

Laura laughed. 'No, no crochet, as far as I know; no sign of any lace doyleys. And no knitting or embroidery either: not so far anyway. She *is* quiet though – I have to watch what I say a bit. I think she doesn't quite know what to make of me. But she's nice really, and she's dying to meet you. So ye'll come on Thursday?'

Another tiny pause. 'Yeah, as long as it suits Cian – he's not home from work yet. I'll check with him and give you a ring back. What time do you want us?'

'Eight-ish, I suppose.' Laura thought of Breffni's appalling timekeeping. 'That does not mean nine-ish, it means half eight. And make Cian drive, so you can have a jar.'

'Oh he'll drive, don't you worry. I drove us to a work do of his last week; someone was retiring after about seventy-nine years in the job.'

Laura laughed again. 'Right, so that would make him, let's see . . . about a hundred and five?'

'Yeah, about that. We got a set dinner and a man with an

accordion entertaining us after; I think he was the office caretaker or something. Everyone was waltzing – it was worse than a wedding. I nearly fell asleep into the pork chops. We were the only two under fifty-five.'

'Serves you right for taking up with a boring old taxman, or whatever he is.'

'Accountant please – give him his correct title. And I assume "boring" refers to his job.'

'You know it does; Cian is a pet . . . .' Laura hesitated – maybe she should say something, after all. 'Look Bref, you are OK about this, aren't you?'

'About what – meeting the love of my life again?' Breffni sounded amused. 'Sure didn't we meet at your wedding, and weren't we fine?'

Laura wondered again if she'd imagined Breffni's earlier hesitation. 'Yeah, of course you were . . . but that was different. This'll be back in Limerick – I thought it might – oh I don't know, stir things up a bit, or something.' She began to feel a bit foolish – she should never have brought it up.

Breffni didn't seem bothered. 'Laur, I appreciate your concern, really I do, but you needn't worry – Andrew and myself are ancient history. Haven't I Cian now? And we were bound to meet sooner or later, with us both back in the same territory – I'm amazed that I haven't bumped into him up to this, actually, when you think that I've been home nearly two years now.'

'Well, you're not exactly living a few doors up from us any more . . . so you don't hate the thought, really?'

'No; I'll rise to the occasion, don't worry.'

'Good . . . and Bref, you won't mention to Ruth about you and Andrew, will you? She's not very confident really – it might throw her a bit.'

The amusement was back in Breffni's voice. 'God, what do you think of me? I'm hardly going to introduce myself as the one who had a fling with her husband when he was young and innocent . . . well, young anyway.'

'I know, I know; I just thought you might say it as a joke, or something – you know what you're like.'

'No worries; my lips are sealed. Talk to you later.'

'See you.' As she hung up, Laura let out the breath she hadn't known she was holding.

✡✡✡

Laura O'Neill and Breffni Comerford grew up five numbers apart in a cul-de-sac just off the North Circular Road, where Breffni's parents, and Laura's mother, Cecily, still lived. For six years, the girls walked to school with one mother and came home with the other. When they reached fifth class, the mothers stayed at home.

As they were growing up, they went through phases of Van Morrison and James Taylor and the Smiths. They agreed to differ on Janis Ian, whom Laura loved and Breffni tolerated. They both threw away the walnuts on the tops of their Walnut Whips, and they lusted after Paul Newman (Laura) and Andy Garcia (Breffni). From fifteen to seventeen they wore only black – apart from their brown school uniforms – and they listened to Leonard Cohen and Billie Holiday in each other's incense-filled bedrooms, and read *Lolita* and *To Kill a Mockingbird* and *Wuthering Heights* and *Brideshead Revisited* till their paperback copies fell apart. They agreed that Colin Firth was the ultimate Mr D'Arcy, and that Madonna tried too hard; and they both had secret tattoos from a holiday in Portugal – a tiny sun on Laura's lower back and a star on Breffni's left hip.

They had their ears pierced at sixteen, and they gave up chocolate at seventeen. Breffni lasted three weeks, Laura almost eleven months. They traded clothes and secrets and diets. They straightened Laura's auburn curls and permed Breffni's silky black hair, to the horror of both mothers.

They tried and failed to smoke. They sneaked out to drink cider from flagon bottles with local lads down by the river on long summer evenings, and were each other's alibis the few times they stayed out all night. Once or twice they recycled boyfriends, but that wasn't a great success. They cried on each other's shoulders when their hearts were broken, and once they held hands and promised God everlasting good behaviour as they waited to find out that Breffni wasn't pregnant.

The year they left school, when Laura was almost nineteen and Breffni a few months younger, they went to San Francisco for the summer and stayed with Comerford cousins that Breffni had met once at a family wedding over six years before. They got a bus around the hairpin bends of Lombard Street and took the ferry out to Alcatraz and rode a cable car up California Avenue. They wandered around Fisherman's Wharf and walked through the Castro district, trying not to stare at the jaw-droppingly beautiful men strolling about hand in hand. They signed up for ten Bikram yoga classes for ten dollars, and staggered home, drenched with sweat, from their first and last class.

'God above – that was like doing it in a sauna.' Breffni flapped the end of her damp pink t-shirt. 'I'm wrecked.'

'I nearly slipped when we were doing that tree thing, my mat was so wet.' Laura quickened her pace to a trot. 'Bags first in the shower.'

'We'll see about that.' Breffni broke into a sudden run and sped past her.

'Hey – you're supposed to be wrecked.' Laura slowed down as Breffni disappeared around the corner. 'Hope you scald yourself.'

They went fishing at dawn one morning in the bay with Breffni's uncle's friend, and watched stripes of crimson and orange and pink lace the sky through the railings of Golden Gate Bridge as the sun floated up to face another perfect day. Later they managed to catch a salmon, Laura frantically trying to manoeuvre the struggling fish into the huge net that Breffni, weak with laughter, was holding over the boat's rail. Their host watched in amusement, ready to take over if the fish looked like escaping.

'Hold that blasted thing steady, would you?' Laura heaved the rod in the direction of the wildly wavering net. 'This weighs a ton.'

Breffni braced herself against the rail, giggling helplessly. 'I'm trying, honest – Jesus, the size of that fish! Don't let him pull you overboard – I've no intention of jumping in after you.' She looked back at the boat owner, still grinning widely. 'Carl, I think the fisherman needs a bit of help here – she's having trouble landing her catch.'

They had barbecued salmon with the cousins that evening on Baker Beach, and belted out a fairly accurate version of 'The Dock of the Bay' after several lite beers.

Back in Ireland, Laura started her commercial art course at the end of September and Breffni, determined never to set foot in an educational institution again, got a job behind the reception desk in a solicitor's office. They met almost as much as ever, keeping up to date with their different lifestyles. Occasionally, Breffni stayed the night in the flat Laura had escaped to after leaving school – thank God Dad had agreed to fund the rent. He could see how things were, how they'd always been between Laura and her mother. As soon as she moved out, Laura got a part-time job in The White House pub, determined not to cost her father any more than she had to.

Over a year later, with Christmas just around the corner, Laura got a phone call.

'Brace yourself – Andrew asked me out.'

'Andrew who?' Laura tried to drag her thoughts away from the department-store logo she was trying to design. She'd never have something ready by Friday.

Breffni snorted down the line. 'What do you mean, Andrew who? Andrew your brother, you eejit. Andrew who grew up in the same house as you.'

'Our Andrew? Andrew my little brother asked you out? You have got to be kidding.' Laura laughed, sure it was another of Breffni's jokes.

Breffni sounded mildly annoyed. 'Why? Why shouldn't he ask me out? What's wrong with me?'

Laura stopped laughing. 'God, you're serious. My brother wants to go out with you.'

'What's so strange about that? Why shouldn't he fancy me?'

Why indeed? Men had always been drawn to Breffni. But Andrew . . . 'I'm not surprised that he fancies you, it's not that; it's just that he's my little brother –'

'Stop calling him your little brother. He's a head taller than you, and he's eighteen, only a year and a bit younger than me. And you know I've always thought he's a right hunk.'

'God, stop – I can't think about him like that. You're not really going to go out with him though, are you?'

Breffni's voice had more than a hint of annoyance in it now. 'Yeah, I am actually. We're going to Gerry Flannery's for a drink tomorrow night.' She paused before addding, 'I hope you're not going to be funny about it.'

Laura considered: her brother and her best friend. It definitely felt . . . odd; but then again, why shouldn't they go out together, just because Breffni was her friend? 'No, of course I'm not going to be funny about it . . . it's just – I suppose it's just a bit . . . unexpected, that's all.'

Breffni's voice softened. 'So you won't disown me if I fall head over heels?'

Laura laughed again. 'With my little – oh sorry, I mean with my much taller brother? Hardly. Ah, what the heck – go for a drink with him. Where's the harm?'

And they did go. And a few days after that, they went to the cinema. And then Laura got used to the idea of her brother and her best friend together, and stopped marvelling at the fact that she'd never seen Breffni so . . . contented. It wasn't that she and Laura spent all day talking about Andrew – on the contrary, it was the first relationship they didn't dissect in great detail – but something had changed in Bref, definitely. There was a sort of excitement there that Laura had never seen before.

She and Andrew met at least twice a week, sometimes more. Occasionally they called in and sat at The White House counter, chatting to Laura – one night the three of them went to see a play at the Belltable – and Laura was just beginning to play with the possibility of her friend and her brother getting serious, when Andrew brought Breffni home to 'meet' his parents.

Of course, Brian and Cecily already knew Breffni well; she'd been in and out of their house practically all her life, sitting at the table during all of Laura's birthday parties, playing in the back garden with other little girls during summer afternoons, spending hours upstairs with Laura when they were older, even occasionally staying overnight on a camp bed in Laura's room.

But this was something new; now she was Andrew's friend.

Laura would have loved to be there, just to see the reaction of her mother, in particular, to this new development. But since she'd moved out, invitations to dinner at home, much to Laura's private relief, had been limited to special occasions – birthday celebrations, Christmas Day, Easter Sunday – so she had to rely on Breffni's account of the night. Apparently Cecily had behaved perfectly all evening.

'We got a gorgeous quiche, and a very posh salad with pine nuts. And strawberries for dessert – only Cecily would produce strawberries at the end of January.'

'But what was it like – what did ye talk about?' Laura couldn't imagine it: Andrew and Breffni sitting down to dinner as a couple, with Cecily playing hostess. Much as Laura adored her father, he couldn't really be depended on to contribute much to the conversation – he usually preferred to leave that to Cecily, who was rarely lost for words. But what on earth would she have found to talk about with Laura's friend, in this unfamiliar social situation?

Breffni was amused. 'Can you not give your mother some credit? We chatted away quite pleasantly, actually – she asked after my parents, although she probably bumps into one of them every time she goes outside the door. Oh, and she wanted to know all about my job – you never told me she was a secretary before she got married. And I asked her about the book club, pretended I was thinking of starting one up with the work crowd. It was grand, really – all very civilised and polite. And, of course, your father was a pet, as usual. Didn't say too much, but kept making sure I had enough to eat – he must have passed me the salad half a dozen times.'

Laura shook her head. 'Well, that's good; you've done the

meet-the-parents thing and survived.' She didn't add *let's wait and see what the verdict is when it comes in*, but she knew Breffni was thinking it too.

And then two weeks later, on a bitterly cold February afternoon, Breffni walked into the travel agency next door to her workplace and bought a ticket back to San Francisco.

Laura was stunned when Breffni called around to her that evening. 'What do you mean, leaving? You can't leave, just like that. What about Andrew?'

Breffni looked straight at her. 'Actually Laur, Andrew finished with me last week.'

Laura's jaw dropped further. 'What? Why didn't you tell me? What happened?' She crouched beside Breffni's chair and put an arm around her shoulder. 'Are you all right?'

'I'll live.' Breffni shrugged. 'I would have told you, but you've been a bit caught up in college stuff lately; I didn't want to distract you.'

'Bref, are you crazy?' Laura looked bewildered. 'As if my stupid course work would be more important than you. What happened?'

Breffni shrugged again. 'Just that, really. He said he didn't think we were going anywhere, blah blah blah. What could I say?'

Laura considered. Andrew and Breffni hadn't been going out for long – six, seven weeks? – but when Laura had seen them together, she'd have sworn that Andrew was just as taken with Breffni as she seemed to be with him. And hadn't everything been fine when Breffni had gone to dinner with Brian and Cecily the other week?

Cecily, of course. Laura could have hit her, the way she ran Andrew's life. Or hit Andrew, for letting his mother dictate to him. There was no doubt in Laura's mind that Cecily was responsible for this latest development. She took Breffni's hand. 'Look, maybe he's just got cold feet; maybe I could talk to –'

'No.' Breffni pulled away from Laura. 'Absolutely not. I'm not having you begging Andrew to take me back. Anyway, I'm quite looking forward to heading back to the States – especially in this weather.' She got up and walked to the window. 'And the job was driving me mad, you know it was. Nothing to do all day except answer the phone and smile at the few people who came in – deadly boring.' She kept her back to Laura, looking out into the dark garden.

Laura was still struggling to gather her thoughts. 'But you could have just got another job here in Limerick – you don't have to go halfway around the world.' It was the first time either of them had made a decision without talking it over with the other; and now Breffni was doing this huge thing all by herself.

When she didn't respond, Laura tried again. 'Look Bref, why don't you wait a while? Maybe we could go back in the summer – I'll be off for three months. We could do a bit of travelling, maybe go up –'

But Breffni shook her head, still looking out. 'Sorry Laur – I've my mind made up; and I have the ticket bought. But do come out in the summer – I'd love that.' She turned around and leant against the window sill, smiling gently. 'You know, the more I think about it, the more I can't wait to go back – remember the buzz of San Francisco? I bet you could be tempted back yourself right now if you weren't up to your armpits in arty-farty stuff.'

Laura considered. 'Well, yeah, I'd love to go back for another holiday – but I don't know about living there . . . you might start doing daily yoga and eating bean sprouts and chanting.'

Breffni shook her head again, made a face. 'Can you see me doing daily anything, except eating? I might do the odd yoga class, but no bean sprouts unless they're in a big fat stir-fry – and definitely no chanting.'

'You might start saying "have a nice day", and talking about your feelings.'

She smiled faintly. 'I won't, honest. No nice days, no feelings.' She turned and looked out into the night again, and after a minute Laura knew, by the way she bent her head slightly, by the subtle change in her breathing, that she was crying.

Laura went over and put an arm around her shoulder. 'I could kill him.'

'Ah no.' Breffni rubbed a sleeve across her eyes and took a deep breath. 'These things happen; don't blame him. I'll survive.'

'But what'll you do there? How will you make enough to live on?'

'Ah, there's plenty of work there. I'll probably look for house-cleaning – remember all the notices we saw in the supermarkets? Looks like they're crying out for cleaners. Or I could babysit, couldn't I?'

'And where'll you stay?'

'With the cousins to start with – I'm sure they won't mind having me back. And then I'll look around for a place once I'm settled.'

'Rents are sky high there – you'll never afford it without a proper job.'

The ghost of a smile flashed across Breffni's face. 'Well, I suppose I'll have to sell my body then. That should make up the shortfall.'

'Bref, be serious.'

'I am serious – about going back, I mean.' Breffni squared her shoulders, and Laura thought that maybe she was right; maybe the change of scene would do her good.

She grinned. 'Hey, remember the secondhand stores, 'Goodwill' and 'Thrift Town' and that huge Salvation Army shop on Valencia Street?'

Breffni nodded, smiled back. 'Remember when I got the Calvin Klein jeans for five bucks? You were raging with me for spotting them first.'

'Remember the giant pizzas in that little place on Twenty-first Street – what was it called?'

'Oh God, yeah – Serrano's. The size of them, as big as the wheel of a High Nelly. Remember the Greek pizza, with the feta cheese and the olives –'

'And Mitchell's Ice-cream Parlour – the ginger ice-cream we couldn't get enough of. And Trader Joe's sourdough bread.'

Breffni nodded, amused at Laura's enthusiasm. 'See? Is it any wonder I'm heading back to all that? Wouldn't you give your eye teeth to be coming too? And anyway, I might only stay a few months – I'm not planning too far ahead. My ticket's valid for three months, and I can extend it up to a year once I'm there, as long as I keep well hidden. I'm sure there'll be plenty of boring office jobs here when I come back.'

But she hadn't come back. Not that year – not even for Christmas, in case they wouldn't let her in again. She wrote to Laura often – long, funny letters full of news and chat about the people she cleaned for.

Georgia is such a typical Californian, therapists for every different part of her life. She can't go to the corner store without some sort of e-mail consultation with one of them . . . Jules and Patrick live in this immaculate apartment they think needs cleaning twice a week – and who am I to argue, at fifteen bucks an hour? I have to hoover – sorry, vacuum

– the ceilings in their two bathrooms. One bedroom, two bathrooms. Only in America, my friend.

She described the characters she met when she took her little babysitting charges to the local parks: Cloud, the gay eighteen-year-old who took obsessive care of Toby, his little half-brother; Teresa, the smiling Mexican nanny with a pair of breath-catchingly beautiful toddler twins dressed from head to toe in designer labels – '*and you may be sure Mamma went nowhere near her local thrift store*'.

Reading Breffni's letters, Laura could see the charming, litter-strewn city again. She could smell the spices wafting from the ethnic restaurants on Mission Street and see the teenage Mexicans gathered on the corners in their baggy pants and hoodies, even on the hottest days, whistling and calling to the passing females.

She could see herself on top of a hilly street at night, looking down at the city lights surrounding the bay. She could close her eyes and wander through Golden Gate Park in the sunshine, catching snatches of an open-air jazz concert or hearing the *thwack* of a baseball against a bat. She could jog along the path by Ocean Beach and smell the sea, more often than not surrounded by the fog that was one of the many quirks of San Francisco. She could walk through streets of pastel-coloured wooden houses and pass beggars wrapped in filthy blankets outside chic little coffee shops and boutiques.

The summer after Breffni went back to San Francisco, Laura took out a bank loan and flew over to join her for a month. She stayed a week in the tiny two-roomed apartment on Lexington Street that Breffni shared with another Irish girl, and then they hired a car and drove across to Yosemite National Park, where they hiked through forests of gigantic redwoods and sat by waterfalls to feel the spray cooling their hot faces.

Back in San Francisco, they went out to dinner with Breffni's cousins and their friends, and the day before Laura flew back to Ireland, they had a picnic on the same beach where they'd eaten barbecued salmon two years before.

That autumn, Donal walked into The White House on a night Laura was working there, and the next time she and Breffni met was a year later in Rome, where Laura and Donal went to get married.

Laura phoned Breffni in San Francisco after she got engaged. 'You're bridesmaid, naturally.'

'Naturally.' Breffni might have been in the house down the road, her voice was so clear. 'Laur, I'm thrilled. But it's kinda quick, isn't it? You haven't known him that long.'

Laura thought of Donal and closed her eyes to relish the deep happiness that flooded through her. 'Long enough to know that he's the one.'

'Gee, you sound so sure. Tell me again what he's like.'

'Gorgeous: you'd love him, dark hair like your Andy Garcia, beautiful smile, very funny. I'll send a photo. And guess what – he's a chef, so I'll never have to cook.'

'Hmm – very important consideration when you're choosing your life partner. And what do the folks think of him?'

Laura groaned. 'God, I was hoping you wouldn't bring that up. Of course Dad is delighted, over the moon. *She* totally disapproves, thinks he's too old.'

'Oh yeah, I forgot about the age difference.'

'It's only fifteen years; it's nothing.'

'You're right – that's nothing; old enough to be interesting, not too old to be past it.'

Laura closed her eyes again, smiling. 'You can say that again;

he knows what he's at in that department.'

Breffni laughed. 'You lucky woman; hang on to him, don't mind Mother. I've just met someone too actually; I was going to write and tell you.'

'Hey Bref, that's great; what's he like?'

'Lovely. No oil painting, but lovely and comfortable to be with, you know? His name's Cian.'

And Laura, who'd been about to ask Breffni if she'd be OK meeting Andrew at the wedding, decided to say nothing. She did wonder, though, if there would be any awkwardness when they came face to face for the first time since the break-up. It was a few years ago, but still . . . was there a danger of something starting up again, being rekindled in the heady Roman air? Andrew was unattached, as far as Laura knew; and it sounded like very early days with this new man, Cian. Could Breffni really be so foolish as to risk fresh heartbreak? Laura was fairly certain that Cecily wouldn't have changed her mind about Breffni's suitability for her darling Andrew. She'd got rid of Breffni once before – she could certainly do it again.

But Laura needn't have worried; there seemed to be no awkwardness when Andrew and Breffni met in the hotel lobby, the evening before the wedding.

'Hey you.' Andrew gave Breffni a mock punch in the arm. 'How's the States treating you?'

'Fine, just fine.' Breffni beamed back at him. 'And you? Still stuck behind a desk in boring old Limerick?' She winked at Laura, looking totally relaxed.

Andrew grinned. 'Limerick suits me fine, thanks – no mosquitoes, no earthquakes . . . I'm quite happy.'

'Hmmm . . . I'm not convinced.' She jerked a thumb in Donal's direction. 'And what do you think of your future brother-in-law?'

And then the elevator doors opened and Brian and Cecily appeared, and they had hardly any time to themselves after that. But it was enough to convince Laura that whatever had been there between them was a thing of the past. Maybe this Cian was more important than Breffni had been letting on; Laura would find out later.

After the wedding ceremony in a little Pallotine church in the Piazza San Silvestro, the small group had champagne and pasta in a chic little restaurant run by Polish nuns. Laura was radiant in simple cream raw silk that stopped just above her ankles; Breffni turned heads in a short, deep-coral shift dress. Cecily was politely distant in pale blue linen. Donal the groom, Tom his best man, Andrew, and Laura's father Brian, who was to fall off a ladder and break his neck only two years later, all wore light grey suits. Apart from Tom, there were no guests on the groom's side: Donal's parents hadn't come, and he had no other family close enough to drag all the way to Rome.

And now it was seven years later, and Breffni had moved back home two years ago with Cian at her side, and Polly had arrived a few months after that. And Laura was godmother to Polly, and got on well with Cian, and was married to the man she adored, and enjoyed her work most of the time.

And every so often, she managed to forget the one thing that stopped her from being completely content.

✡✡✡

'Only me.'

In the sitting room, Breffni pressed the off button on the TV remote control and smiled. Cian's predictability was one of the things that had decided her, after a few disastrous roller-coaster romances, that he was the one she needed to make a life with. She couldn't remember a day when he hadn't let himself into the house with those words: *only me*.

'Hi – in here.' She stood and walked towards the door and met him as he came through, shaking off his jacket. He looked tired; she'd run him a bath after dinner. She leant her head briefly against his chest, pressed her palms into his back, felt the solid bulk of him. He smelt of mint, and the fabric softener she dolloped into the washing. 'Mmmm. Miss me?'

'But of course.' He dropped a kiss on her blue-black hair. 'How's the patient?'

'Ex-patient – totally back to normal. Sang in the bath, demanded two stories in bed.'

He smiled what Breffni called his Polly smile, his whole round face seeming to blur around the edges. 'Is she gone up long?'

Breffni shook her head against his shoulder, dropped her arms. 'She'll still be awake, just about – and dinner's in ten minutes.'

'Thanks, love.' He turned and headed for the door, and she stood and followed the muffled thud of his steps up the stairs and across the landing to Polly's room.

In the kitchen she lit the stub of red candle that sat in an eggcup in the middle of the oval table. They always ate in here, even when they had visitors. The cottage didn't have a dining room, just a biggish kitchen and a slightly smaller sitting room downstairs.

In winter they practically lived in the kitchen, firing up the wood stove and settling down with their books and mugs of tea into the battered old couch they'd inherited with the house. It had been left in the sitting room, but they shoved it into the kitchen to make room for the pair of two-seaters and wooden rocking chair they'd bought. They planned to fire it onto the skip they were waiting for, but somehow it had never made it past the corner near the stove.

It was worn and a bit lumpy, and the cover was threadbare in places, and Breffni would never have chosen a sofa covered in blue and green check, but there was something extremely cosy about collapsing into its depths after a day at work. When they decided to keep it, she bought a big, woolly, dark blue throw and three fat, cherry-red cushions, and hung on to the receipts for a week until she was sure they all worked.

Now, when the weather got wintry and everyone complained about the shorter days, she knew it was only a matter of time before they gravitated towards the kitchen and the long, cosy nights by the stove. Who needed a life full of excitement anyway? That kind of thing only happened on telly, didn't it? What she and Cian had was worth so much more. And so what if he didn't make the earth move, if he wasn't exactly Brad Pitt? Breffni was willing to bet that Jennifer Aniston never stopped worrying about how to hang on to him. No, she and Cian were the lucky ones – secure, settled, relaxed with each other. That was what counted – having someone you knew would always be there, no matter what.

Listen to her – she sounded like Granny Mary. She smiled as she put out cutlery and glasses, and thought: *I must ask her if she can babysit on Thursday night.* She took a bottle of Chardonnay from the fridge and left it on the worktop – that'd go fine with the beef curry. She'd never gone along with that nonsense about matching red wine with red meat, and Cian wasn't a bit fussy either.

As she lifted the saucepan lid and gave the curry a last stir, she imagined Cecily's horror at the thought of serving white wine with beef. She thought of Andrew's new wife – what was her name again? – having to live with her mother-in-law. Cecily was harmless enough really, but the notion of sharing a home with her was pretty intimidating – all that best flowery china and Waterford crystal, having to say excuse me when all you did was cough, using a special little fork to eat a slice of cake, for God's sake. Breffni pictured Cian's face if she handed him a fork with his cake – he'd get a great laugh, before he picked up the slice and took a big bite out of it.

She was tipping the rice into a warm bowl as he came into the kitchen, sniffing the air. 'Mmm – smells fantastic.' She smiled at him. Such a pet – he loved his food, was always so appreciative – and God knew she'd had her share of culinary disasters since they started living together. She remembered two thick fish cutlets that were beautifully grilled on the outside and still perfectly raw in the middle, leathery omelettes, lumpy or cement-thick sauces, and one unforgettable dried-out roast chicken complete with giblets. She was still no Delia Smith, but at least she'd managed not to poison him while she was getting the hang of a few recipes. Poor Cian.

He went to the sink and washed his hands. 'Did you manage much work today?'

She nodded. 'Finished it, finally. I'll send it off tomorrow.'

She freelanced as a proofreader for a few businesses, including a medium-sized publishing house based in the midlands. When they'd moved back from San Francisco, and Cian was hunting around for an accountancy job, Breffni had got a call from her mother one day.

'I've some work for you, pet – nice and easy, just up your alley.'

Breffni was half-amused, half-indignant. 'Ma, I'm not looking for work – have you forgotten I'm heavily pregnant? This is my – what do they call it? – my confinement. I have to take things easy.'

Her mother's snort came clearly down the line. 'Confinement, my foot; you sound like something out of Jane Austen. You're not even five months gone, and you're hardly showing. You're not sick, your ankles aren't swollen, you haven't even got any food cravings.'

'I like Smarties and salt-and-vinegar Taytos together.'

'You've liked that since you were nine. And have you forgotten, my girl, that you've no money coming in, and a baby on the way? Cian hasn't found a job yet, has he?'

'Well no, but he has –'

Her mother sailed on. 'So you've a baby coming and nobody earning. And I know you brought a bit of money home with you from America, but it'll go fast over here – you must have noticed how dear everything has got since you left.'

Breffni had to admit the truth of that. 'But Ma, I can't start a job now – not when I'd be looking for maternity leave so soon.'

'Ah, but it's not a job like that – it's just a bit of reading really. You know how you always loved English at school? You were great at spellings and grammar and things like that.'

'Well, I suppose I liked it, but –'

'So you know Orla Keyes' daughter Rebecca – the middle girl – is in her final year in UCG?' Orla and Breffni's mother had been close friends for years. 'She's just finished her thesis and needs someone to go though it, tidy it up a bit. I told Orla you might have a look at it. And they'd pay; she said they'd insist on paying.'

Breffni didn't want to admit that it did sound tempting – something she could do at home, in her own time. 'What's the subject?'

'No idea – give her a ring and find out. Here's her number.'

So Breffni had said she'd look into it, knowing that she had no choice really, and she'd been amazed by how much she enjoyed trawling through the hundred-odd pages, pouncing on a clumsy phrase, tweaking a sentence here, removing a rogue apostrophe there and generally knocking the thesis into pretty good shape. When the surprisingly respectable cheque had arrived a few weeks later, she'd taken the newly-employed Cian out to dinner and put her idea to him.

'I checked up on Google, and there are courses in England I could do by post, which would fit in perfectly with the baby. And when I got the qualification, I could work from home, whenever I had a few hours free.'

He'd nodded, placid as ever. 'Sounds good – I'd say go for it, if you want it.'

And ten months later she finished the course – Polly's arrival had stretched the original six-month schedule – and now she was a proper proofreader, with enough of an income to justify her occasional splurge in Brown Thomas. And the regular bottle of Chardonnay. 'Will you open the wine, love?' She put the rice on the table as Cian reached for the corkscrew. 'How was your day?'

'Grand, the usual.' Cian never went into detail about what he did in the firm of Chartered Surveyors, and Breffni never pressed him, quite sure that she wouldn't understand a word. On the few occasions that she'd come into contact with his workmates, like the recent retirement do, she got the impression that they weren't what you'd call a barrel of laughs. Still, it seemed to suit him – he headed off happily every morning, after kissing her and catching Polly up in his arms and twirling her around till she screamed with delight.

Breffni often marvelled at how little Cian needed to keep him happy – a good dinner, a sunny day, a lie-in at the weekend – any of these seemed to give him as much pleasure as the iPod Breffni had given him when he'd turned thirty last year, or the helicopter ride they'd taken in the States once. It was another of the qualities that had drawn her to him, this built-in contentment of his.

She sat opposite him now, picked up her fork. 'Oh, nearly forgot. Laur phoned, wants to know if we're free for dinner on Thursday night. You're not planning to whisk me off to Paris for a long weekend, are you?'

He smiled. 'No, that's next month.' He poured wine into their glasses. 'What's the occasion?'

'Andrew and his new bride – can't remember her name – are back from honeymoon. Laur wants us to meet her: and you've never met Andrew either, have you?'

'That's Laura's brother, is it?'

She nodded.

'No, never met him.' He spooned a helping of rice onto his plate, added a generous dollop of curry. 'What's he like?'

Breffni had never told Cian about her fling with Andrew; what would have been the point? 'Nice. Charming. Looks a bit like Laura, from what I remember. I haven't laid eyes on him in years.'

Not since the wedding in Rome, when she'd been all butterflies on the flight over from the States, thinking about the last time they'd met. Her sitting on the plastic seat in the bus shelter in Limerick, trying desperately not to cry as he stood with his hands in his pockets beside her and said that he didn't think it was working out. *Why not*? She'd been dying to ask. What had changed since the week before, when he'd been walking her home after dinner at his parents' house – all of fifty yards away – and he'd stopped halfway between the two houses and leant against a garden wall and pulled her against him and kissed her face all over, and told her softly how beautiful she was? What had happened to change all that?

And how ridiculous it was to be vaguely disappointed when

he'd been so casual in Rome, instead of being relieved that he obviously felt no tension between them. Instead of being glad that they could be friends now, put all that business behind them. Especially when she was just after meeting Cian, who was so different. So lovely and safe.

Looking across at Cian now, mopping up his curry sauce with a chunk of Naan bread, Breffni wondered if things might be about to change a bit. Knowing Laura, she'd be taking care of her new sister-in-law, making sure she found her feet in Limerick. Including the newlyweds in nights out, all six of them off together. Possibly expecting Breffni to do her bit too, have Andrew and the wife over here to dinner whenever Laura and Donal came out.

Which was absolutely fine. She picked up her wine. '*Sláinte*.'

'*Sláinte*.' He looked at her over the edge of his glass. 'So what else did you get up to today?'

She took a drink and told him about Polly's Lego tower.

✡✡✡

'Now, Mags, here's Cecily to talk to you while I get the tea.' Valerie waved Cecily ahead of her into the sitting room.

'Margaret, hello.' Cecily smiled across the room at a fragile-looking white-haired woman. Poor Margaret's ten-year battle with arthritis had aged her terribly; a stranger would have put her at well over eighty, instead of just seventy-three. From her high-backed, fairly solid-looking chair – easier to get out of – she stretched out a tragically swollen-knuckled hand. 'Cecily dear, elegant as ever. Isn't all this rain terrible?'

'Shocking.' Cecily dropped her bag and took the outstretched hand in hers. 'It's probably not doing you any favours.'

Margaret smiled ruefully as Cecily settled into the chair next to her. 'Not really, dear, no, but I'm not complaining. I'm lucky to have Valerie so near – she's a great help.' Valerie was Margaret's niece, a relatively recent addition to the group, and playing hostess tonight for the first time. Margaret leant towards Cecily and lowered her voice a little. 'I have the poor girl run off her feet, if the truth be told.'

'Is that me you're talking about?' The door was nudged open and Valerie reappeared with a tray.

Margaret smiled warmly at her. 'I was telling Cecily how much of a help you are to me, dear. I'd be lost without you.'

'You would not – didn't you manage fine before I arrived?' Valerie began unloading the tray. 'I hope the others will be able to make it; they said on the radio that there are floods out around Corbally.'

Cecily saw with relief that they were getting cups and saucers; she'd suspected that Valerie, the youngest member by far of the reading group, might use mugs. Cecily had never in her life willingly drunk out of a mug, not even a china one. Horrible, clumsy things: suitable only for tradespeople and children. But these cups, while lacking the delicacy of Cecily's bone china, were quite acceptable.

The doorbell rang, and Valerie straightened up. 'Oh good, there's someone else.' She put a plate of fruitcake on the table before leaving with the empty tray.

Cecily looked at the cake. Shop bought, probably. She couldn't see Valerie in an apron surrounded by caster sugar and flour. To be honest, Cecily wasn't sure that Valerie quite fitted into the group. For one thing, there was the age difference. All the other members were over sixty; in fact, before the arrival of Valerie, Cecily had been easily the youngest, by at least three years. Not, of course, that that would have been grounds for refusing entry to Valerie. Indeed not, particularly as she was Margaret's niece.

When Margaret had tentatively broached the subject of Valerie's joining them 'occasionally', they'd all agreed straightaway – of course they had. It was just – well, she couldn't be more than thirty-six or seven; surely she should be mixing with people of her own generation, instead of trying to fit in with a group nearly twice her age? True, she could talk about the books with the best of them, and the couple she'd recommended had been quite popular. But still . . . .

Cecily became aware of Margaret looking questioningly at her and smiled apologetically. 'Sorry, dear, did you say something? I'm afraid I was miles away.'

'Just wondering how the newlyweds are getting on.'

Cecily had mentioned Andrew's wedding at the last monthly meeting; reluctant as she usually was to discuss her private life, she never objected to talking about Andrew. She was so proud of him: such a handsome man, and so charming. Always there for her. Always ready to take her advice on board, if she felt the need to offer it.

Cecily smiled happily at Margaret. 'The newlyweds are fine; they're staying with me until their house is ready. Ruth is a lovely girl – you'll meet her when I'm hosting. She's quite a reader herself actually; I was only saying to her –'

At that moment, the door opened again.

'In you go – I'll just get the teapot.' Valerie's voice was followed by the appearance in the doorway of Dorothy – 'Hello, ladies' – and a man whom Cecily had never seen before.

He smiled at them as Dorothy said, 'Margaret, Cecily, this is Frank, my new neighbour. He's just moved here from Sligo and knows nobody yet. I invited him along to sit in tonight.' Before either woman could respond, the doorbell rang again. Valerie, just arrived in with the teapot, put it down on the table – 'Good, that'll be Emily; we're all here now' – and left the room again.

Cecily put out her hand to shake the one that was stretched towards her; what else could she do? As Frank – such a common name – took it, she hardly heard what he said.

How dare Dorothy take it on herself to bring a newcomer to the group without having the courtesy to mention it beforehand? And what on earth did 'sit in' mean? You couldn't sit in on a book club – the whole idea was to get together to talk about whatever book they'd all read. He'd be bored silly, just sitting there listening to them. And was he going to be a fixture from now on – or worse, assume he could pop along to a meeting whenever he felt like it? Was he going to turn up in Cecily's house next month, when it was her turn to host? Of course, if Margaret hadn't begun it all by foisting that niece on them, this wouldn't have happened; but at least *she'd* had the grace to clear it with them first.

'Not a name you hear too often now.' That man had sat next to her; she couldn't avoid a conversation without being rude. Dorothy had settled herself across from Margaret, peeling off her gloves and asking about the arthritis as if she'd done nothing wrong in parading into the meeting with a complete stranger; the nerve of the woman.

Cecily turned her head and gave Frank her coolest look. 'Sorry, did you say something?'

'Cecily.' Either he'd missed her lack of enthusiasm, in which case he was obtuse, or he'd decided to ignore it, which made him insensitive. 'I had an aunt called Cecily, but apart from that, I don't remember ever coming across it.' He smiled wider then, showing small, even teeth. 'It suits you; genteel, like yourself.'

She couldn't believe the familiarity of the man. She decided not to respond to such a silly comment – genteel, like yourself, indeed; he wouldn't know genteel if it stood in front of him and saluted. She turned slightly away from him; she'd talk to Margaret instead. Let him 'sit in' on that if he wanted.

'Tea, anyone?' He lifted the pot and held it poised over a cup and saucer, smiling at them enquiringly.

Had the man no manners? Imagine insulting their hostess by helping himself to tea; and dismayingly, there were Margaret and Dorothy smiling and nodding. You'd think Margaret had never set eyes on a man before; she was practically blushing, for goodness' sake. Cecily wanted to shake her, arthritis or no arthritis.

Now that man was looking at her again, waving the teapot around like he owned the place. Probably expecting her to dissolve into a simpering teenager too. Well, she wouldn't please him: she tried another ice-cold stare. 'I think I'd rather let it draw a bit, thank you.'

The door opened again and Emily came in – good. Surely she'd say something – she wasn't afraid to air her opinions.

'Sorry I'm late, everyone.' She unwound a soft-looking grey scarf as she walked to the vacant chair across from Cecily. 'The phone rang as I was coming out.' She noticed Frank just as Dorothy introduced him.

Cecily watched, waiting for Emily to frown and remind Dorothy gently that bringing a stranger to the book club without clearing it with the members beforehand simply wasn't done; or if that was a little direct, at least to allow a little disapproval to show on her face. But Emily smiled pleasantly and stretched out her hand. 'Another new member – how nice. Now we'll get the male perspective on our books.'

Cecily couldn't believe it. Emily didn't seem in the least put out by the presence of Dorothy's neighbour; and it was quite clear that Margaret had no objection either. Was she the only member with any standards? Maybe they should go out into the street and drag in the homeless to discuss the latest Ian McEwan.

As Cecily fumed silently, Valerie came back in and glanced around the table. 'Good, you've gone ahead and served yourselves. Cecily, you have no tea; let me pour. Emily, give me that gorgeous scarf and I'll hang it over the radiator. Dorothy, did you try the cake? Thanks so much for the recipe – much more straightforward than my usual one.'

And the September meeting of the book club was officially in session.

✡✡✡

Laura's arm had gone to sleep. She often woke lying on her stomach, with her right arm a dead weight under her head. Now she could hardly move it, it was so full of pins and needles. She manoeuvred it awkwardly out from under her head, and waited. After a few seconds she could wriggle her fingers. When the arm was fully back to life she gave it a shake, then pulled Donal's pillow over to her and snuggled back down with it into the warmth – bliss.

Donal was convinced that if she could work from her bed she would, and she had to admit that the idea sounded very tempting. She loved this time of the day – still half-asleep, tucked up cosily while the rest of the world hurried out to work. If she heard the rain drumming against the window, so much the better.

She opened an eye and checked the clock radio: twenty past eight. Donal would be halfway to the university, flying past the queue of cars on his bike. She pictured him pedalling out the

Dublin road, jacket that he rarely closed flapping behind him.

He'd been on the bike the evening they'd met in The White House. When he asked if he could take her home after she finished clearing up, she of course assumed he meant in a car. She was twenty-one; he was clearly a fair bit older. He'd been chatting to her for about an hour, since he'd arrived in on his own and walked to the counter and ordered a pint.

She gathered in the empty glasses the other barperson was piling onto the counter. 'You don't even know where I live; it could be the other side of the city from you.'

He pretended to consider. 'Hmm. Yes, that's true. I may have to go – let's see now – a whole three miles out of my way.' He smiled, a lovely crinkly-eyed smile, and picked up his pint. 'I think I'll risk it.'

When she'd finally finished up, they went outside and he walked over to the bike, chained to a pole.

She laughed, sure he was joking again. 'OK, where's the Merc?'

'This is much better than a Merc.' He fished a key from his pocket and began to unlock the bike, not a bit put out. 'Like they nearly said in Animal Farm, four wheels bad, two wheels good.' Then he turned back to her, chain in his hand. 'Listen, as you know, I've had a few pints. Aren't two wheels safer than four when your chauffeur's not completely sober?'

And she had to agree that they probably were. Anyway, to tell the truth, she was charmed – she hadn't gone home on the bar of a bike for years. He got on and looked over at her questioningly, patted the bar in front of him.

She walked across and perched up on it, feeling faintly silly, and grabbed onto his jacket as the bike wobbled slightly. 'Hey, watch it – you'll have my father to answer to if anything happens to me.'

'Right, I'd better keep Daddy happy then. Hang on tight and you'll be fine.' He shifted slightly to accommodate her weight, and she was conscious of his nearness – their faces were inches apart – and the musky scent of him.

'What's the aftershave?'

He grinned, raised his eyebrows at her. 'Essence of Donal. Guaranteed to pull the best-looking girl in the pub. Works every time; even without the Merc.'

And right from the start, it had been easy between them. She'd always scoffed at the notion of love at first sight, but now she knew that there *was* such a thing. Maybe it wasn't love, not straightaway, but certainly *something* had happened that night, to both of them. She had known, she'd been certain that he'd ask to see her again; and she knew she'd say 'yes' without thinking. It was as easy as that.

And when he asked her to marry him, just four months later and a week before her twenty-second birthday, she wondered what had taken him so long. He'd taken a piece of his spaghetti – they were in the basement of her favourite Italian restaurant – and made a ring out of it and slid it onto her wedding finger, and she'd looked up from it, laughing, and he'd said 'Will you?' Not laughing at all, for once. And when she realised that he was really . . . that this was really . . . oh my God – she stopped laughing and started crying, tears pouring down her face and frightening the life out of him until he realised what they meant. When she'd recovered, and everyone had stopped looking over at them, she put a hand up to touch his face. 'Thought you'd never ask.'

'Thought you mightn't have me, with only a spaghetti ring and all.' He lifted her hand from his cheek and kissed her palm, and she felt the tears threatening again.

And when the bill was paid they'd gone back to his house in

Westbury and she'd missed lectures for two days.

From the start, Donal and Laura's father had got on fine, were relaxed in each other's company, even if Donal did most of the talking. But Cecily was adamant in her disapproval of Laura's choice; in her opinion, fifteen years was too big a gap. Of course, she congratulated them both when they broke the news to her and Brian, shook hands with Donal, offered him a cool cheek to kiss – but she lost no time in voicing her opinion once she had Laura on her own.

'He'll be fifty-five – well into middle-age – when you're just out of your thirties. Have you thought of that?'

Laura *had* thought of that; she'd thought of everything. She'd pushed away the horrifying fact that he would probably die before her, and she would have to find a way to survive the agony of being without him. But she adored him and so she ignored her mother, whom she did not adore, and married him.

It was Donal who encouraged her to go freelance as soon as she left the Art College.

'But I've no portfolio, apart from the bits and bobs I did in college. I've absolutely no experience. Who'd take me on?' They were sprawled on the couch after a lazy Sunday brunch of soft poached eggs sprinkled with chopped chives, and buttery crumpets. (She'd never tasted a crumpet until she met him; he couldn't last a weekend without a stack of them, getting up to make the batter while she lay in bed with the paper.)

They'd been married six months, and she would have walked barefoot to the moon if he'd asked her.

'What do you mean, who'd take you on? Who in their right mind wouldn't? My darling girl, you've got talent coming out of those beautiful ears.' He took her face in his hands and she gazed back at him, drinking him in. 'Listen; some of the stuff you did in college is as good as any I've ever seen.'

'But you're prejudiced, because you adore me.' She pushed her hand through his tousled dark hair, ran her fingertips over the Sunday-morning stubble on his chin, felt her way down along his faded black t-shirt to rest on one blue-jeaned leg thrown over hers. Her stomach flipped; six months after their wedding, he was still making her stomach flip.

'True, I'm totally prejudiced; but I'm right too.' He traced her cheekbone with a finger. 'And you know what? I'd say Tony and Marie might use you.' Tony was Donal's friend, a sales rep until the company he worked for relocated to Korea, and now in the process of setting up a wedding planner service with the help of his about-town wife and his redundancy cheque. 'They'll need someone to help with the design side of things; that'd be right up your street.'

She looked at him and thought about creating an image for a totally new business venture. That would be some undertaking; and the idea that she might be capable of doing it took her breath away. But Donal seemed to think she could – and even if he *was* a bit biased, maybe he was right too. She *had* got on well in college; her tutors had often praised her work, and she was secretly proud of the various pieces she'd selected for her portfolio. She'd done that kind of stuff all the time in college: why couldn't she do it for real now?

Donal's hand travelled into her hair, twining a single auburn curl around his finger. 'OK, what about this? If you offered to help them out with an overall look for the business, in return for their showing your designs for wedding invitations, or church booklets or whatever, to prospective clients – they'd probably jump at it.'

She smiled at his enthusiasm. 'Donal, it's great that you have such faith in me, but even if I managed to come up with something they liked, I have no idea about business – I could be taken to the cleaners and not realise it. I mean, I wouldn't have a clue what to charge for a wedding invitation design, or booklet, or whatever.'

'Then you can learn as you go along, like a lot of people do. Tony's got a head for business like you wouldn't believe – I'd hate to have to drive a bargain with him. If you were in his camp you wouldn't go far wrong.'

He put a hand on each side of her face, forcing her to look straight at him. 'Look, love, you have to start somewhere – and you've got what it takes to be your own boss; I'm convinced of that. All you need is a bit of confidence. I really think you'd be a fool not to at least give it a try. Couldn't you get in touch with some freelancers and talk about money? I'm sure the college could give you a few names.'

He held on to her face so she couldn't look away. 'At least give it a few months – give it six months, till the end of the year. You're barely twenty-three – a slip of a thing still. You can always look for a job somewhere afterwards if it doesn't work out.' His eyes slid to her mouth. 'If it came to it –' he traced her top lip with his thumb '– I suppose I *could* support you for a while till you got going . . .' she opened her mouth and tasted butter on his thumb '. . . provided that you paid me back in sexual favours of my own choosing. What do you think?' He bent his head and kissed the side of her mouth. 'Will you give it a try?'

She spoke softly, pressing closer to him. 'Hmm, sexual favours . . . I don't know . . .' He kissed the other side of her mouth, and she closed her eyes. '. . . I suppose we could work something out – but you know I don't come cheap. You'd have serious supporting to do if that was how I was paying you back.' As he moved his head down towards the side of her neck – the first of her erogenous zones he'd discovered – her hands crept around his back, slid up under his t-shirt.

He spoke with his mouth on her throat; his words vibrated deliciously against her. 'You're worth every cent, young one. Just promise me you'll think about it.' Then he lifted his head and she opened her eyes reluctantly. 'Let's meet Tony and Marie for a drink and talk to them; you can show them your portfolio.'

She pushed his head down into her neck again and buried her hands in his hair. 'I'll think about it, I promise. Now, where were we . . . ?'

And a few nights later, over drinks in Jury's bar, the four of them had come up with a few jokey ideas for the wedding planner business. And a while after that, she and Marie had got together and sorted out a few more serious ideas.

'Kiss the Bride', Limerick's first wedding planner service, had slotted beautifully into the market gap. Marie and Tony included Laura's designs as part of their overall package, and from then on she was rarely out of work – christening invitations inevitably followed the wedding ones; restaurant menus happened through a contact of Donal's in the catering trade; company brochures came along now and again. Orders for various leaflets and booklets trickled in steadily. And now, thanks to a contact in the Art College, there was a potentially very lucrative schoolbook contract in the offing.

Not all the work appealed to her – illustrating leaflets for the likes of boiler companies, manufacturers of computer components or general hardware stores she found pretty soul-destroying. A few times she was asked to design a brochure for the kind of holiday centres she knew she'd run a mile from. Sometimes she had to work with writers who had quite definite design ideas of their own, and weren't too happy if Laura begged to differ. She stayed up one entire night trying to make a block of horrendous apartments look inviting enough for someone actually to want to live in one.

But every now and again the fun jobs came along: a boutique needing to update its logo, invitations to a children's party, a seaside-themed mural for a fish restaurant owner who was quite happy to let Laura have her way. And sometimes, whatever she was working on, she would find herself stopping and smiling, and thanking whatever lucky stars were responsible for her being able to make a living doing what she loved.

Eventually she found herself sharing a studio with two of her friends from Art College. It was small for three of them, and cold in winter, with not as much natural light as they would have liked, and the rent climbed steadily in return for a glimpse of the Shannon in the distance; but they got on well and had a laugh, and rounded off each week with a few beers in the pub two doors away.

Sometimes, especially when the jobs were plentiful, she felt guilty that it had all been so easy. Donal laughed when she confessed this to him.

'My darling girl, it's your skill that's got you where you are – not luck. You're a talented illustrator, but not any luckier than anyone else – apart from the fact that you're married to me, of course.' She lifted her head from the sketchpad in front of her, but his face was expressionless. 'That was a lucky night, when I walked into The White House and put my eye on you.'

She grinned. 'Yeah, lucky for you, managing to snag the glamorous young barmaid. Be serious, though – you know what I mean. Look at Andrew, slaving away in that horrible computer company five days a week: two weeks off when someone else decides. Same old routine, day in, day out – it must drive him mad. Every day is different for me; unless I've a tight deadline, I can get up when I want, go into the studio or stay and work here, stop when I've had enough. Every job is different from the last one. Why should my lot be so much better?'

He shrugged. 'Look, love, he's your brother and I've nothing against him –'

She shot him a disbelieving look. 'Really?'

He smiled. 'We'll never be best buddies, but I can take him or leave him, you know that. And you and I both know that Andrew likes the easy life: he'll be at that desk in that office till the day he retires. And who's to say that he doesn't enjoy it? I know it would kill you to have to sit in front of a computer screen all day, and it certainly wouldn't be my idea of fun, but it might well suit Andrew – he's obviously got some affinity with computers. And I'm sure he's bringing home a healthy cheque at the end of all those boring weeks – programmers are well looked after.'

She nodded. 'I suppose so.' Donal always managed to make sense of things. She smiled across at him; she was lucky to be married to him – not that she'd ever give him the satisfaction of admitting it, of course.

He'd never learnt to drive – a quirk she secretly found endearing. 'There are enough internal combustion engines polluting the planet without me adding to them. And the bike helps keep me in shape.' He bent his elbow and made a fist, pointing at his barely bulging tricep. 'Feel that for muscle. Go on, feel it.' She tickled under his arm instead, and he grabbed her. 'You're just jealous of my perfectly toned physique. I'm getting you a bike for your next birthday.'

She put her most innocent face on. 'How'll you afford it though, after you've paid for the diamond necklace?'

She got used to being the driver for both of them, had always preferred to drive than be driven anyway. And she had to admire the stance he'd taken: cycling to work at dawn in the middle of an Irish winter couldn't be anyone's idea of fun, however environmentally friendly it was. But he never complained, and it was definitely cheaper – although she wasn't convinced that cycling through all those petrol fumes was healthier than driving through them.

Once, she'd suggested that he wear a mask on the bike, showing him a magazine photo of masked cyclists in Tokyo. 'I hate to think of you inhaling all those fumes every day.'

She was wasting her time – he'd been highly amused. 'Right, I'll pick up the mask when I go to collect the cape and the special powers, OK?' Sometimes he could be too damn smart.

Now she reached out and pressed the slumber button on the radio, and Diana Krall sang 'Cry Me a River' in her chocolaty voice. Laura sank back onto the pillows – ten more minutes. There was an estate agent's brochure waiting to be finished off that should have been gone two days ago; she'd better get it out of the way today.

She started to plan the menu for Thursday night.

✡✡✡

Blast. Andrew O'Neill braked sharply as he reached the traffic lights, just gone red. If the garda car hadn't been in his rear-view mirror he'd have kept going; everyone else did. He drummed his fingers on the steering wheel as he watched the stream of cars crossing in front of him. One person in most of them; no wonder they all crawled home every day. He'd share if anyone suggested it – quite a few of the lads lived around the North Circular – but nobody else seemed too bothered, so why should he? Mind you, the traffic here was still nowhere near as bad as Dublin – imagine the poor sods who had to battle through *that* every day. He'd driven up there only once when he started seeing Ruth; after crawling all the way through Monasterevin, and arriving two hours late to meet her and her flatmates in The Gravediggers, he vowed to switch to the train.

His stomach rumbled; he thought about dinner. Chicken, maybe – they'd had fish last night. With health-conscious Mother doing the cooking, they didn't see a lot of red meat. Not that he was complaining; his mother's meals were up there with the best, no doubt about it. Everything fully planned and meticulously timed, and beautifully presented. Nothing was left to chance in Mother's kitchen.

He remembered watching her when he was a young boy – the way she'd cover the open page of her recipe book with a sheet of acetate to protect it before she started. How she'd peer at the page as she went along, measuring out the ingredients exactly – even quarter teaspoons of salt were carefully calculated. Everything was washed up as she went along; any rare spills were cleaned away immediately.

Then he thought of weekends in Dublin over the past few months, in the poky flat that Ruth shared with Claire and Maura. Their potluck casseroles, where they'd fling in whatever they could find in the fridge and hope for the best – inevitably, with more success some times than others. Every saucepan used; onion skins, red pepper seeds and eggshells littering every worktop. A couple of bottles of not very good wine to go with every dinner, once the few decent ones he'd brought up had run out. A lot more fun, he had to admit, than Mother's perfect meals in Limerick – although he *was* tempted, once or twice, to hint that they try following a recipe occasionally. He'd held his tongue though – they might suggest he do it himself.

He thought about the food in Crete, when he and Ruth first met. Plates of stuffed vine leaves – Ruth went mad for them – salads drenched in salty olive oil, crowned with a thick slab of feta sprinkled with herbs. Tender chunks of chicken wedged between deliciously crisp vegetables on a skewer, slow-cooked lamb, rich with oregano and basil. Inch-thick monkfish steaks that melted in your mouth. Spinach and cheese pies, still warm from the oven, which they brought to the beach every day. He remembered leaning over and licking the flakes of pastry off her bare stomach, and Ruth laughing and pushing him away, probably not wanting him to notice that she wasn't as flat there as she could be.

Funny how he'd ended up marrying someone like Ruth really, when he'd always gone for someone so different. But Mother was right – Ruth had exactly the qualities a man should look for in a wife. She'd look after him, put his needs first, support him in whatever he did. And she'd have children too, without worrying about her figure, or whether babies would interfere with her career – Ruth wasn't a bit like that. Didn't really have a career anyway – you wouldn't call hairdressing a career – so it would be no big deal for Ruth to give it up when the kids came along. Not, indeed, that he was in any hurry for kids – time enough for all that responsibility when they were well into their thirties, like his mother had been – but Ruth had hinted often enough that she wanted a few; he'd be able to put her off for only so long.

He'd enjoyed their fling in Crete, of course – who wouldn't get a kick out of being so patently adored? Andrew was used to his mother's adoration, but to find this in a girlfriend was something new and delightful for him – girls usually played such games. But

Ruth was different – so innocent, so eager to please; really, he'd felt a pang when his two weeks were up and she'd seen his coach off. Waiting for her at Dublin Airport two nights later – no need to tell her that he'd been planning to stay with pals in Dublin for a few extra nights when he flew back anyway, before heading down to Limerick – he'd quite looked forward to seeing her again. And her face when she'd spotted him – well, that was gratifying. That in itself, that depth of feeling that she wasn't experienced enough to disguise, was enough of a novelty to keep him interested. Enough to keep them together for a few months, until Mother started asking him when he was going to bring Ruth down to meet her.

And then, when they'd met, when his mother had taken to Ruth so strongly – well, that clinched it. Mother was no fool; if she thought Ruth would make a worthy wife for him, that was good enough for Andrew. His mother had looked out for him all his life, had kept him from making some disastrous decisions; and while he mightn't always have agreed with her advice – would almost have resented it sometimes – he'd had to acknowledge that she always had his interests at heart. He had always come first with her; he appreciated that. And so he had married Ruth, and made both his women happy.

He wondered how it would be when they moved into their own house. They'd have to work out some kind of a routine when Ruth started working again. If she got a job in town, he could drop her in on his way to work. Mind you, with this traffic every evening, she'd be better off walking home – it wasn't that far out to Farranshone. Give her a chance to put the dinner on, rather than be hanging around waiting for him. And let's face it, Ruth was going to be the one doing the cooking – he was useless at it, never had the chance to learn, with Mother insisting on doing it for him all his life. He wouldn't have minded having a go now and again; he might have been quite good at it actually. But there wasn't much point now, with Ruth probably delighted to do it. And Mother had that fancy cookbook ready to give to Ruth as a house-warming present – that would help her along nicely.

Not that they'd abandon his mother when they moved, of course not. They'd only be a few minutes away anyway – probably go over to her for Sunday lunch or something. Thinking about Cecily's typical Sunday meals – stuffed roast chicken, tender baby vegetables, homemade potato croquettes – his stomach rumbled again. And they could have Mother over to their place some night during the week maybe, Ruth could make a bit of an effort. It might be hard for Mother initially, on her own for the first time in years. But then, she had her book club, and her friends. Such a strong woman his mother had always been. So capable.

He pulled up in front of the house as Ruth opened the front door and walked towards him, smiling. She must have been watching out the window for him.

He noticed that her tan was fading.

✡✡✡

'Mama.' Polly's flour-covered hands reached out as she toddled over to the door, grin almost splitting her fat little face in two.

'Oh great, dinner's here; I'm starving.' Breffni scooped her up and nuzzled into her neck, making munching sounds. Polly shrieked with glee, trying to push Breffni's head away, kicking against Breffni's hip with her miniature trainers. 'Stop, Mama.'

Breffni lifted her head up – 'Hang on; I'm nearly finished. Just a few more bites' – and dived under Polly's chin again. Polly squealed and giggled again, squirming. 'Mama – tiddle, tiddle.'

'Well, I don't know which one of you is worse.' Mary finished filling the teapot and walked over to Breffni, who put her free arm around her shoulders and hugged her.

'Me, definitely. Polly would never eat a person, would you, Pollywolly?' She poked Polly in the side, making her squirm again. 'You'd prefer fish fingers.'

She put Polly down and looked back at Mary. 'I hope she was good for you.'

'She was of course, as good as gold. It's great to see her over that old bug she had.'

'It is – it knocked her sideways for a while. And how are you, Granny Mary? You look great, as usual.'

Mary flapped a hand at Breffni. 'Great, my foot – I look like a holy show. I'm getting a perm on Saturday.' She reached out and stroked Breffni's glossy hair. 'Now if I had your head I'd be fine; you were blessed with that hair. I hope you appreciate it, not having to run to the hairdresser's every month trying to look presentable.'

Breffni grinned – 'God, no – I want a head of blond curls, like Shirley Temple here,' – ruffling Polly's hair. 'Would you ever tell me how Cian and I ended up with a blonde? There's never been anything lighter than dark brown in my family – and none of Cian's relations I've met are fair.'

Mary considered, looking down at Polly, who was rummaging through Breffni's shopping bags. 'I had an uncle who was blond like that – not curly though. And his daughter, a good bit older than me – she went to Canada and settled there – she was fairly light, I think. And actually I was quite fair myself, before age caught up with me and washed it all out. Now the only choice I have is grey or blue, or maybe lilac.'

Breffni laughed. 'Stick to the grey, I think. And what are *you* up to, Missy?' Polly had discovered a stick of French bread; after a struggle, she managed to pull it out of the bag, but the momentum knocked her backwards and she thudded down on her well-padded behind. She looked up at the women and grinned, showing a row of tiny teeth. 'Bump a daisy.'

'I'll take that, thanks.' Breffni whisked the bread away, and before Polly could react, replaced it with a mandarin orange, which she pulled quickly from the bag.

Polly looked at the little fruit in her hand and slowly her smile vanished. 'No.' She threw the mandarin on the floor and it rolled gently under the table.

Mary immediately stretched out her hand towards Polly. 'I think I know what you want, darling. Come with Granny, and we'll get the surprise for Mammy.' Polly immediately struggled to her feet, bread forgotten, and grabbed hold of Mary's little finger. 'We made scones, didn't we, lovey? Let's see if they're ready.' They walked over to the worktop, the older woman leaning down towards the little girl.

Breffni retrieved the mandarin and sat at the table watching them. 'You've her spoilt rotten, Granny. She never gets this kind of love and attention at our house.'

'I don't believe a word of it. She's very lucky to have the parents she has. Now, upsadaisy.' Mary helped Polly onto a chair by the worktop. 'Hold on now, or you'll fall.' Polly stood on the chair and grabbed the edge of the worktop, watching carefully as Mary took a scone from the wire rack and split it.

'Me, Ganny?'

'Yes, darling, this is for you.' She spread it with butter. 'Now, will you sit up at the table with Mammy, and we'll have a little party? Careful now, getting down. Don't fall.' She spotted Polly's floury hands. 'Oh dear, we'd better clean those hands first. Come here, lovey.'

As she took a facecloth and rubbed Polly's hands, Breffni watched with affection, marvelling at how compliant Polly always was with Mary – she'd never have let Breffni wipe her hands so easily. Mary was manna from heaven, no doubt about it. She patently adored her small great-grandchild, and the feeling was mutual. Mary had looked after Polly from the first time Breffni and Cian felt able to leave her. There was never a question of finding another babysitter; Breffni's parents in Limerick were too far away to call on, and they didn't know anyone else well enough in Nenagh, not then. And Granny Mary – really Cian's granny, and one reason why they'd settled in Nenagh after coming back to Ireland – so delighted at the prospect of Polly's arrival, had assured them that she'd be only too happy to help out any way she could.

Breffni had spent the first few weeks of Polly's life wondering why in God's name she and Cian had ever imagined they could raise a child. And why on earth they had bought a house so far from her parents – what was so wrong with Limerick? It didn't help when Cian gently pointed out that they'd got a far cheaper house in Nenagh, that the job he'd managed to find was here, and that his only relative in Ireland was up the road and had nobody else living nearby. And Breffni had come to thank her lucky stars for that relative – if it hadn't been for Mary, Breffni might well have taken Polly and gone back to live with her parents in those first fraught months. Or left Polly with Cian, and gone off herself.

But Granny Mary was a godsend. Somehow she always knew what would help the most, whether it was taking the baby for a walk, sitting down for a quick chat with Breffni if Polly was asleep, or just getting a shopping list and heading off.

And she never came empty-handed. Half a dozen scones, a triangle of brown bread, a little knitted hat or a furry red bear for Polly. Once, after a particularly bad week of teething, she brought a bottle of red wine. Breffni took one exhausted look at it and put her head in her hands.

'I can't do this, Mary, it's too hard . . . I can't do it.' Her shoulders shook.

Mary set the bottle down on the table and sat next to Breffni and put an arm around her.

'You're worn out, you poor creature. I know it seems like there's no end, but believe me, it will get better. I well remember Cian driving his mother to distraction as a baby, and look at him now.' She squeezed Breffni's shoulder and smiled. 'Very well-behaved most of the time.'

Breffni found herself half-laughing, half-crying. 'Sorry, Mary – it was a tough week.' She took a deep breath and wiped her eyes with a sleeve and looked at her saviour. 'I have simply no idea what we would do without you – you do realise that, don't you?'

Mary reached over to the dresser for the box of tissues. 'Rubbish – you'd manage fine, like all new parents; and you're doing a lot better than some, believe me. I'm just happy to be able to help now and again, that's all.'

Breffni pulled a tissue from the box and blew her nose, then reached for the bottle of wine. 'We'll have a glass, Mary – purely medicinal, of course.'

'Indeed we will not, at ten o'clock in the morning. I'm bad, but I'm not that bad.' Mary stood up and took Polly's tiny padded jacket from the hook on the back of the kitchen door. 'You'll put that away till you and Cian find a quiet hour sometime. And now you'll go and have a bit of a lie down, and I'll take this scallywag out for a breath of fresh air that'll hopefully tire her out.'

As she spoke, she whisked the grizzling Polly from her bouncer seat and manoeuvred her flailing arms into the jacket. Then she nuzzled into the baby's chest, talking softly. 'Yes, you little monkey. I'll have you asleep before long, don't you worry. Fast asleep, dreaming of the angels you left behind in Heaven.' She lifted her head and smiled at the baby in her arms, still murmuring softly. 'Won't you go to sleep for Granny Mary? You will. Yes, you will.' And watching Polly looking back solemnly at her, thumb already heading towards her tiny mouth, Breffni didn't doubt it.

It was hard to believe Mary was well into her eighties. Her memory was better than Breffni's, she read everything she could lay her hands on and she was addicted to card games, the more complicated the rules the better. In the time she'd known her, Breffni couldn't remember her ever being sick, apart from the odd head cold.

Mary admitted herself that she'd slowed down in the last few years – 'I used to pass everyone else when I was out walking; now most people fly past me' – but for a woman of her age she was amazingly well preserved. She'd given up driving when she reached seventy-five, sold her ten-year-old Fiat to a neighbour's son – 'I felt I'd had quite enough of that' – and now she pottered around Nenagh quite happily.

Breffni drove her into Limerick about once a month for a shopping afternoon. They had lunch when they arrived, in the Arthur's Quay Centre because it had a crèche for Polly, then they browsed around the shops, sometimes splitting up for an hour or two and meeting again for coffee and cake before heading home.

And any time Breffni invited her parents out from Limerick for dinner, Granny Mary joined them for the night.

'There we go, darling.' As Polly scrambled up onto a chair at the table, Mary put a plate in front of her with half a scone on it.

The butter pooled on its gently steaming surface.

Breffni watched her little daughter as she grabbed the half scone with both hands. 'Mmm – yummy. What do you say to Granny Mary?'

'Ta ta.' Scone poised halfway to her mouth, Polly spotted the bowl of blackcurrant jam in the middle of the table. She stretched the scone towards Breffni. 'Mama, dam.' Breffni reached over and spread a little jam on the scone, and Polly immediately aimed again for her open mouth.

Breffni looked sternly at her. 'Small bite.' Polly opened her mouth wider and lunged at the scone, sinking her tiny teeth into it and covering her cheeks with jam, watching Breffni across the table. She looked so comical that Breffni had to struggle not to smile. '*Small* bite, I said.'

Mary put a plate of warm scones and a little bowl of whipped cream in front of Breffni. 'Live a little.'

Polly eyed the bowl of cream and immediately stretched out her hand with the ravaged scone in it. 'Me.'

'Just a little bit.' Breffni daubed a tiny blob of cream onto Polly's scone before looking up at Mary. 'You're the devil in disguise; I shouldn't be eating this.'

Mary put a knife on her plate. 'Go on, there isn't a pick on you; you're like a model.'

'Model my hat – but you've talked me into it anyway.' Breffni split a scone and spooned a small amount of jam onto it. Then she added a blob of cream – might as well be hung for a sheep – and bit in hungrily as Mary sat across from her and poured tea. 'Mmm, gorgeous.' She couldn't diet this week anyway, with Laura's dinner. 'Oh, that reminds me, Mary. Would you be free to babysit this Thursday night? We've been invited into Limerick for dinner.'

Mary buttered a half scone for herself. 'I will of course, dear; I'd love it.' She always stayed in their spare room when she babysat, leaving them very free.

Breffni talked through a mouthful of scone. 'You're the best. I'll have your room ready.' She turned to Polly. 'Did you hear that? Granny is going to mind you. What d'you say?'

Polly munched her scone, swinging her chubby legs. 'Ta ta, Ganny.'

✡✡✡

Emily reached across the supermarket aisle and waved her hand in front of Cecily's face. 'You're miles away.'

Cecily blinked and turned towards her friend. She hadn't been miles away at all, merely trying to decide on the evening meal. She'd thought about a prawn salad, but the prawns in the fish shop hadn't been very impressive, and they'd sold out of rainbow trout, her second choice. Maybe they'd have something here, although she normally avoided supermarket fish. She smiled at Emily.

'Hello, dear. Any news?'

'Not since I saw you, unless you count pruning the shrubbery, which I spent all yesterday doing. I really need a new pair of gardening gloves; my hands are cut to ribbons.' Emily extended her well-manicured hands, which looked perfect to Cecily apart from a few tiny scratches.

'How are you getting on with the new daughter-in-law? I hope she appreciates that handsome son of yours – not to mention the excellent board and lodging she's getting.'

Cecily laughed. 'Well, it's hardly five star, but everything is going fine. Ruth is very easy to get along with really, no trouble.

You'll meet her soon.' She paused, struck by a thought. 'I might ask her if she'd like to sit in on our next meeting – in fact, I'll be hosting, so she'll be around anyway.'

Emily beamed. 'Lovely.'

'Yes, she'd probably enjoy it; she's quite a reader.' And why shouldn't Cecily bring along someone new, since everyone else seemed to be at it? She kept her smile in place as she watched Emily. 'Have you noticed, by the way, how we seem to be growing in number lately?'

And Emily said, as Cecily knew she would, 'Ah yes – Dorothy's man.'

Cecily waited.

Emily paused. 'He was rather foisted on us the other night, wasn't he?'

Cecily nodded, careful not to look too pleased – Emily seemed to be of the same mind, thank goodness.

'And it looks like he's going to be a permanent fixture – I heard Margaret telling Dorothy to be sure and bring him along in future.' She shrugged her cashmere-covered shoulders. 'He doesn't exactly strike me as the literary type – I suppose we'll just have to see what he makes of the new McGahern.' And that was it. No sign of real disapproval, no indication that she was seriously put out by his appearance at the book club.

Cecily's heart sank; her one hope of an ally was gone. She began to edge away, keeping the polite smile in place with difficulty. 'Well, I'd better get on; can't dally, now that I'm cooking for three.'

'Right, dear. See you Thursday week.' Emily fluttered her fingers and turned away, basket swinging from her arm. Cecily watched for a minute, then made her way towards the fish counter.

She'd get kippers; they'd do fine. She wasn't made of money.

✡✡✡

'Hello?'

Laura's heart sank. She'd been hoping for Andrew or Ruth.

'Hello, Mother. How are you?' Cecily had always been 'Mother'. Never 'Mammy' or 'Mum', even when Laura was very small.

'Oh hello, dear. I'm fine, anything wrong?' *Because there would have to be a reason for me to ring you other than simply to find out how you are. Message received, Mother.*

'No, nothing, everything's fine with us too.' *God, listen to them; they sound like a bad play.* 'I just wanted a quick word with Ruth, if she's around.'

'Ruth.' Cecily allowed just enough of a pause to create tension. 'Yes, I believe she's here somewhere. Hold on.' As if the house was so huge that two people could be unaware of each other's presence. *Try the west wing, Mother.*

While she waited, Laura marvelled at her mother's capacity to make her feel bad with a few well-chosen words – a look, even. She could take the wind out of Laura's sails with a slight lift of one plucked eyebrow. How did the damn woman do it? Why had they never had the kind of relationship Breffni had with *her* mother?

Laura got on so much better with Mona than she ever had with Cecily – easygoing chatter whenever they met, not having to watch what she said all the time, not having to justify her bloody existence. Growing up, she'd envied Breffni the noisy family teas in the Comerford house, everyone talking with full mouths and reaching across the table and planting elbows wherever they wanted. Why wasn't . . .

'Hello?'

'Ruth, it's Laura.' *Because my mother probably didn't tell you who was calling*. 'Just confirming the dinner – Thursday night at my house, around half eight, does that suit? Breffni and Cian are coming.'

'Lovely.' She could hear the smile in Ruth's voice – probably delighted to be escaping the dragon's lair for a night. 'Thanks a lot, Laura. What can we bring?'

'Oh, a bottle of red would be great, and two big appetites.'

Ruth's laugh drifted along the line. 'Fine; we'll see you then. Say hi to Donal.'

'I will. Take care, Ruth.' As she hung up, Laura wondered again how Breffni and Ruth would get on. They were so different – she hoped to God they found some common ground.

Apart from Andrew, of course. She grinned and turned back to her illustration.

✡✡✡

'Darling?' It still felt funny to her, calling someone darling. And even funnier to have someone call *her* darling. But funny in a really nice way.

'Yeah?' He didn't look up from tying his lace.

'Is there a special kind of wine Laura likes?' She reached across the bed and ran her fingers lightly down his back, feeling the knobs of his spine under his blue work shirt. She was wearing an old pyjama top of his, wide purple and white stripes, sleeves rolled up. Her light blond hair was matted where she'd lain on it, like a child's; one cheek was slightly flushed.

He finished tying his lace and stretched a hand over to touch the hot side of her face for a second. 'You look adorable.' She smiled, leant briefly into the coolness of his hand.

He began tying the second shoe. 'Wine . . . she goes for French, I think. Doesn't really matter; none of us are wine buffs, except maybe Donal.' He mimed holding a glass, sticking out his little finger in a mock genteel way, and spoke in a cartoonishly cultured voice. 'Hello, I'm Donal, and I know about wine – and everything else too.'

Ruth laughed, gave him a playful push. 'Andrew, that's mean. I think Donal is lovely; not a bit know-allish.'

He reached around and grabbed her hand. 'My darling wife –' She'd never get tired of hearing him call her his wife; it made her want to purr, like a contented cat '– you'd think Attila the Hun was lovely; or at least misunderstood. You'd be a character witness for Hitler if he asked you.' He leant nearer and pecked her cheek. 'It's one of the thousand things I love about you. See you tonight.' As he released her hand and went to get up, she grabbed quickly on to his wrist.

'Andrew?'

He smiled, half-standing, trapped by her hold. 'That's me.'

'You know how happy you've made me, don't you?' He lifted her hand to his mouth and kissed the knuckles gently.

'My dear, the pleasure has been all mine, I promise you.' He checked his watch. 'And now I must fly. Have fun; see you this evening.' She dropped his hand and he was gone; she could hear him hurrying down the stairs to the egg that Cecily prepared for him each morning.

If Ruth was honest, it did bother her a tiny bit that Andrew's mother was still cooking his breakfast for him. She'd far rather be the one getting up in the morning to see him off, but when she had tentatively offered to do this, the day they came back from honeymoon, Cecily had immediately refused.

'My dear Ruth, it would be pointless to have both of us up at that hour, and I wake at cockcrow every morning anyway, have done for years. I'm used to seeing Andrew off to work. No, you stay in bed, I insist; I know how you young people enjoy your lie-ins.' And Ruth decided that she was imagining the implied criticism; Cecily had been so good to them – of course she wasn't implying anything. And anyway, why would she be critical of Ruth for staying in bed, when she clearly preferred her to – at least until after she'd had Andrew all to herself while he ate his breakfast?

Cecily had been just as adamant about cooking in the evenings, when Ruth had offered to take over some of the meals.

'Thank you, dear, it's sweet of you to offer, but you must allow an old lady her foibles.' Smiling, waiting.

'Mother, you'll never be old.' Andrew's response was delivered right on cue.

Cecily pretended to ignore him, continuing to look at Ruth, but her face softened a little. 'I simply couldn't countenance anyone else in my kitchen. Andrew will tell you that I wouldn't even allow Laura to cook while she lived here.'

Ruth looked obediently at Andrew, who nodded, and Cecily continued smoothly. 'But my dear, if you really want to help, you could of course clear away afterwards.' So every evening, after Andrew and Cecily had moved into the sitting room, Ruth carried the used plates and glasses back into the kitchen and washed them carefully in the sink, terrified of the cut crystal and wafer-thin china. So far, thank goodness, she'd managed not to break anything. And it gave Andrew a bit of time with his mother; she could see how close they were.

Ruth knew – of course she did – how lucky they were to have Cecily to stay with, but all the same, it would be wonderful when they had their own place. Though she'd never have admitted it to Andrew, for fear of offending him, she was a little in awe of her mother-in-law – Ruth would never in a million years have Cecily's confidence and elegance. Sometimes she agonised about this, thinking that Andrew must surely compare them; how could he not? Cecily so suave and self-assured, and she, Ruth, ridiculously gauche and naïve for someone of thirty. Surely, the more Ruth and Cecily were living in such close proximity, the greater the chances of Andrew noticing the huge gulf between them – how long before he realised that he'd chosen a very poor substitute as his wife?

She often wished she could talk to her mother, suddenly so far away in Dublin. Letters or phone calls just weren't the same – she wanted to have Mam beside her, watch her expression as she poured out her anxieties, hear her telling Ruth she was just being silly – of course Andrew wasn't comparing his wife with his mother; anyone could see how much he loved her. She wanted to watch Mam's face as she spoke, see from her face that she meant it.

It was the first time she'd been separated from the family; her married sisters, Siobhan and Mairead, were living within walking distance of their parents, and Irene, the youngest, was still at home. And even when Ruth had moved out of home to share the flat, they all saw each other at least once a week, usually more often. You just dropped in home whenever you were passing, and more often than not, someone else was there too.

When Ruth told her married sisters that she was going to be moving in with her mother-in-law, Siobhan had shaken her head. 'Two women in a kitchen – a recipe for disaster.'

Mairead had nodded. 'And Andrew the only son – you've stolen him from her. She'll make your life hell.'

And then they'd laughed, and newly-engaged Ruth had laughed along with them, knowing they weren't really serious about the doom and gloom. She knew they'd be full of support now if she wanted to have a moan, or just look for a bit of reassurance. But in a way, maybe it was as well that they weren't around – it would give Ruth's silly notions far too much importance if she voiced them out loud, make her sisters feel that something was really wrong, when it wasn't; of course not. She was deliriously happy to be married to Andrew. And it would be much better when they were settled into their own house, only a few weeks away now hopefully.

And when she managed to make some real friends in Limerick. Ruth wondered if perhaps she and Laura might become close; and maybe this Breffni too, she sounded nice. She kept meaning to ask Andrew about Breffni – he must have known her quite well growing up – but with Cecily around most evenings, they never seemed to have much time on their own. The one night Cecily went off to her book club, Andrew had to stay late at work for some audit thing, and he arrived home only a few minutes before his mother.

Not that Ruth had minded too much – she'd actually quite enjoyed the evening on her own, curled up on the living-room couch watching *Coronation Street* and *Fair City*. Cecily rarely switched on the television, preferring to listen to music in the evenings, and Ruth didn't like to ask. It was no harm anyway to do without her soaps – a few weeks wouldn't kill her.

She heard Andrew's car starting up and threw back the duvet. Padding to the window, she saw him manoeuvre the car out of the driveway and in the direction of the North Circular Road. Slowly she walked back and climbed into bed, and picked up her book from the locker; but she didn't open it.

How on earth had Ruth Tobin ended up married to Andrew O'Neill? Till the day she died, she'd never be able to fathom what he had seen in her. Two years older than him, nothing to look at, whatever her mother said, beaten to the altar by two younger sisters. Never in what you'd call a serious relationship, not exactly the life and soul of the few parties she'd been to.

And Andrew so good-looking, he could be on the stage . . . she closed her eyes and remembered the first time she'd laid eyes on him, on the main street of the resort in Crete.

A little taller than her, lightly tanned, thick reddish-brown hair that he pushed carelessly out of his eyes as he punched the buttons on the ATM machine. He wore faded denims, cut off halfway down his thighs, and battered sandals. Grey t-shirt slung across one smooth golden shoulder. She took up her position behind him and rummaged in her beach bag for her card. He turned at the noise.

'Hi. Won't be long.' Irish, with green eyes and a great smile. Lovely even teeth, little crinkle in his left cheek. Two small dark freckles – moles? – across his nose.

'That's fine; take your time.' She wished she'd brushed her hair before she came up from her swim – she must look a holy fright, with it hanging in rat's tails on her shoulders. She could never understand when people complimented her hair; it was so poker straight, no body to it at all.

'But that's what's so great about it; it's like a sheet of gold, the way it falls so perfectly, not a ripple in it. And so shiny; I couldn't get this lot to shine if I covered it in Mr Sheen.' Her flatmate Maura would point at her own ginger curls in despair. 'I'd swap with you in a minute, Ruth, believe me.'

And Ruth would have swapped too – and she'd have thrown in her God-awful freckles while she was at it. Since she'd arrived in Crete, she'd got twice as many as usual – the splodgy beige kind, almost merging into each other on her pink-from-the-beach face. She tucked her sarong more tightly around her – at least she wasn't flaunting her blue-white thighs.

His cash appeared and he pulled it out of the machine and stepped to one side. 'All yours.' He took a wallet from his back pocket and began folding the notes into it.

'Thanks.' She put in her card and immediately, before she'd had a chance to key in her password, it came flying back out again. 'Oh.'

She pushed it in again; again it came straight out. She stood perplexed, wondering what she should do.

'Problem?' He was still there.

She held up her card and made a perplexed face. 'Doesn't want to go in.'

He shoved his wallet back into his pocket and put out his hand, and she immediately placed her card in his palm. He examined it, turning it over in his hands, feeling round the edges. 'Doesn't seem damaged. Let's give it another go.' And the minute he pushed it in, it shot out again. 'Hmm.' He tried again, and this time, miraculously, it stayed in. 'Right, put in your PIN quick, before it changes its mind.' He stepped aside.

'Great – thank you so much.' She beamed with relief, and he bowed deeply, whipping off an imaginary hat. 'My pleasure, Ruth Tobin.' And she realised he'd read her name on the card.

And something – call it too much sun, call it the first moment of madness of her life, she didn't know what to call it – something made her open her mouth and say, 'You'll have to let me buy you a drink . . . or a coffee, or –'

Then her words dried up, and her head filled with *oh my God – he's sure to have a girlfriend waiting for him somewhere with a matching bikini and sarong, and a perfect tan, and not a single freckle.* What had possessed her? And asking him for a drink while it was still blazing sunshine – he'd think she was an alcoholic.

He grinned. 'Great, I could murder a beer – but you'd better get your money out first; otherwise I'll be footing the bill.' And she blushed under her sunburn and tried not to press the wrong buttons as she withdrew fifty Euro more than she'd intended, shocked at her brazenness. *He's coming for a drink; I invited a man for a drink and he's coming.* God, what on earth would they talk about?

Her money came sliding out of the slot and she turned to see him smiling at her and holding out his hand – 'Andrew O'Neill' – and she shook his hand and almost said her name before she remembered he already knew it.

And that was the start of it all. He had ten days left of his holiday, she had twelve. The first day they stayed in the bar for three hours, before she remembered Maura and Claire on the beach and hurried back, tipsy, to find them still there, in practically the same positions, idly wondering where she'd got to.

They were agog when she told them what had happened. Claire sat up, pulling her sunglasses down from the top of her head and fixing the straps of her top. 'Ruth Tobin: you picked up a man at the bank machine – what are you like? Or rather, what's *he* like?'

Ruth giggled. 'Gorgeous, like a film star. He's from Limerick.' Her head spun gently and she moved further under the umbrella – the last thing she needed now was sunstroke. Not when she had just met the most interesting man of her life; and arranged to meet him again in the morning.

The second day, they hired mopeds and drove the ten

kilometres into Chania, wandering through the cobbled Venetian streets, dropping in and out of the higgledy-piggledy shops. They had lunch on the waterfront before heading back, stopping at a little beach to wade into the warm water, fully clothed. When they came out, he gathered up the end of her t-shirt and squeezed the water from it, and she wished she was brazen enough to take it off.

The third night, after a dinner of calamari washed down with several glasses of rough red wine, he brought her back to his studio apartment – the friend he'd travelled with had met a couple of Scottish girls the day before and disappeared with them – and from then on, she lost count. Days of beaches and picnics and sleepless siestas flowed into warm nights full of stars and ouzo and haunting Greek music and moonlit walks by the shore wrapped in each other's arms, and his hands and his mouth awakening something she hadn't known was sleeping.

They were a cliché, caricatures of every couple who've ever fallen in love, and she didn't care.

But, of course, it couldn't last. Waving his airport bus off at two in the morning, she felt all her old self-consciousness come back, and she knew she'd never see him again. It was a holiday romance – that was how they worked. He went home, she went home, end of story. She should be grateful he'd picked her to pass his two weeks with; he could have had anyone. She plodded back to her apartment, wondering what he'd tell his friends, knowing he wouldn't use her phone number – he'd probably thrown it away already – feeling the warm night air pressing down on her, and she climbed into the bed she hadn't seen for over a week and cried herself quietly to sleep under the still-crisp sheet.

Two days later, when she stepped through the doors into the arrivals hall at Dublin Airport, hungover and exhausted, he walked up to her and pulled her into him and she clung on, heart racing, tears of relief spilling down her sunburnt freckled cheeks and onto his shirt.

And now, a year and two months later, they were married. And soon they'd have their own house and she'd find a job and make lots of new friends.

And they'd have lots of children too. She'd always wanted a big family.

She got out of bed and picked up her dressing gown – time to face the day. She had a bottle of wine to buy for Laura; she could take her time looking for that.

✡✡✡

Donal pushed through the swing doors and took a white apron from the row of hooks beside the door.

'Morning.' Paul nodded as he hurried past carrying a tray of croissants. The smell of coffee was heavy in the air.

'Paul, how's it going?' Donal wrapped the apron strings around his waist and tied them at the front. The kitchen at this time was busy as usual, gearing up to the job of getting a few hundred continental breakfasts served up within the next hour or so. Freshly baked croissants, Danish pastries and rolls. Four kinds of cereal, bowls of fruit salad and yoghurt, big jugs of orange and grapefruit juice. Tea, coffee, hot chocolate.

The four chefs split the schedule between them, working one week early, starting at six and finishing at two, and one week late, starting at nine and finishing at five, after the lunches and the coffee breaks and the final clean-up.

Donal preferred the early shift in the summer, relishing the dawn cycle along deserted streets, out the Dublin road as far as the Castletroy Park Hotel, swinging left for UL. Getting up on a bright morning, not having to put the light on while he got dressed – that was easy.

But he could do without leaving his bed at five o'clock on a freezing, pitch-black winter's morning, with a soft and warm Laura still curled up in it. Padding gingerly with his bundle of clothes across the cold wooden floor to the bathroom, trying to get dressed without waking her. Not to mention having to cycle four miles along icy roads with a biting wind cutting through even his sheepskin gloves, slicing down between the back of his neck and his scarf.

And coming home, weaving his way through traffic-clogged streets, tasting the grittiness of the fumes in the back of his throat. Yes, he could certainly do without that.

Still, he'd rather be cycling. He remembered Laura's surprise when she realised he was on a bike the night they met. She never said, but he got the impression that she was slightly amused by what she probably saw as his little oddity. When she asked him why never drove, he told her that he hated what cars did to the environment, which was quite true.

If not the whole story.

He pushed the thought away abruptly and walked across to the sink to wash his hands.

✡✡✡

'Thank you.' Cecily turned around to nod to the man who had reached ahead of her and held the door open – and then her heart sank. It couldn't be.

It was. He smiled at her, palm still splayed against the door. 'Cecily, how nice; I hate to drink alone – even if it is just tea.

Won't you let me buy you a cup?'

Damn – no point in saying she was meeting someone; he'd find out soon enough that it wasn't true. What on earth had made her choose the very café he'd decided on, and at the very same time? She realised that she had no choice but to accept his offer – good manners demanded it.

She smiled stiffly back and inclined her head slightly. 'Thank you.' She walked briskly ahead of him to a table at the back – less chance of being seen by anyone she knew. As she started to take off her jacket, Frank held it for her and hung it carefully over the back of her chair. Not completely without manners, then. And here was a waitress, thank goodness; the sooner they got this over with, the better.

'What can I get you?' The girl stood with a pen poised above her pad, and Frank looked questioningly at Cecily.

'Decaffeinated coffee, please, and a glass of iced water.' *And be quick*, she silently begged the waitress.

He smiled. 'Nothing to eat? A bun?' Yes, he *would* call them buns, not cakes. She shook her head.

'Well then, neither will I.' Frank smiled up at the waitress. 'Just a pot of tea for me, please.' As she turned away, Cecily wondered how on earth they'd manage to keep a conversation going; she couldn't think of one thing she wanted to say to him. He put his hands on the table and gave her an eyebrow-raised smile.

'Decaffeinated coffee? I'd say there's not too much call for that around Limerick.' Instantly, she felt a pinprick of irritation. What business was it of his what she liked to drink? And what did he mean by implying that people in Limerick didn't drink decaffeinated coffee? Did he think they were all unsophisticated buffoons here? But she had to be polite.

With an effort, she kept a neutral expression on her face.

'Actually, given the choice, I always drink decaffeinated; and quite a lot of my friends do too. It may not have made it as far as Sligo yet, but it's widely available in Limerick.' That should put him in his place.

He didn't say anything for a moment, and slowly his smile faded. Then he looked down at his hands and laced his fingers together.

'Cecily, I've offended you.' He raised his eyes and looked directly at her. 'I do apologise. It was entirely unintentional; I wouldn't dream of deliberately saying anything that might cause offence.'

An apology – well, that was something. And gracefully offered too, without any smart remarks. Showed he had some sensitivity at least. Then the faintest of smiles appeared on his face. 'To tell you the truth, I'm a little nervous of you.'

Now she was floored: what a thing to say. The idea that anyone should be nervous of her was quite ridiculous. But at least he'd stopped sounding insincere or cocky.

She'd better make some kind of response. 'There's no need to be nervous of me, I assure you.' How silly that sounded; thank goodness nobody was near enough to overhear them.

He was silent again for a minute, looking back thoughtfully at his hands. She was just beginning, for form's sake, to cast around for a harmless topic to bring up – she supposed books would be a safe one – when he said slowly, 'Cecily, I wonder . . . if I could tell you something?'

Lord, what now? She prayed that he wasn't going to come out with some horribly personal information. Her eyes searched the café for their waitress – some kind of diversion might put him off – but there was no sign of the girl. She waited with dread, determined not to encourage him, but unable to find the right words to put him off politely. She could hardly tell him to keep his private life to himself.

After a few seconds, he started to speak haltingly. 'I – was married for forty-four years to a wonderful woman.' Cecily's heart sank for the second time since bumping into him. Why had he chosen her of all people to unburden himself to? Why not Dorothy – they seemed to get on fine – or anyone else? Anyone who'd been friendlier to him than Cecily had, which was probably everyone else he'd met since he moved to Limerick. She clenched her fists under the table, willing their drinks to arrive so she could finish hers quickly and escape.

Frank was still speaking quietly, not looking at her. 'We had two children, a boy and a girl. When our daughter was twelve, she – got leukaemia, and we . . . lost her.' Cecily's stomach lurched, and again she prayed for some kind of interruption. How dare this man foist his personal tragedies on her? And yet, of course, she felt sympathy – how could she not? Losing Andrew would be the end of her world. Or Laura.

'A few years afterwards, our son . . . was estranged from us under – very difficult circumstances.' He took a deep breath and went on. 'A year ago, Angela, my dear wife, went to bed one night and never woke up.'

He raised his head for the first time since he'd started speaking; Cecily got the impression that he was forcing himself to look at her. 'That's why I moved away from Sligo; I found it too hard to get over her death there. So many people who knew her . . . and in my grief, I found myself dwelling on our earlier tragedies too –' He shook his head slowly. 'It wasn't doing me any good, staying there on my own. My friends – our friends – tried their best, of course, but nothing seemed to help.' He met Cecily's eyes again. 'So I deliberately chose a place where I knew no one;

thought it might help me to . . . pick myself up and move on.' He stopped speaking, lifted his shoulders slightly, gave her a weak smile and let his eyes drift downwards again.

Cecily sat across from him, at a complete loss. Whatever she had expected when they met at the door, it wasn't this. What on earth was one to do in this situation? Her emotions were scattered; pity mixed uneasily with irritation, and she struggled to keep her expression neutral. She felt she must speak; if nothing else, good manners demanded some sort of response.

'I'm very sorry; you've had a lot of hardship.' Her words came out stiffly, sounding insincere to her. She didn't touch him; kept her hands firmly in her lap. She still hardly knew him, despite his having forced his life story on her. Again, she wished fervently that she hadn't chosen this particular café today.

He looked at her and shook his head slowly again. 'Cecily, I'm not telling you this so you'll feel sorry for me. God knows I've had enough sympathy to last me the rest of my life.' His smile was weak, a barely noticeable widening of his lips. 'I just wanted to explain why I may have come across as a little – brash – when I met you the other week. I . . . haven't been out and about for so long, haven't been in any kind of social setting for . . . quite a while now. I suppose I was out of the habit, and nervous of meeting you all.'

Brash – exactly the word Cecily would have used herself. She felt a tinge of embarrassment – if he really had been nervous, his rather silly remarks would of course be forgivable – but how could she possibly have known? No, she wasn't going to be embarrassed; she'd done nothing wrong. She glanced around again; where was that dratted waitress?

He put his chin in his hand, and she automatically registered his elbow on the table. 'Dorothy had to practically drag me along to the book club. She and Liam have been great since I moved here, but I found the thought of meeting a whole new group of people very intimidating. I'd been married so long, you see, with Angela always there beside me.'

Cecily nodded automatically, thinking of herself and Brian as a couple; it had been a kind of comfort to know that someone was always around to do things with, go places with. After he died, the absence of that comfort had struck her quite forcibly. But of course she'd still had Andrew, who'd been wonderful. Frank had had no one – his daughter dead, his son disappeared. Undoubtedly it must have been difficult.

Frank took another deep breath and continued. 'But then I thought, this is why I moved. I knew I'd have to make an effort, if I was to have any kind of life again. So I let Dorothy drag me out.' He smiled again, this time a little wider than before. 'And I must say I really enjoyed myself; but I do apologise if you found me a bit – overpowering.'

She shook her head slightly – what else could she do? He lifted a hand to deny her unspoken comment. 'No, I'm sure I was. Rabbitting on about whatever popped into my head, most of it rubbish.' His smile suddenly became more of a twinkle. 'But you know, Cecily, I'm really not so bad once you get to know me.'

Suddenly he stretched his hand across the table and said 'How do you do? Frank O'Connor.'

Oh, for goodness' sake. She looked down at his hand and smiled, despite herself. And then the waitress came back with their order, and started to unload her tray, and Frank thanked her courteously before asking Cecily what she thought of the McGahern.

And, oddly, it was a little easier after that.

✡✡✡

The doorbell rang just as Laura was about to open the oven door. She turned her head in the direction of the hall. 'Donal? Can you get that?'

'Yeah.' His voice floated down the stairs.

She opened the door and a wave of savoury heat hit her. Mmm – smelt good, and she was starving; she'd added a couple of rashers and a grilled tomato to her breakfast toast, and skipped lunch. She gave the tray of garlicky potato chunks a shake before scattering on the fresh rosemary, and stuck a skewer into the rack of lamb – another ten minutes. Donal's footsteps sounded on the stairs and a few minutes later, Andrew's voice floated in from the hall. Damn – she'd been hoping Breffni and Cian would arrive first, so they'd be there to talk to Ruth and Andrew while she finished up in here. Now she'd have to go in and rescue Ruth from the two men. She'd leave the tartlets till the others got here, and the salad would just have to wait till then too.

She closed the oven door gently, pulled off her apron and raked her fingers through her curls in front of the mirror before going into the sitting room.

'Ah – here she is.' Andrew, just inside the door, put a hand on her shoulder and smacked a kiss on her cheek. 'Hi, sis. Mother says hello.'

Laura laughed. 'Liar. Now go and get a drink from my husband.' She turned to Ruth, perched on the couch next to the fire. 'Ruth, welcome. You look lovely.'

And she did – long straight cream skirt that looked like linen, and a lavender lacy top. She'd clipped back her light blond hair on one side with a cream slide, and her lips were pale pink. There were improvements she could have made – a little mascara, some pencil maybe to bring out her eyes, a darker lipstick, a foundation with a bit more coverage to even out her skin tone and mask her freckles – but Ruth certainly looked very presentable this evening. She blushed slightly at Laura's compliment.

'Thanks – my one and only good skirt.' She looked admiringly at Laura. 'That dress is fabulous.'

'It's my going-away outfit, would you believe? Seven years old now; I just can't bring myself to get rid of it.'

Laura loved it; straight dark wine silk – who'd have imagined wine would suit her hair colour? – sleeveless, with a deep neckline front and back and a narrow waist, falling softly to her knee. Simple and sophisticated. Worth every penny of the startlingly high price that Donal had insisted on paying. She'd tried, half-heartedly, to stop him.

'You'll be broke; we won't be able to afford the wedding.' And still she couldn't bring herself to go back into the dressing room and take it off, kept glancing sideways towards the long mirror.

'Look at it this way. If you don't let me buy it, the wedding's off.'

She'd beamed at him, delighted. 'Well, if you put it that way . . . but remember, you forced me.'

She'd lost count of the number of times she'd worn it, with the plain white gold chain that Donal had given her for their first anniversary, and the matching earrings she'd treated herself to with her first proper pay cheque.

'Laur?' From across the room Donal held up a can of beer. Andrew brought a glass of red wine to Ruth and sat beside her on the couch.

'Hmm – maybe I'll have wine instead.' Laura walked to the drinks table and looked at the bottle. Chateauneufdupape – yummy. Good choice, guys.'

Ruth smiled shyly. 'I asked Andrew what you liked.'

'And I said anything in a bottle.' Andrew grinned, stretching out his long legs, and Ruth gave him an indulgent smile.

'Look at the pioneer who's talking.' Donal filled a glass with wine and handed it to Laura, pretending not to see her warning look.

Andrew looked plaintively at Laura. 'Sis, he's at me again.'

Laura had to smile. 'Now stop it, you two. Ruth, they're always like this; take no notice.' Just then, the doorbell rang again. Laura put her glass on the coffee table. 'Donal, will you pass around the olives? And Andrew, go and talk to Donal. We're going to have a girlie chat on the couch.'

Breffni looked great, as always. Laura had given up trying to compete when she realised that even in her school uniform, without a hint of make-up, Breffni had men doing double takes. Tonight her black hair, always impossibly shiny, fell loose over her shoulders. The trousers that Laura hadn't seen before were the same blue as her eyes, and toned in beautifully with her sleeveless silver-grey top. Tiny diamond studs flashed in her ears.

Laura hugged her. 'You could at least have made an effort; combed your hair or something.'

Breffni hugged her back, smelling deliciously exotic. 'Well, I didn't want to show you up; I knew you'd be in the same old rag you always wear.'

Cian, in his usual sports jacket and chinos, raised his eyes to heaven. 'Stop it, you two – behave yourselves.' He gave Laura a hug. 'Hi there. You look great.' He sniffed. 'And something smells wonderful.'

'That'll be either my perfume or the dinner I've spent the day slaving over. Come in and meet the new bride.'

'See, I told you they were here.' Breffni poked Cian in the ribs. 'It's his fault; we'd have got here half an hour ago if he hadn't been hogging the bathroom.'

Laura grinned and shoved her friend ahead of her. 'Yes, Breffni, I believe you. Get in there.'

Ruth stood quickly as they came in, a polite smile on her face. As Laura made the introductions, Ruth put out her hand. 'Hi, it's nice to meet you both.' She sounded nervous.

Breffni's lightning glance swept over her. 'Nice to meet you too, Ruth; I've been –'

'Hey, long time no see.' Andrew seemed to appear out of the blue.

Breffni swung around to him. 'Hey yourself.' She hugged him lightly. 'Not since Rome, would you believe? And this is my Cian.'

Cian put his hand out to Andrew, wrapping his other arm around Breffni's waist. 'Hello, and congratulations.'

Andrew shook his hand. 'Thanks, mate. And I hear you two have a little girl.' He was looking at Breffni again.

She nodded. 'Polly. Nearly two, and cute as a button; takes after her mother, except for the head of blond curls.' She turned to Cian. 'Get me a glass of red wine, would you, love?'

Laura slipped away – time to get organised. In the kitchen she took the lamb from the oven, then got Donal's bowl of spinach and Gruyère mixture from the fridge and spooned it into the little filo cases that were waiting on a baking tray. She sprinkled on the pine nuts he'd toasted earlier and slid the tray into the hot oven. She was straightening up when a voice behind her said, 'You could have warned me.'

She jumped and turned around. Breffni pushed the kitchen door closed behind her. She held up one of the glasses of wine she was carrying. 'I presume this is yours.'

'You've left poor Ruth with three men? Warned you about what?'

'About the fact that your brother is as gorgeous as ever – and that tan doesn't do him any harm either.'

Laura looked closely at her. 'Are you OK meeting him again Bref, really? I mean, you seemed fine in Rome, and I won't go on about it, but –'

Breffni laughed. 'Yeah, relax, course I am. I'm just saying he's still gorgeous.' She handed Laura the glass and sniffed the air. 'Oh my God, something smells fabulous. I'm so hungry I could eat the hind leg of a diseased pony.'

Laura smiled – when they were growing up, they went through a phase of trying to out-disgust the other by thinking up the worst possible ending to 'I'm so hungry I could eat . . .' The outright winner was Breffni's '. . . the coarsely grated toenails of a gangrenous elephant'.

Laura opened the fridge and pulled out a bag of mixed greens. 'Here – as long as you've deserted poor Ruth, you can find a bowl and chuck that in. There's a jar of Donal's dressing in the fridge, and some cherry tomatoes – but don't add the dressing yet.'

'OK.' Breffni fished under the worktop and came up with a big green bowl. She pulled the bag open and tipped the leaves in. Then she took a sip from her glass. 'This wine is superb.'

Laura took a serving plate from the dresser. 'Isn't it? Ruth and Andrew brought it. Ruth must have picked it out – Andrew's not a bit fussy.'

'Obviously.' Breffni opened the fridge door.

Laura looked at her. 'What's that supposed to mean?'

Breffni turned from the fridge with a little container of cherry tomatoes in one hand and a jar of dressing in the other. When she didn't answer, Laura put her serving dish down. 'Bref, are you having a go at Ruth?'

Breffni took a knife from the block and smiled over. 'Hey, just a joke, keep your hair on.' She began halving the tomatoes, throwing the halves into the bowl. 'But you must admit, she's not exactly in Andrew's league, looks-wise.' When Laura didn't respond, Breffni said, 'Come on, Laur, I'm only stating a fact. She could be vaguely pretty, I suppose, if she made a bit of an effort.' She picked a watercress leaf from the bowl and munched it. 'Bet she can't believe her luck in hooking Andrew.'

Laura looked sternly at her as she ran hot water over the dish. 'Stop, Bref – Ruth is lovely. She's probably much too good for Andrew, actually. Stop being bitchy.'

Breffni grinned, still munching, not at all put out. 'OK, OK, sorry. I'm sure she's grand. I'm sure herself and Andrew will live happily ever after, and have lots of little children to keep Dragon Granny happy.'

Laura had to smile – the thought of Cecily dandling a child on her knee was just too ridiculous. She dried the serving dish and went to check on the starters. 'Anyway, I've never seen why you thought Andrew was so good-looking.'

'Of course you haven't – you're his sister. You're not supposed to think he's good-looking.' She took another sip of wine and watched as Laura lifted out the tray of tartlets. 'Mmm – have they spinach in them?'

'Yeah – Donal made them; I just put them together.' Laura lifted the tartlets onto the warm dish with a spatula. 'Andrew told me that Ruth loved the spinach pies they got in Greece, so hopefully these are something similar.' She picked up a bundle of small plates with her free hand. 'Grab some serviettes and follow me in – and bring my drink.'

In the sitting room, Ruth sat alone on the couch, looking into the fire. The three men were standing in the far corner, chatting. Laura felt a stab of annoyance towards her brother. He *could have kept her company till we got back*. And Donal should have known better too. She signalled for Donal to bring the wine over, then sat beside Ruth and put down her dish of starters. 'Try these; they're a speciality of Donal's.' She handed Ruth a small plate and lifted a tartlet onto it.

'You wanted wine, Madam?' Donal was at her side. She nodded, doling tartlets out onto plates. 'You can leave the bottle, and bring these over.' When he'd gone with his three plates, Laura looked back at Ruth and smiled. 'That'll keep them quiet for a while.' She thought Ruth still looked quite ill at ease – a little wine would relax her. She picked up the bottle and added some to Ruth's glass.

Breffni came in, holding glasses and serviettes. 'Yes please, more yummy wine.' She sat opposite Laura and Ruth and helped herself to a tartlet as Laura topped up her glass. Her scent wafted over as she moved. 'So, Ruth, how do you like living in Limerick so far?' She bit into her tartlet and watched Ruth as she munched.

Ruth blushed slightly. 'Great; it's so easy to get around, after Dublin.' She lifted the plate that Laura had given her, reached for the tartlet.

Breffni swallowed, took another bite. 'By that, you mean it's so much smaller than Dublin?' Her expression was politely innocent, waiting for Ruth's response.

Ruth's smile faltered; her hand paused halfway to her mouth. 'Well, yes it is, of course, but I didn't mean that –'

'Relax – I'm just kidding. I know what you meant.' Breffni lifted her glass towards Ruth. 'Here's to wedded bliss; even if you have to live with mother-in-law for the moment.' She winked at Laura, who was looking at her sternly. 'Great starters, Laur, by the way.' She popped the rest of her tartlet into her mouth, still holding her glass out.

Ruth dropped her untouched tartlet and lifted her glass, smiling faintly. She clinked it against Breffni's and took a quick gulp as Laura stood with the plate of starters. 'I'd better see if they need more; back in a sec.'

Ruth watched her cross the room, then reached for her tartlet again.

'They're specially for you, by the way, to remind you of Crete.' Breffni indicated the tartlet with her head. 'Apparently you ate quite a lot of them over there.'

Ruth blushed deeper. 'Oh, I didn't realise everyone knew that.' She raised the tartlet to her lips and took a tiny bite, holding her plate just under her chin to catch the crumbs.

Breffni watched as she ate. 'That's where you and Andrew met, wasn't it? In Crete. And then you went back there for the honeymoon.'

Ruth nodded, eyes on her tartlet. Her tongue shot out and licked a crumb from the corner of her mouth.

'Very romantic. So –' Breffni smiled again, lowered her voice '– was it love at first sight, or what?'

Ruth giggled nervously. She put her plate down and grabbed her wine glass. 'Kind of.' She took a quick swallow, avoiding Breffni's eyes. 'For me, anyway.' She lifted a serviette and dabbed at her mouth, hoping to God that her lipstick hadn't disappeared, but knowing that it had. Why on earth had she said that – for me, anyway – as if Andrew hadn't felt anything for her initially, as if the feeling had been all on her side? Stupid. She lifted her glass again, conscious of being watched from across the coffee table, forcing herself to look at Breffni and give a too-bright smile.

After a few seconds of silence, Laura reappeared with the last few tartlets and picked up the wine bottle. Breffni held out her glass. 'I'm going to be on my ear – this wine is just too delicious.'

Laura topped up each of their glasses and held the empty bottle up in Donal's direction before sitting down again next to Ruth. 'So what have I missed?'

'Well, I'm grilling Ruth about when she met Andrew, but she's giving nothing away; I'll have to corner him at dinner and get all the juicy details.' Breffni grinned and lifted her glass.

Laura gave her a sharp look – couldn't she see she was making Ruth uncomfortable? She turned to her sister-in-law. 'Ignore her, Ruth – just tell her to mind her own business. What d'you think of the tartlets?'

'They're really delicious.' Ruth took another tiny nibble from hers.

'Mmm, aren't they? Having a husband who can cook has its uses.'

'I told Ruth they were specially for her.' Breffni popped the last of her tartlet into her mouth, licking off the stray crumbs that stuck to her lips. Ruth wondered how she kept her lipstick so perfectly in place.

Laura shot another warning glance at Breffni – was she imagining it, or was Breffni really picking on Ruth? Probably just her idea of fun, but she obviously hadn't yet realised how sensitive Ruth was. Laura would just have to change the subject, and hope Breffni took the hint. She picked up her own half-eaten tartlet. 'Pity they're loaded with calories.'

Ruth gave a wry smile. 'I'd say so; I know I put on weight on holidays.' She bent her head and took another tiny, careful bite. Her pale hair, imprisoned in its clip, looked almost white in the soft light.

Breffni watched her picking at the tartlet, like a rabbit nibbling at a bit of lettuce. What on earth did Andrew see in such a mousy little creature? She turned to Laura. 'Ah, can't you just see herself and Andrew, gazing into each other's eyes over a couple of spinach pies?'

'At least Ruth could eat,' Laura said quickly. 'When I met Donal, I was so besotted I went right off my food – had to force myself to eat these gorgeous meals he cooked for me. I lost nearly a stone; first time in years I fitted into a size ten.'

'And when I met Cian I couldn't eat either, and I still put on weight; I couldn't understand it.' Breffni shrugged her shoulders and looked puzzled.

Laura shot her a sceptical look. 'You, not able to eat? In San Francisco, surrounded by just about every kind of food in the world? Pull the other one.'

Breffni shook her head, wide-eyed. 'No, it's true – ask him. Not a bite for ages.' She paused. 'Unless, of course, you count the odd pizza, to stop me from collapsing – and the buckets of popcorn at the movies, to keep my strength up –' She sipped her wine as Laura exchanged a smile with Ruth '– and a tub of Ben & Jerry's every now and again, just for the calcium.' She looked innocently from one to the other. 'Well I had to have something, didn't I? I couldn't let myself starve, just when I'd found the man of my dreams.'

Laura snorted. 'You – starve? That'll be the day.' She held out the last few tartlets. 'Here, you'd better get another one inside you; you're starting to wilt.'

Breffni immediately took one and bit into it. She spoke through a mouthful of spinach and pastry. 'Thanks; I *was* feeling a little faint.'

'Stop talking with your mouth full – you're spraying all over my good chair.'

Ruth watched them, smiling. Breffni was so beautiful; Laura hadn't mentioned that. And so confident. Not that Laura wasn't striking too, with those auburn curls and the same deep green eyes as Andrew.

But Breffni – she could be a film star. Her skin was so creamy, and it didn't look like she had any make-up on. Ruth wouldn't dream of going out without her tinted moisturiser and lipstick, even if it was gone five minutes later. She felt nervous in the company of these two smiling, confident women – particularly Breffni, even though Breffni had been perfectly friendly to her. She was a bit more direct than Ruth was comfortable with, that was all. It was Ruth's stupid self-consciousness that was making her nervous, nothing else.

Laura stood up. 'Time to feed the starving.' Immediately Ruth stood too, nearly knocking her glass over. 'I'll give you a hand.' She suddenly didn't want to be left alone with Breffni again.

She was aware of being watched as she moved around the room, and she was glad when Andrew reached out and put an arm around her while she was stacking their plates. She smiled gratefully at him and followed Laura into the kitchen.

Cian joined Breffni on the couch, and she rewarded him with a dazzling smile.

✡✡✡

'So how's married life then?' Donal turned back to Andrew after watching Laura and Ruth leave the room.

'Fine; can't complain so far.' Andrew took a handful of nuts from a nearby bowl and began popping them one by one into his mouth. 'Mind you, I've been lucky – never had to fend for myself like you.' He grinned at Donal. 'Always had someone picking up after me.'

'And now you have Ruth.'

Andrew nodded, still smiling. 'Now I have Ruth.'

'And does she realise that she's going to be the one who does all the picking up in this new house?' Donal was smiling too.

'Course she does; she's much better at all that sort of thing than me. And I can't cook to save my life – we're not all Jamie Olivers like yourself.'

Donal folded his arms and regarded Andrew thoughtfully. 'Maybe – and this is just a thought – if you gave cooking a go now and again you might get the hang of it.'

Andrew laughed, not seeming a bit put out. 'God, you're the real new man. Working all day and then going home to cook your wife's dinner. Isn't she the lucky woman?' He popped a few more nuts into his mouth, enjoying himself.

Donal handed him a new can of lager, then opened a fresh can for himself. 'Anway –' he filled his glass and raised it '– here's to Ruth's cooking; for her sake, I hope it's as good as your mother's.'

Andrew tipped his glass in Donal's direction. 'Not yet; but I live in hope. She's got plenty of time to learn.' He put back his head and drank, and Donal watched him, smile fading slightly.

✡✡✡

'. . . Laura, this lamb is fabulous; you must have been cooking it all day . . .'

'. . . Pass the mint sauce, would you Cian? Thanks . . .'

'. . . Ruth, will you have some more potatoes? You've hardly any there . . .'

'. . . Oops, sorry – your good tablecloth. Will it come out, do you think . . . ?'

'. . . I hadn't a notion of it, and I wasn't long telling her either. The nerve of her, expecting me to drop everything . . .'

'. . . Yeah, whole garlic cloves in with the potatoes – not peeled, no . . .'

'. . . He has a new CD out; has anyone heard it yet . . . ?'

'. . . It was my first trip abroad, and I found the heat a bit much really . . .'

'. . . Ah would you look at him, everyone; isn't he the real gentleman . . . ?'

'. . . You're very quiet tonight. Is everything OK . . . ?'

✡✡✡

It hit him like a tidal wave, slamming into the space where he imagined his heart to be, as soon as he laid eyes on her. Catching him completely off guard, forcing him to breathe deeply when nobody was watching him, to try to slow his racing pulse. All through dinner he watched her across the table, mesmerised. Saw her lifting a glass. Putting a forkful of food into her mouth. Talking with her neighbours. Gesturing, laughing. Pushing her hair behind her ear. Propping her chin in her hand. Once or twice meeting his eye briefly, smiling at him when that happened.

He knew how ridiculous it was – he was like a teenager with a crush, for God's sake – but he simply couldn't help himself. Couldn't drag his eyes away from her.

He was careful, of course. Laughed when everyone else did, pretended to be interested in the plate of food in front of him. It was all he could do to eat it; tomorrow he wouldn't remember what was served. He drank water and wine without tasting a difference. Had no idea what they all spoke about, or what he said when anyone addressed him. Felt light-headed long before he'd had enough alcohol to cause it.

He couldn't keep his eyes off her.

✡✡✡

Laura reached across the bed and lifted the phone. 'Hello?'

'Only me, to say thanks a million for last night. It was great, as always.' Breffni's voice sounded rusty.

Laura lay back against the pillows, pulled the duvet up around her shoulders. 'Are you dying?'

'Not too bad. How's *your* head?'

'A little fragile; I'm still in bed. But we cleaned up last night, so I'm entitled.'

Breffni gave a snort. 'Good God – it's half eleven in the morning, woman. Easily known you're childless; Poll was in to us at seven. I've the washing on the line and the bathroom cleaned. I'd have hoovered, but I didn't know if I could bear the noise.'

Laura laughed. 'Ah shut up, you sound like Superwoman. And I don't believe a word anyway; you're probably still in bed yourself.'

'I wish. Anyway, thanks again. My place next, end of the month, yeah? I suppose I'll ask the other two as well.'

'Do – it would be good for Ruth. D'you think she enjoyed the night?'

'Course she did. Weren't we all nice to her?'

'Yeah . . . well, let me know when you're in town. I'm not too busy this week – we could meet for coffee.'

'OK, I might be bringing Mary in on Thursday actually. Take care. Polly sends kisses.'

'Give her one back. See you soon.'

✡✡✡

Easily known you're childless. 'Childless'. 'Barren'. Horrible, dry, brittle words. Whereas 'womb' sounded all round and juicy. Not *her* womb though; hers was withered and brown, deprived of whatever it needed to grow and blossom and bear fruit; *the fruit of thy womb*. Her womb was empty of fruit. It squatted inside her and mocked her each month: *Nothing again, Laura. Better luck next time, Laura. Must try harder, Laura.*

Every twenty-eight days, regular as clockwork, she wrote 'tampons' in angry letters on her shopping list. Each time the blood came, she cried in the bath late at night, when Donal was asleep.

When she visited Cecily, she looked at her and thought: *even you, so cold, so unfeeling; even you could do it.* She watched young girls pushing babies in the street, lifting them carelessly out of their buggies, pushing soothers and bottles into their mouths – and she hated them for being what she couldn't be. She heard about abandoned babies with silent outrage; how cruel, how unfair that was.

She saw Breffni with Polly, the huge, terrifying love between them, and she ached for it. She remembered when Breffni was pregnant, especially in the last month or so, how she'd stop in the middle of a sentence and put her palm to her swollen stomach, and just hold it there with a look that Laura had never seen before. A look that Laura couldn't decipher, as if it was in a foreign language.

And this was why, of course, she couldn't confide in Breffni. How could she possibly cry on Breffni's shoulder about not getting pregnant, when Breffni and Cian had conceived Polly without even trying? Hadn't wanted a baby at all, in fact. Laura remembered Breffni's phone call, over two years ago, as if it had happened last week.

'Laur, I'm in trouble.'

She sounded funny – was she crying? Laura squinted at the

digital face of the clock radio: two thirty-two. Beside her, Donal grunted and turned his face away from the lamp she'd just switched on.

'What's wrong?' She imagined fires, earthquakes, disaster on an epic scale. 'Is Cian all right?'

'I'm pregnant.'

Laura's heart lurched. She drew in a sharp breath. 'God.' Her mind raced. 'Are you sure?'

'Yeah. I did two tests, and I'm a fortnight late. I'm never late.'

Laura groped for something to say. 'What does Cian think?'

Breffni said nothing.

'Bref? You haven't told him?'

'Look, I don't know what I want to do . . . I have to think –'

'You have to tell him; it's his baby too.' Donal stirred again and turned back, watching her through half-open eyes.

'What'll I do, Laur? I don't know what to do.'

Laura took another deep breath. 'You have to tell him. And then you talk about it together. Promise you'll tell him.'

And Breffni had told him, and three months later they'd arrived in Ireland and moved in with Cian's granny Mary until they found a job for Cian and a house for the three of them, having decided that Ireland was a better place to bring up a child.

And Laura had wanted so much to tell Breffni that she and Donal had just started trying for a child of their own, but she couldn't, not when Polly had been unplanned – it would have seemed insensitive somehow. And then, after Polly arrived, and Breffni was struggling with exhaustion and crying if you looked crooked at her, Laura found it even harder. How could she bother Breffni now, particularly with that? And when the first few difficult months had passed, and Breffni finally fell in love with her daughter, and glowed with her new happiness, Laura still said

nothing; at that stage, she simply couldn't. What had turn
the biggest heartache of her life – getting harder to bea
every month that passed – had also turned out to be the one thing she couldn't bring herself to share with the person she felt closest to, after Donal.

And Donal was the last person she could talk to. How could she? It would be like a criticism, an accusation: *Where is our child? Why have you not given it to me? What's wrong with you? What's wrong with us?* She knew how ridiculous it sounded – not able to discuss your fertility problems with your husband – but knowing it sounded ridiculous didn't make it go away.

She often wondered about Donal's family. He told her that he'd been an only child, the surprise arrival in a late marriage. His parents had met when his Australian mother had visited Ireland in her thirties, and eventually, after three years of long-distance courtship, settled in Sligo with her new husband. When Donal was nineteen, his parents decided to emigrate to Australia, where his mother's ageing father lived alone. Of course, they'd wanted Donal to go with them, but he'd chosen to stay in Ireland.

'The last thing I wanted was to up and move halfway around the world. My mother's family lived in this small town – a village really – out in the middle of nowhere. The thought of starting a whole new life in a place like that just didn't appeal to me. And I was in the middle of a catering course; I wanted to finish that.'

'But didn't you miss them? Weren't you lonely?' Laura could not imagine being separated by such a distance from her own beloved father.

Donal shrugged. 'To be honest, we were never much of a family. My folks weren't the touchy-feely types really – I don't ever remember my mother hugging me. And I had pals here, plenty of company. I looked forward to the independence, in fact

– they didn't give me a lot of freedom growing up. The over-protected only child, that was me. Of course, I had quite a job to convince them to go off without me, but eventually I managed it.'

'And you stayed in Sligo, by yourself.' Laura tried to picture it: this teenager, little more than a child really, waving goodbye to his parents as they set off for the other side of the world. Going home afterwards to live in an empty house.

'Well, I was only in Sligo for a few months after they left, as it turned out. When I finished my catering course, I was offered a job in Cruise's hotel here in Limerick – you'll hardly remember it, it's gone years; it was where Cruise's Street is now – and I ended up staying here, sold the house in Sligo after a few months and rented here until I eventually bought the one I have now.'

It all sounded terribly casual to Laura. 'And how come you never write to your parents – or they never write to you?'

He grinned. 'You may not have heard, but we have what's called e-mail now. Quicker, cheaper, less hassle.'

She wasn't satisfied. 'But have you ever been to visit them? What about at Christmas – aren't you ever lonely?'

Donal laughed. 'Now there's a girly question. No, I can't say it's ever bothered me, being on my own at Christmas. When I was in Cruise's, we were rushed off our feet – I hadn't time to worry about not having the mammy at home to cook my turkey. And now –' he grinned '– you might have noticed that I can cook a fair old turkey all by myself.'

Laura wasn't about to be distracted. 'And are you still in regular contact? How often do you hear from them?'

He shrugged again. 'Well, I suppose we've drifted apart over the last while. To be honest, love, it doesn't bother me. I think it's different for guys; they don't need the family as much as females seem to.'

She still thought it strange, to lose contact with your parents so completely. And not even to have them at your wedding – Donal had insisted that neither of them would be able for the trip to Rome.

'They're in their eighties now, both of them. The journey would kill them, believe me.'

And Laura had to agree with that. But she wondered sometimes if there was more to it than he was telling her – if there'd been some kind of a falling-out. Maybe he'd done something so bad that they'd disowned him. Robbed a house, maybe, or left some poor girl at the altar. She supposed she'd never know; have to accept that she'd never get to meet her parents-in-law. Never be able to present them with a grandchild – that was assuming she ever managed to get pregnant, of course.

She and Donal had talked about children when they'd decided to get married. She wanted a big family, full of the squabbles and excitement and noise that neither of them had had growing up.

'Mother was always so – *civilised.* Obsessed with manners – "use a napkin, don't put your knife in your mouth, keep your elbows off the table" – as if any of that nonsense mattered . . . and we could never make noise in the house; if Andrew and I had any kind of row, we had to go out the back to yell at each other. I used to love having my tea at Breffni's, where everyone grabbed what they wanted, and leant across other people's plates and stuff, and Mona never minded if you talked with your mouth full. They had better grub too – mashed bananas on sliced white bread, and fish fingers, and sausages – Mother hated sausages.'

It was a month before their wedding. Laura was lying on the couch in Donal's house, balancing a mug of coffee on her stomach; he was sitting at the end, cradling her bare feet in his hands. He smiled at her chatter, but said nothing.

She lifted her head from her cushion and looked over at him. 'What was it like, growing up in your house? Must have been quiet too, with just you.'

He looked back at her for a minute before answering. Then he said 'Yes, it was quiet, I suppose; I didn't really notice.'

He never seemed to want to talk about his family. Laura wondered again if something had happened to drive them apart. She lifted a foot from his lap and poked him gently in the side with it. 'So you'd like a few children to make our house nice and noisy then?'

He grabbed her foot and held it tightly. 'If that's what you want, I'm happy.' He smiled again, but it was strained. She sat up then and swung her legs down, and slid over beside him and found his hand, and twined her fingers around his.

'Donal, is there anything you haven't told me – anything about your family . . . ?' She faltered as he looked blankly at her.

'Of course not. I'm just not that pushed about having a family of my own. But if you want to, that's OK.'

She wasn't satisfied. 'Darling, you have to want it too. I'm not the boss of you.' She spoke gently, sensing a wariness about him that she hadn't seen before. 'We need to be sure about this.'

Then he reached up and ruffled her hair with his free hand, amused. 'So young and so serious.' The jokey Donal, back again.

She grabbed his other hand. 'Donal, stop. I *am* serious. This is a big thing.'

'OK, OK.' He stopped and looked at her. 'Seriously, if you want children, that's fine with me.' He paused. 'But maybe we could wait awhile? I'd like to have you to myself for a few years.' And of course she loved hearing that – couldn't argue with it. She wanted him to herself too. And she *was* only twenty-two – plenty of time for children.

So they waited, and were careful, and the years passed. And now she was twenty-nine, and they'd stopped being careful two years ago. She'd thrown away her repeat prescription for the pill, and Donal had seemed happy to go for it – or at least, not *un*happy.

And since then, nothing had happened.

The first few months she hadn't taken too much notice. It was bound to take some time, after her being on the pill for so long; they couldn't expect to be successful right away. She'd hold the newborn Polly in her arms and think: *this'll be me soon.*

The day after Polly's first birthday, without saying anything to Donal, Laura had gone to visit the doctor who'd seen her through measles and chicken pox, and a nasty case of shingles one summer. She felt slightly foolish, but the worry that had started as a tiny niggle a couple of months ago had begun to grow; it was time to do something.

Dr Goode had listened without interrupting. Then he told her that there might well be nothing to worry about. He said what she'd been expecting to hear – that her body needed time to return to its normal level of fertility after long-term contraception. He said it would be quite unusual for her to get pregnant straight after coming off the pill. He said that if she wanted, he could do some simple exploratory tests – but he'd need to see Donal too.

Dr Goode said a lot of things that she thought were probably meant to reassure her. She said she'd think about it.

And since then, a year had passed. She'd never told Donal about her visit to Dr Goode; it was the one thing she simply had no idea how to talk to him about. The one thing she desperately needed to talk to him about. He never brought up the subject of children, seemed not to notice that they'd been trying for so long.

Did he care? Was he secretly hoping it never happened?

Next year, Laura would be thirty.

She put down the leaflet on built-in wardrobes that she was supposed to be redesigning; there was no way she could concentrate on that today. She'd have to talk to Donal.

Maybe tonight, after dinner.

✡✡✡

She put a box of Crunchy Nut Corn Flakes into the trolley and felt a tap on her shoulder. She swung around. 'Hey, long time no see. Must be all of what – a week?'

'About that.' He smiled, glancing into her trolley. 'You're stocking up.'

She made a face. 'Yeah, the dreaded weekly shop. I'm seriously thinking of going online.'

He laughed. 'Come on – it's not as if you're feeding the five thousand.'

She grinned back at him. 'I suppose not . . . it was good the other night, wasn't it?'

He nodded. 'Great fun. We should make a habit of it.'

It was only when she saw him walking out through the doors a few minutes later without a bag that she wondered why he was in a supermarket if he hadn't been buying anything.

She watched him walk over to his car. Nice bum.

✡✡✡

She looked even better than she had at dinner.

In the supermarket, he watched her choose a melon, reject unripe bananas, press a loaf of brown bread before tossing it into the trolley. Fill a bag with mandarins. Weigh a cauliflower, chewing on her bottom lip.

He saw her hand reaching up to get the cereal, her multicoloured top pulling away from her low-rise jeans to show him an inch of flat creamy stomach.

Then he went over and touched her shoulder. He hadn't planned to talk to her, but the sight of her bare skin seemed to propel him over. He had no idea what he'd say, how he'd explain his presence. Why he wasn't filling a trolley too – or at least a basket.

He didn't care what she thought. He knew he should run a mile from this madness that had possessed him since the night of the dinner – the compulsion that had brought him to her neighbourhood every day since then in the hope of seeing her – but he found he didn't want to run. Couldn't run.

He was filled with her. She lived in his head all day, and he pulled her out and dreamt her into his nights.

He would have to have her. There was simply no other way.

✡✡✡

Laura looked at Donal reading the paper on the couch and thought: *Now; do it now.* She couldn't wait till after dinner; she'd be far too nervous by then.

She closed her notebook, full of anxious scribbles that were not helping her wardrobe leaflet in the slightest, and got up from the desk and went to sit next to Donal. From the stereo, Robbie Williams was asking them to let him entertain them. The aromas of Donal's special roast chicken – honey, rosemary, lemon – wafted in from the kitchen.

He smiled at her as she sat down – 'Hey you' – and went back to reading his paper again.

'Donal.' She felt her heartbeat quicken.

'Mmm?'

She put a hand lightly on his thigh. 'I need to talk to you about something.'

'Ah.' He looked up and studied her face for a second, then folded the paper and tossed it on the floor. 'I was wondering how long it would take you.'

'What do you mean?' Her eyes searched his face. Could he possibly be talking about the same thing? Had he been worrying about it too? Her heart jumped at the thought that maybe he felt exactly the same; maybe he was just as concerned as she was. She willed him to say what she wanted to hear.

He smiled. 'Oh come on; it's obvious you've something on your mind – you've hardly opened your mouth since I got home. I figured you'd tell me what it was sooner or later.'

So he hadn't been thinking about it too. He had no idea what she wanted to talk about, what had been eating away at her for what seemed like forever. She inhaled a deep breath and let it out slowly. There was no going back now.

She took one of his hands and folded her fingers around it. 'Darling, it's about starting a family.' She watched his face anxiously. 'We've been trying for over two years now and – I'm . . . not getting any younger, and nothing's happening, and – well, I'm a bit worried . . .'

It was coming out all wrong, all twisted up and muddled – not the way she'd planned it at all. Her eyes stayed fixed on his face; she couldn't look away. She held his hand in hers and prayed for him to rescue her.

His smile faded a bit but he said nothing, just nodded slightly and looked back at her, waiting for her to go on. So she tried again. 'I think – the time has come to take some action . . . I mean, to see if we can find out if anything's wrong, if there's anything we need to do.'

She stopped. Waited. Begged him silently to say something.

He pursed his lips, looked at her fingers, wrapped around his hand. 'What action are you talking about?' His voice was neutral, giving her no clue.

She tightened her hold on his hand, wanting to see his eyes. 'We could have tests done – simple tests, to see if either of us . . . if there's anything we need to do . . .' She'd said that already – she was repeating herself. She trailed off again, watching his face closely.

He stood abruptly, pulling his hand from hers. Walked across the room, turned and stood to face her, hands tucked under his armpits. She suddenly felt as if she was on trial, sitting there on the couch. He looked – defensive. And so far away.

He said nothing for a minute – she waited, some instinct kept her silent – and then he said, 'OK.'

She wondered if she'd heard him right. 'OK?'

He nodded, came back to sit on the arm of the couch. 'OK.' He stretched out a hand and ran a finger down her cheek. 'If it means that much to you.'

If it means that much to you. She didn't dare ask what it meant to him. She felt tears of relief threatening to spill out of her, and bit her cheek, hard, and blinked. 'Are you sure you're all right with this?' Her voice felt tight.

'Yeah.' He stood again. 'I'm going to put the spuds in. Want a beer?'

She nodded, then shook her head. 'I'd like a little brandy.'

'OK.' He turned in the doorway. 'You make the arrangements, right?'

She nodded again at the space he left behind, full of a fragile hope.

✡✡✡

'Ruth, dear.' Cecily lifted a sliver of perfectly poached salmon from the serving dish and deposited it on the plate in front of her. 'I've been meaning to ask you if you'd care to attend the next meeting of the book club, Thursday of next week.' She added two cherry tomatoes and a wedge of lemon to her plate before looking over at Ruth. 'It's my turn to host.'

'Thank you, Cecily, I'd be delighted.' Ruth smiled back placidly at her mother-in-law as she lifted a little square of homemade brown bread to her lips. The thought of sitting in on a book-club meeting, with a group of people who were mostly a lot older than her, held far fewer terrors for Ruth than dinner at Breffni and Cian's house this coming weekend.

While she found Cecily's poise and elegance slightly intimidating, it didn't really threaten her. She knew she wasn't under scrutiny, didn't feel under pressure to be witty and charming in Cecily's company. She thought that perhaps her mother-in-law pitied her slightly, knowing that Ruth would never shine, never be confident enough to make an impression in the way that Cecily herself had probably always done. But Ruth could cope with being pitied, or even dismissed as someone of no importance – Cecily's indifference didn't demand anything of her. And Ruth assumed that the other book-club members would be equally polite and non-threatening. It might even be fun, in a sedate kind of way.

Whereas dinner in the company of Breffni . . . Ruth couldn't define exactly why she found Laura's best friend so unnerving; couldn't put her finger on why she was dreading Saturday night's dinner so much. Breffni had been charming and funny all evening at Laura's; she'd had everyone in stitches more than once, especially after what Ruth privately thought were far too many glasses of wine. Mind you, Breffni wasn't the only one – in the taxi on the way home, Ruth had had to practically fight Andrew off; sliding a hand up under her top, nearly ripping her skirt when he lifted it and pushed his knee in between her thighs to part them, laughing when she whispered that the driver could see them. He'd obviously had too much to drink too: anyone could see that. But Ruth didn't mind someone having a few too many once in a while – no harm in that, as long as they didn't get offensive. And it wasn't that Breffni had done, or said, anything at Laura and Donal's that Ruth could object to: it was just that she was one of Them.

Ruth had gone to school with quite a few of Them. The ones who always had the right kind of shoes and lunchboxes and schoolbags; and later, the best-looking boyfriends and the latest CDs and the coolest haircuts. The ones who were always first to see the new releases at the cinemas. Who skipped classes and never got caught. The ones who knew someone who could get them backstage passes at concerts. Who weren't afraid to bring something back to a shop, or to ask for a discount. Who knew, without anyone showing them, how to wear make-up. Who looked good in a school uniform.

And while Ruth had never been bullied at school, never been laughed at, or teased in any way, she'd always been afraid of Them. Always been waiting for one of Them to turn around and sneer at her careful essays and boring shoes and timid smiles. Being ignored was so much less terrifying.

And as soon as Ruth met Breffni, all her old stupid schoolday anxieties had come rushing back. And this weekend, she and

Andrew were going to dinner at Breffni and Cian's house in Nenagh. Compared to that, the book club would be a cakewalk.

Ruth lifted her fork and took a mouthful of salmon and thought about what she'd wear to the night in Nenagh. She'd have to get something new – couldn't wear the cream skirt again, and Breffni was sure to look stunning. She'd go shopping in the morning; maybe ask one of the glamorous assistants behind the counters at Brown Thomas for some advice on make-up. Knew, even as the thought drifted through her head, that she'd never have the nerve.

It mightn't be too bad though; at least Laura would be there. She smiled brightly across the table at Andrew as she passed him the butter.

✡✡✡

'Hello?'

'Andrew, it's me.'

'Hi, Laur. What's up?'

'Just wondering about Saturday night, if you and Ruth want to sit in with us to Nenagh . . . it seems daft bringing two cars.'

'That sounds good – if you're OK about coming to collect us here.'

Because I might have to talk to my mother. 'Yeah, that's no problem. We'll be there between half seven and eight, OK?'

'Fine, thanks; I'll say it to Ruth. Any other news?'

For a second she wondered what he'd say if she told him that she and Donal were going to be tested to see which of them was stopping her from becoming pregnant. 'Nothing strange really . . . how's Ruth?' Laura hadn't met her in a week or so, since they'd had lunch in the pub near the studio.

'Grand – she's sitting in on Ma's book club next week.'

Laura groaned. 'Oh God, the poor thing. I suppose she couldn't get out of it.'

'Actually, she seemed quite happy to be asked.' He sounded mildly annoyed; Laura figured he didn't like her criticising Mother's hobby. 'Ruth's a real bookworm anyway; it'll probably suit her.'

'Are they not all ancient, though?' Laura pictured a gaggle of blue rinses sitting around discussing whichever bestseller they'd managed to find with no hint of sex or violence in it.

'Couldn't tell you; never notice them really when they're around. I suppose we'll find out from Ruth.'

Laura saw Donal coming up the path, and spoke quickly. 'Listen, I have to go. See you on Saturday.'

Donal walked in as she hung up, and she went to him and reached up to kiss his cheek. 'Hi.'

'Hi, yourself; who was that?'

'Just Andrew; I said we'd collect them on Saturday night.'

'Oh, right.' He shrugged off his jacket and hung it on the banisters. He looked tired. She decided to wait a couple of days before she told him about the doctor's appointment. She put her arms around him, leant against his chest, head turned up to see his face. 'Fancy a sexual favour?' It had been a joke between them since that first time.

He smiled gently down at her, encircled her waist. 'You know me – never say no. As long as you promise to do all the work; I'm bushed.'

She grinned. 'Promise.'

✡✡✡

Cecily had deliberated for some time before inviting Ruth to the book-club meeting. She wasn't afraid of offending the others by bringing her along unannounced; certainly not. Clearly, it didn't bother anyone except herself when new arrivals turned up at the drop of a hat.

Neither was she concerned that Ruth might not enjoy it; that was for Ruth herself to decide, surely. And as her daughter-in-law seemed to have her head in a book most of the time anyway, she'd probably fit into the club very well.

No, Cecily had hesitated simply because she was a little – *ashamed* was the wrong word; Ruth was such an inoffensive creature, she couldn't possibly inspire shame – but Cecily wished fervently that there was a bit *more* to her. A bit of colour: someone she could engage in a real discussion – an argument, even. Someone who'd give as good as she got.

But Ruth was so eager to please, so afraid of offending. So . . . *diluted*. She was the perfect wife for Andrew of course, but even so . . .

She imagined Dorothy and Emily exchanging glances behind Ruth's head, pitying Cecily for having ended up with such an insipid daughter-in-law. Wondering what on earth Andrew had seen in her – handsome Andrew, who'd opened the door to a few of them once or twice when Cecily had been hosting, and who'd managed to charm them beautifully.

But when it came down to it, Cecily hadn't had much choice; she'd had to invite Ruth, after having suggested it to Emily in the supermarket. If Ruth didn't appear, Emily would be sure to wonder why. And Ruth herself would probably feel slighted if Cecily didn't include her, seeing as how she'd probably be in the house at the time – she and Andrew seldom went out at night.

But really, Cecily wasn't unduly worried about the meeting. Ruth had seemed quite happy to be asked, so maybe it would all turn out for the best. The meeting might liven her up a bit; or she might talk to Margaret for the night – Cecily felt that Ruth would be very good at listening patiently to accounts of Margaret's arthritis. Or she might hit it off with Valerie, who wasn't that much older than her, after all.

And as for Ruth being able to hold her own when it came to discussing the books, Cecily was confident that any opinion she had was bound to be as worthwhile as those of Frank, who didn't strike Cecily as a particularly literary man.

She hadn't met him since that time in the café, when he had practically forced her to listen to his life story . . . and while of course she sympathised with his losses, she still resented the way he had chosen her, of all people, as his confidante. Had he somehow got the impression that she would provide a shoulder for him to cry on? True, they'd chatted quite pleasantly afterwards, when he'd stopped pouring his heart out to her; and she'd been forced to admit that he wasn't as crass as he'd seemed initially, but still . . . She determined to avoid him as best she could on Thursday night.

Actually, when Cecily thought about it, Ruth might be quite useful at the meeting; she could be positioned between Frank and Margaret, and she could listen to them both all night. Maybe inviting her along hadn't been such a bad idea, after all.

Cecily opened her notebook and started to write her shopping list. Maybe she'd push the boat out and serve a variety of mixed canapés – the little cheese balls rolled in fresh herbs that Emily loved, mini spinach quiches, stuffed mushrooms, maybe some of those rather tasty smoked salmon rolls that she'd served at Andrew's birthday. And afterwards, a selection of homemade biscuits from that nice delicatessen in the shopping centre.

That should make it clear that they weren't all savages in Limerick.

✡✡✡

Donal chewed the chicken thoughtfully, and swallowed. 'Marjoram. Or . . . no, oregano. And probably tarragon. And definitely garlic – but not too strong.'

Breffni looked at Cian. 'Will you tell him, or will I?'

Cian, his mouth full, waved at her to go ahead.

She smiled over at Donal. 'A pack of "Spices Made Simple for Chicken Provençale". All I had to do was cut it open and fire it onto the chopped chicken; haven't a clue what was in it.'

Andrew laughed loudly, and Donal pushed his half-full plate away with a look of horror. 'What – you've served me convenience food? Sorry – as a gourmet chef, it's against my principles to eat anything that comes out of a packet.' He stood up, looking over at Laura. 'Get your coat, darling – we're going home.'

A general burst of laughter then, and from across the table Laura raised her eyes to heaven and pushed his plate back in front of him. 'Sit down and eat, or you're in the spare room for a month.'

'Oh God no, not the spare room. OK, I'll be good.' Donal sat and picked up his fork again, smiling. 'It's very tasty, Breffni, whatever you put into it.' He looked around the table. 'Who's got the rice?'

Andrew passed the bowl across to him. 'God only knows what she has in there – a sachet of "Easy Peasy Rice".'

Breffni picked up a half-eaten bread roll and threw it in his direction. 'No dessert for you, for being disrespectful to your hostess.'

Andrew caught it deftly and put it on his side plate, smiling back at her. 'Oh please, I'd hate to miss the Instant Whip.'

'Bloody cheek.' Breffni turned to Ruth. 'I don't know how you put up with him, Ruth – you must have the patience of a saint.'

'Oh, I don't know about that.' Ruth smiled and looked tenderly across the round table at her husband.

Breffni thought a thicker foundation would do a lot for Ruth – even out her skin tone, hide those freckles. Maybe when they got to know each other a bit better, she could suggest it to her. If she could manage it without causing offence, which might be easier said than done – Ruth seemed the type that you couldn't say boo to. Maybe Laura could do it instead; she was so much better at saying the right thing.

The door to the kitchen was pushed open and Polly stood there, blond curls sticking haphazardly out from her head, a small fist rubbing one eye. A leg of her pale blue pyjamas had ridden up above her knee. She looked up at the table and yawned. 'Mama.'

Cian, sitting nearest the door, bent down and scooped her onto his lap. 'What are you doing out of bed, Missus – and where are your slippers?' She leant against his chest and blinked around the table, smiling sleepily when she caught sight of Laura waggling her fingers at her.

Breffni looked at her daughter. 'Pollywolly Doodle, this is Ruth –' she pointed '– and that's Andrew. Say hello.'

But Polly just burrowed into Cian and stuck a thumb into her mouth, eyelids drooping. Cian stood, gathering her up into him. 'I'll go.'

They all waved at her – Donal blew her a kiss – and she watched them solemnly over Cian's shoulder, sucking steadily on her thumb, as he carried her out.

'She's gorgeous.' Ruth smiled across at Breffni.

'I know.' Breffni picked up her glass and smiled back. 'But hard work – wait till you have your own.'

'Stop putting ideas into her head.' Andrew's voice made them both look over. 'We're only just getting used to being married – give us a chance.'

'Well, just don't take as long as these two –' Breffni indicated Donal and Laura '– or Poll will have no one to grow up with.'

Laura stood abruptly. 'Sorry, need the loo.' She walked quickly to the door and left. In the small silence that followed, Breffni looked questioningly across at Donal, who shrugged back at her.

Then he held out his wine glass. 'Any left in that bottle?'

Later, while Breffni was scooping chocolate ice-cream into bowls at the worktop, Donal collected a few side plates from the table and brought them over. 'It's her time of month; she's a bit sensitive, that's all.' His voice was low enough not to carry over to the table.

'So you're not trying to get pregnant?' Breffni spoke softly too, taking the bundle of plates from him.

Donal spread his hands. 'If it happens, it happens.' Then he raised his voice. 'Let me give you a hand, as the only professional chef here.'

She smiled at him, held out her wine glass. 'You can start by professionally refilling that – there's a new bottle over in that press – and then you can make the coffee; professionally, of course.' She was in a long off-white dress tonight, splashed with huge red flowers, startling against her dark hair and olive skin. Her cheeks were lightly and beautifully flushed, from wine and cooking.

When Donal handed her the refilled glass, she glanced over at the table again. 'So I didn't put my foot in it.' She spoke softly again, lifting shortbread fingers from where they'd been soaking in Bailey's and adding two to each bowl of ice-cream.

He looked blank. 'About what?'

'About you two taking so long to have kids. Donal, is there

really nothing I should know? And feel free to tell me to mind my own business, of course.' She picked up her glass and took a sip.

He shook his head, smiling faintly. 'Nothing to tell; we're just letting nature take its course.' Then he opened the nearest press and peered inside. 'Now, where do you keep the coffee – or the packet of "Easy Coffee Mix"?'

She groaned. 'Enough already – I'm never again going to give away my culinary tricks.' She pointed. 'Coffee in the next press, in the pack that says *real coffee, honest*.'

'And may I say that you look real good tonight.' He reached for the knob of the next press. 'Honest.'

She bowed her head in acknowledgement. 'You may. And now you may make the coffee.' She opened a Flake bar and began crumbling a little into each bowl. 'There – six gourmet desserts coming up.'

Donal smiled.

✡✡✡

'I'd keep an eye on that husband of yours.'

Laura turned to Andrew, a small smile on her face. 'What?'

He inclined his head towards Donal. 'Look how he's leering all over your best friend.'

Laura laughed, dug him in the ribs. 'Shut up, trying to stir things. Behave yourself.'

He lifted a shoulder, turned to Cian across the table. 'I'm just warning Laura to watch out for Donal, making eyes at Breffni over there. What d'you think – should we get worried?'

Cian turned to look at Breffni, approaching the table with two bowls. 'Only about our waistlines, I'd say.' He smiled up at her as she passed him.

'And some of us need to worry a bit more than others about that.' Although Andrew murmured too softly for anyone but Laura to hear, she shot him a sharp look. Really, he could be a bit nasty sometimes; imagine if Cian had heard.

'Ruth, try that and tell me what you think.' Breffni put one of the bowls in front of Ruth and stood beside her, waiting.

Ruth looked quickly around the table before obediently picking up a spoon and scooping up a small amount of chocolate ice-cream. As she ate, she looked up at Breffni and smiled, nodding. Conversation had stopped; all eyes were on her. Breffni stayed standing by Ruth's chair.

'Well? Does it pass?'

'Stop fishing for compliments, you: it's not as if you spent all day with the ice-cream machine.' Laura reached out and grabbed the second bowl from Breffni. 'Here, I'll tell you.' She plunged her spoon into the dessert and took a big mouthful, then closed her eyes in ecstasy. 'Mmm, chocalicious.'

Then Donal came back to the table with two more bowls. 'Who got no Instant Whip?'

'Here.' Cian took both bowls from him and gave one each to himself and Andrew before sniffing into his. 'I see you've been at the Bailey's again, dear.'

Breffni looked sternly across the table at him.

'I'll have you know that's an old family recipe – now you've just told everyone my secret ingredient.'

Across the chatter, Laura watched Ruth put her spoon down carefully beside her half-empty bowl without making a sound.

✡✡✡

He couldn't bear it; he'd go mad.

He'd waited with dread for this night, half hoping that when they met, he'd feel nothing. Of course that hadn't happened; his hammering heart had threatened to burst from his chest all evening. He couldn't understand how nobody had noticed.

She was so close he could touch her – and she might as well be on another planet. He could smell her when she came near, when she bent over to talk to him. Her lips were perfect; he wanted to lean across and taste them, to run his tongue over their softness. He longed to take her and hold her against him, have every part of her pressed into him.

This couldn't go on. This had to go on. He'd go mad if it stopped.

✡✡✡

Donal hung his jacket on the banisters and stood in the hall.

'Laura?' No answer, as he'd expected. He went into the kitchen and washed his hands. Then he pulled open the fridge and took out a greaseproof-wrapped bundle of sliced turkey breast. From the bread bin he pulled half a loaf of crusty, granary bread.

A few minutes later, when he was halfway through his sandwich, he heard the front door opening. 'I'm in here.'

Her head appeared around the kitchen door. 'Hi. Are you here long?'

He shook his head. 'Quarter of an hour. What are *you* doing home?' It was just after three.

She shrugged, still standing in the doorway. 'I decided I'd have an easy Monday; there's nothing too urgent on at the moment, and I still feel a bit tired from Saturday night.' They hadn't left Breffni and Cian's till after three.

'Have we any of that redcurrant jelly from the market?'

'No, I think we're out. There's mayo.'

'Want me to make you one?' He pointed towards the remains of his sandwich.

'No thanks; I'll wait till dinner. Hang on a sec.' He heard her run upstairs and into their bedroom. A minute later she was back, walking into the kitchen with some leaflets in her hand. She sat at the counter opposite him. 'Darling, I called around to Dr Goode last week.'

He put his sandwich down and waited. She put the leaflets on the counter between them and he read *Overcoming Infertility: A Compassionate Resource for Getting Pregnant* on the front of the top one.

'He's given us these to read, and I've made an appointment for us to go and talk to him on Thursday – half four was the latest I could get. You could make that, couldn't you?'

Her voice sounded anxious. He put a hand out and covered hers on the table, being careful not to touch the leaflets. 'Yeah, no problem.' He picked up his glass of milk.

She kept her eyes on the counter. 'And Donal . . . it might be best if we don't have sex in the meantime, in case . . .'

In case I'm given a jar and a dirty magazine and put into a little room to perform. His stomach clenched at the thought. He put down his glass.

'It's OK.' He squeezed her hand. 'I'll try my best to resist you till Thursday.' His smile was wooden.

Her face relaxed. 'Thanks.' She stroked his arm with her other hand. 'I was thinking we might go out to a movie later on, if there's anything worth seeing?'

'Fine; the paper's in the other room.' He looked down at the half-eaten sandwich on his plate, wondering where his appetite had gone.

✡✡✡

Ruth lifted the Aynsley teapot – Cecily's second best – and poured a refill for Margaret and Frank. Then she looked across at Valerie, two chairs away. 'More tea over there?'

'Thanks, Ruth, I'll come and get it in a minute.' Valerie looked around Cecily's sitting room. 'Isn't this lovely and cosy?'

Ruth nodded, although *cosy* wasn't the word she would have used to describe any room in Cecily's house. The sitting room was certainly tasteful, with its pale, thick carpets, and cream and off-white walls. Immaculate bookshelves filled with alphabetically arranged books, and glass-fronted cabinets displaying Lladro and Waterford Crystal and Newbridge silver. Two matching couches covered in pale grey linen, elegant armchairs that weren't designed for curling up in. A coal-effect gas fire in the fireplace – Ruth couldn't imagine her mother-in-law clearing ashes from the grate.

She glanced across at Cecily, who was smiling at something Emily had just said to her. Looking as poised as ever in her soft cream cardigan and straight black skirt, and carefully arranged hair.

The room buzzed with separate conversations; since the general discussion, the seven of them had divided into smaller groups. Cecily and Emily sat side by side on the couch by the window, furthest from the fire. Dorothy and Valerie were chatting on Ruth's other side, leaving herself, Frank and Margaret in the middle.

She lifted the plate of Cecily's meticulously arranged canapés and held them out to Margaret. 'Can I tempt you?'

Margaret shook her head. 'No thank you, dear; I've had two already.'

Ruth turned. 'How about you, Frank?'

'Yes please; my appetite isn't as delicate as Margaret's, I'm afraid.' He put a cheese ball and a smoked salmon roll on his plate, and twinkled over at Margaret. 'I hope you're not dieting, dear; you'll fade away on us.'

Ruth was amused to see Margaret's colour rising slightly; she wondered if she'd still blush when she was Margaret's age – hopefully not. She tapped Frank's arm, smiling. 'Leave her alone.'

He was lovely, really natural and easygoing. He reminded her vaguely of someone, but she couldn't think who it might be. And Margaret was a pet – so gentle and sweet. Ruth sat back and took a sip of tea, totally at ease. She'd enjoyed this evening, sitting with people who had all made her feel welcome. She'd already read the novel they were discussing, so she felt comfortable joining in – hadn't felt at all as if anyone would laugh at her or make her feel uneasy.

Not like last Saturday night. Her stomach still fluttered when she remembered Breffni putting the plate of ice-cream in front of her and demanding to know what she thought of it. Everyone stopping and looking at her – awful. Thank goodness it was ice-cream – anything hot and she probably would have scalded herself, from sheer nerves. And thank goodness for Laura, jumping in to rescue her.

Rescue her: how silly – as if she'd been under attack. Ruth knew that Breffni hadn't meant anything by it. *She* wouldn't have been a bit mortified to have everyone watching her eating, so why should she have thought it would affect anyone else that way? But when Ruth had picked up her spoon, knowing that everyone at the table was watching, feeling their eyes on her – God, it was stupid to have felt so panicky, so afraid she was going to make a fool of herself. It was a spoonful of ice-cream, for goodness' sake.

What a ninny she was.

Andrew hadn't seemed to notice anything, thank goodness. A part of her was still waiting for him to turn around and realise how much better he could have done for himself than Ruth Tobin. But so far, so good. He'd been a bit quiet in the car on the way back, but that was just tiredness – it had been so late. And Laura hadn't said much either, on the way home. They were all ready for bed: particularly Ruth, worn out from the strain of trying to look as if she was enjoying herself.

But there was no strain tonight. She'd warmed quickly to Frank and Margaret, and Valerie seemed very pleasant too; she'd already suggested that Ruth meet her for coffee some afternoon soon. For the first time since her arrival in Limerick, Ruth didn't feel quite so homesick for Dublin and her family. If she and Valerie got friendly, maybe she wouldn't have to meet Breffni that much.

Now Dorothy leant over towards them. 'I think I'll make a move, Frank, if you don't mind. Liam had a bit of a sore throat tonight; I told him I wouldn't be late.'

'That's fine.' Frank stood up and started gathering his book and scarf together. Cecily looked across, then came over. 'Leaving already?' She spoke to Dorothy.

Dorothy nodded. 'I have to get back; Liam's a bit under the weather. Thank you so much, Cecily – it was lovely. You went to great trouble.' She hugged Cecily briefly.

Frank held out his hand. 'Cecily, many thanks. We didn't have much of a chance to talk tonight.'

She shook his hand, smiling faintly. 'But I'm sure you made up for it with my daughter-in-law; looks like you had plenty to talk about.' She looked down at Margaret. 'I hope they didn't tire you out too much, my dear. How's the arthritis?'

As Margaret responded, Ruth thought Cecily sounded a little brusque. What could Frank, such a nice man, have done to deserve that? Maybe she, Ruth, was just being over-sensitive again; she hoped so. She turned to Frank.

'It was lovely to meet you; I hope I'll see you at the next gathering.'

He smiled back at her. 'And you, dear. Take care.' He didn't seem at all upset by Cecily's remark.

After everyone had left, and Ruth was helping her mother-in-law to clear the wafer-thin plates and cups from the sitting room, she found herself wondering again who Frank reminded her of. She was sure she wasn't imagining it; he definitely resembled someone she knew. Hadn't he told her he lived in Sligo till recently though? So she was all wrong, probably – she didn't know a soul in Sligo. Maybe he just reminded her of someone she'd seen on the telly. She picked up a bundle of side plates and carried them gingerly to the kitchen.

✡✡✡

'Hello?'

'Hi, it's me.'

She paused, then answered lightly, 'Hello there; what's up?'

He sounded tense – not a bit like the last time they'd spoken. 'Can we meet? I – I need to talk to you.'

'This sounds very mysterious – what about?' She was careful to keep her tone light, although her heart had begun a gentle trot.

She heard him take a breath. 'I really want to meet you: can we? Wherever you want. I – there's something we need to discuss.'

She counted to three slowly. 'Look . . . I don't think that's a good idea.' Her fingers curled more tightly around the phone.

A long pause at his end. Then, when she was beginning to wonder if he was still there, a long exhalation. 'Right. Sorry, you're right. Let's forget this conversation happened.'

'Of course.'

As she hung up, she realised that her palms were damp. She ran them down along her jeans, then went into the kitchen and sat down heavily and put her head into her hands, heart thumping.

✡✡✡

He held the receiver long after she'd hung up. Finally he replaced it slowly, making hardly a sound. Right: that was it. He'd just have to forget her. Or try to forget her.

Fat chance. He turned abruptly and walked away.

✡✡✡

'Laura?' Ruth put down her fork and looked closely at her. 'Are you all right?'

Laura turned quickly towards Ruth with a too-bright smile. 'Sorry – I was miles away; a few jobs on my mind . . .' She shook her head. 'And too many late nights – I'm a telly addict in the winter, can't tear myself away to go to bed.'

Ruth picked up her fork again and twisted it in her tagliatelle. 'You do look a bit tired; maybe you should take a few days off work, just stay in bed.'

Laura laughed, raked a hand through her curls. 'I wish I could. But that's the trouble when you're working for yourself; you have to take the jobs when they come – and at the moment I'm fairly swamped.' She pushed her chilli around the bowl – she'd had only a few mouthfuls since it had arrived.

'I'm not surprised you're busy; you're very good.' Ruth lifted a forkful of creamy pasta. 'I told you how many people raved about the wedding invitations, didn't I?'

Laura smiled again. 'Thanks, Ruth; yeah, I'm well used to doing wedding stuff – it's how I started out.' Then she put down her fork, picked up her glass of water. 'Enough about me; what about this house of yours? Have you got a date yet?'

Ruth dabbed at her mouth and made a face. 'The last date they gave us was the end of November; they promised. But Andrew called round the day before yesterday and he was told that it'll take a good bit longer than two weeks; at least another month, they said. At the rate we're going, we'll be lucky if we're in by Christmas.'

Ruth and Andrew had bought a house in Farranshone, six weeks before the wedding. It had belonged to an old man who'd spent the last few years of his life in a nursing home, and it was in serious need of refurbishment. They were getting small rooms knocked together to make bigger ones, and units pulled out, and new floors laid, and a small extension to the kitchen at the back. Some walls had to be dry lined, and the attic had no insulation, and the roof was in serious need of retiling. And what was originally supposed to have been finished in what Ruth realised now was a very optimistic two months had already dragged on for over four.

She loved the location – Farranshone was old and friendly, and just a short walk into town – and she knew the wait would be worth it. The house had a big jungly back garden with a gnarly tree in one corner that would be perfect for sitting under with her book when summer came round again. And perfect for children to climb. But she wished it wasn't taking so long . . . the strain of sharing another woman's house, even someone as generous as

Cecily, was beginning to keep her awake at night. If they could only have one or two evenings on their own, cooking dinner together, sitting in front of the telly, watching whatever they wanted . . .

And she could see that Andrew was feeling it too – he'd been distracted lately, not his usual cheery self. Even snapped at her last week, when all she'd asked him was whether he thought they should take Cecily out to dinner sometime.

'Easily known you've nothing better to do than sit at home and plan nights out. Did it occur to you that I mightn't fancy turning around after a hard day's work to go off out to a restaurant?' He wasn't cross exactly, more like mildly irritated, but Ruth was stung by the unfairness of it.

'It wouldn't have to be during the week – we could wait till the weekend. I just thought, with your mother cooking for us every night –' She wanted to add *And I don't sit at home planning nights out – I try to keep busy, in a house where I'm not allowed to cook, and where I'm afraid to clean in case I do it wrong, or I go out and look into the same shop windows I looked into yesterday, and drink coffee I don't want, just to get in out of the rain*, but of course she didn't.

She knew it couldn't be easy for Andrew, trying to cope at work and then deal with the house too; he'd been calling over there quite a lot lately. She'd offered to go with him, but he didn't want the builders to feel they were putting pressure on them – he was afraid it might make them even slower. Ruth was sure he knew best, so she stayed away.

'Don't worry – I'm sure the house will be gorgeous when it's done. I love those white oak floors you're putting in.' Laura picked up her fork again and prodded at her rice. 'You'll have to have a big house-warming.'

Ruth smiled. 'Yes, hopefully it won't be too long more. And once we're moved in, and have some kind of shape on the house, I can look for a job.' That'd help settle her, she was sure of it; a job would give her something to fill her days with.

Laura glanced at her watch and put down her fork. 'I think I'd better get back; I don't want to be working too late tonight.' She stood and picked up the bill. 'My turn.'

Ruth watched as Laura went to the cash desk; she was definitely not herself today. And she looked a bit pale. Hopefully it was nothing major – probably overwork, like she said.

Ruth turned her head to look out the window at the rain. Might as well go home; it wasn't a day for wandering around the shops. She could finish her book for the next club meeting.

✡✡✡

It was going to be a lot worse than Laura had imagined.

Reading the leaflets that she'd got from Doctor Goode, she began to realise that it wouldn't be the straightforward process she'd hoped for. After a few pages, her head was buzzing with *Fallopian tube blockage, laparoscopy, endometriosis, chlamydia, fibroids* – she had no idea there could be so many different possible reasons for infertility, or so many procedures that both she and Donal might have to go through to find the cause of their problem.

She read with dread about male tests for infertility – semen analysis, blood and urine samples, biopsy of the testes. She was well aware that Donal would be happy to let nature take its course: the notion that they might never have children didn't seem to worry him unduly. Would he be prepared to go through the humiliation of such intimate procedures, just to keep her happy?

Because with each month that went by, with each discovery that she still wasn't pregnant, Laura knew that she wouldn't be happy until they'd done everything possible to find the cause – and hopefully, the solution.

What really terrified her, what kept her lying sleepless beside Donal at night, was the notion that maybe there wasn't a cause – or not one that could be discovered. She read with dismay that in around fifteen per cent of cases – fifteen per cent of the one in six couples who had problems – no physical cause could be found. How would she cope if they were given that news – that there was nothing that they could fix, because nothing broken had been found?

She wished there was someone she could talk to, maybe someone who'd been in the same position as herself once. Surely there was a support group for women trying to get pregnant? But no, that wasn't what she wanted – not a group of strangers, more concerned with their own problem than with hers.

Her heart clenched as she remembered Breffni's joke at dinner the other night, about Ruth and Andrew not waiting as long as Laura and Donal to have children. When she said it, when the others had laughed, Laura had felt such a wave of despair that she'd had to get up and leave the room before they noticed. It had taken her a good five minutes, cheeks pressed in turn to the cool bathroom tiles, breathing in slow, steady breaths, before she could face them again. Listening to Cian singing Polly back to sleep in the room next door. Wondering if she'd ever have someone to sing to sleep.

Laura wished again that she could talk about this whole thing with Breffni, but she just couldn't. And the notion of looking for comfort and reassurance from Cecily was so ridiculous that it would make Laura laugh – if she felt remotely like laughing.

The visit to Dr Goode's surgery hadn't been too bad. Thank goodness he hadn't looked for a sample from Donal – she'd been dreading that. He asked them lots of questions – their ages and occupations, what contraception they'd been using, Laura's menstrual cycle, their sexual histories, any previous pregnancies, how often they made love, whether they smoked, took drugs – and Laura did most of the talking for both of them. Conscious of Donal sitting beside her. Listening to her discussing the most intimate details of their life together with a man Donal had just met for the first time.

Laura had known Dr Goode for over twenty years, since he'd taken over when their old family doctor had retired – but Donal had a different doctor, had never had occasion to meet Dr Goode till today. He'd been perfectly polite, in a detached kind of way, when Laura had introduced them; and Dr Goode couldn't have been more sensitive, directing most of his questions at Laura, as though he sensed Donal's silent unease.

They came away with an appointment to see a gynaecologist in a week's time for the first of the tests. Dr Goode prepared them gently for a long wait – some tests, like the semen analysis, would probably have to be done more than once, at intervals of one month – and Laura would be asked to keep a temperature chart for a few months, to make sure she was ovulating. Any more complicated procedures would wait till after that.

Thank goodness he didn't talk about nature taking its course, or everything happening in its own good time. He stuck to practicalities – and he took his time with them; they must have been in with him for nearly three quarters of an hour, even though Laura had counted five people in the waiting room before they went in. When they were leaving, Dr Goode shook hands with both of them.

'Good luck; I hope it works out for you both.'

Laura had wanted to hug him, but that would have been silly. You didn't hug your doctor – even if he was the one you were pinning all your hopes on.

On the way home, she stopped the car outside their local and turned to Donal.

'Is the sun over the yardarm yet?'

He looked over at her. 'Good idea.'

She drank a hot port – it was the first really chilly day, with a promise of winter in the wind that whipped around them – and Donal had a pint. Their conversation was oddly stilted.

'How's that wardrobe job coming on?'

'Finished a few days ago, thank goodness. I started the Carr stuff yesterday.' A cleaning contractor wanted to update his company image; he'd asked Laura to work with a writer and put together a range of new brochures and leaflets.

'Right.' Donal nodded into his pint, and Laura suspected that if she asked him what she'd just said, he wouldn't have been able to tell her. She cast around for something to talk about; they couldn't sit there in silence.

'Andrew rang this morning, some computer virus that they got in all the machines at work. He said I wasn't to open any e-mails from some crowd.'

Donal smiled briefly. 'It's well for him – sitting reading e-mails all day.'

She made a face at him. 'Don't start. It was good of him to warn me. I'd open any old thing that came, just in case it was interesting.'

And they managed to pass the next fifteen minutes not talking about babies and infertility and what might happen when they went to the gynaecologist.

✡✡✡

'Post for you.'

The receptionist handed him a plain white envelope with his name and work address handwritten on it.

His stomach flipped. 'Thanks, Frances.' He hoped to God he looked normal as he slipped it into his jacket pocket. As if it wasn't something that needed his immediate attention.

It was her. He knew it was her. He walked casually to the nearest toilet and locked himself in, and pulled out the envelope and tore it open.

It was a single folded sheet; the writing was hasty. No greeting, no signature, just three short sentences:

> *It's not that I don't want to. It's that it would be a disaster. You must see that.*

His eyes scanned it rapidly, then he read it carefully again, twice.

It's not that I don't want to.

His heart soared: *It's not that I don't want to.* He folded the sheet carefully and replaced it in between the ragged edges of the envelope, and put it back into his pocket.

She felt the same as he did: *It's not that I don't want to.* All that day his mind refused to concentrate; but somehow he managed to get through the work he needed to do.

It's not that I don't want to. Really, exactly the same as *I want to.*

✡✡✡

Ruth picked up a scarf and stroked it thoughtfully. It was deep red and very soft, and terribly expensive – nothing in Brown Thomas was exactly cheap – but they needed to get Cecily something really special for Christmas, to thank her for letting them stay with her for so long; almost four months at this stage.

Two months the builder had promised them in July – Halloween at the very latest – and in their innocence, they'd believed him. Ruth had imagined them unpacking and settling in, with plenty of time for her to get fixed up with a job by Christmas. And now here they were, Christmas just around the corner, and no guarantee that they wouldn't still be living with Cecily at the end of the year.

Ruth's heart sank as she imagined Christmas dinner in her mother-in-law's elegant house – because how could they possibly leave her alone and go to Ruth's family for the holiday? And Laura wouldn't even be there; she'd told Ruth that she and Donal always did their own thing on Christmas Day, apart from a brief visit to Cecily in the morning '– brief by mutual consent, believe me –' so it would be just the three of them sitting down to dinner. Ruth, Andrew and Cecily. Perfectly cooked turkey, all the appropriate trimmings, the right wines with every course, beautifully wrapped gifts – and no fun at all.

No giggling charades, no tins of Quality Street and boxes of Black Magic passed around until everyone felt sick. No slouching in front of the telly in your dressing gown, drinking Buck's Fizz made with Jacob's Creek sparkling wine and watching *Willy Wonka and the Chocolate Factory* and *It's a Wonderful Life*, or playing a very noisy game of Trivial Pursuit. Thinking of all the Christmases with her family in Dublin, Ruth felt a physical stab of homesickness.

She put the scarf back on the shelf; she'd need to check with

Andrew before she bought it, in case he had something else in mind. Or maybe Cecily didn't like red; Ruth couldn't remember if she'd ever seen it on her. As she turned towards the door, she caught sight of a familiar face from the other night.

She walked over, beaming; he was just the tonic she needed right now.

'Hello, Frank. Doing some Christmas shopping?'

His face lit up as he put his wallet back into his pocket and took the carrier bag from the assistant. 'Ruth, how lovely. Yes, I've just got some gloves for Dorothy; she and Liam have been so good to me since I moved here. And you?' He glanced down at her empty hands. 'Just looking?'

'Yes, I'm terrible at making decisions. I'll have to enlist Andrew's help.'

'Well, I'm free for the next hour or two, if I'm any good to you.'

She shook her head, smiling. 'Oh no, I wouldn't subject you to that . . . but –' suddenly the last thing she wanted to do was go home '– would you like to go and get a coffee somewhere?' It would pass an hour if they drew it out, and Frank would be nice easy company.

He beamed again. 'Lovely. There's a place just around the corner.'

When they were seated, he planted his palms on the table in front of him. 'Well . . . how's everything with you, my dear?'

And Ruth took one look at his kind, open face and burst into tears.

✡✡✡

She couldn't believe it, but there it was, sitting on the doormat.

Brazen as you like. She knew it was from him, had to be from him. How dared he? She had a good mind to put it straight into the bin: what if the wrong person had picked it up? She stood looking down at the envelope for a few seconds, frowning.

But what if he was just apologising for the whole business? Maybe he'd come to his senses, and realised what madness it would be, even to think of doing anything . . . She'd never know if she just threw it away. And really, it was her own fault, for sending him that ridiculous note. As soon as it was posted, she'd instantly regretted it. What on earth had possessed her? She should have just done nothing, let it go away quietly. She slid her finger under the flap and lifted it open.

Just a single sheet, like the one she'd sent him. Her eyes darted rapidly over the words:

> *It doesn't have to be a disaster. Who would know except us? Who would we hurt if no one knew? I long for you. Please let this happen.*

He'd underlined 'long'. She put a hand to her mouth. *I long for you.* She closed her eyes and saw his face, imagined his mouth – *no.* She opened her eyes and quickly tore the letter in half, then screwed it into a ball and shoved it deep into the pocket of her jeans. She'd throw it into the first litter-bin she passed when she went out.

She heard a noise from the kitchen and walked towards it.

✡✡✡

So it had begun.

Laura sat on the couch and looked at the blank TV screen.

Donal had gone to meet some pals for a drink – he'd wanted her to go, but she'd pleaded a heavy workload.

'I need to clear the decks a bit for next week.' She'd heard yesterday that she'd got the schoolbooks job – not as big as she'd first imagined, but a nice steady little earner all the same for the next few months. She was expecting the first assignment on Monday.

In a way, she was glad at the prospect of keeping busy for the foreseeable future; it might make the time pass by less unbearably slowly.

Because today they'd begun what Laura knew was going to be a long, agonising wait. At least three months before they'd have any sort of definite information to work with, according to Dr Sloan, the gynaecologist.

'It'll take at least that long to get an accurate reading of your cycle, Laura, and a clear analysis of Donal's semen. We need both of those before we can pinpoint any possible problems.'

Donal had been given his jar and sent to another room; Laura hadn't looked at him as he'd left. Dr Sloan was about Laura's age, maybe a bit older, with a wedding ring. Laura wondered if she had children, but didn't ask. They chatted quite pleasantly until Donal came back, handing Dr Sloan the jar without a word. He was quiet for the rest of the visit, letting Laura do most of the talking again. Dr Sloan had given her a special thermometer – she called it a basal body thermometer – and a series of charts to record her temperature readings.

'This is the first step, before any blood tests or ultrasounds, just to give us some basic information about your cycle. Remember to take it at roughly the same time every day.'

She shook hands with both of them as they were leaving. 'I know it's easily said, but try not to worry. If there's a problem, we'll do everything in our power to identify it and find a solution. Good luck.'

Everyone was wishing them luck. Laura wondered if that was all it took. Maybe every conception was just that – pure luck. One enthusiastic sperm just happening to wriggle away from the millions of others, and head in exactly the right direction to make contact with the impossibly tiny egg that just happened to be ready and waiting for it. If that was the case, she and Donal had been pretty unlucky for the last two years.

She sighed and stood up. Better get some work done; it was going to take a bit more than luck to make *that* happen.

✡✡✡

'More tea, dear?'

Cecily materialised by Ruth's elbow, pot poised. Her insistence on serving breakfast to Ruth, despite her daughter-in-law's repeated assurances that she could easily do her own, never failed to make Ruth feel that she was staying in a very formal boarding house, filled with elderly maidens who all looked like Maggie Smith in *Room with a View*, and who managed never to appear for breakfast at the same time as Ruth. To give Cecily her due, she probably assumed that Ruth secretly enjoyed being waited on – because of course she herself would relish having her lightly scrambled eggs or perfectly grilled bacon – Cecily never called them 'rashers' – handed up to her every morning by a docile servant.

This particular morning, though, Ruth couldn't have cared less if Cecily had appeared in a French maid's outfit, complete with fishnet stockings, and pirouetted across the floor, twirling Ruth's plate expertly over her head. She felt a sudden urge to giggle, and turned it into a discreet cough. 'Thank you,' she said, as Cecily poured her a second cup of Earl Grey tea – Ruth had come to quite like the delicately scented taste. And in seven more days, unbelievably, she would be pouring her own tea – Barry's probably, like they always bought at home – in her own house.

Andrew had come back from a visit to the builders the day before with the news. She just stared at him as it sank in.

Finally she found her voice. 'A week?'

He laughed at her incredulous expression. 'Yes; a week. Seven days. Half a fortnight. A quarter –'

'Stop.' She put a hand over his mouth. 'Are you absolutely sure? It'll be ready for us to move in – no more delays?'

He pulled her hand away and held it. 'Absolutely sure. John promised faithfully – after I threatened to take his ass to court if he was joking.' John was the foreman.

'Andrew, you didn't.' Ruth looked half-amused, half-horrified.

Andrew shook his head, laughing. 'Of course not. But he did promise faithfully – so we'd better start getting our act together. Will you contact your folks about having our stuff sent down? John says we should be able to start moving things in at the weekend.'

They'd bought some furniture in Dublin before the wedding, which Ruth's parents were storing in their garage. And Cecily was going to lend them a few things – kitchen utensils, saucepans, plates – which Ruth was determined would be returned in record time. Laura had a portable telly with a built-in video they could have till they got their own. Everyone was being so helpful – even Breffni had offered to lend them pillows and blankets.

Laura had phoned Ruth a few days ago and told her she was meeting Breffni for coffee in town the following day.

'Why don't you come along? We're meeting at four in that new place in Thomas Street, opposite Davern and Bell.'

Ruth was torn; she hadn't seen Laura in a while, and would have welcomed the chance for a chat. But Breffni would be there too, sitting in silent judgement over Laura's new sister-in-law – *no; stop it.* Ruth determined she was going to cut out this silly paranoia; she was going to give Breffni the benefit of the doubt.

'I'd love that, thanks Laura. Why don't I drop by your studio and we can go there together?' That way there would be no danger of Ruth being alone with Breffni. Just in case she wasn't being paranoid.

She needn't have worried; Breffni had turned up twenty minutes late, just after Ruth and Laura had decided to go ahead and order their cappuccinos. She looked wonderful, as usual, in faded-to-grey black jeans and a dark red ribbed top, with her hair pulled back in a tortoiseshell clip.

'Sorry, I lost track of time in Cruise's Street. Nearly bought a top in Flax in Bloom, but I need a second opinion. Laur, will you come back with me after, and see what you think?' She looked at Ruth and added quickly, 'And you too, if you're not rushing off somewhere.'

Before Ruth had a chance to respond, Laura said, 'I don't know why you always ask me to advise you when you buy clothes – you'll make up your own mind in the end. And anyway, you know everything looks good on you.'

Breffni grinned. 'Ah but still, come and see it; it's not something I'd normally go for.' She watched two frothy cappuccinos appear in front of the others. 'Yummy, I'll have one of those please.' As the waitress turned to go, Breffni rummaged in her bag. 'Oh look, I nearly forgot –' She pulled out what looked to Ruth like three children's colouring pencils. 'They were practically giving these away in Boots, so I got us one each.'

Laura looked at them in amusement. 'Lip liners?'

'Eye pencils, dope.' Breffni held them out. 'Here, you two can choose which colours you want; I'd wear any of them. Pick one, Ruth.'

Ruth looked at the pencils: they were identical, except that each had a different coloured stripe near the end; one was dark green, the second was a kind of terracotta and the third a deep violet. She had never used an eye pencil in her life. Did they go under or over your eyes? How did you know which colour suited you – were you supposed to match it with whatever you were wearing, or go by your eye colour? And how did you put it on? She'd be sure to stab herself if she went near her eyes with one of them.

And as she sat there, pretending to deliberate, another thought struck her – was this Breffni's way of hinting that Ruth needed to make up her eyes? It wouldn't be surprising – it must be obvious that Ruth hadn't a clue about make-up, had never been able to wear mascara without looking like a panda at the end of the night. And any colour she stroked onto her lids just made her clownish. She looked at Laura, willing her to come to the rescue.

And, thank goodness, she did. 'I'd say the rust one would suit your colouring.' Laura took it from Breffni's hand and pulled off the top, then stroked it a few times on the back of Ruth's hand. 'Look, it's nice and warm, it'd go lovely with your grey eyes.' She held it out to her. 'Try it anyway at home, and see what you think.'

Ruth took the pencil from Laura and smiled stiffly at Breffni. 'Thanks.' She put it into her bag, vowing to throw it into the first bin she came to on her way home.

'And I'll take the violet one, Bref – thanks.' Laura turned to the mirrored wall behind her and licked the tip of the pencil before stroking it onto her lower lids. 'Oh yeah, I like it.'

'Mmm – suits you.' Breffni put the green pencil back into her bag as the waitress approached with her cappuccino. 'So Ruth, what about this house then?'

And they'd talked about the house, and Breffni had offered the pillows and blankets, and promised to come along with Laura to help Ruth when moving day came. And Ruth's annoyance faded, and she eventually decided that Breffni was just trying to be friendly, and anyway, it wasn't as if Ruth didn't need help with make-up – anyone could see she hadn't a clue.

So she hadn't thrown away the eye pencil; she'd brought it home and gone straight to the bathroom and tried to apply it like Laura had done, even remembering to lick the top beforehand. It wasn't that hard really, once you got over the feeling of being so near your eye. In the end, she had to admit that it looked quite nice – not clownish at all. Andrew didn't notice anything when he came home from work, but over dinner Cecily told her she was looking very well. The next time she was in town, Ruth went into Boots and bought two more shades, after stroking a few of them on the back of her hand the way Laura had done. The girl beside her was trying on mascara, sweeping it down her lashes as if she'd done it all her life. Maybe Ruth would give that another go sometime – her lashes were far too pale.

Now Cecily smiled as she sat opposite Ruth and poured herself a cup of tea. She added a slice of lemon and stirred. 'You look happy this morning, dear.'

Ruth nodded. 'I am – I'm going over to the house after breakfast. I want to see for myself that it's almost ready.' Then she stopped. 'Cecily, it's not that I'm glad to be leaving here; we're terribly grateful to –'

'It's quite all right, dear, I understand perfectly.' Cecily's hair and make-up were immaculate, as usual – her soft lavender lipstick toned in beautifully with the pale grey sweater that had to be cashmere, it looked so fine. And her eyes were done up too – she'd probably been using eyeliner all her life. 'Naturally, you and Andrew are looking forward to your own place.' She paused. 'Of course, I hope I'll see you both often – I've already told Andrew that I expect you here for Christmas dinner.'

He'd never said a word to her. Ruth's heart plummeted, even though it was what she had expected. She said quickly, 'Thank you, Cecily, we'd love to.' They'd have plenty of Christmases in their own place. Her spirits soared again – their own place. Herself and Andrew – and their children. She tried to imagine Cecily with a grandchild on her knee, and failed. Ah well, maybe she'd pay for their college education instead.

She felt another giggle waiting to erupt – she was just so happy this morning – and dabbed at her lips with one of Cecily's linen napkins, managing a furtive glance at her watch as she did; how soon could she decently leave the table? Then she reminded herself that she had only a week more to go.

One week. Seven days.

✡✡✡

One week. Seven days since he'd written the few short sentences that had taken him three hours to get right. He couldn't believe seven days could seem like such an eternity, the minutes crawling by with excruciating slowness. Seven days that were only marginally less agonising than the seven nights, when his head was bursting with images of her, snatches of her laugh, the smell of her.

He would go mad. Unless he could have her, unless he could

find a way to quench this craving, this hunger he had for her, he would go stark raving mad, screeching like a possessed hyena in his straitjacket, thumping his crammed-with-her head against the walls of his padded cell.

He couldn't understand how he could continue to behave normally, but unbelievably, he did. Some force within him, something stronger than he knew he had, was keeping him from blurting out his secret and falling to pieces. He went to work like he always had, talked to people as usual, ate his meals, made love to his wife. Made love to his wife with his eyes closed, seeing *her* behind his lids. Called his wife 'darling', and 'love', and was careful not to say her name, in case he said the wrong one.

He prayed for an end. He prayed for her to contact him.

✡✡✡

Laura stepped through the shop doors, feeling like an intruder. *Stop being ridiculous*, she told herself. *You've as much right to be here as anyone else.*

She picked a t-shirt from the rail nearest to her. It was blue, with thin white stripes. So tiny; the body was the same length as her hand. She read the label: *0-6 months*. She remembered Polly at six months, still pretty bald, just beginning to sit up by herself, dribbling gummily up at Laura when she held her in her lap.

She put down the t-shirt and found a creamy dress, all ribbons and frills. '6-12 months'. Polly beginning to walk, tottering from Breffni's hand to the edge of the couch, fat little legs thumping across the floor. Losing her balance and plopping down, only to struggle unsteadily to her feet, padded bottom in the air as her podgy splayed fingers pushed against the floor to right herself.

'Can I help you?'

Laura started, almost dropping the tiny dress. An assistant stood beside her with a polite smile, not looking as if she suspected Laura of being mentally deranged at all.

'Er, no thanks. I'm . . . just looking.' Laura put the dress back and moved quickly away, certain that the assistant was watching her curiously. *Damn.* Why hadn't she said she was getting a present for a friend's baby, or a niece or something? You didn't go into a baby shop and just look, did you? It wasn't like going into a grown-up boutique, where you could wander around all you liked – or was it? She knew so little about babies and children, what was accepted and what wasn't. How would she ever be able to raise a child, if the miracle ever happened and she got pregnant?

She risked a glance over her shoulder. The assistant had moved on to another customer, who seemed to be asking her about buggies. Nobody was taking any notice of Laura at all. She relaxed slightly and looked at a row of tiny fleece bootees in lilacs and blues and purples. Polly's first proper shoes had been shocking-pink baby-sized trainers with lime green laces, with a green and pink striped hat to match. Breffni had brought them back from San Francisco. Polly had looked adorable in them.

Laura picked up a pair of miniscule purple bootees. They had a blue felt flower on the outside of each one. '*9-12 months*'. She walked rapidly towards the cash register.

'I'll take these, please.'

The assistant smiled as she took the bootees. 'They're so sweet. Are they a present?'

'No – they're for my own baby.' It was out before she had a chance to think about it. Her face flushed; she hadn't anticipated being asked any questions. Of course it was true; she was preparing for the baby she knew she'd have one day – but imagine if the assistant knew that she wasn't even pregnant yet . . . she stood, heart hammering, as the bootees were put into a bag and the amount rung up.

'Boy or girl?'

Oh God – her mind raced. 'Girl – Emma. She's just six months.' She wondered, in a detached way, how she could sound so calm. There was no sign of a tremor in her voice, no indication at all that she was saying the first thing that came into her head.

The assistant certainly didn't seem to notice anything. 'Ah, I remember my nieces at that age. Is she your first?'

'Yes; but I've just found out that I'm pregnant again.' So calm, as she handed over her debit card. Was her hand shaking slightly? She hoped not.

The assistant's plump, good-natured face broke into a wide beam. 'How wonderful; congratulations.' She took Laura's card and slid it through the machine, then pulled the slip out and put it in front of Laura. 'Just sign there, please.'

Laura's mind was blank as she wrote her name. She thanked the assistant, took the bootees and her card and her receipt, and walked calmly from the shop.

When she was halfway down the street, her legs began to shake.

✡✡✡

'What do you think?'

Frank smiled at Ruth. 'It's a fine house; you've done great work on it.'

'There was an awful lot to be done; I thought we'd never be in.' Ruth wanted to burst with happiness. The day before, she'd been assured by John the foreman that yes, they would definitely be finishing up by the middle of the week: 'Thursday at the very latest.' He'd taken her through the house room by room, and she'd seen, for the first time, what living here would be like.

They'd got the builders to paint the walls off-white throughout, so they could take their time with their own colour schemes. As she walked across the wooden floors, Ruth pictured a red rug here, a pale blue one there. The picture her sisters had given them for their wedding over that fireplace. Laura's telly in that corner. Andrew's computer in the small room at the top of the stairs – they didn't need three bedrooms. Yet.

And this morning Frank had arrived – she'd phoned him and arranged to meet him here, because she was dying to show off the house to someone, and Laura was too busy to come till the afternoon, and she couldn't get through to Valerie. And somehow she sensed that Cecily would rather wait until the house was more presentable. She'd taken Frank through the rooms just as John had done with her, watching for his reaction in each one.

He'd been so good that day in the café, when she'd made such a fool of herself by bursting into tears. The poor man; he hardly knew her. But he hadn't got in the least embarrassed, even though people must have been staring. Just held her hand and passed her paper serviettes till she'd calmed down. And then he listened quietly while she told him how lonely she'd felt since leaving Dublin.

'I know I shouldn't – I have Andrew, of course, and Laura has been so nice, and Cecily couldn't have done more for us, letting us live with her all this time . . . but I miss my family –' The tears threatened again, and she grabbed another serviette and held it to her eyes. 'We've never really been separated, and I know it's only Dublin, not the other side of the world . . . and then not having a job doesn't help, I've so much time on my hands –'

God knew what else she had said, it just seemed to keep pouring out, and Frank had listened patiently until she was empty. Then he leaned slightly towards her.

'Are you actually looking for a job? I mean, actively looking?'

She'd been surprised; it wasn't what she'd been expecting him to say. 'Well, no, not yet . . . I thought – we thought – I should wait until we're in our own house –'

'Why?'

Again so direct. Ruth just looked at him, realising in surprise that she had no answer. 'I don't know.'

'Couldn't you go to work from Cecily's house?'

Of course she could; why on earth hadn't that occurred to her? She felt something stirring inside her, and took a deep breath. 'Yes, I suppose I could. There's really no reason for me to wait –'

Frank shook his head. 'No reason at all. You will have a fair bit of work to do when you eventually move into your house, of course, but other people manage it with a job – why couldn't you?'

He made it sound so simple. Then he said, 'Now, why haven't you been back to Dublin since your wedding?'

And Ruth, beginning to feel slightly foolish, had to admit again that she didn't know.

'So what's stopping you from heading up to the station this minute and getting a train timetable?'

It was as if he'd stretched out a hand and pulled back some kind of curtain, and Ruth could see clearly for the first time in ages.

'Nothing is stopping me.' She smiled a watery smile. 'Frank, I'm so sorry for –'

He lifted his hand. 'Please Ruth, no need to apologise. If I've been any help at all, I'm delighted. I know what it's like to come to a new place: if it hadn't been for my excellent neighbours, I might well have headed back to Sligo after a few weeks. You need a few friendly faces around you when you move to a new city.'

He lifted his cup. 'Now, finish that coffee and head up to the station. You can get yourself a timetable and plan a trip.'

She'd gone straight there, bought a ticket for the following day – why would she need to plan, when her time was her own, she could go anytime? Then she headed home to pack a weekend bag.

And it had all worked out beautifully. When she told Andrew that evening, he nodded, unsurprised. 'Good idea – about time you went back to see them.'

He drove her to the station on his way to work the next morning, and her father was waiting for her at Heuston Station. She stayed two nights, revelling at being back in her old room with the same watermark in the ceiling above the bed, tucking into her mother's hearty meals without worrying about dropping a glass or cracking a plate.

After dinner on the first night, she sat in with her parents and Irene and watched *Emmerdale* and *Coronation Street* and *Fair City*, and answered all their questions about the house and Limerick, and went to bed after tea and biscuits like they always had last thing, and slept soundly all night. The second evening, a Thursday, she went out to the local with Irene and her two other sisters, and met up with Maura and Claire, and showed everyone her honeymoon photos.

And a few days after she got back to Limerick, Andrew came home from work and told her the house would be ready for them within a week.

When she'd rung Frank to invite him to come and see it – he'd given her his number in the café, 'just in case' – he sounded pleased.

'Now, everything is starting to fall into place. How's the job-hunting going?'

'Nothing yet, but I am keeping an eye on the paper.'

'Well, one step at a time. You'll be kept busy for the next while anyway, with the moving.'

Now Ruth opened the back door.

'Right, you've seen the house – let me show you the garden. I must warn you, it's in pretty bad shape. I'd say nothing's been done in it for years.'

Frank followed her out through the back door. 'Yes, I got that impression from the upstairs windows.' He stood and looked around the jungle of weeds. 'It'll certainly need a bit of work to get it into shape. Actually –' his eyes swept around, taking it all in '– I may be able to help you there.' He turned and looked at Ruth. 'I didn't mention that I was a landscape gardener in my previous life, did I?'

Ruth gaped at him. 'Frank – really? No, you never said – would you really like to take it on? We'd be thrilled, I know Andrew would be delighted –'

He smiled at her eager face. 'I'd enjoy getting back to it, I think – and it would certainly keep me out of trouble for a few months. You'd need to discuss it with your husband first, of course.'

'Oh, I'm sure he'll say yes – it's not as if he'd have the time to do it; and he's never mentioned an interest in gardening. No, I'd say he'd be delighted.' Ruth wondered if the day could get any better. 'Can I phone you when I've talked to him, and we can – er – see about payment?'

Frank twinkled. 'Well of course, I don't come cheap. I'd need at least one cup of tea a day, and maybe the odd ham sandwich. How would that sound?'

Ruth laughed, a little embarrassedly. 'We wouldn't dream of letting you work for nothing – but we can fight about it later.'

Frank nodded. 'Of course we can. I'll be seeing you at the book club anyway.' The next meeting was in two days' time, at Dorothy's house. 'You're planning to go, I take it?'

Ruth had hardly thought about the book club since the last meeting; had nearly forgotten the plot of the book they were supposed to be discussing, she'd read so many since then. But she nodded immediately. 'Yes, I'll be there. I'll talk to you then.'

As she walked along Shelbourne Road on the way back to Cecily's house – she didn't think of it as *home* any more, now they had their own – her head was full of all she had to do over the next few days. She felt like skipping; realised that this was the happiest she'd been since she'd moved to Limerick. Her pace slowed a bit as she wondered if that was normal – shouldn't she, as a newlywed, have been walking on air, no matter where she lived? Wasn't the fact that she was with Andrew the important thing? But of course she was happy with him; it was just that living with a mother-in-law would be difficult for most brides, surely. Especially one as . . . perfect as Cecily.

Once she and Andrew were moved in, everything would be great; she just *knew* it. They'd relax and spend lots of time together, and really begin to enjoy married life properly. As she reached the North Circular Road, she quickened her step. So much to do.

✡✡✡

'Hello.'

He turned; knowing who it was before he saw her. Even though she'd spoken softly, even though the place was crowded, and he'd barely heard her above the buzz of people rushing home for the weekend.

For a second, he couldn't speak. She literally took his breath away. Then she turned and walked towards the car park, and he followed her mutely, instinctively keeping a few paces behind her, even though nobody seemed remotely interested in them. He could smell her scent as he followed her; watch her body as it moved.

She reached her car and got in, and he walked around and opened the passenger door and sat in quickly beside her.

For a second, neither of them spoke. He could hear her breathing. Her hands lay loosely in her lap; he could see them from the corner of his eye. He didn't dare look at her, kept his eyes fixed on a small dark car parked in front of them. It could have been black or dark blue, or maybe brown; hard to tell in the sodium lights. He could feel his heart pounding.

Then she spoke, rapidly and quietly. 'You must never write to me or phone me at home. Never.'

He nodded, swallowed, then said, 'OK.' His voice sounded like someone he didn't recognise.

'We never meet anywhere there's the remotest chance anyone would see us. No risks.'

Again he nodded, glanced over. She was staring straight ahead too. Her face looked paper white in the orange light. One hand was on the steering wheel, the other was resting on her thigh.

He reached over and touched it. She caught her breath and glanced at him. With the movement, her scent wafted over to him again. She turned her hand up and wrapped her fingers around his, softly. Her hand was cold.

'What are we doing?' Her eyes looked black in the light. Her fingers pressed against his hand.

'I don't know.' His free hand found her face, the back of his palm stroked her cheek; so incredibly soft. She turned her face into his hand, ran her mouth over his fingers. He felt a sharp stab of desire. 'I just know we have to.'

She nodded, face still pressed against his hand, rubbing up against it like a cat. In front of them, someone got into the dark car and drove off.

Abruptly she straightened up, pulled away from him, placed both hands on the steering wheel. 'I must get back.' She looked over at him. 'I'll make arrangements and contact you. Is it safe to call you on your mobile?'

He nodded, pulled a card from his wallet with trembling fingers and scribbled rapidly on it before passing it to her. Then he forced himself to open the car door. As he was about to close it, he leaned down and said, 'Thank you.'

She smiled then, tentatively. 'You're welcome.' He watched her drive off until her car disappeared out the gates. Then he walked quickly towards his.

✡✡✡

Cecily folded the top of the sheet carefully over the duvet, smoothing it down gently. She took the pillows in their crisp cases from the chest of drawers and arranged them neatly on top, then covered them with the finely crocheted spread that she and Brian had brought back from a distant holiday in the Algarve. Her meticulous washing had preserved it perfectly all these years; it served her well on the cold winter nights.

Her eye fell on a photo on her bedside locker. Andrew was smiling in his usual charming way, sprawled in one of her deckchairs, one hand shielding his eyes against the sun. He wore a navy t-shirt and a pair of light cotton trousers, and he looked so handsome. It was hard to believe that he would soon be leaving home. Oh, she knew she was lucky to have had him with her for so long; other mothers had to wave goodbye to sons barely out of childhood these days, but still . . .

Privately Cecily dreaded the thought of her empty house: she hadn't lived alone for over thirty years. She remembered the noisy times when the children were growing up, and Brian was alive. Friends coming to dinner, birthday parties, first communions . . . always something to plan for, someone to clean the house and cook for.

Laura had been the first to leave, just as soon as she could – straight out of secondary school, if you don't mind. If it had been up to Cecily, the girl would have stayed at home until she had finished college and was earning a salary of her own. What nonsense to throw money away on rent when she could have gone on living here for nothing. But naturally, her father couldn't see sense when it came to his darling daughter; he'd handed over her rent quite happily, month after month. Cecily had long since learnt not to argue with him about Laura – as far as he was concerned, the girl could do no wrong.

And then suddenly Brian was gone too, and it was just Cecily and Andrew. And after she'd mourned her husband for a while, she was perfectly happy with just the two of them: happier, maybe, than at any other time, if the truth be told. Until Andrew had gone on holidays to Crete with a pal from work, and met Ruth.

Cecily had known he'd get married eventually; of course she had. And she supported his choice; in fact, she flattered herself that she might even have influenced him in some small way, who knew? And as soon as Andrew got married, naturally it was only a matter of time before he moved out. But it was one thing knowing that something was inevitable, and quite another being able to deal with it when it eventually happened. As long as Andrew and Ruth were living with her, Cecily had managed to avoid facing up to the fact that her son had begun the process of leaving her forever. But now, with their house finished at last, and the day of their departure – *his* departure – approaching, she found herself struggling to come to terms with it.

And yes, she knew they were only moving to Farranshone, barely five minutes in a car – but it wasn't the distance, that wasn't the point at all. Who would she cook for now? Who would tell her she looked lovely when she sat opposite him at the table in any old thing? Who would protest when she referred to herself as old, tell her not to be crazy, she'd never be old? Who would make her feel as if she really mattered, as if he simply couldn't imagine doing without her?

At least she still had the book club, once a month. And the occasional coffee with Dorothy or Emily in between. No male company though: Cecily had always enjoyed the attention of men. Even if most of them disappointed one, sooner or later, one had to admit that they had their uses. A nice meal out, now and again. Flowers occasionally, or gifts. And it was flattering to be desired – even if the man in question was not in the least desirable.

While Andrew had been living with her, Cecily had been quite satisfied, hadn't felt the need for any other male company. Andrew was attentive, took her out to dinner once in a while, bought flowers and champagne on her birthday – and of course, with her son there was no sense of obligation, as there would have been with another male, sooner or later. They always managed to make one feel under obligation eventually.

But now Andrew was leaving. And Cecily would just have to face up to it, and get used to the fact that from now until the day she died, she would live alone.

She picked up the used laundry and left the room.

✡✡✡

'Hello?'

'Ruth, it's Laura.'

'Oh, hi Laura. You're ringing about the move.'

'I sure am. You're still planning for Tuesday?'

'Yes; the furniture is coming down from Dublin sometime in the afternoon, so I'm going to head over straight after breakfast, around nine hopefully.'

'OK, I'll meet you there around nine thirty, and Bref says she'll come in as soon as Mary arrives to mind Poll.'

'That's great – are you sure you're not too busy with work though?'

'Not really; I've been slogging away for ten days on the trot – I'm owed a day off, and it'd make a nice change.'

'Laura, I really appreciate this; I intend having you and the others over for dinner as soon as we're settled in.'

'Hey, give yourself a chance, no hurry. We'll see you Tuesday.'

✡✡✡

Dorothy picked up the teapot. 'I'd say that's enough book talk for one night. More tea, anyone?' She walked around, filling cups.

Valerie turned to Ruth. 'You must be thrilled; your first house is so exciting.'

'I am – you'll have to come and see it when we're installed.' She turned and nodded towards Frank, sitting next to Cecily at the opposite side of the room. 'And we've already got our gardener lined up; did you know that that's what Frank did all his life?'

Cecily lifted her cup and watched him take another shortbread biscuit from the plate between them. The man certainly had a sweet tooth – that must be his third or fourth. Not that she was taking any notice, despite the fact that he'd made a beeline for her as soon as he'd arrived, bent her ear from the moment he'd sat down. Talking to her as if she was his long-lost cousin, and practically ignoring poor Margaret on his other side – who was, admittedly, busy swapping recipes with Dorothy.

And Cecily had to admit, somewhat reluctantly, that she was finding Frank slightly easier to stomach this evening. She'd been surprised to hear from Ruth that he'd been a landscape gardener; to Cecily's mind, anyone with an affinity to growing things had to possess at least a modicum of sensibility. To be able to see, before it existed, a neatly presented shrubbery, or a tasteful arrangement of patio plants. To know what would thrive in a shady corner, what would cover an ugly wall with the most colour, which plants would work best together in a hanging basket. She wouldn't have credited Frank with that sort of insight. One never knew, really.

Cecily's own medium-sized back garden was immaculate – neatly clipped shrubs, perfectly mown lawn where no dandelion or daisy dared to appear, two well-behaved rose bushes by the end wall, one small flowerbed just outside the patio door where she planted dwarf tulips and daffodils in the autumn and petunias and pansies when spring came around. During the growing season, Andrew mowed the lawn once a week; she suddenly wondered if he'd still do that when he was living in his own house. Surely . . .

'Penny for them; or I suppose I should be offering a cent now.'

Cecily started slightly, then smiled stiffly in Frank's direction. 'Oh, nothing of importance; I was just thinking of my garden.' She felt like telling him that her thoughts were none of his business, but of course, good manners forbade it.

He looked thoughtfully at her. 'I'm sure it is quite lovely, if you are the one who manages it.'

Cecily was completely thrown: what a thing to say. She lifted her cup and sipped her tea, unable to think of a single answer. What in God's name would he come out with next?

'I was wondering if you'd like to have dinner some night.' His voice was deliberately pitched so no one but herself would hear him.

Cecily put down her cup then and looked straight at him. 'Yes,' she said. 'I would.'

✡✡✡

Laura pulled up outside the house and blew the horn twice before getting out and opening the boot. As she hauled the black plastic sack from it, Ruth's head appeared at one of the upstairs windows, which were all thrown fully open.

'Hang on.' She disappeared and opened the front door a few seconds later. 'Hi – is there more in the car?'

'Just the telly, for now. I'm leaving the non-essentials for later; but I thought you might be suffering withdrawal symptoms, after four months of no *Coronation Street*.'

Ruth laughed, imagining herself snuggling up to Andrew in front of the telly on their new deep-red couch – his colour choice, which she'd been unsure of, but which he promised she'd grow to love. Settling down to watch whatever they wanted on telly, whenever they felt like it – just a few nights from now. Or listening to music they'd chosen themselves, putting mugs of coffee – not china cups and saucers – straight down onto the table, without coasters. Or maybe glasses of wine – that one they'd brought to Laura and Donal's had been nice, Chateau something – she'd buy a bottle of that as a treat for their first night here.

Walking back out to Laura's car, Ruth touched her sister-in-law's arm briefly. 'Thanks so much for this – you're very good.'

Laura shook her head. 'No, I'm not; I'm using you as the perfect excuse to skive off work. Don't get me wrong – I'm delighted to have got this schoolbooks job, but Lord, it's pretty soul-destroying. All those bright, cheery, primary-coloured pictures; I'm beginning to feel like a Telly Tubby.'

Ruth laughed again. 'Well, you certainly don't look like one.' If anything, Laura seemed to have lost a bit of weight; her old jeans looked quite loose on her. She was pale too, and Ruth noticed faint dark circles under her eyes. But she seemed in good spirits; Ruth decided to say nothing. She always hated people telling her she looked tired; it always sounded to her like they were really saying that she looked awful.

They deposited the television on the floor in the living room – Ruth had already cleaned it out – and started on the kitchen together. Laura pulled on a pair of rubber gloves and began scrubbing the new worktops – they had a light film of what seemed like plaster on them – while Ruth washed down the wall tiles and wiped the shelves in the presses. She imagined them filled with their things; saw herself reaching up to take down a box of Special K with Red Berries – her weekend treat in Dublin, too expensive to have every morning. Or maybe she'd be rummaging for a jar of honey; she'd adored the Greek yoghurt and honey they'd had most mornings in Crete.

Breffni arrived in her battered Clio half an hour later. Her glossy black hair was in a single perfect French plait that Ruth guessed had taken her about five minutes to do. She wore ancient-looking, threadbare jeans and a baggy red-and-black check flannel shirt, and black, well-worn Doc Martens. She'd probably chosen her oldest clothes for this day of scrubbing; Ruth thought she looked charmingly tomboyish.

'Mrs Mop reporting for duty.' She dropped two full-to-bursting bags inside the front door. 'Didn't know what you'd need in the line of cleaning stuff, so I just brought what I had under my own sink,' she said to Ruth. She pointed to the second bag. 'And that has a bit of lunch when we've done enough slogging to deserve it.'

'I hope there's chocolate in there somewhere.' Laura poked a foot at the bag.

'All in good time. Now –' Breffni planted her hands on her hips and looked enquiringly at Ruth '– am I getting the grand tour before I start, or what?'

'Of course.' Ruth smiled brightly at her. 'I forgot you hadn't been here before.' Like there was the slightest chance of Ruth forgetting. Like she hadn't been dreading this moment – when she would have to go through the house with Breffni and see her reaction to it. She prayed that Laura would come too.

But Laura didn't. 'I'll get on with the scrubbing; don't be too long.' She turned back towards the kitchen, and with sinking heart, Ruth opened the living-room door and stood back to let Breffni in.

And Breffni loved it. Each room seemed to delight her; she found something positive to say about everything she saw.

'. . . Oh look, you could put a window seat in that bay – a nice long cushion, and you could curl up there with your book; when does this side of the house get the sun . . . ?'

'. . . oh wow, a tree out the back – you lucky thing. Our garden is too small, and I'd adore one for Poll. Mind you, she'd probably fall off and break her neck . . .'

'. . . hey, plenty of room in that hot-press. I bet yours will be nice and tidy too – you should see the state of mine. Of course, it's all Poll's fault – she's got more clothes than Cian and me put together . . .'

'. . . Now that windowsill is just crying out for a plant, look how lovely and deep it is – and I've one at home that might suit. It's too big for where we have it, but I think it could be just right there. I don't know the name of it, but it's got lovely purply coloured leaves. I'll bring it next time I'm coming in to the city . . .'

Back in the kitchen, Breffni sounded genuinely enthusiastic as she spoke with Laura. 'Isn't it gorgeous? Did you see the bathroom tiles? And the original fireplace in the living room. And can't you just see a hammock under that tree?'

And Ruth listened, and basked in Breffni's praises, and warmed to her. Why had she ever been wary of Laura's friend? Look how great she was being now. Obviously, she just took a bit of getting to know.

✡✡✡

Fourteenth of December; eleven days to Christmas. Donal closed his eyes and imagined himself and Laura sitting opposite each other at the dinner table. Between them, a duck filled with Donal's special chestnut and orange stuffing, the honey-basted roast parsnips Laura loved, her sherry trifle afterwards – they both detested plum pudding – a bottle or two of their favourite wine, a few candles, a few crackers – and a volume of unsaid words.

When he'd met Laura, the thing about her that had charmed him the most was her openness. She wasn't very confident – she had no faith in her ability as an artist until he'd practically beaten it into her – but she was never afraid to talk about things, because she had nothing she felt she needed to hide. She spoke openly about her strained relationship with Cecily, her deep attachment to her father. When Brian died, two years after Laura married Donal, she'd been desolate for months, crying night after night in his arms; but she'd always been able to talk about her heartbreak, pulling out precious memories to console herself.

'He'd always be the one to bring me to the dentist, never Mother. And on the way home we'd go into Eason's and he'd let me pick out three comics. I'd be sitting in the dentist's chair trying to decide which ones I'd get . . . When I made my confirmation I wanted to wear these shoes that were all the rage, Swedish I think they were, lovely soft leather, very casual-looking. Loads of the other girls had them. But Mother insisted on Clarke's – a hideous black patent pair with a strap and a buckle, like little girl's shoes. I hated them; we had a huge row about it, but of course she won. The day after the confirmation, Dad brought me into town and bought me a pair of the other ones. We had to hide them from Mother for ages; I'd wear the Clarke's ones going out and change at Bref's . . . He brought me and Andrew to see *Star Wars* three times, because we loved it so much. He said he loved it too, but we were fairly sure he was only going for us . . . When I went to see Bref, the time she moved over to San Francisco, I had to take out a bank loan for the fare. He insisted on repaying the loan in full when he found out, told me I could pay him back when I started earning, a Euro a week till I retired . . .'

For Donal, whose life until he met Laura had been a tangle of secrets and unspoken guilt, this ability of hers to vocalise everything was wonderful. She was the breath of fresh air that he desperately needed, and he gulped her in gratefully.

And then, two years ago, it had started to go wrong. It was his punishment – he knew that. He could accept it, it was no more than he deserved. But it was punishing Laura too, and he hated that. Couldn't bear to see the closed look on her face when she thought he wasn't looking. The pain in her eyes as the months went by and she kept on bleeding. He heard her crying late at night, when he was supposed to be asleep, and it broke his heart. He saw her growing thinner, her beautiful cheekbones becoming more pronounced.

And now, they had begun the process that he had dreaded for years. He'd known it would come to this eventually – she'd made no secret of the fact that she wanted children – but he'd refused to think about it, hoping against hope that maybe he'd never have to.

And of course, the worst thing, the most despicable thing, was that all of this was unnecessary. All of Laura's anguish, all her waiting and praying and hoping – all of it was just a huge waste of time. He knew, and he couldn't tell her.

Because if he ever told her, if she ever discovered what he had hidden from her, she would have no choice – honest, open Laura would have no choice – but to leave him.

So he had to wait for her to find out the hard way, through the doctors, and the tests, and the months of trying – and then, when he and Laura were given the news, he would have to pretend that it was news to him too.

He turned away from the calendar, wondering how on earth they'd make it through Christmas.

✡✡✡

She hardly noticed the rain on the windshield, until her vision blurred, and a car coming opposite flashed at her to keep in to her own side of the road. Even at three in the afternoon, the day was dark, with showers falling suddenly and heavily, and not making much difference afterwards to the leaden sky.

She saw the hotel ahead of her, and her heart lurched. It wasn't too late to turn around and go home and forget this insanity. Pretend it had never happened – just something daft she'd dreamt up on an idle afternoon. He'd wait awhile, eventually realise that she wasn't coming. It would all blow over, it would have to. They'd avoid each other as much as they could; they'd survive, and no damage would have been done.

She checked her mirror, indicated, and turned in the gravel driveway. Too late, much too late for that.

She saw his car, parked in the furthest away of the marked spaces. She pulled in four spaces down from his, avoided her eyes in the mirror as she lifted her bag from the floor in front of the passenger seat. When she walked through the front door, he stood and came towards her, and she smiled and put her cheek up to his. You'd swear she'd been doing this all her life.

'Hi.' He looked nervous. 'I've got the key.'

'Let's go then.' She took his arm and they walked through the lobby. She didn't look towards the reception desk.

✡✡✡

Lord, what on earth had possessed her? A dozen times a day since the book-club meeting, Cecily wished fervently that she could pick up the phone and call Frank, make some excuse – anything; she didn't need it to sound genuine, for God's sake – that would get her out of this ridiculous situation. How had it happened, what devil had possessed her, persuaded her to agree to having dinner with him? Had her head been so easily turned by a few silly compliments? Was she that desperate for male company?

But she couldn't phone him; she didn't have his number, and he wouldn't be in the Limerick phone book yet – and anyway, she couldn't remember his last name. In a few hours, she was going to sit into a car beside a man whose last name she didn't know, and let him take her out to dinner. She would be trapped with him for at least two hours, would have to talk to him and listen to him, and in the end, thank him.

One thing she was grateful for – no one else knew. She was quite sure that nobody had been near enough to overhear as they'd made the arrangements, and Cecily intended to keep it that way. When he'd asked her if there was anywhere she would like to go, she'd named a little country hotel, not at all fashionable, almost ten miles outside the city. No chance of bumping into anyone she knew there, she was certain.

And that would be the end of that. One dinner, and a polite but firm refusal if he asked to see her again. She'd acted impulsively, made a mistake; everyone was entitled to that. But she would make quite sure not to repeat it.

One dinner. With a sinking heart she went upstairs to change.

✡✡✡

For hours afterwards, his whole body burned. He marvelled that his voice, when he spoke, sounded so normal, that his hands could do what he needed them to do without shaking. That nobody at all noticed the change in him, or the fact that he'd been missing from work for almost three hours. That it had taken just half of a wintry afternoon in an unremarkable hotel bedroom for him to be certain that nothing would ever be the same.

And in a week's time, they were going to do it all over again.

✡✡✡

Lord, what had she done?

Was she out of her mind? Suddenly she was one of those women who meet men in hotel rooms in the middle of the afternoon. She had gone there knowing what was going to happen, wanting it to happen.

And did she feel guilty now, did she regret the last few hours, did she wish she could turn the clock back to the moment when he'd closed the bedroom door and stepped towards her? Would she wipe it all away if she could, and be glad that it had never happened?

She tried to imagine that – if she'd ignored the letter and stayed away from his work, and if they hadn't spent the last few hours making the kind of love she'd given up on – and she realised that the thought of it never having happened was unbearable. No, she wouldn't turn the clock back, given the chance. She'd turn it forward if she could, to one week from now. Already, she could hardly wait.

And anyway, it wasn't as if she was married.

✡✡✡

Laura opened the bottom drawer – the one Donal never went near, usually full of her winter jumpers – and looked inside. She lifted out the little yellow jumpsuit and stroked the blue furry teddy stuck onto the front: so cute. And the tiny green padded jacket just under it; she'd had a doll once that it would have fit. She pulled out a woolly patterned hat with a giant orange pompom and held it against her cheek: adorable.

One by one, she took everything out and laid them all on the carpet, all the doll-sized clothes and hats and shoes that nearly filled the drawer. There were the bootees that she'd bought the first time. It seemed amazing now, that feeling of guilt she'd had in the street afterwards, as if she'd stolen them. The second time had been easier, when she got the hat. And after that, she didn't bat an eyelid – just strode in as if it was the most natural thing in the world, just another item on her shopping list: *clothes for baby*.

She was glad now she'd bought nothing too frilly, no pale blues or pinks. She had to be careful not to get anything that wouldn't suit her baby; she couldn't put a pink jumpsuit on a boy – or a blue one on her daughter. *Her daughter*: The words sounded wonderful in her head.

Lately she had started dreaming about her babies. Her little girl in yellow dungarees and cute little pigtails, chuckling when Laura tickled under her chin. Her little boy, rosy cheeked, brown hair tousled, digging in his sandpit for treasure. She could see their adorable little faces, smell their baby scents. They clambered onto her lap and covered her face with tiny bird kisses and begged for stories.

After a while, she folded everything carefully again before putting it all back and shutting the drawer quietly. Then she went to her bedside locker and took out her temperature chart. There it was, plain as day: on Wednesday last, her temperature had risen. The gynaecologist had told her that once this happened, ovulation was over. So she *was* ovulating – her body was functioning properly, presenting her with an egg every twenty-eight days, just like it was supposed to. They'd made love nearly every night since the consultation – the odd ones they missed didn't matter; Dr Sloan had told them that sperm remained active inside the woman's body for up to three days – and often again before Donal went to work in the mornings.

And now, Laura was pregnant: she felt certain. And soon she'd be able to prove it, and tell Donal. And Breffni. She imagined how thrilled they'd be, and wished with all her heart that her father was still alive to rejoice too. What a wonderful grandfather he'd have made.

She put the chart back carefully and closed the locker. She checked her watch: lunch time. She knew she should have something, now that she was eating for two, but she hadn't felt hungry for ages. She was too excited.

✡✡✡

Cecily stood at the window of the dark sitting room and watched as Frank drove off. When his car had disappeared in the direction of the North Circular Road, she turned and went into the kitchen. She filled and plugged in the kettle and took her caddy of herbal teas over to the table.

Who would have thought that she would actually have enjoyed herself? She'd been dreading the whole business, not at all relishing the prospect of being in Frank's company for a whole evening, unable to imagine them managing to sustain any kind of conversation over that period of time.

And it had turned out fine. He'd been attentive and polite; the conversation hadn't flagged once. He hadn't been too intrusive, as she'd feared – any questions he'd put to her were quite impersonal. And to her vast relief, the subject of his past hadn't come up once. She'd enjoyed talking about plants with him – he certainly knew what was what. And he was surprisingly well read; no wonder he'd agreed to come with Dorothy to the book club.

He'd insisted on her having a gin and tonic before the meal, ordering mineral water for himself – he told her that he never took a drink when he was driving, which she heartily approved of. The dinner had been quite a pleasant surprise too – she hadn't known what to expect. But her baked cod had been quite tasty, with a well-put-together salad accompanying it – dressing on the side, as she'd requested.

And Frank hadn't once tried to take advantage. In fact, he'd been the perfect gentleman all evening. While she wasn't in the least attracted to him – absolutely not – Cecily had to admit that she was quite looking forward to their next meal out: same time, same place, this night week. Who would have thought it?

O'Connor. His second name was O'Connor.

The kettle started to sing, and she got up for her cup and saucer.

✡✡✡

'Hello?'

'Ruth, Laura here.'

'Hi, Laura, I was going to give you a call later on; we haven't met for a while.'

'I know; I was giving you a chance to get settled in. How's it going?'

Ruth stood in the kitchen and looked out at the rapidly emerging garden; Frank was working wonders. 'Fine – every day a bit more done. I'm not forgetting about having you all over for a meal, but I suppose at this stage it'll have to be in the New Year, with Christmas so close.

'Oh, don't worry about that – wait until you feel ready. I was ringing about a get-together in town, actually. Thought it might be nice for the gang to have a meal out for Christmas – maybe a Chinese, and a few jars after. What would you think?'

'Sounds lovely.' Ruth watched a lone brown bird – a thrush? – landing on one of the bare branches of the tree. Maybe she'd get Andrew a bird table for Christmas. 'When were you thinking?'

'Well, since we've only the one weekend left, I thought we'd try for Friday night. I know Cian has already had his work night out, and Donal's is never till January, so as long as you and Andrew have no plans –'

Ruth watched the thrush flit from branch to branch before suddenly flying away, off over the wall. 'No, we've nothing on this weekend. Andrew's was on a few weeks ago; he said they always have it early. A meal out would be lovely, if we're in time to get a table somewhere.'

'Great; I'll make a booking wherever I can – maybe that new little place on Denmark Street with the funny name; I've heard good reports of it. I'll get back to you and let you know.'

As she hung up, Ruth wondered why she hadn't mentioned her news to Laura. It wasn't that she had forgotten – the letter was sitting on the table in front of her. Short and to the point:

Dear Mrs O'Neill,
We regret to inform you that your job application was unsuccessful on this occasion. We will keep your name on file and contact you should a position that suits your skills become available.
Yours sincerely

And then some indecipherable scrawl – Ruth presumed it was the name of the perfectly made-up woman who'd interviewed her just over a week ago. Another one of Them.

To be honest, she wasn't too put out by the rejection; the salon had intimidated her slightly. Everyone seemed impossibly glamorous – the staff, all leggy blondes or tight-trousered, slim-waisted men, and the customers, flicking through *Vogue* and *Homes and Gardens* as they waited on soft leather couches to be transformed. Ruth's interviewer had probably taken one look at her and decided that she wasn't half stylish enough.

In Dublin, Ruth had worked in a small, friendly salon in her own neighbourhood, with a group of regular customers who'd known Ruth since she was in short socks. She'd started there part-time while she was still at school, washing hair and sweeping up, and the owner took her on full-time after her Leaving, gradually teaching her how to highlight and cut and style. Twelve years on, Ruth felt that she knew a fair bit – she might need a bit of bringing up to date with the latest products and styling aids, but she could attack most hairdressing tasks with some degree of confidence. Obviously, not a view shared by Ms Make-Up.

She took the letter and dropped it into the bin: plenty more salons where that came from. Maybe she should start walking around the suburbs, look for a similar place to Sheila's. But there really wasn't much point in doing any of that before Christmas; she might as well wait now until the New Year. Maybe she'd take another trip up to Dublin then too, go to the sales with her sisters. Pick up a few bargains for the house; they still needed so much.

Laura had sounded in good form – Ruth presumed that whatever had been bothering her lately had passed. The meal out was a good idea; it should get everyone into the Christmas spirit. She could do with a bit of cheering up herself – it was great to be in the house at last, but Andrew had seemed distracted lately, although he kept insisting that nothing was wrong; he'd even arrived home with a big bunch of flowers for her last night. But she still couldn't help feeling that he'd been happier in his mother's house. Was Ruth not looking after him as well as Cecily had? Was he wishing he'd never got married, never gone on that holiday to Crete?

He never asked about her day when he came home, or enquired if she'd heard about the job – didn't it occur to him that she was waiting to hear? Ruth was willing to bet that, if she didn't tell him about the letter that had arrived this morning, he'd never ask. He never suggested going out anywhere, seemed quite happy to sit at home night after night, watching TV or surfing the net.

She shook herself crossly – such negative thinking, when all that was wrong with everyone was probably a big dose of the winter blues. And she and Andrew made love regularly; he was just as enthusiastic as he'd always been in bed. Surely if he was having second thoughts, he wouldn't be interested in that side of things any more?

Just then, she heard the side gate being opened – Andrew had promised to get oil, but he must have forgotten – and she arranged a smile on her face as she opened the back door to Frank.

✡✡✡

'Hey, bro.'

Andrew swung around, smiled at her. 'Am I glad to see you. I need help – female help.'

Laura grinned knowingly. 'You're trying to find a present for Ruth.'

'Yeah – I haven't a clue. Last year was easy; the diamond ring. This year, I'm totally stumped.' He gestured towards the gift boxes of cosmetics stacked in the pharmacy window. 'I was thinking maybe one of those.'

Laura shook her head firmly. 'Absolutely not: she'd throw it at you. Well, Ruth wouldn't, but she should – far too impersonal. What perfume does she like?'

He shrugged. 'Em . . . pass.'

'Ah, Andrew, what are you like? I'd kill Donal if he didn't know mine.' Laura pursed her lips. 'You could go the voucher route; impersonal too, but if you knew her favourite shop . . . ?'

Again he shrugged, shamefaced now. 'Sorry; I just don't notice things like that, Laur.'

No; you're too busy thinking about yourself. She pushed the thought away and tucked her arm into his. 'Come on – you can buy me a coffee while I think about it. We'll come up with something.' As they walked down Cruise's Street, she said, 'By the way, I rang Ruth this morning to ask you to come out for a meal on Friday night, just the six of us.'

He paused for a second, then said, 'Yeah . . . maybe. To be honest, I'm kind of tired lately.'

She shook his arm. 'Ah come on, it's Christmas. You sound like a boring old fart.'

He looked more closely at her. 'And you sound in great form yourself. Anything I should know about? Has Donal been promoted to head chef or something?'

'Shut up; you're so snobby about his job. I'm perfectly happy having a chef for a husband – and anyway, you know well he's already a head chef.'

'Ah yes – head chef at the famous five-star UL canteen.' He caught her scowl and put up his hands in surrender. 'Sorry, sorry, I'm just joking. So, what then? What has you skipping around like a young one?'

Her face cleared – she could never stay cross with him for long. 'I don't know what you mean – I'm always this jolly and friendly.

Hey, you will come Friday night though, won't you? I bet Ruth would love a night out.'

He lifted his shoulders in resignation. 'Looks like I've no choice; she'll hardly go without me.'

'Good.' They reached the coffee shop and Laura steered him towards the door. 'Here we are. Now you can get me a coffee while I decide on the perfect Christmas present for your wife.'

They walked inside.

✡✡✡

'So that's Mam and Dad, John and Colette, yourself, and the three of us. Eight altogether, if you include Polly – who's really only a half.' Breffni finished counting off on her fingers and looked enquiringly at Mary. 'Think I can handle it, and not poison everyone with half-cooked turkey?'

'Of course you can – didn't I have your turkey last year, and live to tell the tale? And anyway, you'll have me to help out – you won't be doing it on your own. And get that man of yours to do his bit too – he's well able.'

'Oh I will, don't worry. Actually, Cian's first job will be to go around to your house and borrow two kitchen chairs.'

Mary nodded. 'Grand. And anything else you need, extra bowls or saucepans, or glasses maybe – make a list and give it to Cian when he's coming.'

'I hear my name – it better be good.' Cian's head appeared around the door, Polly in his arms.

Breffni put her hand out towards Polly. 'Hello, cutie pie.' She looked at Cian. 'We're planning Christmas Day – you're getting a list of jobs.'

Cian nodded placidly. 'Fine. Well, don't let us interrupt – we're off to kick a ball around the park.' He turned to Polly, wrapped in a bright blue padded jacket and dark green hat. 'Say bye to Granny and Mammy.'

'Put on her scarf, Cian – it should be out in the hall.' Breffni waved her fingers at Polly. 'Bye, sweetie. See you later, alligator.'

'See later, al'gator,' echoed Polly, opening and closing her fingers. 'Bye, Ganny.'

'Bye, darling.' When they'd left, Mary turned to Breffni. 'You're looking a bit washed out; anything wrong?'

Breffni shook her head, getting up and going over to the boiling kettle. 'Ah no, just a head full of what I need to get done for this day week. And I suppose I'm a bit anxious about cooking Christmas dinner for the brother's wife; Mam told me Colette is a fantastic cook.' She poured water into the teapot.

Mary took two mugs from the press. 'Ah, will you stop – your cooking is fine. It'll be delicious, wait and see.'

Breffni grinned as she set the teapot onto the table. 'Thanks, Mary – you always say the right thing, even if it is a big fat lie. And anyway, in eight days it'll all be over, so who cares?' She got the jug of milk from the fridge, and groaned as she put it on the table. 'Oh God, I've just remembered that meal in Limerick with Laura and the others on Friday night. I could do without it, to be honest.'

Mary poured tea into the mugs. 'Go on, you know you'll enjoy it. Christmas is a time for going out and meeting the friends. You'd probably be sorry if you hadn't anything planned.'

Breffni smiled. 'I'm sure you're right. And thanks for babysitting, yet again. What would we do without you?'

They drank their tea and listened to Chris Rea on the radio, driving home for Christmas.

✡✡✡

The second time, it was like coming home. No awkwardness, no nervous fumbling. The room was identical to the last one – the only difference was the brass number on the door.

'Oh, God.'

'Shhh.'

And afterwards, when they were still trembling, still damp and hot, he put his mouth to the hollow of her neck and bit gently. She whispered, 'Don't', and pulled his head up so she could kiss his face. Afraid he might leave a mark on her. He wanted to brand her, claim her as his. He couldn't bear the thought that another man looked at her, touched her. He wanted to lock her away for him, only him.

They held hands until they got to the lobby, then she gently pulled hers away. He wanted to weep with emptiness.

She turned to him as she opened her car door. 'See you in the restaurant.'

✡✡✡

'Mmm, guys, you've got to taste this; it's great.' Donal pointed to the dish of beef with his fork. 'The black bean sauce is terrific.'

Ruth spooned noodles onto her plate and passed the bowl to Cian beside her. Then she peered at another dish. 'You had some of that, Andrew – what's it like?'

'Good – fruity.' Andrew speared a cube of chicken from his plate and held it across to Ruth. 'Taste.'

'It's OK, I'll take my own.' Ruth spooned some of the chicken onto her plate.

'Here, I'll try it.' Beside Andrew, Breffni leaned over and ate the piece of chicken from his fork. 'Mmm – wonderful. He's right, Ruth.'

'Who's got the rice?' Laura scanned the round table. 'Here, Donal, pass it over.' She took a small portion of rice and dolloped it on her plate. 'Isn't this great – the gang out for Christmas?' This evening she seemed keyed up; she spoke rapidly and her cheeks were slightly flushed, although she'd ordered orange juice instead of the wine that everyone else except Cian was having.

Andrew had looked at her in disbelief when she'd put her hand over her glass as he was pouring. 'You're not having a jar?'

She'd shaken her head. 'Don't feel like it. Cian and I will stay sober and sensible, and make sure the rest of you drunken louts get home in one piece.'

Now she lifted her glass of juice. 'What'll we drink to – besides Happy Christmas?'

Cian lifted his. 'Happy new house to Andrew and Ruth.'

Andrew shook his head; he was already well into his second glass of wine. 'Ah, not just us – what about a toast to the six of us?' He waved his glass to take everyone in. 'To a great new year together.'

'That sounds good – a happy new year to all of us.' Laura beamed around the table and clinked her glass against Andrew's. In the echoing clinks that followed, Laura met Donal's eye across the table. She held his gaze, smiling brilliantly at him.

'So, Ruth – how's the house coming along?' Cian pushed the serving spoon into the mango chicken and lifted a generous portion onto his plate.

'Great; we're slowly putting a shape on it; and we've a gardener working out the back, would you believe? It's going to be lovely. You'll see it soon, I hope – I'm planning to have you all over for dinner in January.'

'Lovely.' He helped himself to rice. 'Breffni tells me it's great; I think she's seriously considering leaving me and moving into the city – she's mad jealous of you all.'

'And don't think he's joking.' Breffni's voice floated across. She looked around the table. 'I'm sick of being out in the sticks – all the excitement is in Limerick.'

Ruth laughed. 'Oh, I'm sure Nenagh's just as exciting.'

Breffni picked up her glass and smiled at Ruth. 'About as exciting as watching paint dry, actually.'

Cian lifted his hands in mock despair. 'I just can't compete, can I?'

From his other side, Laura spoke. 'Don't mind her, Cian – she's all talk.' She didn't look to be eating much, Ruth thought; her plate seemed pretty full still. But she was in such good form tonight, which was great.

When the plates were all cleared away, Andrew picked up the empty wine bottle in front of him. 'One for the road?'

'Yes please.' Breffni drained her glass. 'None for Cian – he's driving me back to the sticks, God help me.'

'You can join me in a coffee, Cian; they'll all be sorry in the morning.' Laura stood and looked around her. 'Where's the loo here . . . ? Oh, I see it. Back in a sec.'

'Donal?' Andrew indicated the empty bottle.

Donal shook his head. 'Think I'll go for coffee too.'

'Don't forget Ruth.' Breffni inclined her head in Ruth's direction as Andrew held up the empty bottle and signalled to a waiter. 'She'll have some too, won't you, Ruth?'

'Yes please.' Ruth looked at Andrew as she spoke. 'Just as well someone remembered me.'

'And just as well we have a lie-in tomorrow –' Andrew glanced over at Ruth '– unless you have any more jobs lined up for me?'

Ruth smiled briefly and shook her head, feeling a faint stab of annoyance. When had she ever *lined up* jobs for him? He was making her sound like a harridan. The only thing she'd asked him to do – the one job since they moved house – was to get some oil for the side gate, and he hadn't done it; she'd got it herself in the end.

The wine arrived and the waiter made his way around the table, pouring.

'Cheers.' As Breffni clinked glasses with Andrew and Ruth, Donal glanced up to see Laura making her way back towards the table, and immediately his heart sank. She came straight over to him.

'Sorry . . . I don't feel well. I think I want to go home now.' Her voice was low and empty. The slight flush was still in her cheeks, but the earlier sparkle had completely drained out of her. 'Can you call a cab? I don't feel like driving home.'

He stood and put an arm around her shoulders. 'Of course; sit down a minute.' He steered her gently into the chair he'd just left and pulled out his mobile. As he spoke, Laura sat hunched in the chair, eyes fixed on the tablecloth in front of her. From the chair beside her, Breffni put an arm over Laura's.

'Is it your stomach? Did you throw up?'

Laura shook her head, still looking at the tablecloth. 'Just a headache; I need to lie down, get out of the light.'

In the cab, she leant against Donal, crying softly into his chest. 'Why? Why can't I? What's wrong with me?' Her voice was thick with tears.

He held her and whispered, 'I'm sorry darling . . . I'm so sorry.'

He wanted to tell her that everything would be all right, but of course he couldn't.

✡✡✡

'God, I'm stuffed.' Breffni stretched her legs out in front of her and leaned over to turn up the heat.

When Cian didn't respond, she looked over at him. 'Are you all right?' Her words were slightly slurred.

He turned his head and smiled briefly before looking back at the road ahead. 'Fine.'

After a short silence, he said, 'Bref, would you really like to move into Limerick?'

She laughed. 'Are you getting worried that I'll leave you?' When he didn't respond again, she sat up straighter and studied his profile. 'God, you are. Don't be daft; if I was thinking about it, d'you really think I'd be blabbing to everyone?'

He glanced at her again. 'OK.'

'You take everything so seriously . . . lighten up, for God's sake.'

'Right.' He kept his eyes on the road ahead for several minutes after that, and the next time he looked over, when they had to stop at a traffic light, she was asleep. He watched her beautiful face and felt afraid.

✡✡✡

'Stop.' Ruth pushed his hand away, conscious of the taxi driver's eyes in the mirror. 'Darling, please stop.'

Andrew's breath was hot on her face, and smelt spicy. His voice was low, but Ruth knew it wasn't low enough. 'When a woman says stop, she never means it.' He slid his hand up under her shirt again. 'She means don't stop; she means go on.' He tried to wriggle his fingers under the lacy camisole she wore. 'You know you want it, you know it's driving you mad.' His breathing was harsh; his other hand was pulling up her skirt, kneading her thigh painfully, forcing her legs apart. 'My strait-laced little wife – why don't you just go mad for once?' Ruth heard a tearing sound – the stockings she'd paid sixteen Euro for that day.

'No love, please . . . '

The more she struggled, the more it seemed to excite him. His movements became more urgent, his breathing more laboured. He reached further up her leg, grabbing at her underwear. 'Come on, come on . . .' And all the time Ruth was acutely aware of the driver taking it all in, meeting her eyes quite openly any time she looked at the mirror.

She felt a sudden flash of anger. They weren't teenagers, for God's sake, fumbling in the back of a car because they had nowhere else to go. They were married, and could restrain themselves until they were in their own bed.

'I said *no*.' She shoved him away with all her strength, and crossed her legs tightly. 'Stop it, Andrew – I don't want this.' She turned her head and looked out the window, and ignored him for the rest of the journey.

And tried not to feel too nervous about what she'd done.

✡✡✡

The meal had been torture from start to finish. The fact that he could smell her scent, could laugh and joke with her, could say her name and meet her eye – none of that mattered, or it made it worse. She was so close, and he couldn't touch her. Couldn't put his mouth to that perfect skin, run his hand lightly over her smooth stomach. He imagined what the reaction would be if he leaned across and kissed her, and he wished he had the courage to do it.

His only saving grace, the one thing that kept him from putting his head into his hands and howling with frustration, was the thought that, five days from now, she would be in his arms again. He clung to that.

✡✡✡

'Happy Christmas, Mother – from both of us.' Laura touched her mother's cheek with hers for the briefest of seconds. Cecily's skin was cool; she smelled of the Yves St Laurent perfume that always reminded Laura of Arabian nights – heady, exotic, passionate. It astonished her that such a cold-blooded creature as Cecily should favour that scent.

'Thank you, dear – and Donal too, of course.' Cecily took the small silver-wrapped package and opened it unhurriedly, as Laura took a large swallow of her brandy and ginger ale, and waited. Donal caught her eye and winked; Laura gave him a small, brittle smile before turning back to her mother.

'It's beautiful – thank you both again.' Cecily looked down at the delicate gold and silver pendant that had cost half as much as Donal earned in a week. 'I shall treasure it.'

And you shall never wear it – at least, not when you meet us. Laura lifted her glass again and watched as Andrew and Ruth presented Cecily with a soft-looking scarf in a beautiful mauve colour. Cecily immediately wrapped it over her shoulders – 'one of my favourite shades too: how clever of you both' – before standing to refresh all their glasses. Laura glanced at her watch – another half an hour at least before they could make their excuses. And she couldn't even have another drink; as usual, she was driving. She watched Donal accepting a second brandy with a feeling that she took a moment to recognise as resentment. *He* never had to worry about how many jars he had. So handy, not driving.

Stop it. She willed herself to relax, breathed deeply to try to dislodge the knot that seemed to have taken up permanent residence inside her. If she didn't watch herself, she'd end up twisted and bitter. And it wasn't Donal's fault that she wasn't pregnant – at least, they didn't know which of them was to blame yet. Another two months at least to endure before they found out – if they ever did find out. *God, why can't I think about anything else?* Her heart ached; she seemed to be on some kind of awful treadmill, going round and round the same old endless *whys* and *what ifs*.

And no answers. Nobody to tell her that she was being silly – that of course she'd get pregnant, any time now. That it just took longer with some people, that was all. That there was absolutely no problem – none whatsoever.

'Laura, dear?' Cecily was holding out a plate. Laura saw immaculately arranged crackers on which were perched slices of herbed cheese and slivers of cucumber, wafer-thin salami, some kind of pâté topped with olive halves.

'Thank you.' She took a salami-topped cracker – Cecily would probably take it personally if she refused – and placed it on the small china plate on her lap. She felt sure that Breffni and Cian were getting merry on sparkling wine, along with the gang they'd invited to the turkey dinner. No standing on ceremony there; no perching on a spindly-legged chair, forcing down silly, fiddly food you didn't want, listening to operatic music, which Laura had always detested, and trying to look as if you were enjoying yourself.

After what seemed like an eternity, they managed to escape. Laura turned to Donal in the car as they drove off. 'Please let's go on a Christmas break to the sun next year.'

'I promise.' He grinned across at her – probably a bit high on

Cecily's brandy. 'Listen, it could be worse. I'm just glad that she doesn't expect us to stay for dinner. Poor Ruth.' When Laura didn't respond, he put a hand on her shoulder. 'Darling?'

She darted a look at him, unsmiling. 'What?'

'We have each other. We'll always have each other, whatever happens.'

She nodded. 'Yeah, I know.' She felt a tear trickle out of one eye and run slowly down her cheek.

'I love you.' He squeezed her shoulder gently; hadn't noticed the tear.

She nodded again, and then said, 'God, I could use a drink when we get home.'

Donal said nothing, just looked at her as they turned onto the North Circular. After a minute, he took his hand away.

✡✡✡

All day long, she was on autopilot. Doing what was expected of her. Saying all the right things. Dragging her thoughts back whenever they strayed to him. Managing somehow to get through the day without someone looking curiously at her and asking, 'Are you OK?'

A few days ago, the third time. The same room as the first time, when he'd been so endearingly nervous. He was more confident now, more sure of her. Took his time with her. Her hair was damp with sweat, her voice hoarse as she begged him not to stop.

'I adore you . . . you're so beautiful.' His voice was muffled against her neck. 'So unbelievably beautiful.'

She drank in every word, shuddered when his tongue traced her collarbone lazily. *I adore you.* She echoed it back to him in her head, afraid to say it out loud.

Afraid now that this thing they'd started was going to be impossible to stop. Terrified that it would grow and blossom and take control, and destroy everything that got in its way. Already, so soon, she was powerless to resist him. Unable to say *no, stop this, we have to end it.* She couldn't imagine it ending; it could never end.

Somehow, she got through Christmas Day without him.

✡✡✡

'Frank – kettle's boiling.' Ruth drew in her head when she saw him look up and wave. She put spoons on the table, emptied the last few digestives onto a plate, poured steaming water into the teapot.

The back door opened and Frank appeared, shaking his feet out of his battered-looking boots. 'How do you always know just when I've decided that I could murder a cuppa?' He stepped into the pair of shoes on the mat and crossed to the sink. 'It's a perfect day out there, actually quite warm in the sun. Hard to believe it's December.' He turned on the tap and pumped the liquid soap into his hand.

Ruth poured tea into both cups, wondering again why Frank kept reminding her of someone. 'You're doing fantastic work out there. You must have loved your job, did you?'

'I did; never minded getting up in the morning, no matter what the weather was like. Loved getting my hands mucky; the muckier the better.' He put the towel back on its hook and sat at the table. 'Poor Angela was worn out trying to get the grass stains out of my trousers. Didn't matter how much I told her it didn't bother me – 'twas only my gardening gear – she'd still go at them with every kind of cleaner.'

Ruth pushed the sugar bowl over to him, thinking how rarely he mentioned his late wife. 'You must miss her.'

He nodded, spooning sugar into his tea. 'Every day. She was a wonderful woman; always so positive – and God knows, we went through our share of tough times.' He glanced over at Ruth. 'We lost a daughter, you know. Leukaemia.'

'Oh Frank, I didn't know. How terrible.' Ruth instinctively took his hand and squeezed it. 'You poor thing. How old was she?'

'Twelve. Just getting ready to start secondary school.'

'God.' Ruth held his hand tightly. 'Had you . . . have you other children?'

He paused, picked up his cup with his free hand. 'A son, yes.' Another pause; he sipped his tea, put down his cup. 'I . . . we lost touch, years ago.' Then he shook his head slightly and smiled. 'And that's quite enough about me and my dark past. Christmas reminds you of the ones who are gone – that must be why I'm rattling on like this. Now, my dear, I'm admiring your beautiful necklace and guessing it was a present from your husband.'

Ruth smiled, fingered the necklace. It *had* been from Andrew – she'd been delighted when she'd opened it, amazed when he insisted that no one had helped him choose it.

She still felt a lurch of unease when she remembered the other night – how she'd pushed him away in the taxi on the way home from the Chinese restaurant. She knew she had nothing to apologise for – he'd only had himself to blame, pushing himself on her like that, ignoring her protests – but still . . . she was his wife, after all, and he'd had a lot to drink, didn't really know what he was doing. Fortunately, he'd seemed to have forgotten it by the morning – how he'd lurched upstairs as soon as they were in the door, and gone straight to bed without another word to her.

When she reached the bedroom a few minutes later, he was fast asleep in his underpants, clothes tossed in a heap onto the floor. Ruth had picked them up and plonked them on a chair, not attempting to straighten them out. She was his wife, not his mother.

In the morning, he'd turned to her with a groan: 'God, my head's splitting; did I make a total idiot of myself last night?'

'Not at all; you were in great form.' Ruth got up and made him tea in bed, grateful that the little unpleasantness on the way home seemed to have been forgotten.

After Frank had finished his tea and gone back outside, Ruth stood at the kitchen window and watched him digging just inside the back wall, pushing the spade down into the earth, bending to lever it up and turn the soil, cutting into it with the side of the spade. Ruth had asked him about climbers; she wanted to cover the ugly concrete wall. He suggested summer jasmine for scent, and Virginia creeper for the glorious flaming colour it went in autumn, or maybe variegated ivy, if she didn't want it too bare in the winter, and a few sweet peas here and there, because their scent was wonderful too, and their colours so delicately pretty.

He also suggested runner beans, which surprised her until he described the beautiful orange blossoms that covered the plant before the beans appeared. 'And then you'll get a few dinners out of them too; you'll be like the woman on *The Good Life*, remember her, Felicity somebody?'

Ruth had laughed. 'Only the repeats, I'm afraid.'

She watched his slow, systematic turning of the earth; saw him crouching down every now and again to look closely at whatever had caught his attention. She wondered how anyone could survive the loss of a child; and terrible as the death of his daughter must surely have been, wasn't it as bad in its own way not to know where his son was – or even if he was still alive? What on earth could have been so awful for them to have lost contact, to have stayed apart for years? She supposed his son would be in his thirties or forties now. Ruth's heart went out to Frank; she wished there was some way she could help him.

Her eyes roamed the garden; it *did* look like a lovely day, and she hadn't put her nose outside the door yet. She'd finish the few jobs around the house and go for a walk; maybe track down a few local hairdressers. In just three days it would be January – time for some serious job-hunting.

She'd pick up a gardening magazine for Frank somewhere too, when she was out.

✡✡✡

'Only me.'

'In here.' Breffni lifted the throw and draped it over the back of the sofa. As she sat up, yawning, Cian came in. 'What's up – are you sick?'

She shook her head, pulling her fingers through her hair to untangle it. 'I was just grabbing a quick snooze after Poll went up; I think Christmas has caught up with me.'

'Poor you.' He sat next to her and massaged her shoulders. 'Worn out looking after us all. Will I phone for a takeaway?'

'No – it's in the oven, all ready.'

He stood again. 'Well then, you stay there and I'll bring it in on a tray.'

She shook her head, smiling. 'No, I'll come out. I'm fine, honest.' She stood and put her arms around his neck. 'You're far too good for me – I don't deserve you.'

He considered, then shook his head. 'No, you don't. You

deserve someone a lot better-looking, and a damn sight more exciting; not to mention a bit skinnier.'

She dug him in the ribs. 'Stop; I'm serious; you *are* too good for me. And if I wanted a skinny man, I'd put you on a diet.'

He hugged her tightly, chin resting on the top of her head. After a few seconds of silence, he said, 'Bref.'

'Yeah?' She pulled her head back and looked up at him.

'Is it time to think about another baby?'

He felt her stiffen slightly – such a tiny movement; or maybe he imagined it – before she answered. 'Let's leave it a while; Poll's not out of nappies yet.' She watched him with those wonderful blue eyes.

He nodded. 'OK, if that's what you want.' He dropped his arms. 'Can I run up and say hi before she drops off?'

'Do; I'll dish up.' She stood in the middle of the living room and listened to his footsteps for a minute, staring off into the distance. Then she smoothed the cushions on the couch and turned towards the kitchen, wondering how long she could put him off.

✡✡✡

Laura smiled as the toddler wrestled with the bright red plastic cube, trying unsuccessfully to force it through the oval-shaped hole in the lid of the sturdy blue bucket. His face was screwed up with the effort, tiny pink tongue stuck out of the corner of his pursed lips. He suddenly lost his grip on the cube, which shot out of his fat little hand and bounced off Laura's shin before landing beside her.

'Upsadaisy.' Laura bent to retrieve it, then held it out towards the child. He looked from the cube to her face, then back at the cube, but didn't move to take it from her. His face was solemn.

She held it out further. 'Look.' He watched her, unsmiling, as she dropped the cube neatly through the square hole in the bucket lid. 'All gone.'

He looked down at the lid, lifted the bucket and gave it a clumsy shake, patted the top with a podgy palm. Then he picked up a round yellow shape from the collection beside him and banged it against the lid. He looked questioningly up at Laura, who put a finger on the round hole. 'There.' After a few attempts, he pushed the shape through the hole.

'Yah!' He grinned triumphantly at Laura. 'All don.'

She nodded, beaming back at him. 'All gone, good boy.' She picked up a green oval. 'Now, try this one.' She held it out to him and he grabbed it.

'Sorry; I'll take him out of your way.' The young mother – Laura presumed it was his mother – scooped him up and plonked him into a buggy, whisking the bucket out of his arms and replacing it on a low shelf. 'Off we go. Say bye-bye to the lady.'

He flapped cocktail sausage fingers at her and she smiled and waved back. 'Bye.' When they were gone, she picked up the bucket and opened the lid, and replaced all the brightly coloured plastic shapes inside. Then she walked to the checkout desk with it.

'I'll take this, please; it'll be perfect for my little boy. He's just beginning to handle things.'

'They're a great seller – very popular.' The assistant rang up the total. 'That'll be fourteen fifty please.' She wrapped the bucket as Laura rummaged in her wallet. 'Is he your first?'

Why did they always ask that? Laura shook her head. 'No, I've a little girl too, she's four. She'll be starting school next September.' Funny how much easier it got every time. Details just seemed to add themselves. Her son who'd just had his tonsils out. Her little girl who was going to her first birthday party. Her baby who was growing out of everything so fast.

It was all very, very easy.

What was more difficult was finding a place to store everything. When the drawer at home was too full for any more, she'd started filling a big cardboard box under her table at work – quite safe, the girls never went near each other's spaces – but that was full now too. She had to find more space. She wondered about the attic at home – it wasn't big enough to stand up in, no floor on it either, so they really didn't use it for anything. The only time Donal had been up was when they noticed the damp patch on the bedroom ceiling. A box up there would be quite safe.

Sometimes she wondered if Donal would understand. Wasn't she buying them for their baby, who would eventually arrive? Where was the harm in that? If she made up a few stories to amuse herself when she bought them, so what? That was only a bit of fun.

Only of course she knew that it wasn't; fun was the last thing it was. And of course she couldn't tell Donal; there was no way he'd understand that this was the only way she could deal with the heartbreak and frustration and rage. That every time she bought a tiny pair of woolly tights, or a vinyl read-in-the-bath book, it eased the terrible nagging hunger for a while.

She decided to forget the attic for the moment, get another cardboard box instead – it would fit under the studio table beside the first one. And she should be ovulating again in a week or so – maybe this time they'd be lucky. She clutched the bucket in its paper package and made her way back to the studio. She'd already missed the deadline for the first lot of schoolbook illustrations: better get a move on.

✡✡✡

Cecily held the glass out as Frank poured. 'Not too much; the bubbles go straight to my head.' She'd already had her usual gin and tonic before dinner, and a small glass of wine with the food; she wondered if the champagne was overdoing it. But as Frank pointed out, you couldn't celebrate the New Year without a drop of champagne. It wouldn't hurt, just this once.

'Ten minutes to go; I hope you have your resolutions ready.' Frank raised his own glass. 'To friendship.'

'Friendship.' Cecily took a tiny sip. It was deliciously cold, and beautifully dry. Frank had produced it unexpectedly after the meal he had cooked for her earlier. She'd been touched by clear signs that he'd given a lot of thought to the evening; a newly opened bottle of her favourite Gordon's gin, heavy linen napkins that she was sure he'd bought specially, Vivaldi on the stereo – she remembered him asking her about music at the last book-club evening. So thoughtful of him . . . what a surprise he was turning out to be.

And how astonishing to discover that she scarcely missed Andrew in the house, after all. If she were to be completely honest, she would have to admit that she quite relished the peace, the freedom of having the house to herself for the first time ever. Being able to buy the foods she wanted without having to worry about whether others would like them. Coming and going as she pleased, with no explanations to be given to anyone. No need to justify the evenings she was spending with Frank – two meals already in the little hotel outside the city, the third tonight, in his house.

She'd been slightly apprehensive at the thought of coming here – what if she bumped into Dorothy or Liam, just next door? Not that she and Frank had anything to hide, of course, but Cecily preferred to keep her business to herself. No need for anyone to know that they were spending time together, much less how much she was coming to enjoy it. To her relief, she'd met nobody on her way from the taxi to the door. And it had been dark when she'd arrived, so even if Dorothy or Liam had chanced to look out the window, they'd hardly have been able to recognise her.

Earlier, Frank had shown her his collection of books – rather haphazardly arranged on shelves in his sitting room, but interesting nonetheless. She commented on a few titles that sounded interesting, and he insisted on lending them to her. As he was packing them into a brown paper bag, Cecily's attention was caught by a framed photo on the mantelpiece beside the bookshelves.

'Was this your wife?' She was dark, and almost the same height as a younger Frank, arm linked into his, leaning slightly into him. Her other hand was raised to hold windblown hair away from her eyes.

Frank looked up from the bag and nodded briefly. 'That was about ten years ago.'

Cecily's gaze wandered to another framed photo, slightly smaller, yellowing with age. A boy of about ten or eleven held a little girl – eight? nine? – by the hand and beamed into the camera. She wondered if they were Frank's children: the daughter who had died and the son he had lost contact with. Better not to mention them – it might upset the evening. She looked more closely at the boy. Yes, definitely Frank's son; a strong resemblance there, the same chin, and eyes . . .

'Right; just time for a drink before dinner. Gin and tonic, I presume?'

She turned, smiled. 'Lovely.'

He served chicken fillets with a delicious buttery sauce, and stuffed tomatoes. When she complimented him, he admitted that his repertoire was extremely limited. 'Chicken or chops in the oven, wrapped in tinfoil, or a bit of grilled fish – that's about the extent of my culinary expertise. The sauce was the only one I ever mastered, so I serve it with just about everything.' Over cheese and grapes – another thoughtful touch; he knew she never bothered with dessert – they talked about gardens. She described her patio and shrubbery to him.

'I'm afraid I'm not very imaginative; maybe I could get you to have a look at it sometime?' She was cross with herself for how shy she suddenly felt; for goodness' sake, you'd think she was inviting him into her bedroom, instead of looking for a few names of shrubs.

He smiled, nodded. 'I'd be delighted.'

He told her about the orchard they'd had beside their house just outside Sligo. 'My father planted it when he built the house, apple and pear trees. It was great for the kids when they were growing up.'

Except that his daughter had never grown up. The first time he'd mentioned his children since that day in the café, when she'd felt trapped with him as he told her his story. She cut a piece of brie and wondered whether to pursue the topic – she would have liked to ask about his son – but then she decided that it was none of her business. If Frank wanted to tell her, he would.

Later, they counted down to midnight, and wished each other a Happy New Year, and Frank leant across and gave Cecily a chaste kiss on the cheek.

And just for a second, she felt disappointed. How ridiculous.

✡✡✡

'Happy New Year, Andrew.' Laura hugged her brother tightly. 'Let's hope it's a good one.'

'Without any fear.' Andrew hugged her back. 'Are you all right?' he said into her ear. 'You've been very quiet all night.'

'Fine.' She hadn't time to say any more before she felt someone's hands around her waist, pulling her gently from Andrew's embrace.

'Give me back my wife.' Donal turned her towards him and held her close. Andrew went to the stereo.

'You OK?' Donal spoke softly into her hair.

Why was everyone asking if she was OK? She pulled gently out of his embrace and gave him a bright smile. 'Fine – just a bit dry.' She held out her empty champagne glass. 'Fill her up please, chef.'

'Bottle's in the fridge.' Donal gave her a funny look before leaving the room. Laura shrugged; he was probably wondering if she'd make a fool of herself after too much bubbly. Burst out crying and tell Ruth and Andrew how much she wanted a baby. As if.

She turned back to her brother. 'Andrew, how did you escape from Mother tonight? I thought she'd have nabbed you and Ruth for a polite glass of champagne.'

Andrew shrugged, riffling through Laura and Donal's CD collection. 'I thought so too, but the last time I was talking to her, she mentioned she had plans.'

'Mother had plans on New Year's Eve?' Laura looked incredulous. 'What kind of plans could she have?'

Andrew shrugged again. 'Haven't a clue; she didn't say, and I didn't ask.' He considered. 'Maybe some of her book-club buddies were going lap dancing.'

From her armchair, Ruth giggled: she'd definitely had too much champagne; her cheeks were flushed and the line of blue she'd drawn under her eyes – not a colour Laura would have chosen for her – was smudged slightly on one side. 'Or maybe she has a secret lover.' As soon as the words were out, Ruth put a hand to her mouth and giggled again.

Laura burst out laughing. 'Doubt it; can you see my mother in a hotel room in the middle of the afternoon with a balding elderly gentleman?'

Donal came in and filled Laura's glass, then looked at the two giggling women. 'What's so funny?'

'Nothing; just some female rubbish.' Andrew held out his glass. 'Am I allowed some more?'

'Coming up.' Donal poured champagne into Andrew's glass.

Ruth turned to Laura. 'My husband is not amused.' She stood and walked unsteadily over to Andrew. 'Darling, are you not amused?' Her words had begun to slur very slightly. She chucked him under his chin. Laura watched her brother for his reaction. Ruth was definitely a bit more fun after a few glasses of not very expensive champagne, but Andrew had never enjoyed being teased.

He brushed Ruth's hand away. 'You're pissed, woman; go and sit down.' He said it mildly, with just the barest trace of annoyance, but Ruth's smile faded; she suddenly looked like she might cry.

'Andrew, lighten up – we were only joking.' Laura swallowed a mouthful of champagne, thinking: *He's probably annoyed at having his precious mother made the butt of our joke; pity about him.* She turned to Ruth; time to come to the rescue, as usual. 'I was hoping Breffni and Cian would make it in tonight, but Polly's running a temperature; Breffni didn't want to leave her.'

'Poor Polly.' Ruth went back to her armchair and sat down abruptly, still looking subdued. A little champagne sloshed over the rim of her glass and landed on her skirt. 'Oops.' She brushed at it absently.

Andrew took a CD from its case and bent to insert it. 'They don't last long though, do they? Temperatures in kids, I mean.' He slotted in the CD and pressed the 'play' button.

Laura looked over at him in mild surprise. 'Since when are you an expert in children's medicine?' Her tongue got tangled slightly in the last phrase – she probably shouldn't have any more to drink. Then again, it wasn't as if she was pregnant. And it was New Year's Eve.

Andrew shrugged. 'I'm not claiming to be an expert – I'm just saying, aren't kids always getting fevers?' He looked from Ruth, who wasn't looking back at him, to Laura. 'What's so strange about me showing an interest?' Lyle Lovett started to sing about a long tall Texan.

Laura tipped back her glass and drained it. 'You're right actually – Polly often gets a temperature, and it usually disappears very quickly. Pity it had to be today, though.'

She walked to the table and picked up the champagne bottle. 'Ruth?'

Ruth immediately held out her glass. 'Yes please.'

✡✡✡

'Happy New Year, darling.' Breffni dropped a kiss on Polly's head. 'Now, are you ever going to go to sleep for us tonight?'

Polly blinked, droopy-eyed, from her nest of sheets and duvet. 'Night night, Mama,' she said, yawning, thumb wandering towards her mouth. Her cheeks were still lightly flushed, but her temperature had dropped a couple of degrees since dinner. Breffni held her breath as Polly's eyes closed gently. Her rapid little breaths came softly and evenly; Breffni could smell the strawberry-flavoured toothpaste Polly insisted on using.

She tiptoed from the room, leaving the door ajar, and went downstairs to the sitting room.

Cian was just putting a tray with a bottle and three glasses on the table in front of the fire. 'Great – you managed to escape; I was going to relieve you if you weren't down when I brought this in. I take it she's gone off?'

Breffni nodded. 'Just about, thank God.' She slumped into the couch beside Mary. 'I could murder a glass of anything right now. How long to go?'

'Three minutes, just about.' Cian pulled the foil from the sparkling wine and began to ease the cork off. Breffni picked up the remote control and raised the volume a little.

They watched the countdown on RTÉ and exchanged hugs, and toasted absent friends, and shortly afterwards Mary disappeared off to bed. Cian put an arm around Breffni 'You're exhausted.'

She nodded. 'Wrecked. I'll sleep like a log.' As she tipped back her head and drank the last of her wine, Cian watched the muscles in her throat move, saw her hair fall back in a dark sheet behind her. If he lived to a hundred, he would never get tired of looking at her, of marvelling at the fact that this perfect creature had chosen to be with him, out of all the men she could have had.

Could still have.

She lowered her empty glass and he filled it again. 'Thanks. Oh, by the way, I might take a quick run into Limerick tomorrow afternoon.'

He looked at her. 'New Year's Day? Isn't everyplace shut?'

She shook her head. 'Not to shop – I thought I'd run in and see Mam and Dad for a couple of hours, and maybe meet Laura for a quick chat; they invited us in tonight, you know.'

He nodded. 'Yeah, you mentioned it.'

'I've a casserole in the freezer that'll just need to be heated up when I get back, so you can forget about it. And you'll have Mary to help you look after Poll – I invited her to stay for the day and have dinner with us tomorrow night.'

She put her glass on the table and leant back against the couch and closed her eyes.

He nodded again. 'OK.' He'd been quietly relieved when they couldn't go to Laura and Donal's tonight. Chances were the other two were going to be there too, and he really didn't relish another night in the company of Laura's brother – for whatever reason, he hadn't taken to Andrew when they met. Just one of those things, he supposed, although he'd rarely experienced it in the past; found most people no bother to get on with. But Laura's brother wasn't someone who left you feeling good after meeting them. And Ruth seemed very pleasant; funny that she should have gone for him . . . amazing how some couples ended up together, ones you'd never have said were suited. Like himself and Breffni.

He thought back, as he often did, to the first time he laid eyes on Breffni, almost eight years ago now. He'd been where he always was on Friday nights: sitting on a stool on the small stage of the slightly seedy Irish bar at the corner of Sixteenth and Valencia. His repertoire didn't vary much – mostly Christy Moore and Paul Brady, with a bit of the Beatles thrown in for fun – but he always went down well with the regulars, a mix of Irish and Scottish immigrants mainly. Cian enjoyed the few hours at Flaherty's on a Friday night: a nice change from the formality of his junior accountant's job in a downtown firm, where everyone wore suits, even in the hottest weather, and no one took longer than twenty minutes for lunch.

This particular Friday night was just like any other, until he lifted his head at the end of 'The Island' and saw what he thought was probably the most exquisite woman he would ever lay eyes on. And swiftly following on from that thought was another: she would never look twice at someone like him. Slightly overweight from sitting around in an office all day and going home to his mother's dinners; nothing to look at, with his round face and brown hair that, no matter how short he kept it, still stuck up just over his left eye – a cow's lick, someone told him it was called. All Cian McDaid had to recommend him was the fact that he was a half-decent guitar player; but so far that hadn't worked any miracles as far as the opposite sex was concerned.

And Breffni hadn't looked twice at him – not that night, or any of the four Friday nights that followed, until he screwed up his courage, in great form the night of his birthday, and stood beside her at the counter and offered to buy her a drink. And it had taken seven more Friday nights of him hovering at the edge of her group when he went on a break, and grabbing the chance, whenever it presented itself, to talk to her, before she'd asked him when he was going to take her out to dinner. And six months after that before they didn't end the night in separate beds.

And after hundreds of nights together, when she'd come home from her waitressing job one day to their small apartment and told him that she was pregnant, he'd felt such tenderness and love, and gratitude, that it was all he could do not to burst into loud, messy tears. He blessed the mischance that had created Polly, the precious miracle that he still couldn't believe was his, the answers to his secret prayers. What had he ever done to deserve her – this golden baby-child who eclipsed even his love for Breffni? Who caused his heart to stop with joy – he could feel the missed beat – when she smiled up at him, when he held her in his arms, felt her soft baby breath on his cheek, heard her gleeful chuckle.

Breffni had been adamant about contraception, insisted on a condom every time. Kept saying, whenever he brought up the subject, that they didn't want to complicate things with a baby.

'Am I not enough for you?' And every time she asked that, he thought *but it's the other way around*. When she trailed her fingers across his chest, looked up at him with the deep blue eyes he adored, he almost told her why he ached so much for a child with her: because he was terrified, since the day they'd moved in together, that she'd come home one day and say that she was leaving, that this had been a big silly mistake – look at her, for God's sake, and look at him. Cian clung to the hope that a child, their child, would somehow weld them together, keep Breffni from wanting more than good old reliable Cian McDaid – because how on earth could he possibly be enough for her?

And now that they had Polly, he realised that of course there was nothing – not an army of babies – that could guarantee that Breffni would stay. But now he also knew that he'd survive if she left him – because Polly would be his child forever.

He picked up the bottle, lifted it to the light to check the level. Breffni stirred beside him, opened her eyes, yawned.

'Hardly worth putting the cork back.' He divided what was left between their two glasses before lifting his. 'To Polly.'

She smiled, touched his glass briefly with hers. 'To Polly.'

✡✡✡

Laura slid over and ran her fingers lightly down Donal's back. He could feel her nails as they tapped softly along his spine and he shivered pleasantly, half-awake. She lifted her head and put her mouth to the top of his neck, just below his hair, then kissed her way across to a shoulder blade. He could feel the heat of her breath on his skin. His body began to respond, and he turned to face her.

'Good morning.' His voice was croaky with sleep.

'Morning.' She touched his lips briefly, then moved her mouth slowly down along his throat and chest, biting gently when she reached a nipple. He drew in his breath, put a hand on her waist and pulled her in close.

Afterwards, he twined his fingers through her tousled curls and tasted salt on her face, and saw the desperate hope in her eyes, and his heart cracked, like it always did.

✡✡✡

She was there before him; she never arrived this early. He parked right beside her car and practically ran into the hotel. She sat in an armchair by the window, watching without smiling as he approached. He dropped into the chair beside her and took one of her hands – cold – and brought it to his lips. 'Hey.'

She glanced quickly towards the reception desk, then back at him. 'I don't know if I can do this any more.'

It was like being blasted with a shower of icy water, just after stepping out of a steamy bath, all pink and puckered. He felt the shock flash through his body, something thumping down to land heavily at the bottom of his stomach. 'What?'

'It's too hard, I can't . . . we can't do it to . . . it's not right.' Her head drooped, hiding her expression from him. She pulled her hand from his and covered her face. 'I can't, I just can't . . . it's too hard. It makes me feel . . . we're hurting people . . .'

'No.' His head spun – whatever he said now could change everything. 'Listen . . . listen. Come to the room and we'll talk.' He spoke quickly and quietly; he marvelled that his voice didn't shake. He reached across and took one of her hands again, pulled it away gently from her face.

She shook her head, raised her eyes to his. 'If we go to the room . . . you know I can't resist you.' Her hand was trying feebly to pull away from his.

It was going to be all right. He held tightly to her hand. 'We're meant for each other; we need each other. I would die without you.' He watched her face soften, saw her exquisite eyes fill with tears. He wanted to put out a finger and catch one as it trembled on her lower lashes, bring it to his mouth and taste it.

He had to keep speaking, had to convince her to stay. 'It can't be wrong, what we're doing. It feels so right; you know it does. We belong together.' With each word, he could feel her drawing towards him. She blinked, and a single tear slid quickly down her face. Her hand rested in his, stopped pulling away. 'No one will ever know, I promise. No one will ever find out; no one will ever get hurt – we'll make sure of that.' He stood, pulling her gently with him. 'Come on.'

In the room, she wept against him, and murmured his name, and he kissed her tears and rocked her and told her he loved her.

✡✡✡

Ruth put the dish of asparagus on the table, hoping to God that she'd got it right. Imagine, thirty years on this earth and she'd never once cooked asparagus. According to the recipe – taken from page 68 of *Classic Dishes*, presented to her by Cecily when she and Andrew had moved out – the asparagus heads should be cooked in steam, and the ends in water. But it didn't tell you where exactly the water stopped and the steam began. Halfway up? An inch of water in the bottom of the saucepan? Ruth supposed it was asking for trouble, cooking something new for a visitor; she'd played it safe with the salmon steaks, bought already poached and ridiculously overpriced, but at least they'd be edible, and she knew Cecily liked salmon. And the baby new potatoes that some French farmer had managed to grow in January – they should be fine too. Which just left the asparagus.

Andrew picked up a few spears with the little tongs Ruth had bought the day before, and looked questioningly across the table. 'Mother?'

'Thank you.' Cecily accepted the asparagus and waited while Andrew served himself and Ruth. 'Well, this is nice; thank you both.' She picked up her water glass and looked from one to the other. 'I do hope you'll both be very happy here.'

'Thank you, Cecily.' Ruth smiled placidly at her mother-in-law. 'I'm sure we will.' She glanced at Andrew, cutting into an asparagus spear. 'Darling?'

He looked up. 'Sorry – I was miles away.' He lifted his glass. 'It's great to have you here, Mother; we must do it regularly, now that we've settled in.'

Just then, his mobile rang. He put down the glass and stood immediately, pulling it out of his pocket as he went towards the hall. 'Sorry about that; I thought it was switched off.' Cecily and Ruth exchanged a look as he left the room.

In less than a minute, he was back, without the phone. 'One of the lads from work, looking for a lift in the morning. His car is in for a service.' He took his seat at the table, and raised his glass again. 'Here's to my two favourite cooks; I'm a lucky man.' And he tipped back his head and emptied the glass. 'So, Mother, what do you think of our new home? Any decorating ideas for us?'

As Cecily responded, Ruth watched her husband with relief. He'd been so off-form lately, she'd wondered if this dinner was going to be a bit of a strain. Of course she should have trusted him – Andrew was well able to turn on the charm when he needed, especially for his mother.

She turned her attention to Cecily, who was looking out the window in admiration '. . . and I must say, the garden is going to be just lovely.'

Ruth nodded; she was delighted with the way the garden was shaping up. Frank was able to describe so clearly what was going to go where, she could almost see it. And he was full of ideas – camomile seeds scattered on the lawn, so when you stepped on it, you released the scent; lavender planted by the clothesline – 'I came across that in France once; gave the laundry a wonderful smell.' He talked about a winding path down to the shed at the end – 'and of course we must plant some bluebells around the tree' – and a display of wild poppies against the wall just outside the patio window: 'They look magnificent in bloom; a real talking point if you're sitting in the kitchen.'

Ruth must arrange for Laura to call around sometime when Frank was there; she was sure they'd get on. And maybe Laura would spot who Frank looked like – it was still niggling at Ruth; she was sure he reminded her of someone. She thought of asking Cecily if she'd ever felt that, but decided not to; it might sound a bit odd. And anyway, Ruth got the impression that Cecily hadn't much time for Frank – she probably never looked properly at him during the meetings. Pity – he was such a nice man, and Cecily could do with someone to take her out and about, now that she was living on her own. But of course they'd never be suited;

they were far too different.

Listen to her – she sounded like a matchmaker. She looked over at her mother-in-law's plate. 'Cecily, more asparagus?'

✡✡✡

Laura looked up as the waiting-room door opened.

'Now, Mrs O'Neill.' Dr Sloan's young receptionist – surely no older than sixteen – held the door open as Laura closed the magazine she hadn't been reading, and walked through. The urge to urinate was very strong; her full bladder ached dully. Dr Sloan smiled as Laura walked into the surgery.

'Good morning, Laura. All set?'

Laura nodded, forcing an answering smile, resisting the urge to say *I've been set for two years*. She wasn't nervous; she'd often given blood, so that test was nothing new. And the thought of an ultrasound didn't bother her; she'd seen pregnant women having them on TV – a kind of jelly spread on your stomach and a harmless-looking instrument moved backwards and forwards over it. There was nothing to be nervous about. Terrified of what might be revealed, yes. Nervous, no.

Donal had wanted to come with her, but she'd stopped him. 'I'll be in and out very quickly; there's really no need for you to be there. Anyway, you might need time off next week, so it's better if you go in to work today.'

If today's tests proved inconclusive, or didn't provide them with all the information they needed, Dr Sloan would have to perform a laparoscopy. She'd explained the procedure during their initial visit. 'It's a straightforward operation, takes about twenty minutes – just to check that there's no blockage in your fallopian tubes – but it does require you to have a general anaesthetic, so you'll need someone to bring you home when you wake up.' She'd looked enquiringly at Donal.

'He doesn't drive.' As soon as the words were out of her mouth, Laura regretted them. Somehow they sounded like an accusation; another crime that he was guilty of. *Won't give me children, won't drive me home.* And how ridiculous she was being now, making it sound like Donal was doing it on purpose – keeping a child from her just because he felt like it, just because he didn't fancy the thought of being a father. Anyway, it might turn out to be Laura's problem, not his at all. She put out a hand and grabbed his. 'But you'll come in with me, won't you, if I need a laparoscopy? We can get a cab home.'

Dr Sloan had shown them an x-ray of some anonymous woman's uterus, and pointed out the fallopian tubes – impossibly narrow, wiggly threads, hardly visible to Laura's searching eye. So that was the pathway for the egg; all the little turns and twists it had to wriggle through on its journey. So many potential obstacles to herself and Donal creating life . . .

She dragged her head back to the present, where Dr Sloan was releasing the air from the rubber strip around Laura's arm. 'Your blood pressure is down slightly, nothing to worry about.' She unwrapped the strip. 'You also look like you've lost a bit of weight since I saw you last. Is your appetite all right?'

Laura hesitated. 'I've a lot of work on at the moment – I suppose I don't always remember to eat properly.'

'Be careful; you need to keep healthy when you're trying to get pregnant. Make sure you have regular, balanced meals, plenty of green leafy vegetables. Did you start on the folic acid?'

Laura nodded.

Dr Sloan walked to her desk and pulled a pad towards her. 'Now, will you take a seat there for a minute?'

After writing rapidly on the pad, she looked up. 'Laura, there's one other thing. Your husband's semen analysis proved inconclusive. We'll need another sample, so maybe you can discuss this with him? I feel it would be better coming from you.'

'Inconclusive? In what way?' Laura's hands tightened on the strap of her bag.

'Nothing to get alarmed about – we just didn't get an accurate reading, or not one we were completely satisfied with. We need to do a repeat analysis, so we can be sure of our findings.' Dr Sloan paused. 'It's really not something you should worry about, not at this stage. Any number of factors can affect these tests – even a bout of flu from a few months ago. And if Donal prefers, he can produce the sample at home and bring it in to us right away; we'd need to get it to the lab within ninety minutes. Remember to abstain from sex for two days beforehand.'

Driving home, Laura tried to concentrate on the traffic, heavy as usual at this late-afternoon hour. A people carrier full of children drove through an intersection in front of her, seconds after her light turned green. Two cars cut ahead of her as she drove down Henry Street, causing her to brake hard. On the road out to Corbally, she was stuck behind a bulldozer as it crawled along uncaring, before mercifully turning in to a building site.

She was glad of the traffic, relieved not to be able to think, and worry, and despair. Not to be able to wonder, if it did turn out to be Donal, whether they'd survive – because of course they would. Nothing in this world, not even the thought of no children with him, could ever make her love Donal the tiniest bit less.

Nothing at all.

✡✡✡

Ruth dropped the magazines on the table and sat back, leaning her head against the soft plaid behind her. The carriage was empty so far; she closed her eyes and inhaled deeply before letting the air whoosh out of her open mouth. She wondered what the weather was like in Dublin, and imagined stepping out of Heuston Station in two and a half hours, hopping on the LUAS to Abbey Street, and then catching a bus home

She hadn't told anyone she was coming; she wanted to surprise them this time. Behind her closed lids, she imagined her mam's face when she walked in the kitchen door. Would Dad be around, or was he on early shift this week? If he was, she'd have to wait till he came in around two. She and Mam could have a cuppa; Irene might be around too, if Friday was her day off this week.

And she had the whole weekend. Three whole days, almost – she'd get the latest train back on Sunday. Andrew hadn't minded a bit when she brought it up with him.

'Of course go – why not? I'll manage fine.' He put his hands on her shoulders. 'Just remember to come back before you've spent all our money.'

She laughed. 'I'll do my best.' She'd said she was going to have a look in the sales for stuff for the house. She supposed she should be honest with him, give him the real reason, but she wanted her family to know first. Maybe that wasn't how it should be, but she didn't care. She'd tell them first, then come home and tell Andrew. He need never know that he wasn't the first to hear.

She opened her eyes – the carriage was nearly full now – and picked up one of the magazines as the train pulled slowly out of the station.

✡✡✡

'I was afraid you wouldn't come.' His head and one palm rested on her stomach; she felt the words as well as heard them. 'I wondered if you'd change your mind.'

Her hand twined through his hair. 'I thought about it . . .' She sighed deeply, and his head rose and fell again. 'But the thought of finishing it was . . . just not something I . . . but I wish it didn't have to be like this – it makes me feel so . . .' He waited, then he heard her breath catching. He lifted his head, moved up until his face was touching hers; her cheeks felt hot and wet under his. He kissed her eyelids, stroked her face from forehead to chin, wiped at the tears with his thumbs, whispered against her mouth.

'Shh . . . don't . . . don't be sad . . . you make me so happy . . . shh . . . my love . . . don't cry, please don't cry . . . how can it be wrong, when it makes us feel like this? We'll never tell, no one ever needs to know.' And as he spoke, as he said all the things he knew she had to keep hearing, she closed her eyes and lifted her hand to cradle his head, and after a while her tears stopped, and she whispered 'shhhh' and he stopped talking.

In the car park, they stood by her open door. A chilly wind was blowing; her dashboard clock showed five past five. He held her hand, pressed it against his side to keep it warm. 'Can you get away for a full night, soon?'

She looked at him in the orange light from the street. 'I don't know . . . it might be difficult.'

'Try. I love you.' He squeezed her hand and then walked rapidly towards his car.

On her way home, she thought about a whole night with him. Falling asleep beside him. Opening her eyes in the dark and reaching out and finding him there, waking him slowly with her hands and her mouth. She turned the radio up full blast and joined in when Billy Joel sang about an uptown girl.

Her eyes felt tight; when she rubbed them and licked her finger, she tasted salt.

✡✡✡

'Ruth, my dear, that's wonderful news.' Frank beamed at her with such obvious delight that Ruth wanted to hug him. She didn't, of course – what would the others think?

She contented herself with an answering smile. 'I know; I'm thrilled. I start on Monday.'

Valerie came over holding a homemade coffee cake, iced and sprinkled with chopped toasted nuts. 'Look what Dorothy brought; doesn't it look yummy? And what do you start on Monday?'

'My new hairdressing job.' Ruth took the cake and put it on the table next to a little dish of wrapped sweets.

Valerie's face lit up. 'Ruth, that's great – count me in for a cut and blow dry; I'm long overdue. Where's the salon?'

'On the Ennis Road – on the right as you go out from town, just past the school.'

'Oh I know that place; isn't that where you go, Mags?' Valerie turned to Margaret, just approaching with a small bundle of paper napkins. 'That hairdressers on the Ennis Road.'

Margaret nodded. 'Helen's place, yes. What about it?'

'Ruth has just got a job there; isn't that great?'

Ruth stood and listened, and answered questions, and smiled, and nodded. She felt like pinching herself – still couldn't quite believe that she was going to be working again. Earning her own money, meeting new people, going off in the morning like everyone else. Mam and Dad had been thrilled when she'd told them, and Andrew had seemed pleased too, when she broke the news to him – he said they should go out to dinner to celebrate. They'd have gone tonight only it was the book club.

And getting the new job had been so simple. Helen, her new boss, had been lovely when Ruth had walked in off the street, purely on spec; she didn't seem to mind chatting away to Ruth in the middle of putting in highlights.

'Isn't that a good one – you come looking for work just when I'm wondering where I can find someone. Here, Sal, give those to Ruth –' she pointed to the foil strips the junior was holding for her. 'She can do that while you make us a coffee, and I can give her the third degree. Milk and sugar, Ruth?' And just like that, Ruth was having her second job interview in Limerick. As she fed Helen the foil strips, she answered questions about her experiences in Dublin: the kind of training she'd had, the cutting and colouring techniques she was familiar with, the type of salon she'd worked in.

'Actually –' Ruth glanced around her '– it was very like this place.'

Helen laughed. 'What – you mean full of out-of-date mags and old geriatrics like Chris here?' She pointed her little brush in the direction of the customer she was working on, who couldn't have been more than forty.

Chris caught Ruth's eye in the mirror. 'Take my advice – get out while you can. I only come in here because I feel sorry for her. And because she's my sister-in-law.'

Ruth smiled at her, then turned back to Helen. 'I mean it was small and local, like this; everyone coming in knew everyone else, practically. And I knew them all too – I'd grown up close by. I loved it.'

And after a few more questions, Helen had offered to take her on; she was to start on Monday fortnight, when Carol was due to go out on maternity leave.

'It'll have to be on a trial basis, just until I'm satisfied that you can provide the goods; but if you're as experienced as you say you are, I don't see a problem. What do you think?'

'I think that's great; you won't be sorry.' Ruth had practically skipped home, hugging her news to herself. First a new home, now a new job.

All that was missing was a new baby. But that would happen too; she was working on it.

✡✡✡

For the past ten minutes, she hadn't dared to look at Donal. Just kept her eyes fixed on Dr Sloan's face, watching the gynaecologist's mouth opening and closing, searching her expression for clues as to what she was really thinking. The strain of keeping her own face neutral was causing Laura's whole body to feel rigid; her shoulders ached, her jaws were clamped together, her hands, so cold, clutched each other tightly in her lap. She wanted to hit something, hard.

She stopped listening to Dr Sloan talking about alternatives and new advances and plenty of options and high success rates. How could they be expected to take anything else in, how on earth would they ever be able to think logically, behave normally again, after the bombshell that had just been flung at them? Dr Sloan had been as tactful as she could, but every carefully chosen word had struck Laura with the force of a well-aimed lump hammer.

She forced herself to say it again in her head, feel how it sounded: maybe it wasn't as bad as she was making it out to be. *Donal's sperm count is so low as to be practically non-existent.*

She felt her stomach tighten even further; every part of her seemed to be clenched. *Short of a miracle, my husband is never going to make me pregnant. We'll never have a child together*. She willed herself to shut up, clutched her hands tighter, wanting to moan out loud. What made it even worse was that there seemed to be no obvious cause – no previous injury, no heavy drinking, no anti-depressants.

'Nothing that we can point to as the culprit, I'm afraid.' Dr Sloan's voice sounded so normal – so . . . *controlled*. As if she was discussing the latest peace plans in the Middle East, or the rise in prices since the Euro. Not that it mattered really; whatever way she said it, it came down to the same thing – that the only way Laura would ever get pregnant was with another man's sperm.

Suddenly Laura couldn't bear it; couldn't sit there for another second pretending not to be falling apart. She stood abruptly, almost knocking over her chair, vaguely aware of Donal looking at her as she turned and fled. Outside, she took huge gulps of air, hanging on to the low railing that bordered the small front garden, feeling her legs like jelly under her.

'Darling.' His hands came around her waist from behind, his body pressed tightly against hers. For a second she resisted, then she leant back against him, still breathing in deep, shuddering breaths. She felt like she'd never get enough air.

'It's not the end of the world . . . there are things we can do –'

'Stop – I can't. Just stop.' She pulled away from him and started walking fast, out the gate. 'I'll see you at home.' Her legs, still shaky, propelled her forward somehow; away from their car, which she'd parked just outside.

She hadn't a clue where she was going. He didn't follow her, and she didn't know how that made her feel.

✡✡✡

Frank lowered the menu and took off his glasses. 'The steak tonight, I think – one of the few dishes I haven't sampled yet.' He waited as Cecily closed her menu. 'And for you, my dear?'

'I think I'll go for the cod again; they do it so well here.' She watched as he refilled her water glass; she never had wine when they ate out, not wanting to when Frank didn't. He filled his own water glass and then lifted it towards her.

'To our very pleasant nights out; I look forward to them.'

She smiled and raised her glass. Funny, a few weeks ago, she'd have found a remark like that slightly laughable; she'd have scoffed at it. Now, it sounded oddly endearing. Brian hadn't been much of a man for compliments, or sweet talk; he'd always been completely silent during their lovemaking. But it had never bothered Cecily; she'd never craved the kind of talk that she regarded as romantic nonsense – never been that way inclined herself. So it took her by surprise now, how much she enjoyed Frank's easy way with words. He managed to make her feel . . . appreciated in some way, without sounding in the least bit corny or sentimental.

She looked forward too to their weekly nights out – always, except for New Year's Eve, in the same little hotel. They were beginning to be recognised by the waiters; were usually seated at the same corner table, which afforded them a good view of the main dining area without being easily visible themselves. Not that they were hiding from anyone, of course not. Still, it was preferable to be . . . discreet. No need to parade their outings, to risk their becoming the talk of the book club.

At the last meeting, Cecily had deliberately seated herself between Emily and Dorothy, with Frank at the far end of

Margaret's big old dining table. For a while, she wondered if he'd noticed; he chatted animatedly with Ruth when the general discussion had ended. But as she got up to leave, he looked over and smiled a warm farewell.

Tactful. Sensing that she didn't want their friendship broadcast. On impulse, Cecily reached across the table now and touched Frank's hand lightly.

'I look forward to seeing you too.'

And Frank's face softened as she drew her hand back.

✡✡✡

'Oh for God's sake, leave me alone, would you? I'm all right.' Laura swung around, tea towel in hand, and glared at Donal, then turned back to the draining board and picked up another cup and started drying it furiously.

Donal stood for a few seconds, hands dropped to his sides. When Laura continued to ignore him, he swung on his heel and went into the sitting room. After a while Laura heard him rustling the paper.

She sighed deeply and dropped the tea towel, then planted her palms on the draining board and looked out through the window into the black night. The light from the kitchen showed the outline of the stone-flagged patio, the red-brick barbecue that Donal had spent one full summer putting together, beyond it the big old wooden bench with the lovely wide armrests that they'd found in a scrap yard, and that Laura stained with a fresh coat every September. The narrow strip of earth running along beside the fence, just beginning to push up the tiny spears of future daffodils and tulips. The two dwarf apple trees they'd planted at the bottom of the garden, leaf buds still tightly closed now. The rotary clothesline in the opposite corner, red plastic peg-container hanging lopsidedly from one metal arm.

She remembered a barbecue they'd had for her birthday last August. The girls from the studio had come with their husbands, and Breffni and Cian, and a few of Donal's workmates, and a couple from across the road who'd invited them to their house-warming a few weeks before. Andrew and Ruth had been in Dublin, making last-minute wedding arrangements, and Laura had persuaded herself that her mother really wouldn't be bothered attending a party where she'd be the only one of her generation there.

They'd spread rugs out on the grass, and brought the stereo speakers out the window, and served Pimm's, just to be posh, and wine spritzers when the Pimm's was gone. The weather had almost obliged; one quick shower had them grabbing the rugs and scurrying for cover, but then the sun had reappeared, and Donal had spread plastic sheets on the wet lawn, so the rugs could be flung down again.

They'd feasted on Donal's blue-cheese burgers and chicken kebabs and Cajun cod. Afterwards, Donal had put whole unpeeled bananas onto the barbecue, and when they were black all over he had split them open and sprinkled the hot flesh with cinnamon and slathered them with rum mascarpone cream.

When everyone had gone home, Laura and Donal had lain out on a rug and watched the stars flickering on, and listened to Crowded House, and Donal had given her the new Norah Jones CD and the gold daisy in a silver vase on a slender silver chain that she'd admired one day, months ago, when they'd been out together.

He'd knelt on the rug behind her and fastened it around her neck as she leant back against him. 'Happy birthday, flower girl.'

And after that they'd gone to bed and made slow, tender love, and Laura had prayed that it would happen that night, on her twenty-ninth birthday night. But of course it hadn't.

She brushed away the tear that had come out of nowhere, and picked up the tea towel again.

✡✡✡

'Hello?'

'It's me.' Her voice was low, and hurried. 'Can you talk?' He glanced around, checked that no one was close enough to hear.

'Yes. Anything wrong?' Was she having second thoughts again? What they had was so precious . . . and so fragile. He was aware, all the time, how easily he could lose her, and the thought terrified him.

'I – I do want to spend the night with you.'

He was flooded with relief – could feel it coursing through him. 'Wonderful.' He'd do anything, tell any number of lies. 'Let's see what we can arrange then, yeah?'

'Yeah . . . it might take a while to organise.'

He could wait forever. 'OK – see you Thursday; we can talk about it then.'

And she was gone. He pressed the off button and held the phone against his chest. The whole night together. Dinner first in the restaurant, like a real couple. Then a second bottle of wine in the room. No rushing, no checking the time. Candles maybe, maybe a bath . . .

Someone called him from across the room and he turned slowly, hoping to God he looked normal.

✡✡✡

Ruth pushed the basket towards Laura. 'You've had no garlic bread.'

Laura had taken only a small portion of lasagne, and loaded the rest of her plate with the mixed leaf salad, and as far as Ruth could see, she had yet to take a single bite. She *had* managed two glasses of wine, though, while Ruth was still on her first.

'Thanks.' Laura smiled and took a slice from the basket and put it down beside the untouched lasagne. As she picked up her fork again – just to push the salad around, it seemed – Ruth glanced down the table. Breffni and Donal were arguing about the right way to make trifle, and Cian was watching them with a small smile on his face. Andrew had gone out to the kitchen to get another bottle of wine.

Donal was shaking his head at something Breffni had just said. 'You have to let the sherry soak into the sponge first; and then the jelly has to be half-set before you add it, otherwise the whole thing will just go mushy.'

'Not if you use those bourbon biscuits, or whatever they call them – the hard, fingery ones. You have to pour the jelly over them while it's still hot, to soften them up a bit.' Breffni was leaning over the table towards Donal – Ruth wondered if she was aware of how low her top was; Donal's eyes kept wandering down to the blue pendant that swung between her breasts. And the tiny skirt she was wearing – of course Breffni got away with it, with those legs, but still . . . Ruth would have been mortified to go out in such revealing clothes. She was certainly managing to distract the men – Donal was almost gaping openly at her cleavage, and Ruth had spotted Andrew looking at her too. Funnily enough, Cian was the only one who didn't seem to notice Breffni's get-up. Used to it, Ruth supposed.

Donal was shaking his head again. 'No – the sherry will soften the biscuits enough. If you pour the hot jelly over, it dilutes the sherry taste too much. And you're not supposed to use those biscuits anyway; proper trifle is supposed to have cake in it, preferably day-old.'

Breffni made a face, fingers playing with her pendant. 'Yeuk – who wants a trifle with stale cake in it? Even if it is loaded with booze. And speaking of which –' She held out her glass to Andrew, who had just come back with the wine.

He poured, and she smiled up at him, still fiddling with the pendant – couldn't she see that that was just drawing more attention to her low neckline? 'Thank you, darling.'

Andrew smiled back, a little stiffly, Ruth thought. Probably embarrassed at her obviousness. He held the bottle over Laura's glass. 'You're not driving tonight, are you?'

Laura stretched out her empty glass. 'No, I'm not. So yes please, I will. Cheers, everyone.' Without looking around the table, she lifted the glass and took a sip.

'So, Ruth, how's the new job going?' Ruth turned towards Donal with relief; he either hadn't noticed Laura's odd manner, or he was choosing to ignore it. And that suited Ruth just fine.

'Great – I'm really enjoying it.' And she was; Helen couldn't have been better to work with – never pushed her weight around, never let things fluster her. Someone coming into the salon for the first time would find it hard to decide who the boss was. After two weeks in the job, Ruth felt totally at home there – and her new-found independence had given her the confidence to invite everyone around for the long-promised dinner.

She'd played it safe with lasagne, one of the few dishes she felt capable of getting right. The recipes in Cecily's cookbook were all too posh really – she didn't want the others to think she was trying to show off. To go with the lasagne, a couple of packs of mixed leaves that you emptied into a bowl with some nice dressing. And the garlic bread wrapped in tinfoil, eight minutes in the oven. The dessert was safe too – you really couldn't go wrong with apple and sultana crumble and a jug of cream. They'd stocked up on wine and beer, and the fire had been on all day, so the room was lovely and cosy when everyone arrived.

They really couldn't have done more – so why was the evening not going well? Laura had hardly spoken since she'd arrived late with Donal – nearly three quarters of an hour late, leaving Ruth to juggle with the oven temperature: down so the lasagne wouldn't dry out, up again when it was time to put the garlic bread in. Trying to talk to Breffni and Cian when they arrived had been difficult too, with Ruth having to pretend that she didn't notice Andrew ogling Breffni – and who could blame him? She was relieved, though, to see that at least he wasn't drinking an awful lot this evening. That would have been all she needed – a drunken husband, on top of everything else.

And then, when Donal and Laura finally arrived, with apologies and a bottle of expensive-looking wine, Ruth suspected that they'd had a row: Laura looked tense, and Donal seemed much more subdued than usual. And both Breffni and Laura were drinking like fishes now, with Laura looking gloomier as the evening wore on. Altogether, the atmosphere struck Ruth as distinctly strained, and she'd so wanted this meal – their first time entertaining as a married couple, apart from the few dinners with Cecily – to be a success.

But she'd better keep trying; she was the hostess, after all. She pasted a smile on her face and looked over at Laura. 'We must get together for lunch soon – we haven't done it for ages.'

Laura nodded. 'Mmm – but won't it be harder to arrange now, with you working too?'

'Yeah – it'll have to be on my day off, which I can gather is generally going to be Wednesday. How's *your* job going – are you still on the schoolbooks?'

Laura nodded again. 'It's slow going: there's a lot to be got through. And it's fairly tedious, but I shouldn't complain. The money's good – or it will be, whenever I get it.'

No doubt about it, Laura had definitely lost weight. Her black top seemed to emphasise the drawn look on her face, the hollows underneath her cheekbones; her arms in the elbow-length sleeves looked thin. As Ruth watched, Laura picked up her wine glass again and took a long swallow. Then she turned and called down the table. 'Andrew, would you ever take off Leonard Cohen? He's making me suicidal.'

Andrew smiled. 'Blame your husband – he chose it.'

'Oh right; I should have known.' Laura propped her chin in her hand and studied Donal. 'He likes singers his own age – makes him feel less like a dinosaur.'

'Better than being like a kid.' Donal was smiling, but the room was thick with tension. Ruth's heart sank; she wished this miserable night was over. She stood and began to collect the dinner plates, not knowing how to fix things. Andrew got up too, and went to the CD player. 'Now children, stop squabbling. Uncle Andrew will put on something nice and cheerful, and if you're very good, Auntie Ruth will get the dessert she's been baking all day.'

And somehow, it helped. They all laughed; even Laura managed a feeble grin. Breffni got up and reached for the plates nearest to her. 'Here Ruth, I'll give you a hand.' Ruth noticed Andrew's eyes on her again as she walked around collecting plates. In the kitchen, Breffni put her bundle down on the table and then folded her arms, watching Ruth as she opened the oven door. The crumble looked good, nice golden top.

'So – new house, new job. Everything going well for you.'

Her tone of voice was perfectly pleasant, but Ruth felt a stirring of familiar alarm. Even though Breffni had been so helpful when the house move was on, and had chatted away with Ruth whenever they'd met for coffee with Laura since then, Ruth still didn't feel totally at ease in her company; particularly now, on her own with her. And Breffni had had a fair bit to drink tonight – who knew what she might come out with?

Ruth forced a bright smile. 'Yes, everything's fine, touch wood.' She took her oven gloves from their hook and reached in to take the apple crumble from the oven.

'All you need now is a new baby.' Breffni began fiddling with her pendant again, watching Ruth intently.

'Mmm.' Ruth willed her smile to stay in place as she put the crumble on the table and turned to get the jug of cream from the fridge.

'Are you trying?' Perfectly pleasant, eyebrows raised enquiringly.

God, what gave her the right to be so personal? Ruth gripped the cold handle of the jug and looked Breffni straight in the eye.

And her courage failed her. 'Er, we haven't really talked about it.' She wished to God she had the guts to tell Breffni to mind her own business. Why couldn't she stand up to her – why had she never been able to stand up to people like Breffni? She pulled a ladle out of a pottery jar and plunged it into the crumble, then turned to get the bowls.

'Here, I'll take in the cream for you.' Obviously Breffni was bored with Ruth now, wanted to get back to the men.

Just then the kitchen door opened and Laura's head appeared. 'I had to escape; they started talking soccer.' She came in, glass in hand, and spotted the dessert on the table. 'Apple crumble; lovely.'

And Ruth knew she'd take a tiny bit, and poke it around in the bowl for a while, and leave it entirely uneaten.

✡✡✡

'Hi. Sorry nobody's here to take your call. Leave a message for Laura or Donal, and they'll get right back to you.'

'Laur, it's me. Hope the head is OK – mine is splitting, as usual. We hadn't a chance to chat last night – haven't had a proper gossip for ages. You must be working your fingers to the bone. Anyway, call me. Polly says hi.'

'Message for Laura: this is Dan Holloway at Thompson Publishers. I need to speak to you urgently – we really can't extend your deadline any further; our printers are putting a lot of pressure on us. Please call me immediately you get this message. Thank you.'

'Laura and Donal, this is Maria Sloan. I'd like to meet with you again, if you feel ready to talk. Laura, I hope you're coming to terms with the situation – please bear in mind that there are lots of options available to you. Do call my receptionist to arrange an appointment.'

Laura sat on the stairs, leaning against the banisters. Every time the phone rang, she turned her head in its direction, waiting for it to stop, listening to the different voices as they left their messages. The belt of her old blue dressing gown trailed down on either side. Her head felt vaguely itchy. After a while she turned and went back upstairs, slippers flip-flopping. Back to the drawer, because that was all she had now.

✡✡✡

Ruth glanced at the photo on the mantelpiece, then peered more closely. The boy looked about twelve, the girl a bit younger. They must be some relations of Frank's – maybe even himself as a boy, with a younger sister? No, the photo didn't look old enough for that. She turned to the one beside it; now that was definitely a younger Frank, and the woman at his side was surely his late wife. Of course – the children must be his own, the daughter who died and the son . . . she studied him closely again. Yes, the resemblance was there, definitely.

'That's Don and Catherine.'

Ruth started; she hadn't heard him coming back in. 'Sorry – I didn't mean to be nosy . . .'

'Not at all – they're there to be looked at. God knows, I look at them enough.' He held out the gardening book he was carrying. 'Here, take this home and have a browse through it; you might get some ideas for that side bed.'

They were still planning the garden; filling in the shrubbery, deciding what flowers to plant in the new beds, what to choose for the containers that Ruth was going to get for the little stone-paved patio. At least they'd made a start on the end wall – clematis and honeysuckle, and some everlasting sweet pea. Ruth took the book and looked at the riot of colour on the cover. Soon Andrew and herself would have something like that to look out at, to sit in and be soothed by on warm summer evenings. To watch the children climbing the tree, Andrew laughing at Ruth's nervousness when one of the children went too high.

She pulled herself back to the present. 'Thanks a million, Frank – I'll bring it to the meeting on Thursday.' Since she'd started working, she wasn't at home any more when Frank called around to work in the garden, unless he caught her before she went out to do the big weekly shop on her day off. And Frank had never even met Andrew, not once. He never came around at the weekends when Andrew was there, said he preferred to leave them alone then.

He'd met Laura though. She'd dropped by on Ruth's last day off, delivering a dish that Ruth had asked to borrow for the lasagne, and Frank had happened to be there, having his usual tea in the kitchen.

Ruth had introduced them. 'Frank's new to Limerick too; he came down from Sligo a few months ago. He's in the book club.'

Laura nodded. 'You'll know my mother so – Cecily O'Neill.'

'Indeed I do.' Frank's smile was warm. 'A lovely lady.' He turned to Ruth, missing Laura's raised eyebrows. 'So your husband is Laura's brother.'

Ruth nodded. 'Yes. We're a bit like spaghetti, really – all tangled up together.' She looked at Laura. 'And isn't Donal from Sligo too?'

Laura nodded. 'But he's been in Limerick for over twenty years; ever since his parents emigrated to Australia.' She looked out the window. 'This is going to be lovely; is that clematis at the bottom?'

They'd chatted briefly before Laura left, pleading work. Ruth had begun to worry about her sister-in-law; what on earth was up? She wondered if it could be the job that was causing the lines of worry on Laura's face, the weight loss. She hoped it was nothing more serious, nothing wrong between Laura and Donal. Maybe she'd talk to Andrew about it later.

As she walked home from Frank's, Ruth thought ahead to the night out she and Andrew had planned – a visit to an Indian restaurant in belated celebration of Ruth's new job. Belated because Andrew had been working overtime lately – some big project that she didn't even try to understand. No matter – they were finally going; and she was looking forward to having Andrew all to herself for the evening.

Since she'd started working, they'd hardly had a night on their own. When Andrew wasn't working late, it was Cecily coming over for dinner every Tuesday, or the book club, or the awful dinner with the others last week . . . it would be nice to be just the two of them tonight. And afterwards, maybe they'd make love – they hadn't done that in a while either. Andrew hadn't initiated it, and Ruth couldn't imagine making the first move. But maybe tonight, after a nice meal and a few glasses of wine, she'd find the courage, if it looked like nothing was happening . . .

She'd wear her black suit – Andrew liked her in that. And the lacy burgundy-coloured underwear her sisters had got her for Christmas; she'd been saving that for a special occasion.

Yes, definitely tonight. She turned into Farranshone with a light step.

✡✡✡

Donal hardly felt the impact; nothing hurt as he sailed through the air, almost enjoying the feeling of weightlessness. Then the wet road slammed up to meet him, and a lot of things hurt. Everything around him seemed to be floating gently. He tried to get his feet under him to stand up, and when that didn't work, he planted his hands on the ground and pushed. Bad idea. A sharp pain shot up from his right elbow, and that arm immediately buckled, ramming him down on the ground again. He groaned softly.

'God, are you all right?'

He looked up from his prone position into the frightened face of a middle-aged woman. 'I'm so sorry, I – I never saw you, you seemed to appear out of nowhere – are you hurt?' She was the first person he'd ever seen actually to wring her hands. He wondered if she could be his mother; now, what had she looked like again? His mind didn't seem to be working – everything felt scrambled when he tried to think. Like scrambled eggs. He giggled, then winced when his ribs hurt.

'Don't move, stay there, I've called an ambulance.' Another voice, from behind Donal. He attempted to turn his head to see who was there, and then thought better of it. Someone pushed something soft under his head, causing his neck to twinge sharply; someone else covered him with something warm that smelt of perfume. He was dimly aware of voices, car doors slamming, someone speaking agitatedly. He closed his eyes and settled down; might as well let them get on with it. Just a little snooze and he'd be fine.

'Wake up . . . can you hear me?'

Something was hitting his cheek. He opened his eyes; he seemed to be in the back of a van; somewhere too near a siren was blaring – why didn't someone switch it off? A man in a bright orange jacket stopped slapping Donal's face and leant over him. Donal smelt mint. 'Can you hear me? What's your name, son?'

Son – was this man his father? 'Donal.' At least he could talk, even if he suddenly didn't seem to be able to do much else.

The man's anxious expression cleared slightly. 'You were knocked down, Donal. Apparently you ran a red light on your bike. You're lucky the driver wasn't speeding.' He paused. 'You had a few drinks this evening, Donal, I'd say.'

Donal attempted a smile; he must smell like a brewery. 'A few.'

'Are you having any trouble breathing?'

Donal took an exploratory breath; his ribs protested faintly. 'Not too bad.'

'Good; now try not to move about; we're headed for St John's, so it won't be long.'

Donal wondered what St John's was: a hotel maybe. That would be nice, a nice soft bed with clean sheets to go back to sleep in. Room service – some chicken for Dad and himself. 'Thanks.' He closed his eyes again, and immediately the man started tapping his cheek again and said, 'Don't go to sleep. Wake up, Donal. Open your eyes, son.'

✡✡✡

It wasn't until much later, long after the meal and the wine, lying contentedly in Andrew's arms and listening to his steady breathing, that Ruth thought of Frank's son again. Don, wasn't it?

She wondered idly how old he would be now. Did he ever think of his parents? With a shock, she realised that he probably didn't even know that his mother was dead. She supposed he knew about Catherine's death – he didn't look that much older than her in the photo, and if she was only twelve when she died, he'd have been in his mid-teens at the most – surely whatever had caused him to lose contact with the family had happened later than that.

So sad . . . she wished again that she could do something to help Frank – but what? If his son had wanted to find him, he could have, even after Frank had left Sligo; presumably some people up there would have a forwarding address, or there'd be some relatives he could contact, surely. It must be easy to find someone in a place as small as Ireland. Then again, the son might not even be living in Ireland any more – or he could be dead, like his mother and sister. She still wondered who Frank reminded her of; when she looked at him, it was as if something was nagging at the back of her mind, waiting for her to realise . . . she must remember to ask Laura if she thought Frank looked like anyone they knew, now that she'd met him too.

Andrew stirred, and Ruth waited until he'd settled again before putting her hand back on his stomach. Tonight had been lovely . . . just like she'd wanted it to be. They'd both drunk a little too much with the meal, getting nicely mellow, laughing at silly things. In the taxi, Andrew had put an arm around her shoulder, lips against her forehead, and Ruth had turned her face up to his, stroking his thigh gently. At home they'd gone straight upstairs, and he had lifted her top over her head and she had unzipped her skirt, feeling a bit brazen in her new underwear, letting his hands move over her body as she began to unbutton his shirt.

And even when he fell asleep immediately afterwards, Ruth wasn't put out. Nothing could ruin this night for her. She sighed deeply and stroked his stomach gently. He loved her, of course he did. He wasn't regretting their marriage – it was just settling into the new house, getting used to life as husband and wife. Anyone would find that hard to do.

Everything was going to work out fine; she knew it was.

✡✡✡

'Hi. Sorry nobody's here to take your call. Leave a message for Laura or Donal, and they'll get right back to you.'

'Laura, it's Andrew. Listen, I've just got a call from St John's – they tried to get hold of you. Donal's been in an accident; he was knocked off his bike. I haven't any –'

He heard the phone being picked up. 'Oh God, is he OK?'

'They didn't tell me anything – I'll come and get you now and we'll go to the hospital together.'

'No, that'll take too long. I'll drive myself.'

'Laura, hang on – that's not a good idea. Laura?' But she was gone.

✡✡✡

'Hello?' Cian's voice was slurred with sleep. Was it the middle of the night? Laura had no idea.

'Cian, it's Laura – I need to talk to Breffni.'

Mercifully, he didn't ask anything. 'Hang on.' She heard muffled thumps – steps on stairs – and an agonisingly slow few seconds (minutes? hours?) later, the phone was picked up.

'Laura? What's –'

'Donal's been knocked down, he's in St John's. I'm just going there; can you come?' It spilt out in one rapid breath.

'Oh God, I'm on my way. See you there.'

✡✡✡

'The thing that probably saved him from much worse injuries – and you needn't quote me on this – was the fact that he had a fair amount of alcohol in his system.' The doctor looked from Andrew to Laura. 'He didn't tense his body when he hit the ground, so apart from the broken arm, and a fractured collarbone, he got off pretty lightly really – a couple of bruised ribs and a few cuts here and there.'

'And he's been checked for any . . . internal injuries.' Andrew had an arm firmly around Laura's shoulders – she was quite sure she'd have collapsed in a heap on the grey carpet tiles without it.

Thank God he'd got to the hospital just after her. She clung on tightly to his jacket, willing the doctor to shut up and take her to Donal.

'No internal injuries; we've done all the tests, and he seems fine. Obviously we'll keep him under observation for the rest of the night, and we'll review his situation in the morning.'

'You know he's allergic to penicillin?' She found her voice from somewhere, but didn't recognise it when it came out.

The doctor nodded. 'Don't worry – we saw the bracelet.'

And suddenly she couldn't wait any longer. 'Please, I want to see him.' Her whole body felt as if it were shaking.

'Of course.' The doctor walked ahead of them down the corridor. 'He's on a trolley, I'm afraid – the beds we have are all in use – but he's been sedated, so he's getting some sleep. Don't be alarmed at the cuts; they're all pretty superficial.'

And there he was, lying on his back, hooked up to some kind of beeping machine, bruised and bandaged. And asleep. The broken arm, plaster-casted from wrist to elbow, lay on top of the sheet that covered him. All his knuckles were grazed. He looked pale, and sad. His stubble stood out starkly against his white face. Laura put out a shaking hand and stroked the cheek that hadn't a gash.

She blinked hard, took a deep breath and turned to Andrew. 'I'll stay with him. You go home.'

'No, I'll stay.' They were whispering.

Laura shook her head wearily. 'Breffni is coming; I'll be OK.'

Andrew's arm was still cradling her shoulders. 'Well, I'll stay until she comes; she might be delayed. I'll wait for her outside – give a shout if you need me.' And without waiting for a response from her, he walked off down the corridor.

The doctor left her, promising to send someone with a cup of tea, and Laura was alone with Donal, finally able to let out the tears that had been threatening since she'd heard Andrew's voice on the answering machine. She leant over him and let them come, and they spilled onto the sheet and onto his sad, battered face.

'Sorry . . . I'm so sorry . . .' The tears flowed out and she wiped them from his face with her fingers. 'It's all my fault, I'm sorry . . .'

His eyes fluttered open, and his face creased awkwardly into a faint smile. 'Hey.' His voice was hoarse.

She made no attempt to stop crying; she didn't think she could stop if her life depended on it. 'I'm sorry . . .' She gulped the words out through her sobs. 'I've been such a bitch; this is all my fault . . .' The tears plopped onto his good hand as he lifted it to touch her face.

'Hey – I'm the one who should be crying. Look at the state of me.' His words were slurred.

She knew he was trying to make her smile, but it only brought more tears. 'You could have died . . . you could be dead now.' She put a hand to her mouth, letting the tears run over it.

'Shh – you'll wake the nurses; they're trying to sleep. I'm fine, just a bit battered. Serves me right for getting legless.'

Still her tears poured out. 'You wouldn't have got legless if I hadn't driven you to it . . . I've been a right bitch to you.' She wiped her wet face and sniffed noisily, rummaging in her pocket for a tissue.

'Use your sleeve – or the sheet.' Donal reached for the hand nearest to him, gave a weak grin. 'See? Made you come back to me.'

She laughed, half-hysterical with relief and shock. 'Stop joking about it.' She held on to his hand tightly. 'You did make me come back though.' She'd come so close to losing the best thing in her life; served her right for being so wrapped up in herself, so sorry for herself. Allowing her obsession to take over, blinding her to the precious thing she already had. Pushing him away whenever he tried to get near. Saying the most horrible, bitchy things; ignoring him, even. She'd shut him out, blamed him for her unhappiness, when it wasn't his fault – there was nothing he could do about it. It was his unhappiness too, wasn't it?

He groaned quietly, and she clutched his hand. 'Are you OK?'

He closed his eyes. 'Don't suppose there's any chance of an Alka-Seltzer? My hangover's started.'

And somehow, that made her cry all over again.

✡✡✡

'He's fine; no serious injuries, thank God.' Breffni pulled the red strip from around the packet of digestives and shook a few onto the plate in front of her. She was still in her dressing gown, up late after the broken night.

'Thank God is right. I don't know how anyone cycles around that city – I'd be terrified. I wouldn't even chance Nenagh.'

Breffni grinned as she pushed the plate in front of Mary. 'With all due respect, Granny, I think you'd terrify the drivers far more, whizzing around Nenagh on a high Nelly.'

'Biccy?' Polly eyed the plate hopefully, chubby fingers gripping the edge of the table.

'Oh go on, then.' Breffni handed her a biscuit. 'Just one – dinner is coming. What do you say?'

'Ta.' Polly grabbed the biscuit and disappeared under the table.

Breffni sniffed the air cautiously, then made a face. 'Sorry, Mary – I think she forgot the potty again. This training seems to be lasting forever.'

'Ah, not to worry. They all seem to do it in their own time. I know all of mine were different; and Polly is still very young.'

'Hmm, I suppose. C'mere, you.' Breffni ducked under the table and came up with a munching Polly in her arms. 'Did you forget your potty?'

'Potty.' Polly looked at Breffni and munched on, crumbs scattering over her blue and yellow top.

'Yes, lady – potty. You'll have to do potty – Granny doesn't want to mind a smelly girl.' She turned at the door. 'Back in a minute, Mary – sorry about this.'

'Not at all, dear – has to be done.' Mary took a biscuit and bit into it as she listened to Breffni's steps on the stairs. Polly was chattering away as usual. Such a happy child, always laughing.

Mary hoped that whatever was bothering Breffni didn't communicate itself to the child before it got sorted out. Little children were often like old people that way; they could sense things other people didn't.

But of course it would get sorted out, whatever it was. Everything did, sooner or later.

✡✡✡

'Ruth, would you give Sal a shout and ask her to take Mairead over to the basin please? I'll be finished with Caroline in a minute.' Helen had to raise her voice to be heard over the noise of the dryer she was aiming at the newly cut, glossy blond hair of her customer.

'Right.' Ruth turned towards the door that led into the back of the salon. Sal was sorting new stock, coming out only when they called her to wash hair or sweep up.

Three months into the job, Ruth still looked forward to going in every day. She'd got to know most of the regular faces at this stage, although she still mixed up the odd name. No one seemed to mind though; people obviously looked forward to their visits to Helen's. Everyone seemed in good humour, sitting under dryers or waiting to be washed, or cut, or highlighted. And they all seemed to know each other; conversations constantly flew around the salon.

'Helen, would you ever invest in some up-to-date magazines – I'm sick of reading about last year's scandals.' This from a plump, dark-haired woman on the couch – Ruth thought her name was Shirley, or maybe Stacey.

'Last year's – that's a good one. I just read about Charles and Di getting married.' A voice from a head that could barely be seen under one of the big dryers – Mrs McCoy from next door, who'd been Helen's very first customer. Ruth marvelled that she could hear anything under there.

'Listen, you lot – you're lucky I have any mags at all, the pittance you pay me.' Helen held a section of hair out with her brush and aimed the dryer at it. 'If I was in the city centre, I'd be charging twice as much.'

'And paying twice as much rent.' Shirley/Stacey again, rummaging through copies of *Hello!* on the coffee table. 'Oh look, here's one that's only six months old – wonderful.'

Helen looked across at Ruth. 'Listen to them – they walk out their doors and they're here in less than a minute. They get top-class service, free coffee, and all the latest neighbourhood news, and they're still not happy.'

'You should take on a man, spice the place up a bit.' Mrs McCoy winked at Ruth as the dryer was lifted from her head. 'We could do with a bit of hanky-panky in here, couldn't we, girls?' Ruth smiled; Mrs McCoy was eighty if she was a day.

And on it went, laughter and cups of coffee, and Saturdays so busy sometimes that all you had for lunch was a sandwich grabbed in the back room when you had a minute, and people rushing in, wanting a wash and blow-dry without an appointment, and Helen always squeezing them in. Ruth loved every minute, and thanked her lucky stars that she'd ended up there.

And it was good at home too. Frank had almost finished in the garden, and declared himself well pleased with how it was turning out. 'You'll have a fine bit of a garden in a couple of years' time, when those shrubs start to mature a bit, and the climbers take off. The tree adds a bit of character too.'

'D'you think there's any hope of apples?' He'd told her he thought it was a Cox's Pippin.

'Hard to say; it looks quite ancient. And of course it would depend on whether there are other trees in the vicinity. But we'll live in hope.'

The house was practically fully furnished – Ruth had picked up a few nice bits in the Dublin sales – and they were getting to know a few of the neighbours too. Mrs O'Brien, on their left, limited herself to a nod and a brief smile if they passed each other on the path, but the Phelans on the other side were much more chatty. Betty Phelan arrived during their first week with a still-warm apple tart, and Jim, her builder husband, had already offered them the use of his van if they had any furniture shifting to do.

Farranshone was so handy for town too – every place was so close by in Limerick, compared to Dublin. And even the weekly visit to Cecily's, and her mother-in-law's return visit, seemed to have got easier. Was Cecily mellowing, or was Ruth becoming more used to her?

Or was it simply that, for the past week, nothing at all was bothering Ruth?

✡✡✡

'I think I can manage next week.'

His mouth felt dry. 'Really?' Next week, after an eternity of waiting and hoping. After several attempts to slot all the factors into place, to leave no loose thread that could be unravelled by a curious partner.

She nodded. 'If nothing happens in the meantime. I've made . . . arrangements for Wednesday night.' She took the hand she was holding and kissed the tips of his fingers, one by one. 'The whole night.' She sucked his little finger gently, and he closed his eyes and turned to press against her, ran his other hand along the back of her thigh.

She slid his finger from her mouth. 'Will you manage it?'

'Yes.' Yes, yes, yes. If he had to crawl here on his hands and knees, if he had to swim the Atlantic in a hurricane, he'd manage it. 'We can have dinner downstairs first.'

He felt her stiffen slightly. 'Do you think that's wise?'

'Why not? We're miles from anyone we know. I want to show you off to a crowd of perfect strangers.'

He heard the smile in her voice. 'You just want to get me sloshed so you can have your wicked way with me.'

He grinned and opened his eyes. 'Er . . . darling, you may not have noticed, but we've been having our wicked ways with each other stone-cold sober for quite a while now.'

'Mmm . . . we have, haven't we?' And she ran her nails lightly down his back, and he started to breathe faster.

✡✡✡

'So, how are you enjoying having the house to yourself?' Emily used the side of her fork to cut through the layers of custard and flaky pastry on the plate in front of her. A creamy-yellow blob of custard came oozing out the edge.

'Very well; in fact, I'm really surprised at how much I'm relishing the freedom.' Cecily paused to sip her Earl Grey tea, and then lifted her serviette to dab lightly at her lips. She marvelled that Emily could eat that sugary, fatty creation – even enjoy it, by the looks of her – and still keep her perfect figure.

'Yes, it's nice to have a bit of space to yourself. I must say, I'm quite happy when Derek heads off for his evening of bridge; thank goodness he's given up asking me to take it up.' Emily's narrow, meticulously plucked eyebrows rose. 'I couldn't think of a duller way to pass the time.' She forked a small portion of pastry to her lips.

'They say it's very interesting, the ones who play it. There must be something in it.'

'Well, if it amuses them, I suppose – oh lord, don't look now –' She broke off and ducked her head behind a hand, and Cecily risked a small look behind her.

Immediately Emily hissed, 'Don't – he'll spot us.'

'Who are you – oh.' He was standing at the checkout, paying his bill. Not looking remotely in their direction; and now walking away from them, towards the door of the coffee shop, tucking his wallet back into his jacket as he went. Cecily liked that jacket – the dark green in the small check suited his colouring.

She turned back to Emily. 'He didn't see us.' Something made her add, 'Anyway, I thought you had no objection to him.'

Emily picked up her fork again. 'Not at the book club, I suppose. He actually seems to have some worthwhile opinions from time to time. But my dear –' her eyebrows travelled again in the direction of her hair, '– he's not really our sort, is he? I mean, seriously, could you see yourself socialising with him?' Her laugh tinkled. 'It would be a bit like Lady Chatterley and her groundsman.'

And Cecily watched her put another dainty piece of pastry into her elegant mouth and thought, *what a silly creature.*

✡✡✡

'I'm so glad you decided to come back and see me.'

Laura smiled at Dr Sloan. 'We've spoken about it, and we feel ready now to . . . explore the alternatives.' Beside her, Donal gave her hand a squeeze, and she returned it. 'We're wondering about . . . a donor.'

Dr Sloan nodded. 'Yes, that's the direction I would be recommending. There's a high success rate, although it could take some time – you could be looking at between five and ten treatments before you get pregnant. On the plus side, donor insemination is quite cost-effective, and it's a simple enough procedure . . .'

As the gynaecologist continued, Laura glanced over at Donal. The bruises on his face had all but disappeared, and the cut on his cheek was healing nicely. His arm was still in a cast – it was due to come off in a couple of weeks – but otherwise, he was pretty much back to normal.

And thanks to the shock of the accident, they were pretty much back to normal too. Back in that place they'd been after he'd proposed, when they were everything to each other. When her thoughts were full of him, even when he was with her. And the second time round, it was even better.

She didn't deserve him; but mercifully, he'd stayed. And now they'd work it out, she was sure. Today they were taking their first, shaky step. And while the thought of being inseminated with another man's sperm, of creating a baby with a stranger, still made her stomach lurch with disappointment, she'd cope. *They'd* cope. She had to focus on the baby – picture herself and Donal raising the child that would be legally his. And hers. *Her baby*.

She thought of the drawer of tiny clothes at home, and the boxes under her desk at work, and her heart lifted. They'd cope. Whatever it took, they'd cope together.

✡✡✡

As she took the white envelope, Ruth looked questioningly at Andrew. He smiled and shook his head. 'No hints. Open it.'

She laughed in delight – she loved surprises – and looked at the front. Blank, no clues there. Turning it over, she put a finger into the small opening at the edge and slid it across. The vellum came apart raggedly. She put in a hand and pulled out four thin pieces of blue paper. *Gate Theatre: Admit One*, she read on the top one. *April 22nd, 8.00pm*. The date was for the following Wednesday night. She flipped through the other three tickets – all the same night, four seats in a row.

'What's all this?' She looked up at him, the smile still playing on her lips. 'Theatre tickets – in Dublin?'

Andrew shrugged his shoulders. 'A surprise, a belated present for the new job, a moment of madness – call it what you like. I thought you were due a trip to see the family; and I'm sure you can persuade the three of them to go to the play with you.' He pointed at the tickets. 'It's Brian Friel – you like him, don't you? And I assume your boss will let you off a bit early to get the train up; you work through enough lunch breaks there.'

He seemed almost nervous – did he think she wouldn't like the present? She kissed his cheek. 'Darling, thank you so much, that's . . . a lovely thing to do – and yes, I'm sure Helen will let me off early – I'll just have to change my day off from Wednesday to Thursday.'

'What?' He looked at her in dismay. 'I thought your day off was Thursday – that's why I booked them for Wednesday night – damn.'

He looked so crestfallen, Ruth wanted to laugh. Trust him to forget which day she had off – he really could be awfully absent-minded sometimes. She smiled up at him. 'Don't worry – I'm sure it won't be a problem. Helen won't mind me changing, just for one week. She's so easygoing.' She looked down at the tickets again. Dear Andrew – he'd been so thoughtful; and *The Faith Healer* was one of her favourite plays. Mam and Dad would be delighted with the night out – and Irene too, she was sure.

A thought struck her. 'Why don't you come too? We could go with Mam and Dad – Irene wouldn't have to go – or we could get an extra ticket for her. You could get Thursday off, couldn't you?'

He shook his head. 'I'd love to, but I can't; it's going to be mad at work all next week – the auditors are due and it's all hands on deck. I'll probably be working late a couple of nights as it is.'

'Oh, right. Well, no harm – we'll certainly use them ourselves.' She put her arms around him. 'Thanks, darling, it was very sweet of you. I'll talk to Helen tomorrow.' She kissed his cheek. 'Now, be quick if you want a shower – dinner's ready.' She listened to the running water upstairs – was he whistling? She smiled as she took the potatoes over to the sink to drain, and thought of going up to Dublin again, much earlier than she'd expected.

Then another thought occurred to her: she could tell them when she was up. A bit sooner than she'd planned, but she didn't think she could meet them and not say it. She imagined their reactions, and her smile widened.

But she wouldn't tell Andrew yet. She wanted the moment to be just perfect when she did that.

✡✡✡

Laura sat back and studied Breffni's expression. 'Stop looking so shocked.'

'Sorry – I'm not shocked really . . . well, no, actually I am.' Breffni leant forward, elbows propped on the table. 'I had no idea, Laur – you never said a word.'

'I know, I . . . just couldn't. It was the one thing I couldn't bring myself to tell anyone – least of all someone with a baby, I suppose.'

'But this is me; I'm not anyone – and I'm not just "someone with a baby".'

'I know.' Laura leant towards her. 'Look, don't be hurt. I didn't even talk about it to Donal for ages, which was pretty pathetic, when you think about it. It's not as if he wasn't involved.'

Breffni took Laura's hand. 'I'm not hurt – I'm sorry. I'm supposed to be your best friend. I should have guessed.'

'No, don't be daft – how could you? It's not something you can figure out – no outward signs to be seen. Although sometimes I felt that everyone must guess, it felt so important to me. I'd see all these babies everywhere I looked, and I'd wonder if the mothers knew how jealous I was of them.'

She was so relieved to be able to talk about it at last. It was as if a giant stone had been lifted off her, and she could breathe happily again after years of gasping and choking. She picked up a slice of pizza and bit into it, relishing the sweetness of the pineapple and the creaminess of the warm mozzarella – even her appetite had come rushing back. She'd put on two pounds in a week.

'So – what's the next step then?' Breffni emptied the last of her beer into the glass. 'Have you any timescale?'

Laura chewed and swallowed. 'Actually, it could start quite soon; within a few weeks, if everything goes according to plan.'

'God – that quick? You mean, you could be pregnant in a month's time?'

Laura laughed at her excited expression. 'Calm down, will you? In theory, yes, I could get pregnant the first time; but the gynaecologist warned us that it could take much longer – as much as ten tries, which would be ten months.'

'But she's saying that you will conceive eventually?'

'Well, I suppose nothing's certain, but I seem to be functioning normally – ovulating and everything – so there's no reason why I shouldn't get pregnant. I suppose I've as good a chance as anyone now.' Laura picked up her beer glass. 'Better make the most of this, while I still can.'

'Absolutely – in fact . . .' Breffni raised her empty bottle and held two fingers up to the barman, who nodded over at her.

'Just a quick one, so – I've to go back to work.' She'd phoned the publishers and crawled a bit – used Donal's accident as part of her excuse, which she felt slightly guilty about – and managed to get one last extension on the deadline, and since then she'd been working flat out to get the illustrations done. She picked a pineapple chunk from the last slice of pizza. 'So, lady of leisure, what are you doing for the rest of the day?'

Breffni shrugged. 'Oh, no big plans. I'll shop for a bit, and then call over and see Mam and Dad for tea. I've told Cian I might even stay the night – Dad hasn't been that well lately, and Mam could do with a break. Granny Mary is sleeping over with Cian and Poll, just in case.'

'Well, give a ring later on if you're staying in Limerick – I could call over and see your folks. It's ages since I met them.'

'Actually, Laur, I might not, if you don't mind. If Dad isn't feeling great, I'm hoping Mam will take an early night with me there. And to be honest, I could do with an early night myself – haven't been sleeping all that well.'

'Oh, poor you. Well, tell them I said hello.'

Then the beers arrived, and Phil the barman, who knew Laura from coming in for lunch, distracted them for a while.

✡✡✡

Paul looked up as the kitchen doors opened. 'Hey, the warrior returns.' He walked over and clapped Donal on the back. 'How're you feeling?'

'Grand – never better.' And he did look good. The cuts had healed, and the plaster cast was finally off – which meant that he could cycle again, and cook again.

And Laura was happier, which was all that mattered. The haunted look he'd tried not to see was gone from her eyes. She was eating properly again, and working again. And they were OK again.

He still felt like a failure, and a fraud. Still hated that it was his fault she'd had to go through so much – and that she would never discover the whole truth. Hated that he could never tell her, never. Whatever happened in the future, whatever joy, or fresh sorrow, lay ahead of them, she could never know.

It was something he'd have to live with; and he would live with it. He'd managed to bury it deep, years ago, and he could shove it way down again now, and never think about it any more. He'd survive.

And this time next year, incredibly, he might be looking

forward to becoming a father. After he'd accepted, years ago, that it could never happen to him. How lucky was he?

'Right; time I started earning my keep around here.' He grabbed his apron from the hook and followed Paul over to the stoves.

✡✡✡

And Ruth, on the train to Dublin, suddenly looked up from her magazine and said 'oh', and stayed staring straight in front of her, mouth slightly open, eyes unblinking, for a long time after that.

✡✡✡

Frank placed his knife and fork side by side on his plate, empty except for a sprig of dill. 'Well, I'm glad you persuaded me to try the fish; it certainly was delicious.'

'You should listen to me, Frank; I'm always telling you.' Cecily smiled across at him, and Frank thought again how attractive she was when she forgot to keep what he privately called her 'correct' face on.

'And how was your lamb?'

'Lovely.' She put down her cutlery and dabbed at her lips. 'Very tender.'

She hadn't mentioned seeing him in town the other day; he might wonder why she hadn't made her presence known. She'd left the place herself as soon as she could after that, making some excuse to Emily about expecting Andrew to call around. Imagine being so snobby – *not our type*, indeed. What gave Emily the right to pass judgement on such a kind, caring man? Cecily wondered what she had ever seen in Emily, with her notions of grandeur.

She glanced around the room as Frank looked at the dessert menu – such a sweet tooth he had; thank goodness he'd long since given up trying to persuade her to have something too. She'd never had much of a taste for sweet things, even as a child. The only –

Her thoughts came to a sudden halt as a man walked into the dining room. He was immediately approached by a waiter, who exchanged a few words with him before leading him to a table by the window, on the far side of the restaurant from where Cecily and Frank were seated.

Andrew. What on earth was Andrew doing out on a Wednesday night? Hadn't they told her at dinner the evening before that Ruth was going to Dublin today? Maybe he was meeting someone from work, grabbing the chance while he was free – but what had brought him out to this hotel, half an hour from the city? She saw him glance casually around and lowered her head quickly, took up her water glass and sipped.

'Would you like anything else, dear?' Frank, attentive as ever.

She shook her head, keeping it turned as much away from the front of the room as possible. 'No, thank you.'

As Frank looked down at the menu again, she dared a quick glance over. Andrew was looking out the window, chin on hand, elbow on the table. A menu sat unopened in front of him. Waiting for someone, surely.

And as Cecily watched, Laura's friend came in and walked straight over to his table. And in front of the entire restaurant he stood and kissed her deeply, hands cradling her head, before helping her off with her coat.

And Cecily, dumbfounded, thought, *so that problem wasn't solved, after all.*

✡✡✡

'Laur? Glass of red?' Donal's voice floated in, on top of a spicy smell that was making her mouth water. He was doing his own take on a creamy mushroom stroganoff, full of spinach and paprika and toasted flaked almonds, and chunks of strong red onions. She loved when he ignored the cookbooks and went with his instincts – so far, they hadn't failed him.

She dropped her brush into the pot of green-grey water and picked up a rag. She thought she'd heard the sound of a bottle popping open a while ago; and a glass of full-bodied red would go down a treat right now. 'Mmm, yes please.' Just one more day should finish it; thank goodness she'd made this last deadline – she knew she wouldn't have got any more time. It had meant working all hours, bringing stuff home to do in the evenings, which she usually tried to avoid, but it would be worth it.

Donal was being brilliant; insisted on doing all the cooking so she could concentrate on the illustrations. Washed up too, wouldn't hear of her lending a hand. She thought again of how close they'd come to disaster, and shuddered. Never again. Whatever happened, she'd never again jeopardise what they had together.

Her period was due any day now. She smiled at the thought that she was actually looking forward to it, instead of hoping against hope that it wouldn't arrive. But this time was different; the sooner it started, the sooner they could start calculating, and working towards her first treatment.

'Half an hour to dinner; hope you're hungry.' Donal put a glass of wine on her desk, well away from the paraphernalia, and looked at the almost-completed illustration in front of her. 'That's great.'

She dug him gently in the ribs. 'You always say that.'

He caught her hand and pulled it around his waist. 'That's because it's always great.' He kissed the top of her head. 'Half an hour, I said.'

'It smells fantastic.' She pulled her hand back and reached for the glass, sipped at the wine. 'Mmm, that's nice.' Then she took the brush out of the water, picked up a tube of yellow paint.

'That's thirty minutes we have to wait.' He was still standing beside her. 'Everything's cooking away, no need to keep an eye on it.'

Keeping her eyes on her page, she began to smile slowly. 'OK, fine.' She squeezed half an inch of yellow onto her saucer, dipped the brush in, swirled it around.

He began to massage the back of her neck gently with one hand. 'Yessir, thirty whole minutes. Nothing to do but wait.' His voice was slow, almost a murmur. He placed his own glass next to hers and began kneading the sides of her neck with both hands. They felt warm and strong; she turned her head slightly to accommodate his touch. 'Just wait, that's all.' He started to whistle along under his breath to the Coldplay CD on the stereo.

She laughed softly, dabbing yellow into the little girl's dress. 'Donal O'Connor, I'm busy here.' But she didn't want him to stop – she could feel her muscles relaxing deliciously.

'I know.' He stroked out towards her shoulders now, thumbs circling steadily. 'You just carry on; don't mind me.' Lazy circles, all around her shoulder blades. She breathed deeply, relishing the sensation.

'I know what you're doing, and it won't work.' She arched her back slightly, allowing him to knead more deeply. 'You're not going to distract me.' She added yellow dots carefully to the ribbon in the girl's hair.

'Me? Distract you? I've no intention of it.' He brought his hands back to the base of her skull and began kneading deeply up under her hairline. Slow, lazy circles.

She took another deep breath, dipped her brush back into the water. 'Stop it.' But she was still smiling, her head dropping slightly as he pressed up under her hair in a slow steady rhythm.

'Stop what?' He pushed her hair to one side, then bent and put his mouth to the top of her neck, one hand still massaging her skull. 'I don't know what you mean.' She felt his tongue lightly on her skin; his free hand dropped down, crept around her waist, began to inch up under her top. His breath was hot on her neck. 'You just carry on – don't let me disturb you.'

She dropped the rag she was holding. 'Oh God, OK, OK, I give up.' She stood and turned around to him, laughing. 'You're insatiable.'

'And you're so easy.' He pulled her after him, towards the couch. 'Now, we've got twenty-five minutes left; let's see what we can do.'

✡✡✡

'I'm home.'

Polly looked up, dropped her Lego with a clatter, and slid off her chair. 'Mama.' She toddled rapidly towards the kitchen door as Breffni came in and scooped her up.

'Hi Pollywolly. I missed you.' She buried her face in the blond curls, and Polly giggled, squirming. 'Tickle.'

'Down you go; make me something nice with your Lego.' Breffni deposited her back on a chair. 'Hi, Mary – everything go OK?'

'Fine; but you look tired. Sit down and I'll get us a cuppa.'

Mary filled the kettle and lit the gas under it.

Breffni stayed standing, watching Polly's attempts to build a Lego tower. 'We had a late night – I stayed talking with Mam till all hours.'

'How's your Dad?'

'Fine, really. I was glad to find him as good as I did; the way Mam was talking, I thought he'd be worse. But he was up out of bed when I arrived, talking away.'

Mary smiled. 'That's great; he's on the mend so.'

Breffni nodded. 'Yeah. He had a fine tea as well, so the appetite is coming back.'

'Good.'

Breffni turned towards the hall. 'I'd better just give Cian a call, tell him I'm back.'

When the door had closed behind her, Mary put two cups and a jug of milk on the table, then opened the press where the biscuits were kept. Breffni was looking a lot more contented this morning; maybe all she'd needed was a good chat with her Mam. She should go and see her more often, if it cheered her up.

Breffni came back in from the hall and beamed at her. 'Isn't it a gorgeous day?' She sat beside Polly and picked up a Lego piece. 'Now, let's see what we can make here.'

✡✡✡

When the phone on his desk rang, he knew it was her. His heart leapt.

'Hello?'

'Andrew, I've got your wife on the line.' Disappointment flooded his body. As he waited for Ruth's voice, his grip tightened on the receiver. *Pull yourself together*.

'Andrew?'

He made a supreme effort to sound cheery. 'Hi, darling – you're back then.'

'Yeah; I just got in the door.'

'Well, did you enjoy it?'

Her voice was enthusiastic. 'It was great; and the others loved it too. Thanks so much, darling.' There was a pause, then she asked, 'What time are you going to be home?'

An image of Breffni lying naked beside him the night before flashed into his head. Tonight he would be making small talk with Ruth. 'Not sure . . . about six, I'd say.'

'OK – I'll aim for dinner at seven then. Will you bring a bottle of wine?'

Funny – she didn't usually look for wine in the middle of the week. 'If you like, yeah. Red or white?'

'Red, please. That nice South African one we had at your mother's the other day, if you can get it.'

'OK . . . see you later then.'

After he hung up, he dropped his head into his hands and pressed the heels of his hands against his closed eye sockets. If anyone saw him, they'd assume he was taking a break from the screen; they all did that every now and again.

And she was there in the darkness, smiling at him. Bewitching him. All his senses responded; he could smell her, taste her. Stroke her perfect skin. His own skin rose with goose pimples at the memory of the night. At the sound, still echoing in his head, of her whispering 'I love you' for the very first time.

And at his grateful promise, in response, to leave Ruth for her.

✡✡✡

How long had Cecily been standing there? If anyone saw her, gazing through the window, they'd probably assume that she was thinking about the garden, maybe searching for the first petunia bud in the window box. Or wondering if she should prune the shrubs now, or leave them alone till later. No one would guess that she didn't even see the garden – wasn't remotely interested in what was happening out there. It could have shrivelled up and died for all she cared.

She wondered if Frank had noticed anything. He'd probably been slightly surprised when she told him, after he'd practically finished his slice of lemon cheesecake, that she'd changed her mind – she would like a glass of wine, after all. It must have sounded a little peculiar to him: she never had wine on their nights out – it wouldn't have felt right, with Frank not taking a drink – and ordering a glass of wine when she'd already finished her meal was certainly not the done thing. But it was the only thing she could think of that would delay their leaving. Frank knew she never had tea or coffee that late at night, except for herbal tea, which the hotel didn't provide. And at all costs they mustn't leave the table; she couldn't face them, not until she had decided how to cope with this shocking discovery.

So she and Frank sat on, presumably having some kind of conversation, although if her life depended on it now, she wouldn't be able to recall a single word. While she had attempted – she must have attempted – to behave with a semblance of normality, her thoughts were racing: questions were whirling around in her head. *When did it begin again? Am I the only one who knows about it? And what in heaven's name can I do about it this time?*

She watched them finally leave the table – mercifully, they hadn't lingered – and she watched Andrew's hand reach out and pull Breffni close to him as they walked from the restaurant. When Cecily and Frank left some time later – she'd drawn her glass of wine out as long as she possibly could – there was no sign of Andrew and . . . that creature.

Cecily's mouth curled now at the thought of Breffni. Her daughter's best friend from the time they could walk, playing in each other's gardens, going off to school – and later town – together, disappearing upstairs when they were older, to laugh at Cecily behind her back, you could be sure. Cecily had never trusted that lady, all innocent smiles and flicking her hair back and '*Yes, Mrs O'Neill*' when you met her, but Cecily had seen her, giggling with Laura at the carefully planned birthday parties, ridiculing her neat little sandwiches, mimicking Cecily's polite way of eating when they thought she wasn't looking. Oh yes, Cecily had known girls like that when she was young – smart madams who thought they were entitled to whatever they wanted. Hussies who could charm the birds off the trees with a bat of their eyelashes, who imagined the rest of the world existed for their amusement.

Oh yes, Cecily knew the type.

And then, when Laura and her smart-alec friend began to go to the tennis club hops – what rows *that* had caused between Cecily and Brian – it wasn't long before a string of young fellows started turning up, sniffing around Laura's friend like cats in heat, walking her home at some ungodly hour. Cecily had seen her passing the house, wrapped around some spotty boy, giggling like an imbecile, allowing him to grope her when they stopped at the gate – disgusting. Laura, of course, would have been home at a reasonable hour – Cecily had managed to ensure that, at least – but there seemed to be no such curfew in the other house.

The business with Andrew had been inevitable, of course;

Cecily had seen it coming a mile off. He was so handsome, so charming – she knew it was just a matter of time before that hussy tried to get her claws into him. The way she'd sidle up to him, put a hand on his arm, brush her hair off her face, or twirl it around her finger as she spoke to him – in a way, it was almost a relief when he finally brought her home to dinner, their so-called 'relationship' made official.

Cecily didn't hold it against Andrew in the least – what was he do to in the face of such blatant temptation? Mind you, it had taken a lot of persuasion on Cecily's part – far more than she'd needed in the past – to convince him that that girl was all wrong for him. Andrew had resisted his mother's arguments for once, insisting that Cecily didn't really know Breffni, that once she got to know her, she'd see . . . Cecily had almost laughed in his face at the thought of their ever being friends. But she hadn't laughed; she was too frightened at the notion of losing him, of having him turned against his mother by that sly missy.

So she'd kept up her arguments, being careful not to let her aversion to that creature show – she must seem to be quite impartial, at all costs – and in the end, thank heavens, he'd seen reason and finished with her. When Breffni had gone back to the States, Cecily had felt relieved; now Andrew would get over her – he'd really been quite smitten, silly boy. And then, before he'd met someone suitable, she'd returned, unmarried and pregnant – another scenario Cecily had seen coming a mile off. But the father seemed to be standing by her – probably thrilled with himself, poor fool – and they settled far enough away for it not to be a worry. And then Ruth had come along, and she'd been perfect for Andrew, and Cecily had made sure that she stayed.

And now, when everything should have been safe, that woman had somehow managed to bewitch Andrew all over again; turn his head with her whorish ways. Probably bored with her own wimp of a partner. Cecily had met Cian once at Laura and Donal's house – he hadn't had a lot to say for himself. Nothing much to look at either. And she seemed to remember a bit of a weight problem; obviously didn't bother looking after himself. So the little tramp had decided to spice things up a bit, go after Andrew again – never mind that he was married now, or that she was a mother. No, none of that would have bothered her. She'd batted her eyelashes at Andrew, used her vulgar prettiness to flirt like mad with him probably, when poor Ruth wasn't looking. What man, let alone a healthy young man like Andrew, could be expected to resist temptation like that? Everyone knew that men were weak, for goodness' sake. It was up to the woman to be strong, to show moral courage if she was attracted to a married man. Of course, that was assuming that the woman in question had any morals to begin with.

And now, what was Cecily to do? Because she had to do something; that was clear. It was up to her, as Andrew's mother, to save him, and to save his marriage. She owed it to poor Ruth, if nothing else.

She wished she had someone to turn to for help – but of course that was out of the question. This wasn't something Cecily intended discussing – with anyone. God alone knew what people would make of it; she'd be the talk of Limerick if it ever became public knowledge. She could imagine Emily relishing the drama of it all, gossiping about it with her silly friends, delighting in Andrew's fall from grace: '– and my dear, if you heard Cecily talk about him, you'd think he was a god.' No, that was not going to happen. Cecily was not going to let that happen.

Somewhere during the long sleepless night that followed her awful discovery, Cecily had come face to face with the distasteful possibility that Andrew had really fallen for this woman – that he might even imagine himself in love with her. So if Cecily managed somehow to bring an end to it, he would be devastated. And if he ever discovered that she'd had a part to play in it, he would undoubtedly hold it against her. But how strong would his resentment be? Might it cause him to turn away from his mother completely? Cecily wasn't blind to the irony; all the years of making sure that he didn't end up with the wrong person – all her efforts to ensure that no woman took him away from her – and now, if she succeeded in getting rid of Breffni, she might lose him anyway. The thought terrified her; she knew it would kill her if Andrew turned against her. He was all she had. Laura had never been a daughter to her; it had always been only Andrew.

Standing at the window, Cecily squared her shoulders. She had no intention of losing him. She was damned if that witch was going to win this time. So, at all costs, Andrew must never know. Somehow, Cecily had to find a way to bring this catastrophe to an end without Andrew's knowledge of her role in it. She stared unseeing out the window, mind racing.

✡✡✡

Andrew held the bottle over Ruth's glass. 'Drink up; I don't know why you asked me to get it.'

Ruth smiled as he topped up her barely-touched drink. 'Sorry, darling – but you're enjoying it, aren't you?'

He topped up his own glass and put down the bottle. 'It's great, yeah – and the dinner was lovely too. You went to a lot of trouble.'

So he *had* noticed; she'd wondered, when he didn't comment all through the fillet steaks, and carrots with ginger and orange butter, and roasted potato chunks with garlic and rosemary. She had gone to a lot of trouble; she wanted the whole evening to be just perfect. Because she was going to tell him this evening.

Mam and Dad had been thrilled, as she'd known they would be. Made a big fuss of her, phoned the others to tell them; they'd barely made the play, with all the excitement. In the dark of the theatre, Ruth had hugged her happiness to herself, hardly noticing what was happening on stage. And in the train on the way back this morning, she found herself smiling at strangers sitting nearby, not minding a bit if they thought her odd.

And when she finally managed to drag her thoughts away, somewhere between Portlaoise and Roscrea, she remembered the other thing that had preoccupied her on the way up to Dublin. The amazing discovery she'd made, just out of the blue. The thought that had popped from nowhere into her head, slotting neatly into the space that she hadn't known was waiting for it, and making her look up suddenly from her magazine with a surprised 'oh'.

Now, getting used to the new information, the only surprise she felt was that it hadn't hit her sooner. The evidence she needed had been under her nose all the time; how had it taken her so long to connect the dots? And was she absolutely sure that she'd got it right? Had she put two and two together and come up with six?

No, she was right – she was certain. It all made sense, and she couldn't deny the proof that was staring her in the face. All she had to do now was figure out the next step to take. Then another thought struck her – it wasn't meddling, was it? It was really none of her business . . . what if they didn't want her help? What if they threw it back in her face, told her that she'd no right? But if she did nothing, she'd never know . . . and she thought of the wonderful surprise it would surely be, the joy that she was going to be able to bring – it must bring joy, mustn't it? – and her heart lifted. She must be careful though, and do it right. She must figure out a plan of action.

But not tonight. Tonight was for her and Andrew; and she decided she couldn't wait any longer – let the Viennetta stay in the freezer for another night. She reached out to the hand that was resting on the table and covered it with hers and squeezed. 'Darling, I have something to tell you.'

Andrew took a sip – more a gulp, really – of his wine. 'What is it?'

She gave him a radiant smile and said, 'I'm pregnant.'

✡✡✡

'Hello?'

'Bref, it's me.'

'Hi – what's up?'

'Nothing – just felt like calling.' Laura giggled. 'Actually I'm real restless today – can't settle.' More giggling. 'I must be in love.'

Breffni closed her eyes. 'That must be it.'

'I know it sounds ridiculous, but I feel like Donal and I are falling in love all over again, you know?' Quick, breathless words.

Breffni nodded, smiled, eyes still closed. 'That sounds great.'

'It is.' Another giggle. 'We can't keep our hands off each other. Oh, by the way, it hasn't come yet.'

'What hasn't come?' Breffni twined the phone cord around her fingers.

Laura laughed. 'Sorry, I shouldn't expect everyone to be as one-track minded as I am right now. My period, I mean – wouldn't you know, the one time I'm waiting for it.'

'Murphy's Law. You're probably delaying it, thinking about it all the time.'

'Yeah – but I'm not that bothered really; it'll come soon enough. Somehow, I just know –' Laura paused, serious now '– Bref, I've got a real good feeling about this; I really feel it's going to work out OK for us.'

'Absolutely; of course it will.' Breffni opened her eyes, untwined the cord. 'You and Donal are due a break.'

'I know; that's what I feel. It has to turn out right, doesn't it?'

Breffni nodded at the opposite wall. 'Of course it does. Let me know as soon as you've any news, right?'

'OK. Talk to you soon.'

The phone went dead in Breffni's hand, and she hung up and walked back slowly into the kitchen.

Laura, all excited about getting pregnant. Andrew, promising to tell Ruth this weekend. Herself, trying to figure out how to break it to Cian that she's leaving him and taking Polly with her.

All go, these days.

✡✡✡

'Hello?'

'Laura, it's me.'

'Andrew – what's up?'

'I . . . I need to speak to you.'

He sounded odd. 'Fine – why don't you come around this evening? We'll even feed you.'

'No – I want to talk to you on your own. Can you meet me after work, in that little pub near the studio?'

Curiouser and curiouser; she began not to like the way this was going. 'Yeah . . . OK; I'll give Donal a ring and say I'll be a bit late. But Andrew, what's –'

'Say you'll be a lot late. Tell him to expect you when he sees you.'

'Andrew, what is it? What's going on?'

'I'll talk to you later, OK? What time can you finish?'

She checked her watch. 'I can be out of here at five thirty; how's that?'

'OK. See you then.' No goodbye, no explanation.

Laura hung up, her good mood draining away.

✡✡✡

He'd cried. Wrapped his arms around her and cried. She'd never seen him cry before. Never seen anyone cry with happiness before, let alone a man.

She was so glad that he was thrilled; she knew he would be. Knew that deep down, he longed for children just as much as she did. Lying in his arms that night, Ruth had felt completely happy. What had she ever done to deserve this? A man she never dreamt would be interested in her – let alone interested enough to marry her – a lovely home, a job she enjoyed, and now a baby on the way.

They had everything. They were the luckiest people in the world. And the next morning, after waving Andrew off to work, Ruth picked up the phone to break the news to her mother-in-law.

✡✡✡

The doorbell rang as Breffni was mopping up Polly's Ready Brek spill. Polly immediately slid from her chair and tottered towards the front door, always delighted at the prospect of visitors.

'Hang on, baby – I'm coming.' Breffni threw the dishcloth into the sink and walked towards the door, wiping her hands on the legs of her faded jeans.

Cecily wore an expensive-looking camel-coloured coat that stopped just below her knees. She was holding a matching bag and not smiling. For a second, Breffni stared at her, feeling something swooping unpleasantly inside her. Then she said, 'Mrs O'Neill, hello. Come in.' She scooped Polly into her arms and stood back to allow the older woman to step into the hall.

'Come through to the kitchen; it's warmer.' She closed the front door and walked ahead of Cecily down the hall, and held the kitchen door open with the hand that wasn't wrapped around Polly's waist. 'Sit down; can I get you anything? Tea or coffee?' Damn that she hadn't cleared the table, that Polly's scatterings – milky Ready Brek bowl, half-chewed toast – were still on show. That a knife was sticking out of the pot of apricot jam. 'Please excuse the mess; I was just about to clear up.'

Cecily sat on the edge of the nearest chair and held her bag in her lap. 'No, thank you. This is not a social call.' She didn't look at Polly, who had stuck two of her fingers into her mouth and was watching their visitor curiously. Cecily didn't acknowledge her presence at all, just looked past her at Breffni. Still unsmiling.

Breffni's heart began to quicken. She turned to Polly. 'Darling, will you play with your Lego while I talk to the lady? It's in the sitting room.' She forced her voice to stay calm as she put Polly down gently, praying that she wouldn't act up.

Polly stood, one hand planted on Breffni's thigh, looking uncertainly at Cecily.

'Go on, lovie – I'll be in in a minute.' Breffni pushed her gently towards the door. 'Make a castle, OK? For the queen.'

Polly's face cleared, and she trotted obediently towards the hall. Breffni followed her to the door, pushed it almost closed after her, turned to face whatever lay ahead.

'You know why I'm here.' Cecily's voice was ice cold; the words sounded like they were being bitten off before they were finished. She had a twisted expression around her mouth, as if she'd eaten something that didn't agree with her.

Breffni said nothing; she was literally struck dumb. She folded her arms and leaned against the wall, heart racing, forcing herself to meet Cecily's stare. *Oh God, she knows. She's found out.*

Cecily waited a few seconds, watching her, then nodded slowly. She settled back slightly into the chair, crossed her legs at the ankles. Breffni watched her and thought, *she's enjoying this*. She pressed her arms tightly across her chest and waited. Hoping to God that Polly didn't come in; ready to swoop on her if she did, and bundle her back out.

'I know what you're doing with my son.' Still in that clipped, cold voice.

Oh God. Even though she had known it was coming, hearing the words out loud still made Breffni feel something plummet inside her. She wished to God she'd sat down now; crossing to a chair at this stage would look like an admission of guilt. She'd have to stay where she was. She could feel her heart pounding inside her tightly locked arms.

'You're nothing but a dirty little whore.' So hard, so cold. Cecily may as well have reached out her carefully manicured hand and whipped it across the other woman's face. To Breffni's horror, tears sprang to her eyes; she blinked quickly and bit her lip, glanced quickly towards the door.

'Oh, she'll find out soon enough what kind of mother she has.' Cecily's voice began to rise slightly; her words flew out faster.

'You threw yourself at him, forced yourself on him. He didn't want you, you stupid woman. He only did what any man would do if it was offered to him on a plate.'

Breffni unlocked her arms, put up a hand to brush across her face, didn't know what to do with her hands then, jammed them into her pockets to stop them shaking. She shook her head and found her voice; it came out cracked and low. 'No – you're wrong; he loves me . . . he was the one –'

'Shut your trap.' Cecily's voice snapped like a whip across the room. 'He doesn't love you, he loves his wife. Remember his wife, the one he goes to bed with every night? The one he chose for better or worse, for the rest of his life?' When she stopped speaking, her harsh breathing filled the kitchen. Spots of faint colour had appeared in her cheeks.

Breffni shook her head again, curled her hands into fists in her pockets. She opened her mouth to speak, then closed it again. Cecily's mind was made up – Breffni was the Jezebel, Andrew the innocent darling son. There was no point in trying to reason with her, tell her how Andrew had pursued Breffni, how she'd done her utmost to resist him. She simply wouldn't be believed.

'Now listen to me, you stupid little tramp.' Cecily's voice lowered again; Breffni heard the menace in it. 'I've got some news for you.' She paused, and again, it seemed to Breffni that Cecily was taking pleasure from this awful scene.

Cecily leaned forward, stretching her mouth now into what was probably meant to look like a smile, but came out like a grotesque smirk. 'Good news, in fact. I'm going to be a grandmother.' She paused, watching Breffni intently. 'And it's not Laura who's pregnant – it's Ruth. Andrew's wife.' She sat back again, eyes locked on Breffni. Awful smile still in place. 'She's going to have his baby.'

'No.' Breffni's voice was barely more than a whisper; the word flew out of her mouth and disappeared. 'No, that's not true.' Her throat ached, her heart beat painfully against her chest. Her head started turning from side to side; she couldn't seem to control it. *No, no, no.* Her face crumpled, mouth open in anguish. 'No.'

Cecily nodded, smile rigid. 'Oh yes, isn't it wonderful? And how did I hear this delightful news? Why, my son phoned me, of course, just last night.'

No, no, no. It kept pounding inside Breffni's skull, clanging like a demented bell. Was she saying it out loud? In her pockets, her nails were digging into her palms; she welcomed the pain, dug in deeper.

Cecily's voice was coming at her in waves, fading, getting louder. 'Andrew was in tears, in fact. So happy at the thought of becoming a father.' Cecily put her head on one side, almost whimsically. 'He'll make a good father, don't you think?'

NO. With an enormous effort, Breffni stopped shaking her head, found her voice. 'It's not true. You're making this up. He's telling Ruth everything this weekend.' The words tumbled out in gasps; she was breathless after every little phrase. But what did it matter now what she told Cecily? Soon everyone would know. How on earth did Cecily think her pathetic lie would change anything? She squeezed her fists tighter, gathering strength. 'You're lying – Ruth's not pregnant.'

Cecily seemed genuinely amused. 'Why don't you call her up then, and ask her?' She gestured towards the hall. 'Go on, I'll wait here.' When Breffni didn't move, she gestured again. 'Go on. Phone her.' She sat back, hands folded on her bag.

A trickle of doubt crept into Breffni's head. Could it be possible? Could this monster be telling the truth? But Andrew had told her that Ruth didn't care for sex, had never enjoyed it. He'd insisted that they hadn't made love since he and Breffni . . .

'Go on. What are you waiting for?' Cecily sat there, smile playing gently on her lips. 'Why don't you congratulate her? I'm sure she'd be thrilled.'

Something snapped in Breffni – the pleasure that Cecily was taking, coming here and trying to destroy what she and Andrew had . . . and then, suddenly, she thought *but wait – what if it is true?* Maybe somehow Ruth had tricked him into having sex at just the right time, and he'd been too ashamed to tell Breffni. That didn't matter, none of that mattered – they still loved each other, they were still going away together – and Polly was coming with them.

She stood straighter, gathered herself together to launch her attack. 'It won't work. Even if Ruth is pregnant, you won't break us up. We love each other – we're going away together; it's all arranged.' Her voice sounded steady, reasoned. She took a deep breath, ready to plunge on, ready to order this woman out of her house.

But Cecily got there first, smile vanished as if someone had taken a cloth and scrubbed it roughly away. 'You idiot. Can't you understand yet? How do you think I found out about your dirty little affair?' She was hissing now, eyes narrowed, cheeks spotted with colour again. 'I saw you at your sneaky little dinner date last week, when Ruth was safely out of the way. I saw you groping him under the table, like the slut you are.'

Breffni drew her breath in sharply. Cecily had been in the hotel, had watched them throughout their meal, when they'd been so happy, so excited at the thought of the night ahead. Had seen her put a hand on Andrew's thigh . . . Colour flooded her face; of all the people who could have found them out, it had to be Cecily.

'So naturally, when he called me last night with the good news,

I had to tell him what I'd seen.' Cecily's immaculately made-up face was contorted with rage; watching her, Breffni marvelled at Laura's endurance – still alive, still sane after growing up with this monster. 'And when he realised that I knew, Andrew broke down, told me everything. How you ran after him like a tart, wouldn't leave him alone, kept calling him at work, begging him to meet you.' Her mouth curled with disgust. 'He said you found the hotel, set it all up, told him you'd be waiting for him. Even paid, he said –' that horrible smirk was back '– you obviously don't know how prostitutes normally operate.'

But Andrew had always paid, insisted. Always had the bill settled before she arrived. Breffni didn't bother saying it out loud, just stood against the wall and waited for this nightmare to finish.

Cecily's voice dripped with scorn. 'So it looks as if history is about to repeat itself. You come sniffing around my son, he weakens for a while, and then he sees reason and drops you.' She laughed harshly. 'Poor Breffni – the only man you can hang on to is a boring slob.'

And, watching the older woman's triumphant face, Breffni suddenly realised – or had she known it all along? – that it hadn't been Andrew who'd 'seen reason' all those years ago; it had been Cecily who'd poisoned his mind against Breffni, telling him that she wasn't good enough for him. Wearing him down until he'd had no choice but to give in, and give her up.

Breffni remembered her bewilderment when he'd dropped her, just like that. The tears she'd wiped away silently as he finished with her, mumbling his reasons, not looking at her once.

And then, meeting him in Rome, discovering how attracted to him she still was, struggling to speak casually to him. Sitting as far from him as possible in the restaurant after the ceremony – because she had no intention of going through that heartbreak again. Flying back to the States, running back to the safety of Cian McDaid, who was really quite endearing, and who would never dream of breaking her heart.

But of course, it had all been for nothing. They'd been powerless to resist the pull between them, once they were meeting again regularly. Even with Cian, even with Polly to keep her safe from him. None of that had mattered. 'I must have been mad to let you go,' he'd said to her, that first afternoon. 'Stark, staring mad.'

No, not mad: weak. No match for his mother's strength. Too weak then, when he was just eighteen, and certainly too weak now to struggle against his mother – not with Ruth on her side. And his unborn baby. Because of course Cecily was telling the truth about Ruth's pregnancy – Breffni understood that now.

She forced herself to look directly at Cecily. 'You've said what you came to say. Now I'd like you to leave.' Her voice was low, and didn't shake.

Cecily stood up. 'If you tell him I was here, I'll deny it, of course. And I think you know who he'll believe.'

Breffni felt a stab of anger; could Cecily seriously imagine Breffni would try to see Andrew again, after this? She kept her voice low. 'You're welcome to your precious son; you deserve each other. And for the record, I've had plenty of better fucks.' She was rewarded with Cecily's flinch. 'Now get out.' Her voice rose slightly as she held the kitchen door open. 'Get out of my house, you mad bitch.'

Just then Polly trotted out of the sitting room, clutching a higgledy-piggledy arrangement of Lego. 'Mama, look.'

✡✡✡

'God.' Laura pushed her hands through her curls and looked across at her brother in horror. 'How could you have done that? How could you? I can't believe it.'

At least he had the grace to look ashamed. 'I don't know . . . I was stupid, I don't know. But Laura –' he paused, spread his palms up helplessly, '– I love her.'

'Which one?' Laura's voice was hard.

'Breffni, of course.' He looked beseechingly at her. 'Please try and understand – I'm totally in love with her.'

'And Ruth? Where does she figure? Or had you even thought about your wife in all this?' Laura glared at him. 'Your *pregnant* wife?'

He hung his head. 'Of course I've thought about Ruth; I feel as guilty as hell about her.' He looked up again, pleading for Laura to see it his way. 'But it was a mistake; the marriage was a big mistake. I should never have . . . we should never –'

'Oh, right.' She tried to control her voice; didn't want it to start shaking with rage. 'You made a mistake; so you're just going to walk away from it? You're going to walk away from your own child? And, speaking of children –' her eyes blazed into his '– have you considered Polly in all this?'

'Yes, of course we have.' He let a hint of exasperation creep into his voice. Laura knew it was because she wasn't saying what he wanted to hear. Wasn't sympathising with poor Andrew, wasn't trying to find a way to help him out. 'Polly will come with us, of course. You didn't think Breffni would leave her behind?'

'And you think Cian will let her go.' She said it flatly, staring at him.

His confused expression gave her some satisfaction; maybe at last she was getting through to him. 'What?'

Laura picked up her glass, took a sip; her mouth felt

desperately dry. 'Why would you imagine he'd give up his daughter to his adulterous partner?'

'I . . . didn't think he'd have a choice. I mean, it's not as if they're married . . .'

'So what – you assumed the mother would automatically get the child, even though she's the home-wrecker?' Laura shook her head. 'Sorry; that may have been true in the last millennium, but not now.'

He looked at her for a few seconds without speaking, then lifted his glass and drained it. He wiped his mouth with the back of his hand and nodded at Laura's empty glass. 'Want another?'

She nodded shortly. He'd been right – this was going to take some time. She sighed deeply as she watched him walk to the bar, saw two young females turn to look at him. What a mess he'd managed to get himself into – planning to run off with his sister's best friend, just after his new wife discovered she was pregnant.

Laura had always known that Andrew was selfish. All his life, things had come easily to him – with his looks and his charm, he'd never been short of friends, or girlfriends; and he'd walked into his job straight after college – but her sister's eye had allowed her to see him for what he really was. And when you thought about it, who could blame him for being selfish? Andrew had grown up believing the myth that Cecily had built around him: that he was perfect, that he deserved anything he wanted.

Laura loved him, of course; they'd always got on, despite the obvious difference in the way they were treated by Cecily. Laura had never held their mother's favouritism against him; it wasn't his fault. And they'd had lots of good times, growing up. But he certainly wasn't the saint that Cecily – and probably poor Ruth – believed him to be. He was spoilt and self-obsessed, and he took whatever he wanted without a thought for the consequences.

And even as she shoved aside a stab of jealousy at the thought of Ruth's pregnancy, Laura's heart went out to her. Poor, innocent Ruth. Believing herself loved by her husband, no doubt thrilled to discover that she was carrying his baby. Dreaming of their perfect future together – with maybe lots more children to come. Poor, stupid Ruth. She deserved someone better.

But she had chosen Andrew. And now that he'd forced Laura into his confidence, wasn't it her duty to help Ruth? Didn't her sister-in-law deserve someone on her side in this awful situation?

Laura watched as Andrew came back towards her with the drinks, and realised, with dread, what she would have to do.

✡✡✡

'Is everything all right, my dear?' Frank looked over at Cecily with concern. 'You've hardly touched your chicken; is it not to your liking?'

Cecily looked down at her plate and knew that she wouldn't manage another bite, even though she'd eaten nothing since a half slice of brown toast at eight this morning. She shook her head slightly as she laid down her knife and fork beside one another. 'I'm sorry, Frank, I don't seem to have much of an appetite this evening.' She looked around the unfamiliar restaurant; she should have known that the new surroundings wouldn't make the slightest difference. Being out again with Frank only served to remind her of the last terrible night, when she'd seen her son across the room with another woman.

Since she'd driven away unsteadily from that awful scene in Nenagh the other morning, Cecily's thoughts had been in turmoil. Her delight when Ruth had phoned her with the news – here was exactly what she needed – had started to evaporate as soon as she'd stepped into Breffni's grubby little kitchen. Oh, she'd said what she'd come prepared to say, had invented Andrew's confession just like she'd planned, and it had all sounded so plausible to her. It seemed, too, that Breffni was swallowing it all – after her initial denial, which Cecily had expected, of course. And her parting shot, her crude put-down of Andrew, had definitely seemed genuine. It sounded like she really wasn't intending to contact him again.

But maybe she was a better liar than Cecily was giving her credit for. Maybe even now she was back with him, telling him everything, discovering that Cecily hadn't confronted Andrew with her discovery after all.

Tossing in her bed at night, Cecily imagined the two of them laughing at her, sneering at her well-meant intervention. Despising her for trying to separate them.

It had been a mistake to come out with Frank tonight; there was nowhere they could go where she could feel comfortable. Until this dreadful situation was resolved, Cecily was going to be no company for him. She looked across at his concerned face. 'I think I'd like to go home.'

'Of course.' He was on his feet, signalling to the waiter for the bill, taking her coat from the back of her chair and helping her into it. She imagined telling him everything, and knew she wouldn't dream of it – even though he'd probably be full of understanding and sympathy. And. of course, telling Laura was completely out of the question.

No, this was something Cecily would have to cope with alone. She had done what she could; now all that was left was to wait, and hope, and pray.

✡✡✡

'You're in rare form today.' Helen smiled at Ruth across the row of chairs.

Ruth beamed back. 'It's this spring in the air; I always get a lift when I see the days getting longer.'

'Oh right.' Helen nodded. 'It's got nothing to do with the brand new house, and the hunk of a husband then?' Andrew had collected her from work one rainy evening, and since being introduced to him, Helen and Sal had missed no opportunity to tease Ruth good-naturedly about the man with the film-star looks she'd married.

'Well, I suppose they have something to do with it.' Ruth grinned happily, thanking her lucky stars for the millionth time that she'd chanced to call in here looking for a job. Mind you, she'd be out of work when Carol, the stylist Ruth had replaced, was ready to come back after her maternity leave. But by then, Ruth would be getting ready to have her own baby – the thought of the tiny creature growing inside her caused her the same thrill that it always did – the same thrill she'd felt when she'd held the pregnancy test wand in trembling hands and seen the precious blue line. She was dying to tell Helen – wanted to tell the whole world, but it was still a bit soon.

Helen glanced at the clock. 'Hey, it's your lunch time. Go out and skip in the sun for yourself.'

Ruth laughed. 'Maybe I will. By the way, I'm going to the post office – have you anything you want me to drop in?'

'Oh, hang on – I have, actually.' As Helen went into the back, Ruth looked out the window. Blue sky, hardly a cloud. Still cool enough to need a jacket, but definite spring weather, full of everything bursting into life. She hugged herself, wondering if she could bear all this happiness.

✡✡✡

'Hello?'

'Breffni – it's me.'

A pause, then, 'Oh, hi there.' Another pause. 'How're things?' Her voice sounded flat.

'Fine . . . actually, I have some good news.' *Right, here goes.*

Breffni said nothing, just waited.

'Ruth is pregnant; isn't that great?' Laura prayed that her voice didn't sound as horribly false as it felt.

Nothing. No sound from the other end.

'Breffni? Are you there?'

'Yeah, no, that's great . . .'

Was that a stifled sob? 'You sound like you've a cold.' No way was she going to give sympathy.

'Mmm – all stuffed up . . .' Another muffled sob.

Suddenly Laura thought *this is ridiculous*. 'Breffni, I know. Andrew told me.'

Loud sobbing now. 'God, oh Christ . . . Laura, I'm so sorry . . .' Her voice was ragged, thick with tears. 'I'm so sorry . . . Jesus . . .'

'How the hell could you? How could you do it?' Laura felt a rising anger. 'Could you not keep your hands off him? He was just married, for Christ's sake. What's *wrong* with you?'

No response, just loud sobbing, then the phone put down, gently.

Laura stood holding the dead phone, trying to breathe the anger out of her. She heard Donal's key in the front door and hung up.

Donal walked in. 'Hey babe, gossiping as usual.'

She nodded, kissed his cheek. 'Can't beat a good old gossip. Come on; lunch is on the table.'

✡✡✡

He parked in his usual space, checking for her car. No sign yet: good. He liked to arrive before her, have the bill settled before she walked in. He wondered why it felt like a million years since he'd been here last. It was just over a week since they'd spent the night together, in a room not a hundred yards from where he stood. Nine days since he'd held her in his arms, breathing in the scent of her hair, wrapping his body around hers, drowning in her.

Today, they were back to their usual afternoon arrangement. They'd decided to wait till this week to meet again, in case there were any repercussions from their night together. He'd just about managed to survive nine days without her, nine days with no contact – they'd agreed it would be safer. And now . . . his heart soared at the thought of seeing her again. Today, they could start to make plans.

He still smarted when he thought about the meeting with Laura the other night. He'd assumed she'd take some persuading to see it from his point of view, but he'd been fairly sure that eventually she'd come round to his way of thinking, that she'd be able to understand that what he and Breffni had was too important to ignore. Instead, Laura had insisted that he was wrong, that his affair with Breffni had to end, that he had to concentrate on making his marriage work. So, of course, he'd promised – what else could he do? If Laura thought he was going to go ahead and make plans for a future with Breffni, she might decide to take matters into her own hands and try to turn Breffni against him, or something.

And of course she'd been wrong about Polly – of course Breffni could take Polly with her when they went off together; she was the child's mother – that had to count for something. And Cian surely wouldn't want the responsibility of bringing up Polly alone. His family were all in the States, except for his ancient grandmother – she wouldn't be around for much longer. And he'd still see Polly from time to time; they wouldn't want to deny him that. It would be awkward for a while, obviously, but they'd sort it out – they were civilised people.

And Ruth – she'd cope too. She'd probably go back to Dublin – she'd never wanted to leave her family anyway – and she'd have plenty of help there to bring up her child. He couldn't think of it as 'his' child, or even 'their' child. It was Ruth who'd wanted it – Ruth who'd pushed him into it. He remembered the night it must have happened, when they went out for that meal, and Ruth kept refilling his wine glass, getting him all worked up in the taxi on the way home. She'd obviously planned it all meticulously. He'd been careful up to that, watching for signs that she was having her period, avoiding sex when he knew she was at the dangerous time of the month, feigning sleep if he thought there was any chance that she could get pregnant. There'd been a few times, after nights out with the others, when he'd wanted Breffni so badly, he'd turned to Ruth in desperation – but he'd been lucky up to this. Really, Ruth had brought this on herself, forcing him into something he hadn't wanted – not with her.

The only thing that he dreaded in all this business was his mother's reaction; how would she take it when the truth came out? Would she understand that he and Breffni had been powerless, that they'd been swept up in something that was huge – far bigger than either of them had anticipated? Could he make Mother see that they hadn't acted out of malice, hadn't set out to hurt anyone? Would she, in time, come to accept Breffni as his new partner, when she'd been so decidedly against her the last time around? He hoped so – hoped he'd be able to explain it all to her some day, when she'd got over the initial shock.

He settled his bill in cash, as usual, glanced at his watch as he walked to a couch by the window. Breffni was late; something must have held her up. He imagined her face when she heard that Ruth was pregnant. He'd tell her as soon as they went upstairs, get it out of the way. He hoped to God he'd use the right words, make sure she understood that he hadn't wanted it, had hoped fervently that it wouldn't happen. He'd insist that it was all Ruth's doing, too much wine one night, just a horrible mistake.

He'd explain that it wasn't going to make any difference to their plans, that he still wanted to go away with her. That nothing had changed. He'd show her how much he still loved her.

Hurry up. He willed her to arrive, impatient to see her. He pulled out his mobile – no messages. Where was she? He debated ringing her, even though he'd promised never to, and then forced himself to relax.

She'd be here. She was just a bit late, that was all.

✡✡✡

The face that looked out at Breffni from the bathroom mirror was hardly recognisable. Eyes so puffy that they were practically shut. Face blotchy from all the tears. Hair hanging in damp strands, trailing limply down each side of her empty face.

Empty face – empty of hope, robbed of joy. She ducked her head and turned the cold tap on full blast. Scooping handfuls of water, she splashed her face again and again, oblivious to the puddles she was making on the tiles. Her hair dripped into the sink, the neck of her t-shirt became soaked. The water made her gasp; before long, her hands were so cold she couldn't feel them any more. Shivering, she groped for a towel and tipped her head upside down while she rubbed her hair roughly, then stood upright and mopped her face. When she'd done the best she could, she used the towel to soak up the worst of the water on the floor before dropping it into the laundry basket. Then she peeled off her soaking t-shirt and threw that in too.

She risked another look in the mirror – marginally better, face not quite so blotchy, although now her half-dry hair stuck up at wild angles, making her look like a demented cavewoman. She picked up her wooden comb and began to coax it through, grateful that Polly and Cian weren't due home for at least another hour.

Thank God Mary had already collected Polly when Laura rang, just under two hours ago. She couldn't imagine how she would have coped if they'd still been here. How could she have explained the tears that had poured out of her since then, the sobs that had threatened to rip her in two, leaving her gasping for breath, making her chest hurt with their intensity?

Since Cecily's visit two days before, Breffni had been clinging desperately to the hope that it had all been a pack of lies – that Ruth wasn't pregnant, that Andrew hadn't betrayed Breffni to his mother, making it seem like he'd been lured into some sordid affair against his better judgement. He couldn't have done that – what they had was far too special, whatever weird influence Cecily might have over him. And if he *was* a little weak, and a little in thrall to his mother – well, that was hardly a crime. He wouldn't be human without some weakness. He'd been so much younger too, last time around – it would have been easy for someone as scheming as Cecily to persuade him to give up Breffni. No, the more she thought about it, the more convinced Breffni became that this was all some horrible gamble on Cecily's part. Having discovered that Andrew was having an affair, she'd been desperate to break them up, keep Andrew married to wimpy Ruth, who'd never come between Cecily and her darling son. So she'd concocted this myth, Ruth getting pregnant, Andrew seeing the light, throwing himself on his mother's mercy, promising to mend his ways.

And when Breffni discovered – as she would, of course, in time – that Ruth wasn't pregnant after all, the damage would hopefully have been done. The seeds of suspicion would have been sown. For all Breffni knew, Cecily could have spun a similar yarn to Andrew – told him she'd seen Breffni out with another man, or something. Anything, to drive a wedge between them, to stop them from seeing each other. She wouldn't put anything past that woman.

And Breffni's mind whirled on and on in anxious circles, one minute convinced that Andrew would never betray her, that everything was going to be all right – the next terrified that she'd discover that it was all true. That Ruth *was* pregnant, and that Cecily had all the ammunition she needed to keep Andrew away from Breffni forever.

The only way she'd find out, of course, was to go to the hotel as usual for their next meeting – so what if Cecily found out? It really didn't matter now – and see if he was there. If he was, then she had nothing to worry about. He'd have told Ruth, and she'd go home and tell Cian, just as they had planned. And some day she might even tell him about Cecily's visit, and maybe they'd be able to laugh at it.

Maybe.

And just two hours ago, after Breffni had waved goodbye to Mary and Polly, as she was preparing to shower herself before leaving to meet her lover, she'd picked up the phone and Laura had told her that Ruth was pregnant.

And it was all over.

✡✡✡

Laura heard the faint rattle of the letter box and checked her watch as she went out to the hall. Twenty past two; it got later every day. She gathered up the three envelopes and went back into the kitchen to finish her lunch. Lovely to be able to take the odd day off again; wonderful that she'd got the latest batch of illustrations finished finally. Fantastic that they'd got such a good reception from the publishers.

Great that she could forget about all that now, and focus on getting ready for what lay ahead. That's if her period ever arrived; as of this morning, she was eight days late. Wouldn't you know, the one time she wanted it to come. No doubt Breffni was right – all her thinking about it was probably holding it up. But how could she not think about it, and what it was going to set in motion, once it eventually arrived?

Her stomach flipped, as it always did when she thought about taking the first step towards having a child of their own. Maybe, if they were terribly lucky, the only step she'd have to take before becoming pregnant. Who was to say it wouldn't work the first time? She and Donal could do with a bit of luck, after two years of disappointment.

But even if it didn't, she could go on trying, again and again. And eventually it would happen; it had to. She wasn't thirty yet – they had plenty of time for it to work. She thought of herself and Donal shopping for an actual baby, picking out tiny clothes and toys for real; not pretending like she'd done before. Last week she'd emptied the upstairs drawer and the boxes under her table at work and brought everything to the charity shop. They were for a different baby – one who'd been created out of misery and desperation, by a woman Laura hardly recognised now.

She longed for it all to begin – for all this waiting and hoping to be over at last. But it was a different kind of longing now – a kind of butterflies-in-the-tummy Christmas Eve excitement, knowing that what you were wishing for was just around the corner. And she couldn't remember when she and Donal had been this happy; it was almost as if taking the decision to get the treatment had somehow signalled an end to their misery, had taken a weight off their shoulders and allowed them to move on.

And any day now . . . she smiled as she looked down at the envelopes. A phone bill, a mailing from the University Concert Hall, and – she turned the last one over. Plain white, typed address, both their names. She ripped it open and pulled out the single, folded page. Just one sentence, also typed:

Don's father is living in Limerick now.

Underneath, a phone number. Laura stared at the page for a few seconds, completely at a loss. What did it mean? Why was there no name, no signature – and who was Don? Her first thought was that it had been sent to them by mistake. She looked at the envelope again – *Donal O'Connor and Laura O'Neill.* Donal, not Don. Laura had never heard anyone call him Don. She turned the page over; the other side was blank. She read it again, trying to make sense of it: '*Don's father is living in Limerick now.*' But Donal's father was in Australia, wasn't he? Could he have moved back, after all these years? And no mention of his wife, Donal's mother. This was all very strange.

Well, only one way to solve the mystery. She stood up, holding the letter and went to the phone.

✡✡✡

'Hello?'

Breffni listened to the silence in the hall, then Cian again: 'Hello?' Another silence, then she heard him hanging up.

'Must have been a wrong number. I hate when they just hang up like that; they could have the manners to say something.' He sat back down on the couch and picked up his paper. She bent her head, pretending to be engrossed in her book. A few minutes later, the phone rang again. She jumped up.

'I'll go this time.'

Her hand shook as she reached out for the phone. 'Hello?' She prayed her voice would sound normal to Cian.

'Breffni, what's wrong? Why –'

'Sorry, wrong number.' She hung up quickly and took a deep breath before removing it from the hook. Then she wiped her palms on her jeans and opened the kitchen door.

'Same again. I've taken it off the hook for a while. I'm just going up for a bath.' She barely managed to keep the tears from falling until she'd closed the bathroom door softly.

✡✡✡

And in Frank's house, the phone began to ring and he stood up to answer it. As he spoke, and listened, and shook his head briefly, his placid expression changed to mild bewilderment, before his whole body stiffened with shock, and he put one unsteady hand to his mouth. After a few minutes, no more, he nodded once, picked up a pen from the table, scribbled on the notebook beside it. Then he replaced the receiver gently and stood leaning heavily against the wall, hands over his face, shoulders slumped.

✡✡✡

'Only me.'

Breffni dropped the tea towel onto the worktop and turned to face the kitchen door. 'In here.'

Cian appeared, went over to kiss her. 'Hi, babe.' He dropped his briefcase and looked around the kitchen. 'Where's Poll?'

'Mary took her; she'll bring her back later.' Breffni's heart was thumping; she picked up the tea towel again and wiped her damp palms. 'Want a drink?'

'I'll get it. You?' Cian opened the fridge and took out a beer can, waving it in Breffni's direction.

She shook her head, indicated the worktop. 'I have wine.' Her second big glass; she needed a buzz for this. She picked up the glass and took a big swallow.

'You OK?' He walked over and put a hand on her shoulder.

She nodded, then shook her head. 'Sit down, will you? There's something I need to tell you.'

He felt his heart sink to the floor as his daughter's face flashed into his head.

✡✡✡

Frank looked at the house, checked his piece of paper. *This one.* He opened the gate and walked up the drive, conscious of the noise his footsteps were making. They sounded so firm, as if the person taking them knew exactly where he was going.

No indication that he was more nervous than he ever remembered being in his life.

He reached the door, pressed the bell quickly, before he had a chance to change his mind and walk away from God knew what was waiting for him inside.

When the door opened, his first thought was *but I know her*. Reddish brown hair, attractive – they'd already met somewhere, quite recently. But Don hadn't been there. And she looked too young, surely, to be married to Frank's son, whose forty-fourth birthday Frank had remembered last year, like he remembered every birthday since Don had stormed out. Had this all been a terrible mistake then?

But his date of birth had matched. And the mole behind his right knee, and the fact that he was left-handed, and allergic to penicillin. Which all left precious little room for mistakes.

'Frank?' Her hand came towards him and he took it automatically. Her voice was low and pleasant. 'But I know you; we met at Ruth's.' So she'd already spoken to Donal's father, and never known. Had imagined him to be a feeble old man in his eighties, when this man standing in front of her could hardly be more than mid-sixties.

It came back to Frank abruptly, the meeting in the kitchen. 'And you're Cecily's daughter.' And Ruth was married to Laura's brother, so she must know Don too. Why did the word 'spaghetti' pop into his head? He shook her hand, and couldn't think what to say next. What on earth did you say to a daughter-in-law you hadn't known existed an hour ago?

They stood facing each other for a few moments, and then she stepped aside, pulled the door open wider. 'Sorry – please come in.' He realised that she was as apprehensive as he was – just as much in dread of what this new, unnerving development might bring. As Frank stepped into the hall, Laura added quickly, 'He's not here, he's at work. He won't be back for another hour, at least.'

In the kitchen she offered him coffee, and he asked if it would be very ill-mannered of him to look for tea instead, and she said of course not, sorry, she should have given him the choice. They were both carefully, nervously polite.

As she filled the kettle, she spoke with her back to him. 'So you never lived in Australia.' There was something heartbreaking in the flatness of her voice, as if she was trying hard not to care that her husband had lied to her. As if she wasn't terrified at what Frank might be about to reveal to her.

Frank shook his head, wanting to spare her any pain this conversation might cause – would surely cause – but what could he do? She'd waited long enough for the truth. 'No. We lived in Sligo all our lives.'

'No.' She shook her head too – of course not. She'd known, as soon as she spoke to Frank on the phone, as soon as she'd been sure that he was Donal's – Don's – father, that Australia had been a lie. She made herself open presses, take out cups, saucers, sugar bowl, reach into the fridge for milk.

And when everything was assembled, when the tea was made, when she had run out of reasons not to sit at the table, she sat. Took the spoon from her saucer and held it tightly.

Outside it began to rain heavily, in one of those sudden downpours – more like a tipping up and emptying out of the clouds than a normal shower. Laura turned quickly towards the window, still so nervous that Frank wanted more than anything to say something to reassure her. But there was nothing he could say.

Finally, she looked back at him, gave a brittle smile. Picked up the teapot and poured tea into both their cups. Frank thought of Cecily – his son's mother-in-law, he realised with a fresh shock – drinking tea so daintily at the book-club meetings. Dabbing her lips after every sip. She knew Don too. All these people knew him, lived with him every day.

'Well.' Laura had no idea what to say next. What did you ask, how could you possibly find a question that didn't sound ridiculous? *Tell me about my husband. Explain why he kept you hidden for years. Make sense of this for me; give me a plausible reason for his lie – and for the lies I don't know about yet.*

Because, of course, there were more. Oh God, she didn't want to hear more. But she had to hear more.

'I'm assuming you don't know the reason for our . . . separation.' Frank's voice was gentle. When Laura didn't respond, just picked up her spoon again, he interlaced his fingers, looked thoughtfully at them.

'When Don was fifteen, his sister died.' He heard Laura's sharp intake of breath, looked up at her white face. 'You didn't know about Catherine.' It wasn't a question.

Laura shook her head quickly. 'He told me he was an only child. He said that you and his mother were older when you met . . .' Her voice was barely audible. Outside, the rain still fell heavily. Neither of them touched the tea, added milk, or sugar.

'I was twenty-four when Don was born. My wife was twenty-six.' Frank hated what his son was forcing him to do. Hated the empty look in Laura's white face. Forced himself to continue; all he could do to help her now was to tell her everything.

'Catherine was born three years later. When she was twelve, she contracted leukaemia, was dead within six months.' Always, whenever he said the words out loud, they caused an anguish so sharp, still, after all these years. He paused, swallowed. Added milk to his tea, took a sip.

Laura sat there, stunned. Afraid to take her eyes off Frank, afraid to open her mouth . . . and what would she say anyway? Beg him to stop, when she knew she had to hear whatever there was? Donal had a sister . . . he'd lied to her about his dead sister.

Frank was speaking again; she listened dumbly. 'After that, Don went off the rails a bit . . . started hanging around with a different crowd . . . Angela and I weren't too aware of what was happening, to be honest. We were still in shock, I suppose . . .' Frank stopped, took another sip of his tea. Laura watched his hands on the cup; they had the same shaped hands, Donal and his father. Outside, they both heard a distant peal of thunder. Both ignored it.

'They'd been very close, the children. Don took Catherine's death very hard . . . and we weren't able to help him. We let him down.' Laura watched his hands, lying one on top of the other on the table now, afraid to look up at his face.

Frank's voice was steady; he raised it slightly to be heard above the rain, lashing now against the window. 'We had warnings, I suppose. A call from the school, wondering why he hadn't been in for almost a week. A neighbour letting us know that he'd seen Don with a few lads in the park, drinking. We had rows, plenty of rows . . . but we didn't do anything really, to help him.' He shook his head, picked up his cup again. 'We saw it coming, and did nothing to stop it.'

As he drank, Laura waited. *Here it comes, the reason for all the lies*. She looked towards the window, needing something real, something ordinary. The rain had stopped as suddenly as it had begun; in the late-afternoon light the garden looked freshly washed, everything clean again. A bird flew across the garden, landed briefly on an arm of the clothesline. She wanted to be out there among the sodden shrubs, walking on the drenched grass, anywhere but here.

Frank put a hand out and covered Laura's. She felt the warmth of it, bit her lip, kept looking determinedly out the window.

'One day, Don left the house with a bottle of vodka. He stole a car in town, after he'd finished the bottle, and crashed it into another car. The driver of the other car was eight months pregnant; they were both killed.' His hand squeezed Laura's gently.

Her head turned slowly from side to side, still watching the garden. No, he was wrong there; that didn't make any sense at all. They couldn't both have been killed – Donal was still alive. Then Laura realised what Frank meant, and her hand flew out from under his and up to cover her mouth. The baby – the tiny, almost-born baby. A drawer full of liquorice-allsorts-coloured clothes slid into her head. A tear rolled down her cheek, bumped into her hand, still pressed against her mouth. Donal had killed a baby.

And still Frank's mouth was opening and closing – what more could he say, what other horrors lay waiting for her to discover?

'Don escaped relatively uninjured, a few broken bones, lots of cuts and bruises. But he fractured his pelvis, and there were some internal injuries there . . . we were told that it might have repercussions later, when he wanted a family.'

And as he said that, something slotted into place. A last piece being added to the jigsaw, the whole picture clear now. *Yes, that explains that.* Her throat was so dry . . . Laura reached for the milk jug, poured some into her cup, then lifted it and took a gulp, coughed as it went down too fast. A few more tears spurted out.

Frank waited until she was listening again. *Nearly there*, he wanted to say. *This is nearly over*. 'He was put into a correctional home for two years, until he was eighteen. We visited him, but he wouldn't talk to us. When he was let out, he left Sligo, and I haven't seen him since.'

Laura closed her eyes, ignoring the tears that were pouring down her face. Found her voice again. 'Your wife?'

'She died just over a year ago – brain haemorrhage. He may know, if he kept an eye on the death notices.'

Laura opened her eyes again, noticed that Frank's hands were trembling slightly – had they been, all along? She tried out a few sentences in her head. *Donal wasn't an only child. His parents didn't move to Australia. His sister died when she was twelve. He crashed a stolen car while he was drunk and killed a woman and her baby. He was left impotent after the accident.*

And after that, more thoughts came. *He knew. All the time, he knew, and he never told me. He left me to hope and pray, and despair, and he never told me. He came to the doctor, and to the gynaecologist, and he sat beside me and he held my hand. And pretended he didn't know.*

After a while she wiped her face with her sleeve, lifted her eyes from Frank's hands. They sat across from each other, waiting, not talking any more. And eventually, when the tea left in the pot was completely cold, the door opened and Donal walked in. And they both turned and looked at him.

✡✡✡

Dear Frank,

I felt it necessary to contact you in view of the recent revelations regarding the identity of your son, which my daughter Laura rightly thought I should hear. While I am, of course, happy for your sake that you have become re-acquainted, and while I hope that you can put the events that caused the original separation behind you both – Laura has not supplied these details, nor do I wish to hear them – I feel that to continue our friendship under the circumstances would be inappropriate. I trust you can see my point of view; indeed, you may fully agree with it.

As we shall no doubt come face to face in the future,

given the connection that now exists between us, I would appreciate your cooperation in keeping our previous meetings from the rest of the family, as it is not something I wish to have discussed.

Yours sincerely,

Cecily O'Neill
PS I shall not be attending future meetings of the book club.

after

Ruth pulled her key out of the door. 'Hello?'

Her mother's head poked out from the kitchen. 'In here, love – he's been as good as gold.'

Ruth smiled – her mother always said that, even if Gerard had yelled his head off from the minute she left. She followed her mother into the kitchen, headed straight over to the baby carrier on the table. Her son looked up at her, sucking intently on his blue soother, arms flapping as he recognised her. *He has his father's eyes*, she thought, as she bent her head to nuzzle against his chest. *Gorgeous green eyes, just like Andrew*.

'What kind of a day had you?'

'Grand – the usual.' Ruth wriggled a finger into her son's tiny fist, felt his strong grip. 'Two body waves, two highlights, a few cuts. Mrs O'Carroll was in; her nephew won five thousand Euro with a scratch card last week, imagine.' She tickled Gerard under his chin, and he gurgled and grabbed her hand.

'You're joking; I didn't think anyone won those. I hope he treated her to the hairdo.'

Ruth laughed. 'If he did, she didn't mention it.' She disentangled her hand and lifted Gerard's bag from the chair, marvelling again that babies needed so much luggage when they went anywhere. Then she turned back to her mother. 'What about you – what did you two get up to?'

'We made a cake, didn't we, lovie?' Her mother smiled down at her grandson and he gurgled at her, soother slipping sideways. 'He was a very good helper. And here –' she lifted a tinfoil-wrapped package from the table '– before big Gerard eats it all.'

'Poor Dad – all his cakes come in halves now.' Ruth took the bundle and tucked it into her bag. 'Thanks, Mam.' She slung the bag over her shoulder, lifted the baby carrier with the other arm. 'Well, we'd better get going, give this little man his dinner.' She put her free hand on her mother's shoulder, kissed her cheek lightly. 'Thanks again, Mam. See you Thursday.'

'Mind yourself, love.'

Driving back to the apartment – she still couldn't think of it as home, although her tiny garden was just beginning to bloom; that would help – Ruth thought *beans on toast*. That would do her fine: such a relief not to have to worry about cooking for someone else any more. Gerard was easy – just open a jar of Heinz. She wondered idly what Cecily was cooking for Andrew tonight. Something wonderful, as usual. With wine and silverware and cut crystal. She shuddered, remembering her terror when she'd done the washing-up in her mother-in-law's house; such a long time ago, it seemed now. Thank God she'd never broken anything.

In the seat beside her, Gerard crowed happily. Ruth glanced across at him. 'Yes, darling. I'm happy too.' And miraculously, she was. She never thought she would be again, when everything had come suddenly, terrifyingly crumbling down around her last

May. When Andrew had walked in from work one day – hardly a week after she'd told him she was pregnant – and announced that he'd been having an affair.

With Breffni.

Even now, almost a year later, Ruth felt slightly sick whenever she allowed herself to think about that horrendous day. Standing there, face rigid with horror, listening to her husband taking her dreams and squeezing the life out of them – she'd felt her world shattering, had had to reach out and grab on to a chair, to touch something solid and hang on to it.

And Breffni. Of course it had been Breffni, with her shiny hair and her perfect face and her lip gloss that stayed in place all evening. Breffni, who'd lent them bedclothes and towels, and who'd given Ruth an eye pencil, to help her make the best of herself. Knowing that if Ruth was worked on from top to toe by the greatest make-up artist in the world, she'd never hold a candle to Breffni.

It was a miracle she hadn't lost Gerard. How had he survived it all? That horrible scene, Andrew's look of disbelief, his hands going up to protect himself as his wife, his docile, eager-to-please wife had screamed and scratched and thumped, wanting him to hurt too. And after that was over, after she'd shouted herself hoarse, after she'd demanded that he leave, not caring where he went, or what anyone would think – what did any of that matter now? What did it matter if he was telling the truth when he said the affair was over? – the great outpouring of her grief that began, the tears that just wouldn't stop, as she lay alone in their double bed.

And in the morning, when she'd found the strength to drag herself out of the bed, exhausted, she'd pulled her suitcase from the top of the wardrobe and started putting clothes into it. She'd been sitting on the train when she realised that she hadn't called Helen to tell her she wouldn't be in to work; halfway to Dublin before she remembered it was Wednesday, her day off.

And then the months when Dad and Mam had taken over. Settling her back into her old room, answering the phone so they could tell Andrew that she was out. Getting a cushion for her back, an antacid for her heartburn. Tissues for her tears. And finally, one day, she'd stood up and answered the phone herself when it rang.

'Ruth, God . . . I'm so sorry –'

She hardly recognised his voice; it was like listening to someone you knew you'd heard somewhere before, but couldn't for the life of you remember where. For the first time ever, Ruth interrupted, ready with the words she'd been practising for days.

'Save your apologies; I'm not interested. In a few days you'll get a letter giving details of my new bank account, and the name and address of my solicitor.' Her palm was pressed against the bulk of her stomach; she was bigger than him now, in every way. 'You will sell the house and pay half of whatever is left into my account. When the baby is born, my solicitor will contact you to work out access. I have nothing more to say to you.'

He was speaking as she hung up; cutting him off, silencing him, was deeply satisfying – and the flood of tears that followed soon after seemed, for the first time, to be more healing than sorrowing.

Over the next few days, she wondered where this new strength was coming from. Was it the thought of the child inside her, was he giving her the courage to stand up for them both? Or was it the image of Breffni and Andrew together, was that finally turning her grief to rage, making her powerful with it? Determining that They would never again make life miserable for Ruth Tobin? Not Ruth O'Neill any more – she was changing it back to Tobin. And her baby was going to be Tobin too: another small triumph.

Not that she was over it – far from it. Her parents would lie sleepless for many nights to come, listening sadly in the next room to the sobs that were still too harsh to be hidden. But the healing process had started; she was going to survive. She and her baby would survive.

And as the months went on, Ruth began to wonder what she'd ever seen in Andrew. Was it just his good looks – could she really have been that shallow? Because now she realised that that's all there was to him – just a pretty face. God, she'd been so naïve. So taken in by a handsome man's attention that she'd never looked beyond it. So grateful that he'd wanted to marry her, so sure that no one would ever want her in that way. What a pathetic creature she'd been, the old Ruth Tobin.

Gerard had been born two days late, on the twenty-ninth of December. And looking at his screwed-up pink face, stroking his impossibly tiny fingers, touching his spike of thick black hair – no wonder she'd had such bad heartburn – Ruth had felt something so much stronger than she'd ever felt for Andrew. She'd cradled her child in her arms, oblivious to her sweat- and tear-stained face, deaf to her mother's excitement, hardly seeing the flash of her sister's camera, and thought wonderingly *so this is love*.

Two months after Gerard was born, Ruth dropped in to see Sheila in the old salon – Mam had told her that Ruth was back – and asked if there was any part-time work going, and Sheila had taken her on immediately, three days a week. Mam minded Gerard while Ruth was at work, and Maura and Claire, Ruth's old flatmates, called around often to the apartment, and Ruth's younger sister Irene doted on her little nephew, begged to take him out on walks.

Occasionally Ruth found herself wondering what had

happened between Donal and Frank. At least she'd done her bit to help them find each other again, even if an anonymous letter was the best way she could come up with. She hoped things had worked out all right – Laura had always been good to her. But Ruth never asked Andrew about her; never asked about any of his family when they met. It was better to cut all those ties now.

She stopped at a red light, looked over at Gerard again. Everything was fine; they were happy now. And she'd always have Gerard – he'd always be hers.

✡✡✡

'Only me.'

'In here.' Breffni stretched her arms over her head, yawned hugely, struggled to her feet. Cian came in as she was combing through her hair with her fingers. There seemed to be so much more of it when she was pregnant; something about it not falling out as much. Maybe she should think about getting it cut, although Cian loved it.

'How're you feeling?' He dropped a kiss on her forehead.

She made a face. 'Like an elephant who's been bingeing for about seven months.'

He grinned. 'Poor you. Not long to go now.'

'Thank God. The sooner he's out, the better.' They'd asked and been told that it was a boy.

'Right, I'm off for Poll. D'you need anything when I'm out?' There was a little Spar near Mary's house.

Breffni shook her head. 'No, we're OK till tomorrow.' Cian had been doing the weekly shop on his way home from work for the past month or so, since Breffni had become too exhausted to consider it.

As she heard the front door slam behind him – why could he never close a door quietly? – Breffni thrust her feet into her slippers and padded slowly towards the kitchen, wincing slightly as she felt an enthusiastic kick. *Steady, buster*.

She turned the oven up a little, started to lay the table for their dinner. No wine – Cian had assured her that he wasn't pushed whether they had some or not, and she couldn't face even one glass these days.

He was so thoughtful really. Even after everything, still so attentive to her, so considerate. Listening, not interrupting, as she'd told him about Andrew – almost as if he'd been expecting it. And after, not a word of reproach. Asking her what she wanted to do. What *she* wanted to do.

She'd looked at him, the tears drying on her face. 'Well, I . . . I assumed that you'd want me to leave.' Suddenly realising that that was the last thing *she* wanted. Hardly believing when he replied that he'd really prefer if she stayed – if she wanted to stay with him. If it really was over between Andrew and herself. And she'd wept again as she'd promised that it was.

And then, Cian answering every phone call until Andrew tried again, and the low conversation in the hall that seemed to go on for a long time, but that probably hadn't. He'd never told her what had been said, and she'd never asked, and Andrew hadn't phoned again.

And after a few months had gone by, and she was still struggling with her guilt, and still discovering what she'd so nearly thrown away, she'd nervously suggested that they have another baby.

Of course she'd lost Laura. That was the worst of all. She'd been afraid to ring her for the longest time, and then one day she'd plucked up her courage and called her mobile, and Laura had listened without comment to Breffni's stuttered apologies, and declined politely when Breffni had suggested that they meet, saying sorry, that she was extremely busy with work. And when Breffni had taken a deep breath and asked how the fertility treatment was going, Laura had paused before answering, 'I really don't think that's any of your business', and hanging up.

And Breffni had thought how like Cecily she sounded.

She was still grieving for Laura when her mother told her about Andrew's move back to his mother's house.

'Of course I didn't hear it from Cecily – that woman would hardly give you the time of day. But his car is there all the time, and there's no sign of the wife. So sad; that marriage lasted no time. I'm sure Cecily is pleased to have Andrew back though – they were always very close. Didn't you two have a thing for a while when you were teenagers?'

Breffni heard the front door again, and Polly's quick patter towards the kitchen. 'Mum?'

'Hi there.' She stooped carefully towards her daughter and planted a loud kiss on her cheek. 'How's Granny Mary?'

Polly pulled off her summer jacket and handed it to Cian, who hung it on the back of the door. 'Fine. We made scones, an' I had two.'

✡✡✡

And Cian sat at the table and propped his chin in his hand and watched the light of his life as she chattered with Breffni, and didn't think beyond the fact that she was still with him now.

✡✡✡

'More coffee, darling?' Cecily stood with the cafetière poised.

Andrew shook his head briefly. 'No thanks.' *She knows I never have more than one cup, and every night she still asks if I want another*. He rustled his newspaper, hoping she'd take the hint and go back to her book.

'Don't forget, Laura's at eight, if you want to change.'

Right, so she doesn't consider what I'm wearing suitable. Hear you loud and clear, Mother. 'Mm-hmm.' He thought again about seeing Breffni on the street last month. As beautiful as ever, blooming with pregnancy. Holding Polly by the hand, looking in the window of a toy shop. Pointing to something in the window, turning to Polly with a smile.

He wondered if she was having a boy or a girl.

'You're going to see Gerard next week, aren't you?'

He sighed loudly, lowered the paper just enough to look over it at her. 'Yes, as usual.' She knew he went once a month, for God's sake.

Cecily lowered the cafetière carefully onto its stand, picked up her book, settled herself back down into her armchair again. 'I was wondering if I might go with you this time.' She smiled brightly at him.

Lord, that was all he needed. As if his visits weren't hard enough. He folded the paper slowly. 'I'm not sure that that would be a good idea, Mother – not right now. Ruth is still . . .' What? Ruth was still what? Still the sweet little creature he'd married? Not a bit of it. 'Look, leave it another while; I'll talk to Ruth. She might let me bring him down here for a night when he's a bit older. At the moment she's still . . . a bit mixed up about everything.'

He saw the quick disappointment, the way she managed to replace it just as rapidly with the same bright smile. She'd just have to wait, that was all; the last thing he needed was Cecily witnessing his treatment at the hands of Ruth. So cold, so aloof when they met, not even a cup of tea offered, or a drink, in that cramped little flat. No pleasant conversation, no how are you, how's life in Limerick.

Which was a bit much, when you thought about it. He'd offered to stand by her and Gerard, after all. Do the decent thing – wasn't that what it was called? – that awful night when he'd been so honest with her and come clean about everything.

And it wasn't as if Ruth knew about the unpleasant phone conversation with Cian the night before, threatening all sorts if Andrew ever tried to make contact with Breffni again. As far as Ruth was concerned, her husband was confessing his crime and attempting to make amends, end of story.

But Lord, that awful scene, flinging him out of the house, going running back to her parents the very next day, leaving Andrew looking like the big bad wolf. And then insisting that he sell the house – not that they hadn't made a fair profit; house prices were still climbing steadily in Limerick. But by the time he'd paid off the mortgage, given Ruth her half, and sorted out child support – a surprisingly large amount, it seemed to him – there wasn't a whole lot left over. Certainly not enough for him to consider buying someplace else, not just yet.

So he was back with Mother, for the time being. And of course it was fine – she'd always looked after him so well. And in time, he'd start looking at places in town – a small apartment maybe, on the river. But there was no hurry. For the moment he was fine where he was; almost as if he'd never left sometimes. Funny that Mother had never really questioned his abrupt return to the house; had accepted his tale of Ruth suddenly deciding that she couldn't settle in Limerick, that she wasn't happy with him.

Funny that Mother never seemed curious about his future either, never asked him what he planned to do. Which was just as well really, as he didn't know himself. Play it by ear, that was the best thing. No hurry.

Would be nice to have a bit of time to himself though, now and again. Since she'd given up the book club, Mother rarely went out in the evenings. Maybe he'd suggest that she give that friend of hers a call – what was her name again? – and go to a play or a concert sometime.

Maybe he'd get two tickets and present them to her; she'd have to go then.

✡✡✡

Cecily watched him over the top of her book. Such a handsome boy still, despite all that he'd had to go through this last year. Who could have possibly imagined that Ruth would turn out to be so headstrong, so demanding, so unforgiving? Surely a wife should be able to overlook her husband's weaknesses, put that sort of thing behind her and soldier on? No one had ever said that marriage was a bed of roses, for goodness' sake. Women these days didn't know when they were well off – if Ruth had pulled herself together, instead of running back to Dublin like a hysterical ninny, she would have realised which side her bread was buttered on. How many women would give their eyeteeth to have Andrew? On reflection, Cecily decided that they were better off without her: silly creature.

But the yearning to see her grandson had taken her completely by surprise. Ruth had sent photos when he was born, and Cecily's eyes had filled with tears as she looked down at the tiny creature. Her flesh and blood, Andrew's son . . . she found herself thinking about him often in the months that followed, wondering what stage he was at, if he was sleeping through the night, whether he'd started teething. She'd sent a card to Ruth, which she'd known wouldn't be acknowledged. And now Andrew seemed against the idea of her going with him to visit Gerard, which Cecily could half-understand, given Ruth's ridiculous attitude, but still resented. What a tragedy that she, Cecily, the innocent party, was being denied the pleasure of seeing her only grandson grow up.

And as much as she loved her other grandchild, it didn't make her loss of Gerard any less painful . . . Cecily thought about the evening ahead at Laura's, about seeing Frank again. She'd been horrified to discover that he was Laura's father-in-law; stunned when Laura had told her. Somehow, the whole business seemed sordid – humiliating in some way. So of course Cecily had cut ties with Frank: impossible for them to keep meeting like before.

And naturally Frank had respected her wishes, hadn't tried to contact her again. They'd already met a few times at Laura and Donal's, in fact, and Frank had behaved impeccably, chatting pleasantly as if he and Cecily were simply casual acquaintances. And if she felt a pang when she remembered their evenings out, those very pleasant dinners together, well, that would pass in time. And who knew? Maybe in the future they could . . . well, it would be perfectly acceptable for them to share an evening together now and again, wouldn't it? Just as friends, of course. Perfectly respectable.

Especially now that she had given up the book club too – imagine Emily's glee when she discovered that Andrew's marriage had finished. Oh, she would have been all sympathy to Cecily's face, but think of the whispers behind her back . . . No, it was entirely out of the question to put herself through that humiliation. This Thursday the club would be meeting – perhaps she and Andrew could go to see a film instead; he rarely went out these days. Yes, that might be a good idea.

'Darling,' she said.

He counted to three, slowly, before looking up.

✡✡✡

And Frank, checking the clock on the kitchen wall, saw that he was due at Laura and Don's – Donal's – in less than an hour. And he hurried upstairs to change out of his gardening clothes and clean himself up, hoping to God that he'd remember to take the bottle of wine out of the fridge before he left.

Dying, as usual, to see the person who'd brought him back to life.

✡✡✡

'Remind me again why we're putting ourselves through this.' Donal's voice floated out from the open bathroom door.

Laura smiled into the mirror. 'You know very well it's our turn – Mother has had us twice in the past month. Although I must admit I'm having second thoughts myself – I look like a whale. Come out and do up the zip for me, and I'll see if I can still breathe.'

He appeared in the mirror behind her. 'A damn sexy whale, if I may say so. Here –' He eased the zip of her dress up slowly, while Laura attempted to pull in her stomach.

'Thanks – if I just pretend to eat I'll be fine.' She turned sideways, pressing her hand to her abdomen as she examined herself in the mirror. 'Three months – and still a long way to go.'

Donal grinned. 'I'm blue in the face from telling you you're fine

– what is it with women that they have to look like sticks? We men want something to grab on to, you know.'

Laura thumped his arm. 'Shut up – I want to be a stick, OK? Doesn't matter what *you* want. Don't let me have dessert.'

He nodded, still smiling. 'Fine. Now how long have we got before the hordes descend?'

'Three people are hardly hordes. And about ten minutes; have you checked the dinner – and will you make sure the fire is OK?'

Before Donal could answer, a wail erupted from the corner. They met each other's eyes before turning simultaneously towards the cot.

'I'll get her.'

'No, you go down – it's my turn.'

And Laura, bending over her daughter's cross, red face, smiled a smile of such pure happiness that Catherine was charmed into silence. She snuffled up at Laura and grabbed one lilac-socked foot, pulling off the sock and bringing it towards her mouth.

'Oh no you don't, you little rogue.' Laura lifted her into her arms and rescued the sock, turned to find Donal still standing by the door, arms folded, watching them.

She stood and looked back at him. 'Want a go?'

He nodded, walked over and took his daughter from Laura. His daughter, his miracle child, conceived against all the odds. Sitting quietly in Laura's womb as Laura heard how her husband had deceived her. Waiting to be discovered when Laura, full of hurt and fear and pain, had gone for help to Dr Goode – not noticing, in her anguish, that her period was now well over two weeks late.

And Catherine *was* a miracle – she'd saved them from falling apart. How could they not survive, now that they had started a baby between them? She was the glue that had kept them all together. And when she was born, the incredible joy that Frank especially had got from Catherine, named in memory of his beloved daughter . . . seeing that, how could Laura not forgive the past, and move on?

And incredibly, Catherine had brought Laura and her mother closer together. It wasn't the cosy, easy relationship that Breffni had with her mother – it would never be that – but it was better between them, definitely. Cecily was warmer, doting on Catherine, bringing expensive toys and clothes whenever she called around, telling Laura about a new baby alarm she'd seen advertised. She'd even offered to babysit, the last time they'd been to her house for dinner, but so far they hadn't taken her up on it – they couldn't bear to leave Catherine yet.

'Hon.' Donal looked up from the baby.

'Yeah?'

'What about giving Breffni a ring? Just to catch up, bury the hatchet?'

She didn't answer immediately, looked back into the mirror, concentrated on getting the dress to sit right. Smoothed down the front of it with her palms.

'I don't know.' How could she contact her again, how could they ever be friends again, with all that had happened?

Something that Ruth had said once swam suddenly into Laura's head – something about them being like spaghetti people, all tangled up together . . . and they *had* been, twining in and out of each other's lives. She and Ruth, Donal and Cian, Andrew and Breffni . . . and she hated that Breffni had wrenched it all apart, destroyed Ruth's marriage for the sake of a fling. It had to have been a fling, hadn't it, when they hadn't gone off together like Andrew had been planning? Laura had never spoken about it to him after that one time, had been glad when he'd never brought it up again, just acted his usual confident self.

Poor Ruth.

But still . . . Laura missed her friend badly sometimes, missed her so much it nearly hurt. When she'd found out she was pregnant, her first thought had been *must phone Bref*, before she remembered. And now Bref didn't even know that she'd had Catherine, that she hadn't had to have the treatment after all. And *she* knew nothing about Bref – had she left Cian? Was that relationship destroyed too? And if it was, who would Bref have had to turn to, without Laura?

Maybe she'd call her. Maybe in a while she'd call her.

She turned from the mirror. 'Right, let's get this show on the road – they'll be here any minute. Gimme –' She stretched out her arms '– go and do your thing downstairs. I'll give this one a clean nappy so she won't disgrace us.'

As Donal handed over Catherine, Laura met his eyes. 'You're a good man.'

And with a pang, she saw the lightning flash of pain on his face before he turned to go downstairs.

Putting Out the Stars
Points for discussion

1. Who would be your favourite and least favourite characters, and why?
2. Does Cecily's relationship with Andrew ring true? If so, do you think the notion of a mother idolising her son is a uniquely Irish one?
3. I originally intended one of the main characters to die at the end, until my editor dissuaded me! Which of the characters would you have killed off, and how would you have done it?
4. Is Ruth's character credible? And could she ever have landed herself a man like Andrew in real life?
5. As you read the book, did you come to change your attitude towards any of the characters?
6. As I was writing, I attempted to give the story a parochial feel – did I succeed?
7. Did you enjoy the atmosphere created by the intimate dinner parties? Did they make you hungry?
8. How long did it take you to guess the identities of the lovers? Who else did you suspect of having the affair?
9. Was the infidelity issue adequately handled? Were Laura's actions ones you could see women carrying out in that situation?
10. And finally...the title *Putting Out the Stars* was chosen to reflect the darkparts of the book, particularly with reference to the female characters: Laura's loss of hope when Donal's condition was made known to her, Ruth's shock when Andrew confessed his infidelity, Breffni's devastation when she realised that the affair was over. Do you think that it reflected the content of the book? Could you suggest other possible titles?

Thank you so much for choosing my book; I hope you enjoyed it.
Roisin Meaney

✂---

If you are in a reading group and you would like information about new releases, discounts and reading guides, please send this form to: Reading Groups, Gill & Macmillan, Hume Avenue, Park West, Dublin 12, or contact read@gillmacmillan.ie.

Name ____

Address ____

____

Signature   Daytime telephone number

_________________   ______________

e-mail address ____

Also by Roisin Meaney

A wonderful heroine, sparky writing and an absorbing storyline from the Tivoli 'Write a Bestseller' competition.

Lizzie seems to have it all: loving parents, a nice creative sideline in mouth-watering cakes, and the most eligible man in Kilmorris waiting to marry her. But one day she stumbles across something that will change her life, and soon she's chucked a backpack into her car and set off into the Wild West – of Ireland, that is – in search of adventure. She's in for a few surprises – there's sexy Pete for a start, a charming new home, true friendship and an offer that will make her sweet dreams a reality. She begins to think that things could hardly be more perfect. And then she meets Joe, who's about to turn her life upside down...

'A warm engaging debut from a name I'm sure we will be hearing a lot more about'
Irish Independent

Available wherever books are sold
or order online at **www.gillmacmillan.ie** to save 20%